smart, original thriller, destined to keep people reading on into the night." —*Gazette*

"Armstrong has a definite talent for sensual descriptions. The wolf creatures are vividly created in gestures and behaviour, and most of the sexual encounters would knock one's socks off (not to mention other things)." —*National Post*

"*Bitten* is hip and postmodern.... Those who enjoy the vampire books of Anne Rice, or Canadian vampire writer Nancy Kilpatrick, will love it." —*The Globe and Mail*

"A very contemporary, funky supernatural thriller with a particularly provocative heroine." —*Hello*

"A hair-raising story for the she-wolf in us all."
   —Shannon Olson, author of *Welcome to My Planet*

"Entertaining new take on an old thriller story form. Makes Buffy look fluffy." —*Daily Express*

"A tasty confection of werewolves, sex and vendettas... After the first nibble it's quite hard to stop.... Elena and her acid repartee successfully steal the show throughout; she has bags of charm. Gory, sexy fun." —*SFX*

"Good slick fun; expect the television series soon."
   —*Guardian*

STOLEN

"Elena Michaels, the only known female werewolf, cavorts on a more fully cultivated supernatural playing field in this sure-footed sequel to *Bitten*.... [*Stolen* is] a prison-break story spiffed up with magic.... Armstrong leavens the narrative with brisk action and intriguing dollops of werewolf culture that suggest a complex and richly imagined anthropologic backstory. The sassy, pumped-up Elena makes a perfect hard-boiled horror heroine.... This novel will please not only horror fans but also mainstream readers who like strong female characters." —*Publishers Weekly*

"In *Stolen*, Kelley Armstrong delivers a taut, sensual thriller that grips from the first page. Elena Michaels is at once sublime and sympathetic, a modern heroine who shows that real women bite back." —Karin Slaughter, *New York Times* bestselling author of *Blindsighted* and *Kisscut*

"Like *Bitten*, *Stolen* paints a perfectly convincing portrait of a woman who quite literally runs with the wolves.... Armstrong has created a persuasive, finely detailed otherworldly cosmology—featuring sorcery, astral projection, spells, telepathy and teleportation—that meshes perfectly with the more humdrum world of interstate highways and cable news bulletins.... More than just a thriller with extra teeth, *Stolen* is for anyone who has ever longed to leap over an SUV in a single bound, or to rip an evil security force to shreds, or even just to growl convincingly."
—*Quill & Quire*

"The narrative veers between clever, scholarly distinctions among different sorts of magical powers and a lot of action movie-style sex and violence.... What's interesting are the twists and turns along the way, boosted by bits of philosophy and arcane knowledge Armstrong adds to her strange brew.... We meet enough truly entertaining creatures along the way to make us wish that this will not be the last romp for Elena and her pack." —*Toronto Star*

"Armstrong is a clever writer ... [and *Stolen*] grabs you at the outset." —*Winnipeg Free Press*

"*Stolen* is a delicious cocktail of testosterone and wicked humour.... Too earnest to attempt parody, [Armstrong's] take on the well-travelled world of supernatural beings is witty and original. She's at her best when examining the all-too-human dilemmas of being superhuman.... [*Stolen*] bubbles with the kind of dramatic invention that bodes well

for a long and engrossing series. . . . This can only be good news for the growing Michaels fan club."
—*The Globe and Mail*

"Mesmerizing . . . the 'otherworldly' atmosphere conjured up by Armstrong begins to seem strangely real. Armstrong is a talented and original writer whose inventiveness and sense of the bizarre are arresting." —*London Free Press*

Also by Kelley Armstrong

STOLEN

BITTEN

DIME STORE MAGIC

HAUNTED

BROKEN

INDUSTRIAL MAGIC

KELLEY ARMSTRONG

SEAL BOOKS

Seal Books and colophon are trademarks of
Random House of Canada Limited.

INDUSTRIAL MAGIC

Seal Books/published by arrangement with Random House Canada
Seal Books edition published November 2004
Seal Books reissue May 2007

ISBN 978-1-4000-2528-2

Cover illustration © 2004 by Franco Accornero
Cover design by Jamie S. Warren Youll

Seal Books are published by Random House of Canada Limited.
"Seal Books" and the portrayal of a seal are the property of
Random House of Canada Limited.

Visit Random House of Canada Limited's website:
www.randomhouse.ca

PRINTED AND BOUND IN THE USA

OPM 10 9 8 7 6 5 4 3 2 1

To my mother-in-law, Shirley . . . thank you
for being proud of me

Acknowledgments

With thanks . . .

To my agent, Helen Heller, for always keeping me on track.

To Anne Groell at Bantam US, for helping me bang this one into shape.

To Antonia Hodgson at Time Warner UK, for suggesting the perfect "kick" for my flat ending.

To Anne Collins at Random House Canada, for her ongoing support.

To Random House Canada marketing manager Constance MacKenzie, and my publicist, Adrienne Phillips, for their continued efforts to get this series into as many hands as possible.

To Taylor Matthews, my Florida connection, for reading through my scenes of Miami and the Everglades, and giving me some great advice.

And finally, a special thanks to Ary, who created the wonderful RPG site based on the Otherworld series (www.kaotherworld.com). And thanks to Jen, Matt, and Raina, who help her maintain this ever-growing site. You guys do an amazing job!

INDUSTRIAL MAGIC

Prologue

"GOT ANOTHER *CSI* QUESTION FOR YOU," GLORIA SAID AS Simon walked into the communication hub with an armload of papers. "If you're not busy."

"Perfect timing," Simon said. "I'm just about to start my coffee break." He started pulling a chair to Gloria's workstation, then hesitated. "Can I get you something?"

Gloria smiled and shook her head. Simon moved the chair beside hers, being careful not to block her view of the digital-display city map on the side wall. That's what Gloria loved about shamans, they were so damned considerate. You want a nice guy, you get a shaman. You want a self-centered jerk, you get a half-demon.

Her shift partner, Erin, hated it when Gloria said that. Racial discrimination, she called it. Of course Gloria didn't really believe every half-demon was a jerk—she was a half-demon herself—but that didn't keep her from saying so to Erin. Night shift in the communication hub could get deathly dull, and there was nothing like a good political correctness debate to liven things up.

Gloria pushed her chair back, one eye still on her monitor. "Okay, so I'm watching *CSI* last week, and they trick this guy into giving them DNA. Then, like five minutes later, they tell him it's a match. Can you really analyze DNA that fast?"

"Can *they*? Or can *we*?" Simon said. "For a municipal crime lab, it's damn near impossible. With our lab, though, there's no political wrangling about overtime and budgets and case precedence. We can't analyze a DNA specimen in five minutes, but—"

Gloria's headset beeped twice: an incoming call on the emergency line. She lifted a finger to Simon, then swung around. Even before the call connected, data began flashing on her computer screen as the call tracer went to work. She glanced over her shoulder to see the map of Miami replaced by another city: Atlanta.

Gloria reached for the button to page Erin back from lunch, but Simon beat her to it, simultaneously grabbing Erin's headset to put it on.

The line clicked.

"Cortez emergency services," Gloria said.

A female voice came on, shrill and garbled with panic. "—help—park—man—"

Gloria soothed the caller with reassurances that help was on its way. She could barely make out a word the caller said, but it didn't matter. The computers had already pinpointed the location, a pay phone in an Atlanta park. The Cabal had an office in Atlanta, which meant they had an emergency crew there, and the computer automatically dispatched them the moment it located the call's origin. Gloria's only job was to keep the caller calm until the team arrived.

"Can you tell me your name, honey?"

"D—na M—ur."

Sobs punctuated the words, rendering them unintelligible. Gloria glanced at her monitor. The computer was analyzing the voice, trying to match what it heard against the roster of Cabal employees and employee families. A list of several dozen names appeared. Then the computer factored in gender, an age estimate, and the call location. It came back with a list of five names. Gloria focused on the top one, the computer's best guess.

"Dana?" she said. "Are you Dana MacArthur, honey?"

A muffled "Yes."

"Okay, now, I want you to find someplace—"

The line went dead.

"Damn!" Gloria said.

"The Atlanta team just phoned in," Simon said. "Ten-minute ETA. Who is it?"

Gloria waved a hand at her screen. Simon leaned over to look at the photo. A teenage girl grinned back.

"Ah, shit," he said. "Not another one."

The driver swung the SUV into the park and dowsed the lights. Dennis Malone stared out the window into the overcast night. He turned to tell Simon they'd need good lighting, and saw that the crime-scene tech was already fiddling with his flashlight, replacing the batteries. Dennis nodded, stifled a yawn, and rolled down the window for some air. On the jet, he'd loaded up on caffeine, but it wasn't kicking in. He was getting too old for this. Even as the thought flitted past, he dismissed it with a smile. The day he retired without a fight would be the day they found him cold and stiff in his bed.

He had the best damned job a cop could want. Head of the finest investigative unit in the country, with the kind of resources and funding his old buddies in the FBI could only dream about. And he didn't just get to solve crimes, he got to plan them. When the Cortezes needed to get rid of someone, they came to Dennis and, together with his team, he'd devise the perfect crime, one that would stump the authorities. That was the best part of his job. What he was doing tonight was the worst. Two in one week. Dennis told himself it was a coincidence, random attacks unconnected to the Cabal itself. The alternative . . . well, no one wanted to consider the alternative.

The SUV stopped.

"Over there," the driver said, pointing. "To the left, behind those trees."

Dennis swung open his door and stepped out. He rolled the kinks from his shoulders as he surveyed the site. There was nothing to see. No crime-scene tape, no television crews, not even an ambulance. The Cabal EMTs had been and gone, arriving silently in an unmarked minivan, then speeding back into the night, headed for the airport, where they'd load their passenger on the same jet that had brought Dennis and Simon to Atlanta.

Over by a stand of trees, a flashlight signaled with an on-off flicker.

"Malone," Dennis called. "Miami SD."

The light went on and a heavyset blond man stepped out. New guy, recently come over from the St. Cloud Cabal. Jim? John?

Greetings were a brief exchange of hellos. They only had a few hours until daybreak, and a lot of work to do before then. Both Jim and the driver who'd brought them from the airport were trained to assist Dennis and Simon, but it would still take every minute of those remaining hours to process the scene.

Simon moved up behind Dennis, camera in one hand, light source in the other. He handed the light source to the driver—Kyle, wasn't it?—and pointed out where he wanted Kyle to aim it. Then he started snapping pictures. It took a moment for Dennis to see what Simon was photographing. That was one advantage to having shaman crime techs—lead them to a scene and they instinctively picked up the vibes of violence and knew where to start working.

Following the angle of Simon's camera lens, Dennis looked up to see a rope dangling from an overhead limb, the end hacked off. Another length lay on the ground, where the EMTs had removed it from the girl's throat.

"It took me a while to find her," Jim said. "If I'd been just a few minutes faster . . ."

"She's alive," Dennis said. "If you hadn't been that fast, she wouldn't be."

His cell phone vibrated. He took it from his pocket. A text message.

"Have you updated Mr. Cortez?" he asked Jim. "He hasn't received a site report yet."

From Jim's expression, Dennis knew he hadn't sent one. With the St. Cloud Cabal you probably didn't phone anyone in the family at three A.M. unless the Tokyo stock market had just crashed. Not so when you worked for the Cortezes.

"You've filled out a preliminary report sheet, right?" Dennis said.

Jim nodded and fumbled to pull his modified Palm-Pilot from his jacket.

"Well, send it to Mr. Cortez immediately. He's waiting to notify Dana's father and he can't do that until he knows the details."

"Mr. . . . ? Which Mr. Cortez?"

"Benicio," Simon murmured as he continued snapping pictures. "You need to send it to Benicio."

"Oh? Uh, right."

As Jim transmitted the report, Simon moved back to photograph the rope on the ground. Blood streaked the underside of the coil and Dennis flinched, imagining his granddaughter lying there. This wasn't supposed to happen. Not to Cabal children. You worked for a Cabal, your kids were protected.

"Randy's girl, wasn't it?" Simon said softly behind him. "The older one?"

Dennis could barely picture Randy MacArthur, let alone know how many kids he had. Simon was almost certainly right, though. Lead the man once around a corporate picnic, and the next day he'd be sure to ask Joe Blow in Accounting whether his son's cold was improving.

"What is her father?" Jim asked.

"Half-demon," Simon said. "An Exaudio, I believe."

Both Jim and Dennis nodded. They were half-demon, as were most of the Cabal's policing force, and they knew what this meant. Dana would have inherited none of her father's powers.

"Poor kid never had a chance," Dennis said.

"Actually, I believe she *is* a supernatural," Simon said. "If I'm not mistaken, her mother is a witch, so she would be one as well."

Dennis shook his head. "Like I said, poor kid never had a chance."

That Cortez Boy

I SAT IN A HOTEL ROOM, ACROSS FROM TWO THIRTY-something witches in business suits, listening as they said all the right things. All the polite things. How they'd heard such wonderful accounts of my mother. How horrified they'd been to learn of her murder. How delighted they were to see that I was doing well despite my break with the Coven.

All this they said, smiling with just the right mixture of sadness, commiseration, and support. Wendy Aiken did most of the talking. While she did, her younger sister Julie's eyes darted to where Savannah, my thirteen-year-old ward, perched on the bed. I caught the looks Julie shot her, distaste mingled with fear. A black witch's daughter, in their hotel room.

As Wendy's lips moved in rehearsed platitudes, her gaze slipped past me to the clock. I knew then that I would fail . . . again. But I gave my spiel anyway. I told them my vision of a new Coven for the technological age, linked by sisterhood instead of proximity, each witch living where she chooses, but with a full Coven support system only a phone call or e-mail away.

When I finished, the sisters looked at each another.

I continued. "As I mentioned, there's also the grimoires. Third-level spells, lost for generations. I have them and I want to share them, to return witches to their former glory."

To me, these books were my trump card. Even if you didn't give a damn about sisterhood or support, surely you'd want this power. What witch wouldn't? Yet, as I looked at Wendy and Julie, I saw my words wash right over them, as if I was offering a free set of steak knives with the purchase of a complete living-room suite.

"You're a very compelling saleswoman," Wendy said with a smile.

"But . . ." Savannah muttered from the bed.

"But we must admit, we have a problem with the . . . present company you keep."

Julie's gaze slid toward Savannah. I tensed, ready to leap to her defense.

"That Cortez boy," Wendy said. "Well, young man, I should say. Yes, I know he's not involved with his family's Cabal, but we all know how things like that turn out. Youthful rebellion is all very well, but it doesn't pay the bills. And I hear he's not very successful in that regard."

"Lucas—"

"He's still young, I know, and he does a lot of pro bono work. That's very noble, Paige. I can see how a young woman would find it romantic—"

"But," Julie cut in, "like Wendy says, it doesn't pay the bills. And he *is* a Cortez."

Wendy nodded. "Yes, he is a Cortez."

"Hey," Savannah said, standing. "I have a question." She stepped toward the sisters. Julie shrank back. "When's the last time you saved a witch from being murdered by Cabal goons? Lucas did that just last month."

"Savannah . . ." I said.

She stepped closer to the two women. "What about defending a shaman set up by a Cabal? That's what Lucas is doing now. Oh, and Paige does charity work, too. In fact, she's doing it right now, offering two-faced bitches like you a spot in her Coven."

"Savannah!"

"I'll be in the hall," she said. "Something in here stinks." She wheeled and marched out of the hotel room.

"My god," Wendy said. "She is her mother's daughter."

"And thank God for that," I said, and left.

As I drove out of the city core, Savannah broke the silence.

"I heard what you said. It was a good comeback."

The words "even if you didn't mean it" hung between us. I nodded and busied myself scanning traffic. I was still working on understanding Savannah's mother, Eve. It wasn't easy. My whole being rebelled at the thought of empathizing with a dark witch. But, even if I could never think of Eve as someone I could admire, I'd come to accept that she'd been a good mother. The proof of that was beside me. A thoroughly evil woman couldn't have produced a daughter like Savannah.

"You know I was right," she said. "About them. They're just like the Coven. You deserve—"

"Don't," I said quietly. "Please."

She looked at me. I could feel her gaze, but didn't turn. After a moment, she shifted to stare out the window.

I was in a funk, as my mother would have said. Feeling sorry for myself and knowing there was no good reason for it. I should be happy—ecstatic even. Sure my life had taken a nasty turn four months ago—if one can call "the end of life as I knew it" a nasty turn—but I'd survived. I was young. I was healthy. I was in love. Damn it, I should be happy. And when I wasn't, that only added guilt to my blues, and left me berating myself for acting like a spoiled, selfish brat.

I was bored. The Web site design work that had once fired a passion in me now piled up on the desk—drudgery I had to complete if anyone in our house intended to eat. Did I say house? I meant apartment. Four months ago, my house near Boston had burned to cinders, along with everything I owned. I was now the proud renter of a lousy two-bedroom apartment in a lousier neighborhood in Portland, Oregon. Yes, I could afford better, but I hated digging into the insurance money, terrified I'd wake up one day with nothing in the bank and be forced to spend eternity living beneath a deaf old woman who watched blaring talk shows eighteen hours a day.

For the first two months, I'd been fine. Lucas, Savannah, and I had spent the summer traveling. But then September came and Savannah had to go to school. So we set up house—apartment—in Portland, and carried on. Or, I should say, Savannah and Lucas carried on. They'd both lived nomadic lives before, so this was nothing new. Not so for me. I'd been born near Boston, grown up there, and never left—not even for school. Yet in my fight to protect Savannah last spring, my house hadn't been the only thing to burn. My entire life had gone up in smoke—my business, my private life, my reputation—all had been dragged through the tabloid cesspool, and I'd been forced to relocate clear across the country, someplace where no one had heard of Paige Winterbourne. The scandal had fizzled out quickly enough, but I couldn't go back. The Coven had exiled me, which meant I was forbidden to live

within the state boundaries. Still, I hadn't given up. I'd
sucked in my grief, dried my tears, and marched back into
the fight. My Coven didn't want me? Fine, I'd start my
own. In the last eight weeks I'd met with nine witches.
Each one said all the right things, then turned me down
flat. With each rejection, the abyss widened.

We went out for dinner, followed by an early movie. My
way of apologizing to Savannah for inflicting another
witch-recruitment session on her.

Back at the apartment, I hustled Savannah off to bed,
then zoomed into my room just as the clock-radio flipped
to 10:59. I grabbed the cordless phone, jumped onto the
bed, and watched the clock. Two seconds after it hit
11:00, the phone rang.

"Two seconds late," I said.

"Never. Your clock must be running fast."

I smiled and settled back onto the bed. Lucas was in
Chicago, defending a shaman who'd been set up by the
St. Cloud Cabal to take the fall for a corporate espionage
scheme gone awry.

I asked Lucas how the case was going, and he filled me
in. Then he asked how my afternoon had gone, specifi-
cally my meeting with the witches. For a second, I almost
wished I had one of those boyfriends who didn't know or
care about my life outside his sphere of influence. Lucas
probably noted all my appointments in his Day-Timer, so
he'd never do something as inconsiderate as fail to ask
about them afterward.

"Shot down," I said.

A moment of silence. "I'm sorry."

"No big—"

"Yes, it is. I know it is. However, I'm equally certain

that, given the right circumstances and timing, you'll eventually find yourself in a position where the number of witches clamoring to join your Coven will far exceed your requirements."

"In other words, give it time and I'll need to beat 'em off with a stick?"

A soft chuckle floated down the line. "I get even less coherent after a day in court, don't I?"

"If you didn't talk like that once in a while, I'd miss it. Kind of like I'm missing you. Got an ETA for me yet?"

"Three days at most. It's hardly a murder trial." He cleared his throat. "Speaking of which, another case was brought to my attention today. A half-demon killed in Nevada, apparently mistaken for another who was under Cabal warrant for execution."

"Whoops."

"Exactly. The Boyd Cabal isn't admitting their mistake, let alone conducting a proper investigation and proce- dural review. I thought perhaps you might be able to as- sist me. That is, if you aren't busy—"

"When can we leave?"

"Sunday. Savannah could spend the night at Michelle's, and we'd return Monday evening."

"Sounds—" I stopped. "Savannah has an orthodontic appointment Monday afternoon. I'd reschedule, but . . ."

"It took six weeks to get it, I know. Yes, I have it marked right here. Three o'clock with Doctor Schwab. I should have checked before I asked." He paused. "Perhaps you could still come along and leave early Monday morning?"

"Sure. That sounds good."

The words came out empty, the elation that surged only a moment ago drained by this sudden glimpse of my future, calendar pages crammed with orthodontic appointments, Saturday morning art classes, and PTA meetings stretching into eternity.

On the heels of that thought came another. How dare I complain? I'd taken on this responsibility. I'd wanted it. I'd fought for it. Only a few months ago, I'd seen the same snapshot of my future and I'd been happy. Now, as much as I loved Savannah, I couldn't deny the occasional twinges of resentment.

"We'll work something out," Lucas said. "In the meantime, I should mention that I took advantage of a brief recess today to visit some of Chicago's lesser-known shopping venues, and found something that might cheer you up. A necklace."

I grinned. "An amulet?"

"No, I believe it's what they call a Celtic knot. Silver. A simple design, but quite elegant."

"Sure. Good . . . great."

"Liar."

"No really, I—" I paused. "It's not a necklace, is it?"

"I've been told, on good authority, that jewelry is the proper token of affection. I must admit I had my doubts. One could argue that you'd prefer a rare spell, but the jewelry store clerk assured me that all women prefer necklaces to musty scrolls."

I rolled onto my stomach and grinned. "You bought me a spell? What kind? Witch? Sorcerer?"

"It's a surprise."

"What?" I shot upright. "No way! Don't you dare—"

"It'll give you something to look forward to when I get home."

"Well, that's good, Cortez, 'cause God knows, I wasn't looking forward to anything else."

A soft laugh. "Liar."

I thumped back onto the bed. "How about a deal? You

tell me what the spell does and I'll give *you* something to look forward to."

"Tempting."

"I'll make it more than tempting."

"That I don't doubt."

"Good. Now here's the deal. I give you a list of options. If you like one, then you can have it when you get home if you tell me about the spell tonight."

"Before you begin, I really should warn you, I'm quite resolved to secrecy. Breaking that resolve requires more than a laundry list of options, however creative. Detail will be the key."

I grinned. "You alone?"

"That goes without saying. If you're asking whether I'm in my hotel room, the answer is yes."

My grin broadened. "Good, then you'll get all the detail you can handle."

I never did find out what the spell was, probably because, five minutes into the conversation, we both forgot what had started it and, by the time we signed off, I crawled under the covers, forgetting even the most basic nighttime toiletry routines, and promptly fell asleep, my curiosity the only thing left unsatisfied.

Death before Dishonor

COME MORNING, I BOUNDED OUT OF BED, READY TO TAKE on the world. This would have been a positive sign had I not done the same thing every morning for the past two weeks. I awoke, refreshed, determined this would be the day I'd haul my ass out of the pit. I'd cook breakfast for Savannah. I'd leave a cheerful message of support on Lucas's cell phone. I'd jog two miles. I'd dive into my Web site projects with renewed vigor and imagination. I'd take time out in the afternoon to hunt down season-end tomatoes at the market. I'd cook up a vat of spaghetti sauce that would fill our tiny freezer. The list went on. I usually derailed somewhere between leaving the message for Lucas and starting my workday . . . roughly around nine A.M.

That morning, I sailed into my jog still pumped. I knew I wouldn't hit two miles, considering I'd never exceeded one mile in my entire running career, which was now in its fifth week. Over the last eighteen months it had come to my attention, on multiple occasions, that my level of physical fitness was inadequate. Before now, a good game of pool was as active as I got. Ask me to flee for my life, and we could be talking imminent heart failure.

As long as I was reinventing myself, I might as well toss in a fitness routine. Since Lucas ran, that seemed the logical choice. I hadn't told him about it yet. Not until I reached the two-mile mark. Then I'd say, "Oh, by the way, I took up running a few days ago." God forbid I should admit to not being instantly successful at anything.

That morning, I finally passed the one-mile mark. Okay, it was only by about twenty yards, but it was still a personal best, so I treated myself to an iced chai for the walk home.

As I rounded the last corner, I noticed two suspicious figures standing in front of my building. Both wore suits, which in my neighborhood was extremely suspicious. I looked for Bibles or encyclopedias, but they were empty-handed. One stared up at the building, perhaps expecting it to morph into corporate headquarters.

I fished my keys from my pocket. As I glanced up, two girls walked past the men. I wondered why they weren't in school—dumb question in this neighborhood, but I was still adjusting—then realized the "girls" were at least forty. My mistake arose from the size differential. The two men towered a foot above the women.

Both men had short, dark hair and clean-shaven, chiseled faces. Both wore Ray-Bans. Both were roughly the size of redwoods. If there hadn't been a one-inch height difference between them, I'd have sworn they were identical twins. Other than that, my only way of distinguishing them was by tie color. One had a dark red tie, the other jade green.

As I drew closer, both men turned my way.

"Paige Winterbourne?" Red Tie said.

I slowed and mentally readied a spell.

"We're looking for Lucas Cortez," Green Tie said. "His father sent us."

My heart thumped double-time, and I blinked to cover my surprise.

"Fath—?" I said. "Benicio?"

"That'd be the one," Red Tie said.

I pasted on a smile. "I'm sorry, but Lucas is in court today."

"Then Mr. Cortez would like to speak to you."

He half turned, directing my gaze to a king-size black SUV idling just around the corner, in the no-stopping zone. So these two weren't just messengers; they were Benicio's personal half-demon bodyguards.

"Benicio wants to talk to me?" I said. "I'm honored. Tell him to come on up. I'll put on the kettle."

Red Tie's mouth twisted. "He's not going up. You're going over there."

"Really? Wow, you must be one of those psychic half-demons. Never met one of those."

"Mr. Cortez wants you—"

I put up a hand to cut him off. My hand barely reached the height of his navel. Kind of scary if you thought about it. Luckily, I didn't.

"Here's how it works," I said. "Benicio wants to speak to me? Fine, but since I didn't request this audience, he's coming to me."

Green Tie's eyebrows lifted above his shades.

"That's not—" Red Tie began.

"You're messengers. I've given the message. Now deliver."

When neither moved, I cast under my breath and waved my fingers at them.

"You heard me. Shoo."

As my fingers flicked, they stumbled back. Green Tie's

eyebrows arched higher. Red Tie recovered his balance and glowered, as if he'd like to launch a fireball at me, or whatever his demonic specialty might be. Before he could act, Green Tie caught his gaze and jerked his chin toward the car. Red Tie settled for a glare, then stomped off.

I reached for the door handle. As the door swung open, a hand appeared over my head and grabbed it. I looked up to see the green-tie-wearing bodyguard. I expected him to hold the door shut, so I couldn't escape, but instead he pulled it open and held it for me. I walked through. He followed.

At this point, any sane woman would have run for her life. At the very least, she would have turned around and walked back out onto the street, a public place. But I was bored and such boredom has a detrimental effect on my sanity.

I unlocked the inner door. This time, I held it open for him. We walked to the elevator in silence.

"Going up?" I asked.

He pushed the button. As the elevator gears squealed, my resolve faltered. I was about to get into a small, enclosed place with a half-demon literally twice my size. I'd seen too many movies not to know how this could turn out.

Yet what were my options? If I ran, I'd be exactly what they expected: a timid witch-mouse. Nothing I did in the future would ever erase that. On the other hand, I could step on the elevator and never step off. Death or dishonor? For some people, there's really no choice.

When the elevator doors opened, I walked on.

The half-demon followed. As the doors closed, he took off his sunglasses. His eyes were a blue so cold they made the hairs on my arms rise. He pressed the Stop button. The elevator groaned to a halt.

"You ever seen this scene in a movie?" he asked.

I looked around. "Now that you mention it, I think I have."

"Know what happens next?"

I nodded. "The hulking bad guy attacks the defenseless young heroine, who suddenly reveals heretofore unimagined powers, which she uses to not only fend off his attack but beat him to a bloody pulp. Then she escapes"—I craned my head back—"out that handy escape hatch and shimmies up the cables. The bad guy recovers consciousness and attacks, whereupon she's forced, against her own moral code, to sever the cable with a fireball and send him plummeting to his death."

"Is that what happens?"

"Sure. Didn't you see that one?"

His lips curved in a grin, defrosting his icy gaze. "Yeah, maybe I did." He leaned back against the wall. "So, how's Robert Vasic?"

I blinked, startled. "Uh, fine . . . good."

"Still teaching at Stanford?"

"Uh, yes. Part-time."

"A half-demon professor of demonology. I always liked that." He grinned. "Though I did like it better when he was a half-demon priest. Not nearly enough of those around. Next time you see Robert, tell him Troy Morgan said hi."

"I—I'll do that."

"Last time *I* saw Robert, Adam was still a kid. Playing baseball in the backyard. When I heard who Lucas is dating, I thought, that's the Winterbourne girl. Adam's friend. Then I thought, whoa, how old is she, like, seventeen, eighteen . . . ?"

"Twenty-three."

"Man, I'm getting old." Troy shook his head. Then he

met my gaze. "Mr. Cortez isn't leaving until you talk to him, Paige."

"What does he want?"

Troy arched his brows. "You think he'd tell me? If Benicio Cortez wants to relay a message in person, then it's personal. Otherwise, he'd save himself the trip and send some sorcerer flunky. Either way, half-demon bodyguards are not in the know. The only thing I do know is that he really wants to talk to you, enough that if you insist on inviting him upstairs, he'll come. The question is: Are you okay with that? It's safe. Hell, I'll come up and stand guard if you want. But if you'd feel more comfortable in a public place, I can talk to him—"

"No, that's fine," I said. "I'll see him if he comes up to the apartment."

Troy nodded. "He will."

An Offer I Can Refuse

THE MOMENT I STEPPED INTO MY APARTMENT, I HAD TO grip my fists tight to keep from slamming the door and throwing shut the deadbolt. I was about to meet Benicio Cortez. And to my shame, I was afraid.

Benicio Cortez headed the Cortez Cabal. The comparison between Cabals and the Mafia was as old as organized crime itself. But it was a bad analogy. Comparing the mob to a Cabal was like comparing a gang of teenage neo-Nazis to the Gestapo. Yet I feared meeting Benicio, not because he was the CEO of the world's most powerful Cabal, but because he was Lucas's father. Everything that Lucas was, and everything he feared becoming, was embodied in this man.

When I'd first learned who Lucas was, I'd assumed that, having dedicated his life to fighting the Cabals, Lucas wouldn't have any contact with his father. I soon realized it wasn't that simple. Benicio phoned. He sent birthday gifts. He invited Lucas to all family functions. He acted as if there was no estrangement. And even his son didn't seem to understand why. When the phone rang and Benicio's number appeared on the caller ID, Lucas would stand there and stare at it, and in his eyes I saw a war I couldn't imagine. Sometimes he answered. Sometimes he didn't. Either way, he seemed to regret the choice.

So now I was about to meet the man. What did I truly fear? That I wouldn't measure up. That Benicio would take one look at me and decide I was't good enough for his son. And the worst of it? Right now, I wasn't sure he'd be wrong.

A single rap at the door.

I took a deep breath, walked to the door, and opened it. I saw the man standing there, and my heart jammed into my throat. For one second, I was certain I'd been tricked, that this was not Benicio but one of his sons—the son who'd ordered my death four months ago. I'd been drugged and, coming to, the first thing I'd seen were Lucas's eyes—a nightmare version of them, their deep brown somehow colder than the icy blue of Troy Morgan's stare. I hadn't known which of Lucas's half-brothers it had been. I still didn't know, having never told Lucas what happened. But now, as I stared into those eyes, the steel in my spine turned to mercury and I had to grip the door handle to steady myself.

"Ms. Winterbourne."

As he spoke, I heard my mistake. The voice I'd heard that day was riveted in my skull, words bitten off sharp, staccato, and bitter. This one was velvet-soft, the voice of a man who never has to shout to get anyone's attention. As I invited him inside, a harder look confirmed my error. The son I'd met had been in his early forties, and this man was another twenty years older. It was an understandable mistake, though. Smooth some of the deeply etched lines on his face and Benicio would be a carbon copy of his son. Both men were wide-shouldered, stocky, and no more than five seven, in contrast to Lucas's tall, rail-thin physique.

"I knew your mother," Benicio said as he crossed the room. No "She was a good woman" or "I'm sorry for your loss" tacked on. A statement as emotionless as his stare. His gaze swept the room, taking in the secondhand furniture and bare walls. Part of me wanted to explain, and another part of me was horrified by the impulse. I didn't owe this man an explanation.

Benicio stepped in front of the couch—part of a perfectly serviceable if threadbare set. He looked down at it as if debating whether it might soil his suit. At that, a small inkling of the old Paige bubbled to the surface.

"Don't bother sitting," I said. "This isn't a tea-and-crumpets kind of visit. Oh, and I'm fine, thank you for asking."

Benicio turned his empty stare on me and waited. For at least twenty seconds, we just looked at one another. I tried to hold out, but I broke first.

"As I told your men, Lucas is in court, out of town. If you didn't believe me—"

"I know where my son is."

A chill tickled the nape of my neck as I heard the unspoken qualifier: "I *always* know where my son is." I'd never thought of that, but hearing him now, there was no doubt in my mind that Benicio always knew exactly where Lucas was, and what he was doing.

"Well, that's funny," I said. "Because your men said you had a message for him. But if you know he's not here, then . . . Oh, I get it. That was only an excuse, right? You know Lucas is gone and you came here pretending to want to deliver a message, hoping for a chance to meet the new girlfriend. You wouldn't want to do that with Lucas around, because you might not be able to control your disappointment when you confirm that your son is indeed dating—whoops, living with—a witch."

"I do have a message," he said. "For both of you."

"I'm guessing it's not 'congratulations.'"

"I have a case that might interest Lucas," he said. "One that might be of particular interest to you as well." While we'd been talking, his eyes had never left mine, but now, for the first time, he truly seemed to be looking at me. "You're developing quite the reputation, both for fending off the Nast Cabal's attempt to take Savannah and for your role in ending that business with Tyrone Winsloe last year. This particular case would require someone with such expertise."

As he spoke, a thrill of gratification rippled through me. On its heels came a wave of shame. God, was I that transparent? Throw a few empty words of praise my way and I wriggled like a happy puppy? Our first meeting and Benicio already knew what buttons to press.

"When's the last time Lucas worked for you?" I asked.

"This isn't working for me. I'm simply passing along a case that I believe would interest my son—"

"And when's the last time you tried that one? August, wasn't it? Something about a Vodoun priest in Colorado? Lucas turned you down flat, as he always does."

Benicio's cheek twitched.

"What," I said, "you didn't think Lucas told me about that? Like he didn't tell me how you bring him a case every few months, either to piss off the other Cabals or to trick him into doing something at your request? He's not sure which it is. I'm guessing both."

He paused. Then he met my gaze. "This case is different."

"Oh, I'm sure it is."

"It involves the child of one of our employees," he said. "A fifteen-year-old girl named Dana MacArthur."

I opened my mouth to cut him off, but couldn't. The moment he said "fifteen-year-old girl," I needed to hear the rest.

Benicio continued. "Three nights ago, someone attacked her while she was walking through a park. She was strangled, hung from a tree, and left to die."

My gut clenched. "Is she . . . ?" I tried to force out the last word, but couldn't.

"She's alive. Comatose, but alive." His voice softened and his eyes filled with the appropriate mix of sorrow and indignation. "Dana wasn't the first."

As he waited for me to ask the obvious question, I swallowed it and forced my brain to switch tracks.

"That's . . . too bad," I said, struggling to keep my voice steady. "I hope she recovers. And I hope you find the culprit. I can't help you, though, and I'm sure Lucas can't, either, but I'll pass along the message."

I walked toward the front hall.

Benicio didn't budge. "There's one more thing you should know."

I bit my lip. *Don't ask. Don't fall for it. Don't—*

"The girl," he said. "Dana MacArthur. She's a witch."

We locked gazes for a moment. Then I tore mine away, strode to the door, and flung it open.

"Get out," I said.

And, to my surprise, he did.

I spent the next half-hour trying to code a customer feedback form for a client's Web site. Simple stuff, but I couldn't get it to work, probably because ninety percent of my brain was endlessly cycling through what Benicio had told me. A teenage witch. Strangled and strung up from a tree. Now comatose. Did this have something to do with her being a witch? Benicio said she wasn't the first. Was someone targeting witches? Killing witches?

I rubbed my hands over my eyes and wished I'd never let Benicio into our apartment. Even as I thought that, I realized the futility of it. One way or another, he'd have made sure I knew about Dana MacArthur. After all these years of bringing cases to Lucas, he'd found the perfect one, and he wouldn't quit until we knew about it.

A faint rustling from the kitchen interrupted my brooding. My first thought was "We have mice," followed by "Well, doesn't that just make my day complete." Then the loose floorboard by the table creaked, and I knew whatever was in the kitchen was a lot bigger than a rodent.

Had I fastened the deadbolt? Cast the lock spell? I couldn't remember, but somehow I suspected I'd been too overwhelmed by Benicio's visit to take care of such mundanities. I mentally readied two spells, one to deal with a human intruder and another, stronger spell, for the supernatural variety. Then I pushed up from my chair and crept toward the kitchen.

A dish clattered, followed by an oath. No, not an oath, I realized as I recognized the voice. Simply a wordless exhalation of pique. Where anyone else would mutter "shit" or "damn," this was one person who never uttered even a profanity without first considering its appropriateness to the situation.

I smiled and peeked around the corner. Lucas was still dressed for court, wearing a dark gray suit and equally somber tie. A month ago, Savannah had bought him a green silk tie, a splash of color she declared long overdue.

Since then, he'd made three trips out of town, each time packing the tie and, I was certain, never wearing it.

When it came to his appearance, Lucas preferred the disguise of invisibility. With wire-rimmed glasses, dark hair cut short, and an unexceptional face, Lucas Cortez didn't need a cover spell to pass through a room unnoticed.

Now he was trying very hard to be silent as well as invisible as he poured coffee from cardboard cups into mugs.

"Playing hooky, Counselor?" I said, rounding the corner.

Anyone else would have jumped. Lucas only blinked, then looked up, lips curving in the crinkle I'd learned to interpret as a smile.

"So much for surprising you with a midmorning snack."

"You didn't need that to surprise me. What happened with your case?"

"After the debacle with the necromancer, the prosecution began pursuing a twenty-four-hour recess, to find a last-minute witness. Initially I was reluctant, wanting to end the matter as quickly as possible, but, after speaking to you last night, I decided you might not be opposed to an unexpected visit. So I decided to be magnanimous and agree to the prosecution's request."

"Won't it hurt your case if they find their witness?"

"They won't. He's dead. Improper handling of a fire-swarm."

"Firearm?"

"No, fire-swarm."

I shook my head and sat down at the table. Lucas placed two scones on a plate and brought it over. I waited until he took his first mouthful.

"Okay, I'll bite. What's a fire-swarm and what did it do to your witness?"

"Not *my* witness—"

I tossed my napkin at him. His quarter-smile broadened to a grin and he launched into the story. That's one thing about being a lawyer to the supernatural. The pay is crap and the clientele can be lethal, but any time you take supernatural events and try to present them in a human courtroom, you're bound to get some great stories. This time, though, no story, no matter how amusing, could distract me from what Benicio had said. After the first few sentences, Lucas stopped.

"Tell me what happened last night," he said.

"Last—?" My mind slowly shifted gears. "Oh, the Coven thing. Well, I gave them my spiel, but it was pretty obvious they were more interested in not missing their dinner reservation."

His gaze searched mine. "But that's not what's bothering you, is it?"

I hesitated. "Your father came by earlier this morning."

Lucas stopped, fingers tightening around his napkin. Again he searched my eyes, this time looking for some sign that I was making a very poor joke.

"He sent his guards in first," I said. "Supposedly looking for you, but when I said you weren't here, he wanted to talk to me. I...I decided it was best to let him. I wasn't sure—we'd never discussed what I should do if—"

"Because it shouldn't have happened. When he found I wasn't here, he shouldn't have insisted on speaking to you. I'm surprised he didn't already know—" He stopped, eyes meeting mine. "He knew I wasn't here, didn't he?"

"Er, uh . . . I'm not sure really."

Lucas's mouth tightened. He shoved back his chair, strode into the front hall, and pulled his cell phone from his jacket. Before he could dial out, I leaned into the hall and lifted a hand to stop him.

"If you're going to call him, I'd better tell you what he wanted or he's going to think I refused to pass along the message."

"Yes, of course." Lucas tucked the cell phone into his pocket, then pinched the bridge of his nose, lifting his glasses with the motion. "I'm sorry, Paige. This wasn't supposed to happen. Had I thought he might come here, I would have forewarned you, but no one from my father's organization was supposed to contact you or Savannah. He gave me his word—"

"It was fine," I said, managing a smile. "Short and sweet. He just wanted me to tell you he's got another of those cases that might interest us—well, you."

Lucas frowned and I knew he'd caught my slip.

"He said it would interest both of us," I said. "But he meant you. He was just throwing in the 'us' part to pique my curiosity. You know, get the new girlfriend intrigued and maybe she'll pester you to give in."

"What did he say?"

I told him Benicio's story. When I finished, Lucas closed his eyes and shook his head.

"I can't believe he'd—no, I *can* believe he'd do that. I should have warned you."

Lucas paused, then steered me back into the kitchen.

"I'm sorry," he said. "These last few months haven't been easy for you, and I don't want you affected by this part of my life any more than necessary. I know I'm the reason you can't find any witches to join your Coven."

"That's got nothing to do with it. I'm young and I haven't proven myself—well, not beyond proving that I can get kicked out of the Coven. But whatever their hang-ups, it's got nothing to do with you."

A small, wan smile. "Your lying hasn't improved."

"Well, it doesn't matter. If they don't want—" I shook my head. "Why are we talking about me anyway? You have a call to make. Your father is already convinced I'm not going to relay his message, so I'm going to hound you until you do."

Lucas took out his phone, but only stared at the keypad. After a moment, he looked over at me.

"Do you have any critical projects to complete this week?" he asked.

"Anything due this week would have been done last week. With Savannah around, I can't let deadlines creep up on me, or an emergency could put me out of business."

"Yes, of course. Well..." He cleared his throat. "I'm not due in court until tomorrow. If Savannah was able to stay at a friend's tonight, would you be able—or should I say *willing*—to join me on an overnight trip to Miami?"

Before I could open my mouth, he hurried on, "I've postponed this long enough. For your own protection, it's time to formally introduce you to the Cabal. I should have done this months ago, but . . . well, I hoped it wouldn't be necessary, that I could take my father at his word. Apparently not."

I looked at him. It was a good excuse, but I knew the truth. He wanted to take me to Miami so I could hear the rest of Dana MacArthur's story. If I didn't, worry and curiosity would gnaw at me until I found some way to get the answers I needed. This was the reaction Benicio wanted, and I desperately didn't want to give it to him. And yet, was there really any harm in hearing what had happened, maybe seeing this witch and making sure she was all right? Benicio said she was a Cabal employee's daughter. The Cabals looked after their own. That much

I knew. All we had to do was say "No, thanks," and the Cabal would launch an investigation, and Dana MacArthur would get her justice. That was good enough for me. It had to be.

So I agreed, and we made plans to leave immediately.

Mastermind of Manipulation

WE BOOKED SEATS ON A FLIGHT FOR MIAMI. THEN WE arranged for Savannah to stay at a friend's house overnight, called her at school, and gave her the news. An hour later, we were at the airport.

We hadn't had a problem booking last-minute tickets, and we hadn't expected to. Just over a month ago, terrorists had driven planes into the World Trade Center, and many travelers opted not to fly the not-so-friendly skies if they could avoid it. We'd arrived early, knowing that passing through security wouldn't be the speedy process it had once been.

The guard opened Lucas's bag and rifled through it, then pulled out a cardboard tube. He passed his metal detector over it, then gingerly removed the end cap and peered inside.

"Paper," he said to his partner.

"It's a scroll," Lucas said.

Both men glowered at him as if this might be a new street name for an automatic rifle.

"A sheet of paper bearing ancient text," Lucas said.

One guard pulled it out and unrolled the scroll. The paper was brand-new, gleaming white, and covered in precise, graceful strokes of calligraphy. The guard screwed up his face.

"What does it say?" he asked.

"I have no idea. It's Hebrew. I'm transporting it for a client."

They handed it back, unfurled and creased. As they checked out my laptop and overnight bag, Lucas straightened the scroll and rolled it. When they finished, Lucas hoisted both bags and we headed toward the boarding area.

"What *is* that?" I whispered. "My spell?"

"I thought you might need a distraction after today."

I smiled up at him. "Thanks. What does it do?"

"I'm choosing option two."

I remembered the option game and laughed. "Too late, Cortez. The deal was that you had to tell me last night. You're home now, so the scroll is mine, option-free."

"I would have selected an option, had you not distracted me from my purpose."

"What, my listing the options prevented you from choosing one?"

"Most effectively. Option two."

"Hand it over, Cortez."

He thumped the scroll into my outstretched hand. "I've been robbed."

"Well, there is a solution. You could get me another spell."

"Greedy," he said, steering me to a quiet spot along the wall. "An unquenchable thirst for spell-casting power and variety. This does not bode well for our relationship."

"Why? Because you're just as bad as I am?"

With a fluid two-step, Lucas moved from my side to my front, and turned to face me. He arched one brow.

"Me?" he said. "Hardly. I'm a disciplined and cautious

spell-caster, well aware of my limitations and with no desire to overcome them."

"And you can say that with a straight face?"

"I can say everything with a straight face, which makes me a naturally gifted liar."

"So how many times did you try my spell?"

"Try your spell? That would be wrong. Grievously impolitic, not to mention impolite, rather like reading a novel before you wrap it as a Christmas gift."

"Twice?"

"Three times. I would have stopped at two, but I had a modicum of luck with the second effort, so I tried again. But, sadly, a successful cast eluded me."

"We'll work on it. So what does it do?"

"Option two."

I socked him in the arm and started unrolling the spell.

"It's a rare gamma-grade sorcerer ice spell," he said. "When cast upon an object, it acts much like a beta-level ice spell, freezing it. However, if cast upon a person, it induces temporary hypothermia, rendering the target unconscious. There were four options, weren't there?"

"Three . . . no, the movie theater makes four."

"Four options. Ergo, if I provide you with four spells . . ."

"Now who's greedy?"

"I'm only asking whether the implied promise of one spell for one option could be reasonably translated to mean four spells would get me—"

"Oh, for God's sake, pick an option already. It's not like you wouldn't get any of them anytime you wanted."

"True," he said. "But I like the added challenge of attaining it. Four spells for four options."

"That wasn't—"

"There's our flight."

He picked up our carry-ons and headed for the boarding area before I could get in another word.

The official "meet-the-parents" visit. Has there ever been a greater torture in the history of dating? I speak from hearsay, not experience. Sure, I'd technically met plenty of old boyfriends' parents, but never through the formal introduction process. More like bumping into them on the way out the door. The "Mom, Dad, this is Paige. See ya" kind of introduction.

I'd met Lucas's mother, but there hadn't been a lead-up. She'd appeared at our door one day, housewarming gifts in hand. Had I known she was coming, I'd have been terrified. Would she disapprove because I wasn't Latino? Wasn't Catholic? Was living with her only child after exactly zero weeks of dating? It didn't matter. If Lucas was happy, Maria was too.

The Cortezes were another matter. Benicio had four sons, of whom Lucas was the youngest. The older three worked for the Cabal, as was traditional for all members of the central family. So Lucas was already the odd man out. His position wasn't helped by the fact that Benicio and Maria had never married, likely because Benicio had still been married to his wife at the time of Lucas's conception, which would make Lucas . . . not the most popular guy at family reunions.

In a Cabal central family, like any "royal" family, matters of succession are all-important. It is assumed that a son of the CEO, usually the oldest, will inherit the business. Not so with Benicio. While his three eldest sons spent their adult lives toiling to improve the family fortunes, who had Benicio named as his heir? The illegitimate youngest son who had devoted *his* adult life to destroying the family business, or at least buggering it up real good. Does this make any sense to anyone besides Benicio? Of course not. Either the man is a mastermind of family manipulation or just plain fucked in the head. I don't use that word much, but in some cases, nothing else fits.

We took a cab from the airport into the city. Lucas had the driver let us out in front of a café, where Lucas suggested we stop for a cold drink because it was at least ninety degrees and, with the full sun beating down, felt more like a hundred, especially after the chill of an Oregon autumn. I argued that I was fine, but he insisted. He was stalling. I scarcely believed it, but after twenty minutes of sitting on the café patio, pretending to drink our iced coffees, I knew it was true.

Lucas talked about the city, the good, the bad, and the ugly of Miami, but his words were rushed, almost frantic in their desperation to fill time. When he took a sip of his drink, more reflex than intention, his cheeks paled and, for a moment, he looked as if he might be sick.

"We don't have to do this," I said.

"We do. I need to make the introduction. There are procedures to be followed, forms to be completed. It must be official. You aren't safe if it isn't." He lifted his gaze from the table. "There's another reason I've brought you here. Something else that's worrying me."

He paused.

"I like honesty," I said.

"I know. I'm just afraid that if I pile on one more disadvantage to being with me, you're going to run screaming back to Portland and change the locks."

"Can't," I said. "You put my return ticket in your bag."

A soft laugh. "A subconsciously significant act, I'm sure. By the time today is over, you may very well want it back." He sipped his coffee. "My father is, as we expected, less than overjoyed by our relationship. I haven't mentioned this because I felt there was no reason to confirm your suspicions."

"It was a given, not a suspicion. I'd be suspicious if he *was* overjoyed at the thought of his son dating a witch. How loudly is he complaining?"

"My father never voices his objections in anything above a whisper, but it is an insidious, constant whisper. At this point, he is merely raising 'concerns.' *My* concern, though, is that with his trip to Portland he appears to already be assessing your influence over me. If he decides that your influence will negatively affect his relationship with me, or my likelihood of becoming heir . . ."

"You're afraid I'll be in danger if your father thinks I'm coming between you two?"

Lucas paused.

"Honesty, remember?" I said.

He looked me square in the eye. "Yes, I'm concerned. The trick, then, is not to allow him to think that will happen. It would be even better if I could convince him that my happiness with you will be beneficial to him. That the strength of our relationship might bolster, rather than tear down, the other relationships in my life."

I nodded, as if I understood, but I didn't. Nothing in my own life had prepared me to understand a parental relationship where a simple visit home had to be planned with the strategic cunning of a military engagement.

"I hope this doesn't mean you're planning to accept this case," I said.

"No. My intention is simply not to refuse as vehemently as I normally do, or he'll blame you, however illogical the reasoning. I will hear him out, and I will endeavor to be more receptive to his paternal attentions than is my wont."

"Uh-huh."

Lucas smiled. "In other words, I'll make nice." He pushed his half-filled glass to the middle of the table. "We have a few blocks to walk. I know it's hot. We could call a cab—"

"Walking is good," I said. "Though I can just imagine what the humidity has done to my hair. I'm going to meet your family looking like a poodle with a live wire shoved up its butt."

"You look beautiful."

He said it with such sincerity, I'm sure I blushed. I grabbed his hand and tugged him to his feet.

"Let's get this over with. We meet the family. We fill out the forms. We find a hotel, buy a bottle of champagne, and see if I can't get that spell working for you."

"*You'll* get it working?"

"No offense, Cortez, but your Hebrew sucks. You're probably mispronouncing half the words."

"Either that or my spell-casting simply lacks your expert proficiency."

"Never said it. Well, not today. Today, I'm being nice to you."

He laughed, brushed his lips across my forehead, and followed me out of the café.

I'd never been to Miami before, and coming into the city by cab I hadn't been impressed. Let's just say, if the taxi had got a flat tire, I wouldn't have left the vehicle, not even armed with a passel of fireball spells. Now, though, we walked through the southeast section of the downtown core, along a dramatic row of steel and mirrored-glass skyscrapers overlooking the impossibly blue waters of Biscayne Bay. The tree-lined streets looked like they'd been scrubbed clean, and the only people hanging out on the sidewalk were sipping five-dollar coffees on café patios. Even the hot-dog vendors wore designer shades.

I expected Lucas to lead me to some seedy part of town, where we'd find the offices of the Cortez Corporation cleverly disguised in a run-down warehouse. Instead, we stopped in front of a skyscraper that looked like a monolith of raw iron ore thrust up from the earth, towers of mirrored windows angled to catch the sun and reflect it back in a halo of brilliance. At the base of the building the recessed doors opened to a street-front oasis with wooden benches, bonsai, overhanging ferns, and a circular waterfall ringed with moss-covered stones. Atop the waterfall was a carved granite pair of Cs. Over the double-width glass doors a brass plate proclaimed, with near-humble simplicity, "Cortez Corporation."

"Holy shit," I said.

Lucas smiled. "Reconsidering that vow never to be the CEO's wife?"

"Never. Co-CEO, though, I might consider."

We stepped inside. The moment the doors closed, the noise of the street disappeared. Soft music wafted past on an air-conditioned breeze. When I turned around, the outside world truly had vanished, blocked out by dark mirrored glass.

I looked around, trying very hard not to gawk. Not that I would have been out of place. Just ahead of us, a gaggle of tourists craned their necks in all directions, taking in the twelve-foot-high tropical aquariums that lined two of the walls. A man in a business suit approached the group and I tensed, certain they were going to be kicked out. Instead, he greeted the tour guide and waved them over to a table where a matron poured ice water.

"Tour groups?" I whispered.

"There's an observatory on the nineteenth floor. It's open to the public."

"I'm trying not to be impressed," I said.

"Just remind yourself where it all comes from. That helps."

It did, dowsing my grudging admiration as quickly as if someone had dumped that pitcher of ice water over my head.

As we veered near the front desk, a thirtyish man with a news-anchor smile nearly knocked his fellow clerk flying in his hurry to get out from behind the desk. He raced toward us as if we'd just breached security, which we probably had.

"Mr. Cortez," he said, blocking our path. "Welcome, sir. It's a pleasure to see you."

Lucas murmured a greeting, and nudged me to the left. The man scampered after us.

"May I buzz anyone for you, sir?"

"No, thank you," Lucas said, still walking.

"I'll get the elevator. It's running slow today. May I get you both a glass of ice water while you wait?"

"No, thank you."

The man darted ahead of us to an elevator marked "Private." When Lucas reached for the numeric pad, the clerk beat him to it and punched in a code.

The elevator arrived, and we stepped on.

The Wages of Sin
Pay Very Nicely Indeed

INSIDE, THE ELEVATOR LOOKED AS IF IT HAD BEEN CARVED from ebony. Not a single fingerprint marred the gleaming black walls and silver trim. The floor was black marble veined with white. How much money does a company need to make before it starts installing marble floors in the elevators?

A soft whir sounded and on what had appeared to be a seamless wall, a door slid open to reveal a computer panel and small screen. Lucas's fingers flew over the keypad. Then he pressed his thumb against the screen. The computer chimed, the panel slid shut, and the elevator began to rise.

We exited on the top floor. The executive level. At the risk of sounding overimpressed, I'll stop describing the surroundings. Suffice to say it was exquisite. Simple and understated, yet every surface, every material, was the best money could buy.

In the middle of the foyer, a marble-paneled desk rose, as if erupting from the marble floor. A beefy man in a suit sat behind a panel of television screens. When the elevator chime announced our arrival, he looked up sharply. Lucas steered me off the elevator and toward the left side of the foyer. A solid wood door on the left side of the foyer swung open. Lucas glanced at the guard, nodded, and led me through the door.

We headed into a long corridor. As the door behind us closed, I slowed, sensing something out of place. It took a moment to realize what it was. The silence. No piped-in Muzak, no voices, not even the clatter of keyboards. Not only that, but the hall itself was unlike any office corridor I'd ever seen. There were no doors along either side. Just a long hallway, branching off in the middle, and ending in a huge set of glass doors.

As we passed the midway intersection, I snuck a glance down each side. There were actually two diagonal corridors off each side, each ending in a glass door. Through each of the four glass doors I could see a reception desk and secretarial staff.

"Hector's office to the left," Lucas murmured. "My eldest half-brother. To the right, William and Carlos's offices."

"Who has the other office?" I asked. "Beside Hector's?"

As soon as I said the words, I knew the answer, and wished I hadn't asked.

"It's mine," Lucas said. "Though I've never worked an hour in it. An absurd waste of prime real estate, but my father keeps it staffed and stocked, because any day now I'm bound to come to my senses."

He tried to keep his tone light, but I could hear the tightness creeping in.

"And if that ever happens, which office do I get?" I asked. "'Cause you know, I'm not going to be one of those silent-partner wives. I want a seat on the board and an office with a view."

He smiled. "Then I'll give you this one."

We'd come to the end of the hall. Through the glass door I saw a reception area three times as large as the ones I'd glimpsed down the side hallways. Though it was now past six o'clock, the office was manned by a squadron of secretaries and clerks.

Like the other door, this one was automatic, and, like the last time, someone had it open before we came within ten feet. As the doors opened, the sea of staff parted to give us a path to the reception desk. The younger secretaries heralded our arrival with unconcealed gapes and stammered hellos. The older ones welcomed us with subdued smiles before quickly returning to their work.

"Mr. Cortez," the receptionist said as we approached the desk. "A pleasure to see you, sir."

"Thank you. Is my father in?"

"Yes, sir. Let me——"

"He's in a meeting." A heavyset man walked from an interior hall and headed for a bank of filing cabinets. "You should have called."

"I'll buzz him, sir," the receptionist said. "He's asked to always be notified of your arrival."

The man across the room shuffled papers loudly enough to draw our attention. "He's busy, Lucas. You can't show up unannounced and drag him out of meetings. We're running a business here."

"Hello, William. You're looking well."

William Cortez. Middle brother. I could be forgiven for not reaching that conclusion earlier. The man bore little resemblance to either Lucas or Benicio. Average height and about seventy pounds overweight, with soft features that might have been girlishly handsome once, but had faded into doughy blandness. William turned to us for the first time, zapping Lucas with an irritated glare. His gaze crossed over me with only a small head shake.

"Don't page my father, Dorinda," William said. "Lucas can wait like the rest of us."

She glanced at her fellow secretaries for help, but they worked harder, pretending not to notice her sinking into the quicksand of conflicting authority.

"Perhaps we should ascertain the exact nature of the request," Lucas said. "Did my father say he *could* be notified or that he *should* be notified?"

"Should, sir. He was very clear on that." She snuck a sidelong glance at William. "Very clear."

"Then I'm sure neither William nor myself wishes to get you into any trouble. Please notify him that I've arrived, but tell him I'm not here on a matter of any urgency, so I can wait for his meeting to end."

The receptionist fairly sighed with relief, nodded, and picked up the phone. While she called, Lucas steered me over to William, who was still at the filing cabinet.

"William," Lucas said, dropping his voice. "I'd like to introduce you to—"

William slammed the drawer, cutting him short. He hefted a pile of folders under his arm.

"I'm busy, Lucas. Some of us work here."

He turned on his heel and stalked out the main doors.

"Mr. Cortez?" the receptionist called from the desk. "Your father will be right out. He'd like you to wait in his office."

Lucas thanked her and led me down the hall to the glazed-glass double doors at the end. Before we reached them, a door to our left opened and a trio of men in standard-issue middle-management suits strode out, then stopped to stare at Lucas. After a quick recovery, they offered welcomes and handshakes to the crown

prince, their greetings falling just a hair short of obei-
sance. I snuck a peek at Lucas. As someone who normally passed through life unnoticed, what was it like to
be recognized here at every turn, to have VPs twice his
age falling over themselves to pay their respects?

Once they were gone, we headed through the double
doors, into a small reception room, and through yet another set of double doors before we reached Benicio's inner sanctum. Had I seen a picture of his office earlier, I'd
have been shocked. Now, having seen the rest of the
building, it was exactly what I'd expect. Simple, understated, and no larger than the office of the average corporate VP. The only remarkable thing about it was the view,
made all the more spectacular by the window itself,
which was a single pane of glass stretching floor-to-
ceiling across the entire wall. The glass was spotless and
the lighting in the room had been arranged so it cast no
reflection, meaning you saw not a window, but a room
that seemed to open right into the bright blue Miami sky.

Lucas walked to his father's computer and typed in a
password. The screen blinked to life.

"I'll print off a copy of the security forms while we
wait," he said.

While he did that, I perused the photos on Benicio's
desk. The first one to catch my eye was of a small boy, no
more than five, at the beach, staring at the camera with
the most serious expression any five-year-old at the
beach has ever had. One look at that expression and I
knew it was Lucas. Beside him, a woman pulled a face,
trying to get him to smile, but only making herself laugh
instead. The broad grin infused her plain face with something approaching beauty. Maria. Her grin was as unmis-
takable as Lucas's sober stare.

What did Benicio's other sons think when they saw

their father's former mistress's picture so prominently displayed, yet none of their own mother, his legal wife? Not only that, but of the three photographs on Benicio's desk, Lucas occupied two while the three of them shared one group portrait. What went through Benicio's head when he did something like that? Did he just not care what anyone thought? Or was there a deeper motive at work, purposely fanning the flames between his legitimate sons and the "bastard heir"?

"Lucas."

Benicio wheeled through the door, a broad smile lighting his face. Lucas stepped forward and extended his hand. Benicio crossed the room in three strides and embraced him.

The two bodyguards who'd accompanied Benicio to Portland slipped inside, surprisingly unobtrusive for men of their size, and took up position against the wall. I smiled at Troy, who returned it with a wink.

"Good to see you, my boy," Benicio said. "This is a surprise. When did you get in?"

Lucas extricated himself from his father's embrace as he answered. Benicio had yet to acknowledge me. At first, I assumed this was an intentional slight, but as I watched him talk to Lucas, I realized Benicio hadn't even noticed me there. From the look on his face, I doubted he'd notice a raging gorilla if it was in the same room as Lucas. I searched his face, his manner, for some sign that he was dissembling, putting on an act of fatherly affection, but saw none. Which made everything else all that much more inexplicable.

Lucas stepped back beside me. "I believe you've met Paige."

"Yes, of course. How are you, Paige?" Benicio extended

a hand and a smile almost as bright as the one he offered his son. Apparently Lucas wasn't the only Cortez who could make nice.

"Paige told me you wanted to speak to me," Lucas said. "While that could, of course, be easily accomplished by telephone, I thought perhaps this would be a good time to bring her to Miami and ensure the proper security clearance forms are completed, so there is no misunderstanding regarding our relationship."

"There's no need for that," Benicio said. "I've already sent her vital stats to all our field offices. Her protection was assured the moment you told me about your . . . relationship."

"Then I'm simply clarifying it with a paper trail, to please the insurance department. Now, I know you're busy, Father. When would be the best time to discuss the details of this case?" He paused, then pushed on. "Perhaps, if you don't have plans, the three of us could have dinner together."

Benicio blinked. A small reaction, but in that blink and the moment of silence that followed, I read shock, and I suspected it had been a while since Lucas had voluntarily shared a meal with his father, much less extended an invitation to do so.

Benicio clapped Lucas on the back. "Perfect. I'll make the arrangements. As for discussing these attacks, though, we'll leave dinner as social time. I'm sure you're both anxious to hear more—"

A rustle at the door cut him short. William stepped in, gaze riveted on his father, probably so he didn't have to acknowledge us.

"I beg your pardon, sir," William said. "But as I was dropping off the Wang report, I overheard Lucas's offer and wanted to remind you that you have a dinner engagement with the governor."

"Hector can take my place."

"Hector's in New York. He has been since Monday."

"Reschedule, then. Tell the governor's office that something important came up."

William's mouth tightened.

"Wait," Lucas said. "Please don't rearrange your schedule on my account. Paige and I will be staying the night. We can have breakfast together."

Benicio paused, then nodded. "Breakfast tomorrow then, and drinks tonight if I can get away from the governor early enough. As for this other matter—"

"Sir?" William said. "About breakfast? You have an early morning meeting."

"Reschedule it," Benicio snapped. When William turned to leave, he stopped him. "William, before you go, I'd like you to meet Paige—"

"The witch. We've met."

He didn't so much as glance my way. A line creased between Benicio's eyebrows and he rattled off something in Spanish. Now, my Spanish was pretty good, and Lucas had been helping me improve—if only so we could talk without Savannah listening in—but Benicio spoke too fast for my translation skills. I didn't need an interpreter, though, to guess that he was upbraiding William for his rudeness.

"And where is Carlos?" Benicio said, reverting to English. "He should be here to see his brother and meet Paige."

"Is it past four?" William said.

"Of course it is."

"Then Carlos isn't here. If you'll excuse me—"

Benicio turned away, as if William had already left. "Where was I? Yes. This other matter. I've convened a meeting in twenty minutes to provide you with all the details. Let's get Paige a cold drink and we'll head to the boardroom."

Familial Violence Insurance

TWENTY MINUTES LATER, LUCAS OPENED THE CONFERence room door for me. His eyes slanted a silent question my way. Did I want him to go first? I shook my head. Though I wasn't looking forward to confronting what I knew lay within that meeting room, I had to do it without hiding behind Lucas.

As I stepped inside, my gaze swept across the dozen or so faces within. Sorcerer, sorcerer, sorcerer . . . another sorcerer. Over three quarters of the men in the room were sorcerers. Each pair of eyes met mine. Chairs shuffled and voices murmured wordless noises of disapproval. The word "witch" snaked through the room on a chorused whisper of contempt. Every sorcerer in the room knew what I was without being told. One look in the eyes, and witch recognized sorcerer, sorcerer recognized witch, and the introduction rarely pleased either.

Benicio waved Lucas and me to two empty chairs next to the vacant head of the table.

"Good afternoon, gentlemen," he said. "Thank you for staying late to join us. You all know my son Lucas."

The men within handshaking distance extended their

hands. The rest offered spoken salutations. No one looked my way.

"This is Paige Winterbourne," Benicio continued. "As I'm sure most of you know, Paige's mother, Ruth, was Leader of the American Coven. Paige herself has been a member of the interracial council for several years, and I'm pleased to say, in that capacity, she has expressed an interest in the MacArthur case."

I held my breath waiting for some comment about my exile from the Coven or my embarrassingly short term as Leader. But Benicio said nothing. As much as he might dislike me, he wouldn't upset Lucas by insulting his girl-friend.

Benicio gestured toward a stocky man near the foot of the table. "Dennis Malone is our head of security. He's most familiar with the case, so I'll ask him to begin with an overview."

As Dennis explained, Dana MacArthur was indeed the daughter of a Cabal employee but not, as I'd assumed, of the Cabal witch. Like Savannah, Dana claimed super-natural blood from both parents, her father being a half-demon in Cortez Corporation sales. Randy MacArthur was currently overseas establishing a commercial foot-hold in the newly capitalist areas of Eastern Europe. Dana's mother was a witch named Lyndsay MacArthur. I'd hoped to recognize the name, but I didn't. Coven witches had little contact with non-Coven witches. Even my mother had only taken notice of outside witches when they'd caused trouble. One of the many things I'd wanted to change about the Coven, and now never would.

According to the background information Dennis pro-vided, Dana's parents were divorced and she lived with her mother. Dennis mentioned that her mother lived in

Macon, Georgia, and the attack had taken place in Atlanta, so I assumed Dana had been traveling or visiting friends. She'd apparently been out walking by herself around midnight—which seemed very strange for a fifteen-year-old girl, but I'd get an explanation later. The important thing was that during that walk, she'd cut through a park and been attacked.

"Where is Dana now?" I asked when Dennis finished.

"At the Marsh Clinic," Benicio said.

"That's a private hospital for Cabal employees," Lucas explained. "It's here in Miami."

"And her mother is with her?" I said.

Benicio shook his head. "Unfortunately, Ms. MacArthur has been...unable to come to Miami. We have every hope, though, that she'll change her mind."

"Change her mind? What's the problem? If she can't afford airfare, I'd certainly hope someone would—"

"We've offered her both commercial airfare and a flight on our private jet. Ms. MacArthur has some...concerns over air travel at this time."

At a noise from across the table, my gaze slid down the row of faces until it came to the youngest attendee, a sorcerer in his thirties. He met my gaze with a half-smirk. At a glare from Benicio, the smirk changed into a cough.

"Concerns over air travel," I said slowly, trying to wrap my head around the idea that a witch would let anything stop her from racing to her daughter's sickbed. "That's not unusual these days, I guess. A bus ticket might be—"

The smirking sorcerer cut in. "She doesn't want to come."

"There's been some estrangement between Dana and her mother," Benicio said. "Dana had been living on her own in Atlanta."

"On her own? She's fifteen—"

I stopped, suddenly aware that a dozen pair of eyes were on me. I could imagine nothing more humiliating for a witch than this, to sit in a room filled with sorcerers telling you that one of your race, who pride themselves on their family bonds, had let her teenage daughter live on the streets. Not only that, but she didn't even care enough to come to her daughter's side when she lay comatose and alone in a Cabal hospital. It was inconceivable.

"Maybe if I could speak to her," I said. "There might be a misunderstanding . . ."

"Or we could be lying," the sorcerer said. "Here's my cell phone. Anyone got Lyndsay MacArthur's number? Let the witch—"

"Enough," Benicio said, his voice sharp enough to cut diamonds. I'd heard that tone before . . . from his son. "You are excused, Jared."

"I was only—"

"You are excused."

The sorcerer left. I struggled to think of some way to defend my race. Lucas's hand squeezed my knee. I looked at him, but he'd turned to the table, mouth opening to speak for me. I quickly interrupted. As much as I longed for the support, the only thing that could make this worse would be for him to jump to my rescue.

"Is Dana's father aware of the situation?" I said.

Benicio shook his head. "Randy has been in Europe since spring. If he'd known about Dana's estrangement from her mother, he would have requested leave to come home."

"I meant the attack. Does he know about that?"

Another head shake. "He's currently in a very unstable location. We've tried contacting him by telephone, e-mail, and telepathy, but haven't been able to deliver the news. We expect him to be back in a major city within the week."

"Good. Okay. Back to the case, then. I'm guessing we're here because you want Dana's attacker found."

"Found and punished."

Somehow, I doubted that punishment would involve the local authorities, but after hearing what had been done to Dana, I couldn't bring myself to care.

"But the Cabal can investigate by itself, right?"

A reedy voice from down the table answered. "Mr. MacArthur is a class C employee."

I looked at the speaker, a specter-thin, specter-pale man dressed in a mortician-black suit. Necromancer. It's a stereotype, I know, but most necros have a whiff of the grave about them.

"Paige, this is Reuben Aldrich, head of our actuarial department. Reuben, Ms. Winterbourne isn't familiar with our designations. Would you explain for her please?"

"Of course, sir." Watery blue eyes looked my way. "Employees range from class F through A. Only class A and B employees are entitled to familial violence insurance."

"Familial . . . ?"

Lucas turned to me. "It's insurance that covers corporate investigations into criminal matters such as kidnapping, assault, murder, psychic wounding, or any other dangers one's family might face as a result of their employment with the Cabal."

I looked at Reuben Aldrich. "So Mr. MacArthur, being class C, isn't entitled to a paid investigation into his daughter's attack. So why bring it to us—to Lucas?"

"The Cabal is offering to hire him," said the man beside me. "The reallocation of resources and man-hours would make the cost of an internal investigation prohibitive. Instead, we're offering to retain Mr. Cortez in a contract position."

Lucas folded his hands on the table. "Paying for an outside investigation into an assault not covered by the benefit package is a generous and considerate offer, but—" He met his father's gaze with a level stare. "—unlikely to meet corporate profitability standards. You mentioned to Paige that the attack on Miss MacArthur wasn't the first."

"There's a second, possibly related, case," Benicio said. "Dennis?"

Dennis explained. Eight days ago another Cabal employee's runaway teen had been attacked. Holden Wyngaard was the fourteen-year-old son of a shaman. Someone had followed him for several blocks at night, then jumped him in an alley. Before anything could happen, a young couple had wandered into the alley and Holden's attacker had slipped away. The Cabal was not investigating.

"Let me guess," I said. "Mr. Wyngaard is a level C employee."

"Level E," Reuben said. "Substance-abuse problems have caused his status to drop. He is currently on suspension, and therefore entitled only to the most basic health-care benefits."

"But you think the cases are connected?"

"We don't know," Benicio said. "If we had clear proof of a pattern, we'd conduct our own investigation. As it stands, it's a troubling coincidence. While the expense of a full-scale investigation isn't warranted, we'd like to be proactive and hire Lucas to look into the matter."

"Not me," Lucas said, his voice soft, but firm enough to carry through the room. "Paige."

"Of course, if Paige was interested in helping you—"

"I'm currently in the midst of defending a client, and

couldn't possibly pursue this in the timely manner you'd require."

Benicio hesitated, then nodded. "Understandable. You have other obligations. I can't argue with that. If you'd like to set Paige on the case then, and supervise—"

"Paige doesn't require my supervision. You approached her with this case, hoping it might interest her because it concerns a witch. Whether she decides to take it is her choice."

Every pair of eyes turned to me. I felt the eager words of agreement leap to my throat. No one in this room gave a damn about Dana MacArthur. She needed someone on her side, and I longed to be that someone. Yet I locked my mouth shut and gave my brain time to override my heart.

One tragedy, and one near-tragedy, both involving the runaway kids of Cortez Cabal employees. Did I think they were related? No. The streets were a harsh and violent place for teens. That's a cold fact. I had to make an equally cold decision. I had to let someone else find justice for Dana. If I took this case, it would involve Lucas, if only by forcing him to act as middleman between the Cabal and me. I wouldn't do that to him. So I thanked everyone for coming out . . . and turned them down.

Time to Empty the Minibar

AFTER THE MEETING, BENICIO WALKED WITH US BACK to his office to get our overnight bags.

"I'd like you to take Troy tonight," Benicio said. "I'm concerned. If someone's targeting Cabal children—"

"I believe I'm a decade or so above fulfilling that requirement," Lucas said.

"But you're still *my* child. You know Troy; he'll be as unobtrusive as possible. I just . . . I want you to be safe."

Lucas lifted his glasses and rubbed the bridge of his nose, then glanced over at me.

I nodded.

"Let me take a guard from the security pool, then," Lucas said. "You should keep yours—"

"I'll still have Griffin," Benicio said, nodding at Troy's partner. "That will be enough tonight."

When Lucas finally agreed, Benicio slid in a few more "requests." He wanted to pick up the tab for our hotel, to compensate for bringing us here. Lucas refused. Benicio backed off, but followed with another demand. With the combination of this new threat and 9/11, he didn't want Lucas flying on a commercial airline. He'd make sure the corporate jet was fueled up to take us home. Again Lucas refused. Now Benicio dug in his heels, and kept them dug in until Lucas finally agreed to accept the hotel room, just to get us out of there.

By the time we escaped to the street, Lucas's forehead had gained ten years of stress-furrows. He stood beside the garden, closed his eyes, and inhaled.

"The sweet smell of freedom," I said.

He tried to smile, but his lips faltered and fell into a tired line. He squinted up and down the street, then headed east. Troy fell into position two paces behind. After a few yards, Lucas glanced over his shoulder.

"Troy? Please, walk beside us."

"Sorry," Troy said, striding up. "Habit."

"Yes, well, when a two-hundred-and-fifty-pound half-demon follows me, it's never a good thing. Fleeing for my life is usually involved."

Troy grinned. "You need a bodyguard."

"I need a saner life. Or faster feet. Right now, though, we need . . ."

"Wheels," I said. "Followed by stiff drinks."

"Uh, sir?"

Lucas winced.

"*Lucas,* I meant," Troy said. "The parking garage is beside the office. We needed to take the walkway across to get the car."

Lucas sighed. "Now you tell me."

"Hey, it's not my place to think. That's for you sorcerer guys. Me? I'm paid to keep my mouth shut, glare at strangers, and, on a good day, break a couple kneecaps."

"Cushy job," I said.

"It has its moments. The kneecap-breaking gets a little stale, though. I've tried tossing in the occasional jaw-busting and skull-smacking, but Mr. Cortez, he's a knee-cap man."

Lucas shook his head and headed back toward the building.

At the hotel, Troy cased our room before allowing us inside. Seemed like overkill to me, but that was his job.

"All clear," he said, coming out. "There's a door between our rooms. Knock if you need me. If you go out to dinner . . ."

"We'll tell you," Lucas said.

"I'll keep out of the way, sit at a corner table, whatever."

"We'll probably have a quiet night, order room service."

"Hey, it's all paid for, so go for it." Troy caught Lucas's look. "Yeah, I know, you don't like using the old man's money, but you're his kid, right? If it was my dad . . ." He grinned. "Well, if it was *my* dad, I suppose he'd be offering me a lifetime supply of fire and brimstone, and personally, I'd prefer the cash, but that's just me. Seriously, though, take advantage of it. Clean out the minibar, rack up the room-service bill, steal the bathrobes. Worst thing that can happen, you'll piss off the old man and he won't talk to you for a year."

"Not the worst punishment I can imagine," Lucas murmured.

"Exactly. So live it up. And call me if you need help with the minibar."

I closed the door, cast a locking spell, and collapsed on the couch.

"I'm sorry," Lucas said. "I know that was difficult for you, turning them down."

"Let's just—let's not think about it. Not now. Maybe in

the morning . . . Will we have time to stop by the hospital in the morning? See how she's doing?"

"We'll make time."

"Good. I can make sure she's okay, see if there's anything I can do from that angle and try to forget the rest. Now, let's help ourselves to that drink."

I started pushing to my feet, but Lucas waved me down.

"Stay there. I'll get it."

He glanced at the minibar, then at the door.

"The minibar's closer," I said. "And if you go out for booze, you'll have to take Troy. Your father brought us running down here, the least he can do is pay for our hotel and a drink."

"You're right. First, the drink. Then dinner. We'll order in—" He stopped and shook his head. "No, we're going out. Someplace nice. Followed by a show or a walk on the beach or whatever you want. My treat."

"You don't have to—"

"I want to. And, though I neglected to mention it earlier, I have money. Well, some money. I received payment on a legal matter, and I am, for the first time in months, reasonably flush."

"Is this for the case you're working now? With the shaman?"

"No, this is from a few years ago, a client whose financial situation has improved and who wanted to repay me. As for the current case, there is the possibility of a payment. A barter, so to speak. He has—" Lucas paused, then shook his head. "A matter we can discuss later, if and when it comes to fruition. For now, I have enough money to treat you to a proper evening out, and pay the rent for the next few months. Let me mix that drink, then I'll tell Troy we'll be leaving for dinner within the hour."

I didn't miss the "pay the rent" part, however skillfully he slipped it in. I paid the lion's share of the household expenses. Paid them by choice, I should add. I knew this bothered Lucas—not in an "I am man; I am breadwinner" kind of way, but as a subtler matter of pride.

Lucas barely earned a living wage. Most of his court and investigative work was pro bono, helping supernaturals who couldn't afford a lawyer or PI. What little money he made usually came from doing legal paperwork for wealthier supernatural clients, many of whom could easily and more conveniently have hired a local lawyer, but who retained Lucas as a way of supporting his pro bono efforts. Even that made Lucas uncomfortable, smacking too much of charity, but his only alternative would be to stop taking nonpaying cases, which he'd never do.

It hurt like hell to see him sleeping in fleabag motels, barely able to afford public transit, saving every penny so he could pay part of our expenses. I had enough for both of us. But how could I turn down his contributions without belittling his efforts? Yet another kink in the relationship we had to work out.

We stumbled back into the hotel room just before midnight, having followed dinner with a few rounds of pool and more than a few rounds of beer. Definite advantage to the whole chauffeur/bodyguard deal: built-in designated driver. The downside, though, was that Troy beat me in two out of three pool games, a serious blow to my ego. I blamed it on the booze. Deadened my reflexes . . . though it did wonders for helping me forget the rest of the day. As for Lucas, he was feeling better, too.

"I did not cheat!" I said, struggling to wriggle free of

the upside-down over-the-back-of-the-sofa position in which I found myself pinned.

He pulled my blouse from my skirt and tickled my ribs. "You *so* cheated. Second game. Seven ball, left corner pocket. Minor telekinesis spell."

I squealed and swatted his hands. "I—the ball rolled."

"With help."

"Once. Only once. I—stop—" Another embarrassingly girlish shriek. "You—third game—the eight ball. You moved it out of the way of your shot."

He toppled us over onto the couch and slid a hand under my skirt.

"Diversionary tactics, Counselor," I said.

"Guilty." He hooked his fingers over my panties and peeled them off.

"Not so fast, Cortez. You promised me spell-casting."

"I think you did enough of that at the pool hall."

He stifled my sputtering with a kiss.

"Wait. No—" I wiggled sideways and dropped to the floor, then scooted out of reach. "How about a game? Strip spell-casting."

"Strip—?" He rubbed at his smile. "Okay, I'll bite. How do you play?"

"Just like strip poker, only with spell-casting. We take turns trying the new spell. Each time we fail, we remove a piece of clothing."

"Given the difficulty of that spell, we'll likely both run out of clothing first."

"Then we'll have to get more creative."

Lucas laughed and started to say something, but a knock cut him off. He looked at the main door. I pointed at the one linking our suite to Troy's. Lucas sighed, heaved himself to his feet, and peered around. I picked up his glasses from the floor.

"Thank you," he said, taking them. "I'll be right back."

"Better be. Or I'm starting without you."

Lucas buttoned his shirt on the way to the door. I crawled onto the sofa, straightened my skirt, and stuffed my panties between the cushions.

Lucas pulled open the adjoining-room door.

"There's been another attack," Troy said.

"Where?" I said, popping up from the sofa.

"Here. In Miami." Troy ran a hand through his hair. His face was pale. "I just got the page. They—I'm on call this week. No one took me off the list tonight. Can you phone in and let them know I can't make it?"

"Come in," Lucas said.

"I need—I've got some calls to make. It's—it's Griffin. His oldest boy. Jacob. I should—"

"You should come in. Please." Lucas closed the door behind Troy. "Are you saying Griffin's son has been attacked?"

"I—we don't know. He called the emergency line and now he's missing. They've sent out a search team."

"Why don't you go with them?" I said. "We'll be fine."

"He can't," Lucas said. "He'd be severely reprimanded for leaving me behind. A problem easily solved if I go along. Care to join us?"

"You need to ask?" I said, getting to my feet.

"No way," Troy said. "Dragging the boss's son and girl-friend along on a search-and-rescue wouldn't get me reprimanded, it'd get me fired. Or worse."

"You aren't dragging me anywhere," Lucas said. "I'm going to help, therefore you're obligated to follow. I'll phone in for details on the way."

Welcome to Miami

I SAT IN THE FRONT SEAT OF THE SUV, GIVING LUCAS PRI-
vacy in the back as he called the security department for
an update.

A drizzling rain pattered on the roof, just enough to
make the road slick and shimmery in the darkness. Our
windshield, though, was dry, improving Troy's visibility
tenfold. Seeing that, I understood how Troy knew Robert
Vasic. Like Robert, Troy was a Tempestras, a storm demon. The name, like many half-demon cognomens, tipped
into melodrama and bordered on false advertising. A
Tempestras couldn't summon storms. He could, however,
control the weather within his immediate vicinity, calling
up wind, rain or, if he was really good, lightning. He could
also, like Troy, do something as small but practical as
keeping rain off his windshield. I thought of commenting,
but one glance at Troy's taut face told me he was in no
mood for a discourse on his powers. He was so intent on
his driving, he probably didn't even realize he was shunt-
ing the rain from the windshield.

"Can I ask something?" I said quietly. "About Griffin's
son?"

"Hmm? Oh, yeah, sure."

"Is he a runaway?"

"Jacob? Shit, no. They're tight. Griffin and his kids, I mean. He's got three. His wife passed away a couple years ago. Breast cancer."

"Oh."

"Yeah, Griff's great with his kids. Real close." Troy eased back in his seat, as if grateful for the chance to fill the silence with something other than the patter of rain. "Griffin comes off like an asshole, but he's a good guy. Just takes the job too serious. He used to work for the St. Clouds, and they run things different. Like the fucking military . . . pardon my French."

"The St. Clouds are the smallest Cabal, right?"

"Second smallest. About half the size of the Cortezes. When Griffin's wife was sick, the St. Clouds made him use vacation time for every minute he took off driving her to chemo and stuff. After she died, he gave two weeks' notice and took an offer from Mr. Cortez."

At a click from the backseat, Troy glanced in the rearview mirror.

"Any news?" he asked.

"They have two search teams out. Dennis—" Lucas looked my way. "Dennis Malone. You met him at the meeting today. He's been called in to coordinate the operation from headquarters. He advises that we begin several blocks from where Jacob phoned. The teams are currently searching the blocks on either side of that point."

I twisted to face Lucas. "Do we have any idea what happened to Jacob?"

"Dennis replayed his phone call for me—"

"Nine-one-one?"

Lucas shook his head. "Our personal emergency line. All Cabal employee children are given the number and told to call it instead. The Cabals prefer to avoid police involvement in any matter that may be supernatural in nature. An employee's family is told that phoning this number ensures faster response times than calling nine-one-one, which it does. The larger Cabals have security and paramedic teams ready to respond twenty-four hours a day."

"So that's who Jacob called."

"At eleven twenty-seven P.M. The call itself is indistinct, owing to both the rain and poor cellular reception. He appears to say he's being followed, after leaving a movie and becoming separated from his friends. The next part is unclear. He says something about telling his father he's sorry. The operator tells him to stay calm. Then the call ends."

"Shit," Troy said.

"Not necessarily," Lucas said. "The cellular signal may have been disrupted. Or he may simply have decided he was making too big a deal out of the matter, become embarrassed, and hung up."

"Would Griffin let him go to a late movie with his friends?" I asked Troy.

"On a school night? Never. Griff's real strict about stuff like that."

"Well, then, that's probably it. Jacob realized he'd be in trouble for sneaking out and hung up. He'll probably crash at a friend's place, and call his dad once he works up the nerve."

Troy nodded, but didn't look any more convinced than I felt.

"Jesus," Troy said as he pulled into the area where Dennis had advised us to park.

He'd squeezed the SUV between two buildings and come out in a tiny parking lot only a few feet wider than the alley itself. Every building in sight was rife with boarded-up windows, the boards themselves rife with bullet holes. Any security lights had long since been shot out. The rain swallowed the glow of the new moon overhead. As Troy swung into a parking spot, the headlights illuminated a brick wall covered in graffiti. My gaze swept across the symbols and names.

"Uh, are those . . . ?"

"Gang markings," Troy said. "Welcome to Miami."

"Is this the right place?" I said, squinting into the darkness. "Jacob said he was at a show, but this doesn't look . . ."

"There's a theater a few blocks over," Troy said. "A gazillion-screen multiplex plopped down in the middle of hell. Just the place you want to drop off the kiddies for a Saturday matinee." He shut off the engine, then dowsed the lights. "Shit. We're going to need flashlights."

"How's this?" I cast a spell and a baseball-size blob of light appeared in my hand.

I opened the car door and lobbed the light out. It stopped a few yards away and hung there, illuminating the lot.

"Cool. I've never seen that."

"Witch magic," Lucas said. He cast the spell himself, conjuring a weaker ball of light, and leaving it in his palm. "It has a more practical orientation than ours. I'm not as accomplished at this spell as Paige yet, so I'll keep my light at hand, so to speak. If I throw it out . . . well, it rarely cooperates."

"Splats on the sidewalk like an egg," I said, tossing him a quick grin. "Okay, then, we have the flashlights covered. Troy, I'm assuming you can handle umbrella duty. So we're all set."

*   *   *

We walked to the edge of the parking lot. The skeletal remains of a building rose from a vacant slab of land at least the size of a city block. Scrubby trees, half-demolished walls, piles of broken concrete, ripped-open trash bags, discarded tires, and broken furniture cluttered the landscape. I bent to lift a sodden sheet of cardboard draped over a large lump. Troy kicked a syringe out of the way and grabbed my hand.

"Not a good idea," he said. "Better use a stick."

I peered across the field, in one glance picking out a score of places where Jacob could lie low and wait for help.

"Should we try calling him?" I asked.

Troy shook his head. "Might attract the wrong kind of attention. Jacob knows me, but he's a smart kid. If he's hiding out here, he's not going to answer us until he sees my face."

Though none of us said it, there was another reason for not just calling his name and moving on. He could be injured, unable to answer. Or worse.

"The rain is easing and Paige's ball casts sufficient light for us all to search," Lucas said. "I suggest we split up, each taking a ten foot swatch, and make a thorough sweep." He stopped. "Unless . . . Paige? Your sensing spell would be perfect for this."

"A spell?" Troy said. "Great."

"Uh, right. The only problem . . ." I glanced at Troy. "It's a fourth-level spell. Technically, I'm still third-level, so I'm not . . ." God, this stung. "I'm not very good—"

"She's still refining her accuracy," Lucas said. That sounded so much better than what I was going to say. "Could you give it a try?"

I nodded. Lucas motioned for Troy to follow him and start searching, giving me privacy. I closed my eyes, concentrated, and cast.

The moment the words left my mouth, I knew the spell had failed. Most witches wait for results, but my mother had taught me to use my gut instinct, to feel the subtle click of a successful cast. It wasn't easy. To me, intuition always seems like some flaky New Age thing. My brain seeks the logic in patterns; it looks for clear, decisive results. As I move into harder spells, though, I've been forcing myself to develop that inner sense. Otherwise, with the sensing spell, if I didn't detect a presence, I wouldn't know whether it was because no one was there or because the spell had failed.

I recast. The click followed, almost as a subconscious sigh of relief. Now came the tough part. With a spell like this, I couldn't just cast it and leave it on, like the light-ball. I needed to sustain it, and that took concentration. I held myself still and focused on the spell, measuring its strength. It wavered, almost disappeared, then took hold. I resisted the urge to open my eyes. The spell would still work, but I'd rely too much on what I was seeing instead of feeling. I turned slowly, and sensed two presences. Troy and Lucas. I pinpointed their location, then peeked to double-check. There they were, exactly where I'd sensed them.

"Got it," I said, my voice echoing through the silence.

"Good," Lucas called back as they headed my way.

"So how does this work?" Troy asked.

"If I walk slowly, I should be able to detect anyone within a twenty-foot radius."

"Great."

I inhaled. "Okay, here goes."

I had two choices. Be led around with my eyes closed,

like some wack-job spiritualist, or open my eyes and keep my gaze on the ground. Naturally, I went for option two. Anything to avoid looking like an idiot.

Lucas and Troy followed. After a few yards, I felt the spell waver. I told my nerves there was no need to panic, no pressure here. They called me a liar, but agreed to fake it for a while. I relaxed and the spell surged to full strength.

Weak presences tickled at the edges of awareness. When I focused on them, they stayed amorphous. Small mammals, probably rats. An image flashed through my mind: a novel a friend and I had "borrowed" from her older brother when we'd been kids. Something about rats going crazy and eating people. There was this one scene with...I forced the image back, my gaze skittering across the ground looking for rat turds.

The spell fluttered, but I kept walking. We finished one twenty-foot strip and started up the next. I weaved through a minefield of beer cans and around the black scar of a campfire pit. Then I picked up a presence twice as strong as the others.

"Got something," I said.

I hurried toward the source, climbed over a three-foot wall remnant, and startled a huge gray tabby. The cat hissed and tore off across the field, taking the presence I'd sensed with it. The spell snapped.

"Was that it?" Troy said.

"I can't—" I shot a glare at Lucas. I knew he didn't deserve it, but couldn't help myself. I stamped off to the end of the swath, grabbed a stick, and poked at a pile of rags.

"Paige?" Lucas said, coming up behind me.

"Don't. I know I'm overreacting, but I hate—"

"You didn't fail. The spell was working. You found the cat."

"If I can't tell the difference between a cat and a sixteen-year-old boy, then, no, it's not working. Forget it, okay? I should be looking for Jacob, not field-testing spells."

Lucas moved up behind me, so close I could feel the heat from his body. He dropped his voice to a murmur. "So you uncover a cat or two along the way. Who cares? Troy doesn't know how the spell's supposed to work. We have a lot of ground to cover."

Too much ground. We'd been here at least thirty minutes and barely searched a thousand square feet. I thought of Jacob being out there, waiting for rescue. What if it was Savannah? Would I be plodding through the field, bitching at Lucas then?

"Can you guys keep up the manual search?" I whispered so Troy couldn't overhear. "I don't want . . . I don't want you relying on my spell."

"That's fine. We'll cover ground faster that way. We have my light spell, as poor as it is. You take yours, go to the opposite side of the field, and start there."

I nodded, touched his arm in apology, and headed off with my light-ball trailing after me.

This time the sensing spell worked the first time. Or, I thought it worked, but something was wrong. The moment I cast, I felt a presence, a dozen times stronger than the cat's. I broke the cast, and tried again. Failure, then success. But the presence was still there, down a narrow alley between two buildings. Should I alert Lucas and Troy? And what, drag them over to help me uncover a whole litter of cats? This I could check myself. No sixteen-year-old boy would be scared off by the sight of me.

I ended the sensing spell and directed my light-ball to

stay around the building corner. There it would cast a dim glow, enough to see by, but not enough to spook a kid who likely knew little about the supernatural.

I slipped into the alley. The presence had come from a few yards down, along the east side. Less than ten feet away I saw a recessed doorway. That'd be it. I picked my way through the refuse, making as little noise as possible. Beside the doorway, I pressed myself against the wall. A smell wafted past. Cigarette smoke? Before I could process the thought, my body followed through on its original course of action, swinging around the doorway. There, in the shadows, was a teenage boy.

I smiled. Then I saw another boy beside the first, and another behind him. Something rustled behind me. I turned to see my exit blocked by another bandana-wearing teen. He said something in rapid-fire Spanish to his friends. They laughed.

Something told me this wasn't Jacob.

The Local Wildlife

ATTITUDE IS EVERYTHING. THEREFORE, WHEN FACED WITH four—oh, wait, there's another—five inner-city gang members, the worst thing you can do is turn tail and run. And why should you? Well, the presence of lethal weaponry might answer that question, but that's not how I see it. These are kids, right? People, just like everyone else. As such, they could be reasoned with, so long as one took the right stance. Firm, but polite. Assertive, but respectful. I had every right to be here, and furthermore, I had good cause. A cause that they might be able to assist.

"Hello," I said, standing tall and looking up to meet the eyes of the one I assumed was the leader. "I'm sorry to disturb you. I'm looking for a teenage boy who went missing around here. Have you seen him?"

For a moment, they just stared at me.

"Yeah?" one in the back said finally. "Well, we're looking for some money. Have you seen any? Maybe in your purse?"

A round of snickers. I turned to the speaker.

"As you've probably noticed, I'm not carrying a purse. I—"

"No purse?" He turned to his friends. "I think she is

hiding it, under her shirt. Two big purses." He made the universal male gesture for large breasts.

I waited through the inevitable guffaws and resisted the urge to tell them that, as boob jokes went, this was one of the lamer ones I'd heard.

"He's sixteen," I said. "Tall. Dark hair. White. Someone was chasing him. He may be hurt."

"If we saw him, he would be hurt. No one comes here and just walks out again." He met my gaze. "No one."

"Ah," a voice said behind us. "Well, perhaps this evening you gentlemen could make an exception." Lucas took my arm. "We apologize for the misunderstanding. Please excuse us."

The thug behind me stepped up to Lucas and flicked open a switchblade, keeping the knife down at his side, a covert threat.

"Nice suit, *pocho*," he said, then dropped his gaze over my skirt and blouse. "Where did you two come from? The fucking mission?"

"Out of town, actually," Lucas said. "Now, if you'll excuse us—"

"When we're done," the knife-thug said. "And we aren't done."

He smirked at me and reached out his free hand toward my breast. I started murmuring a binding spell, but before I could cast it, Lucas lifted his hand and blocked the youth's.

"Please don't do that," Lucas said.

"Yeah, and who's gonna stop me?"

"I am," a voice rumbled.

Everyone looked up—way up—to see Troy. He plucked the knife from the thug's hand.

"The mission bodyguard," I said. "Sorry, guys, but we

have work to do. Thanks for your cooperation, and don't stay out too late. It's a school night."

A chorus of muttered Spanish, none of it complimentary I'm sure, followed us from the alley, but the kids stayed in their doorway.

When we were out of earshot, Lucas glanced over at Troy.

"You realize, of course, that you robbed me of a rare opportunity to display my martial prowess, and win untold weeks of feminine appreciation."

"Sorry 'bout that."

I grinned and squeezed Lucas's arm. "Don't worry. I know you were mere milliseconds from blasting them with an energy-bolt spell."

"Absolutely." He glanced over his shoulder at Troy. "You'll have to forgive Paige's overenthusiastic attempt to befriend the local wildlife. Not many of their type where she comes from."

"Hey, we have gangs in Boston."

"Ah, yes. I believe they're particularly bad down by the wharf, where they're liable to descend upon the unwary, surround him with their yachts, and shout well-chosen and elegantly elocuted epithets."

Troy laughed.

Lucas continued, "When dealing with gang members, Paige, it's best to treat them as you would a rabid dog. Whenever possible, avoid their territory. If you inadvertently run into one, avoid eye contact, back away slowly . . . then blast them with a good energy bolt."

"Got it."

"Shall we continue—"

Lucas's cell phone beeped. He answered it. Fifteen seconds later, he hung up.

"They found him?" Troy said.

Lucas shook his head. "Just checking in to see if we had."

"Like we wouldn't call if we did." Troy gazed around the field. "Aw, fuck this. He's not here. You know what? I think you're right. I think he's lying low at a buddy's house. Griffin knows all about the other attacks. That's why he gave Jacob the cell phone, and told him to report anything unusual. Jacob probably spotted one of the neighborhood bad boys, panicked, and phoned it in. Then he felt stupid and took off."

We looked at one another.

"So," I said. "Do you guys want to take the north end again and I'll cover the south?"

They nodded. We were just about to split up when Lucas's phone buzzed. Another brief conversation.

"Griffin showed up in the second sector," Lucas said.

Troy winced. "Oh, shit."

"Precisely. He's making things difficult for the searchers. Unintentionally, of course, but he's quite distraught. They're understandably concerned, considering his abilities."

"What kind of half-demon is he?" I asked.

"A Ferratus," Lucas said.

Not one of the more common half-demons. So rare, in fact, that I had to translate the name from Latin before I remembered it. Ferratus. Iron-plated. A one-trick half-demon, but that one trick was a doozy. When a Ferratus half-demon invoked his power, his skin became as hard as iron. No wonder Benicio had snapped up Griffin from the St. Clouds. He was the perfect bodyguard . . . and the last guy you'd want going on a rampage.

"Dennis has asked me to intercede," Lucas said. "They're only a block over. I suggest we walk, and cover the intervening area along the way."

"I could stay here and—" I began.

"No," both men chorused.

I followed them into the alley.

As we walked, I drifted behind Lucas and Troy. So long as we were moving, I might as well cast my sensing spell and see whether I picked up anything. No reason to let them know what I was doing—that would only increase the pressure to provide results. Since they were both examining every nook and cranny on the way, they assumed I was doing the same and didn't notice as I fell farther behind.

I found two more alley cats. My alternate career with Animal Control was looking bright. On the positive side, as soon as I sensed kitty number three, I knew it was feline, which meant I was learning to distinguish between presence strengths.

I'd just finished finding my fourth stray cat when a distant voice hailed us. I peered down the alley to see several men approaching Troy and Lucas. The second search party. I quickened my pace. I'd gone about ten feet when I sensed another presence. Stronger than a cat, but . . . I stopped walking and concentrated. No, too weak to be human. I took another step. My feet felt lead-weighted, as a niggling uncertainty plucked at my brain. Too strong to be a cat, too weak to be human. So what was it?

Ahead, the men stood in a huddle, voices carrying to me only as waves of sound. Lucas saw me, but didn't wave me over. Tacit permission to continue searching. So no harm in checking out that presence. I traced it to an adjoining alleyway. I turned to show Lucas where I was going, but he'd left the group. Gone to find and calm

Griffin, no doubt. I'd zip down the alley and be back before he noticed I was gone.

I tracked the presence along the connecting alley to a doorway. The door had been propped open by a wadded-up piece of cardboard. Wet cardboard, bracing a door that opened inward. I checked the door itself for signs of dampness, but it was dry. A windless night and a drizzling rain wouldn't explain the sodden cardboard, meaning it had been brought in from the alley within the last hour or so.

I hesitated outside the door, readied a fireball, then shifted my light to the entrance, where it would illuminate the room within. I eased around the doorway. The room was empty, save for a pile of rags in the corner. The presence I was sensing came from that corner, somewhere under those rags. As I pulled the light-ball closer, I saw that the heap wasn't rags, but a moth-eaten filthy blanket. Protruding from under it was a high-top sneaker emblazoned with the ubiquitous Nike swoosh.

I ran across the room, dropped to my knees, and yanked away the blanket. Underneath was a man, curled in fetal position. I touched his bare arm. Cool. Dead. The presence had weakened even more since I'd first detected it. Dissipating as the last traces of body heat faded. A pang of sadness ran through me, chased by a guilty surge of relief that this wasn't the boy I was seeking.

I moved back. As I did, my shadow fell from the man's face, and I realized it wasn't a man at all. The size had fooled me, but now, seeing the soft features and frightened eyes, I knew I was looking at Griffin's son.

My hands flew to his neck, feeling for signs of life, but I knew I'd find none. I rolled him onto his back to check for a heartbeat. As his arms fell from his chest, I inhaled, seeing the bloody patchwork of his T-shirt, crisscrossed with stab wounds.

"Paige!" Lucas called from somewhere outside.

"In—" My voice came out as a squeak. I swallowed and tried again. "In here."

I got to my feet, then caught sight of Jacob's bloodied shirt and bent to pull up the blanket. His wide eyes stared at me. People used to believe you could see the last moment of a man's life imprinted in his eyes. I looked into Jacob's eyes and I did indeed see that last moment. I saw bottomless, impotent terror. I bit my lip and forced myself to tug the blanket up.

A noise at the door. A large shadow filled the door frame.

"Troy," I said. "Good. Keep everyone else back until I've had a chance to tell Lucas—"

The man crossed the room in a few long strides. Even before I saw his face, I knew it wasn't Troy.

"Griffin," I said, jumping back to block Jacob's body. "I—"

He grabbed me by the shoulder and threw me out of the way. I hit the floor. For a moment, I lay there, dazed. That moment was just long enough for Griffin to kneel beside his son and pull back the blanket.

A howl split the air. A curse, a scream, another howl. The slam of fist against brick. Another. Then another. I looked up to see a fog of brick and mortar dust and, through it, Griffin beating the wall, each blow punctuated with an unearthly howl.

"Griffin!" I shouted.

He was past hearing me. I cast a binding spell, too quickly, and it failed. From outside came the sound of voices and running feet, then Griffin's enraged grief drowned them out. A hail of broken brick pelted down, mingled with slivers of wood and stone. A falling shingle glanced off my shoulder as the building quaked under the force of Griffin's blows.

In a few minutes, something would give—the roof, a wall, something. Through the dust, I could see the open doorway, beckoning me to safety. Instead, I closed my eyes, concentrated, and cast the binding spell again. Halfway through the incantation, a chunk of brick hit my arm, and I stumbled backward. More brick rained down, larger pieces now, big enough to hurt. I gritted my teeth, closed my eyes, and cast again.

The pounding stopped. I held the spell for a few seconds before I dared to open my eyes. When I did, I saw Griffin, his fist stopped in midair. He grunted, then snarled, trying to break free, but I put everything I had into holding him still. Our gazes met. His eyes darkened with rage and hate.

"I'm sorry," I said.

Lucas and the others swung through the doorway.

Evidence of a Pattern

TWO DRAINING HOURS LATER, WE RETURNED TO THE SUV. The EMTs had taken Jacob's body to the Cabal morgue for examination and autopsy. A forensics team was processing the scene. Investigators were combing the area for witnesses and clues. Standard procedure for a murder investigation. Yet every one of these professionals, from the coroner to the photographer, was a supernatural, and a Cortez Cabal employee.

None of this would ever make the six o'clock news. The Cabals were a law unto themselves in the purest sense of the phrase. They had their own legal code. They enforced that code. They punished the transgressors. And nobody in the human world knew any different.

"Do you want to stay with Griffin?" I asked Troy as he escorted us to the car. "I'm sure we could grab another bodyguard from the security team."

Troy shook his head. "They're taking Griffin to see his kids. He doesn't need me there."

As we neared the SUV, Troy lifted the remote. Heavy running footfalls sounded behind us. It was Griffin.

"I want to talk to you," he said, bearing down on Lucas.

Troy put up a hand to stop him, but Lucas shook his

head. I readied a binding spell. Griffin stopped inches from Lucas, well within anyone's personal comfort zone. Both Troy and I visibly tensed. Lucas only looked up at Griffin.

"I want to hire you," Griffin said. "I want you to find whoever did this."

"The Cabal will investigate. My father will see to it."

"Fuck the Cabal."

"Griff," Troy warned.

"I mean it," Griffin said. "Fuck the Cabal. They won't do shit until some sorcerer's kid gets hurt. I want you to find this son of a bitch and bring him to me. Just bring him to me."

"I—"

"I can pay you. Whatever the going rate is for a PI, I'll double it. Triple it." He raised his fist for emphasis, then looked at his hand, shoved it into his pocket, and lowered his voice. "Just tell me what you want, and I'll get it."

"You don't need to do that, Griffin. My father will order an investigation, and he has resources I can't match."

"I'm class C. I'm not *entitled* to an investigation."

"But you'll get one."

"And if I don't?"

"Then I'll do it," I said quietly.

Griffin glanced over, as if he hadn't noticed me there. For a long minute, he just looked at me. Then he nodded.

"Good," he said. "Thank you."

He turned and walked back into the night.

"Oh, God, what did I just say?" I murmured, thumping my head back against the leather rear seat. I looked at Lucas, buckling his seat belt beside me. "I am so sorry."

"Don't be. If you didn't say it, I would have. You set his

mind at ease. That's what he needed. As for following through, that won't be necessary. My father will call for an investigation, if for no other reason than to reassure his employees that the Cabal is taking action."

This time when Troy searched our room, he found someone there. Benicio. Lucas took one look into the room and slumped, as if the strain of the night had just hit him full force.

"Minibar?" I whispered.

"Please."

Benicio and I traded nods, and I skirted past him to the bar fridge. I took out two glasses, then stopped and turned to Benicio.

"Can I get you something?"

"Water would be fine," he said. "Thank you, Paige."

I fixed drinks as the two men talked behind me.

"I wanted to thank you for joining the search," Benicio said. "It meant a lot to everyone, having someone from the family helping."

"Yes, well, you're welcome. It's been a long night. Perhaps—"

"I couldn't get your brothers there on a direct order, let alone voluntarily. They think leadership is showing up at the office every day, issuing orders, and signing papers. They have no concept of what the employees expect, what they need."

I peeked at Lucas. He stood there with the pained expression of a child forced to sit through the thousandth rendition of his father's favorite lecture.

"I'm sure Hector would have gone."

Benicio snorted. "Of course Hector would go. He'd go

because he knows I'd want him to. He'd have killed the boy himself, if he thought it'd win my favor."

Lucas winced. I handed him a straight scotch. He mouthed a thank-you. I gave Benicio his water and he nodded his thanks before continuing.

"We've had more evidence of a pattern. A St. Cloud VP got wind of our problem, prompting a call from Lionel. One of their necromancer's daughters, who was living with relatives after some family trouble, was attacked last Saturday, the night before Dana."

"Is she okay?" I asked.

Benicio shook his head. "Like Jacob, she managed to place a call to their emergency line saying she was being followed but was dead when they found her. I've placed calls to Thomas Nast and Guy Boyd asking whether they know of any attacks on employees' children. Thomas tentatively confirmed that they've had two incidents, but he wouldn't provide details over the phone. The Cabals are meeting in Miami tomorrow to share information."

"They're launching a joint investigation, I presume," Lucas said.

"Yes, which is why I'm asking you to reconsider."

"Reconsider?" I said. "If the Cabals are investigating, you don't need us."

"No. If the Cabals are *jointly* investigating, I need your help more than ever. As Lucas can tell you, an intra-Cabal operation—"

Lucas lifted a hand. "We're tired, Papá," he said softly. "It's been a very long night. I understand this new concern, and I agree that it *is* a concern. May I ask, though, that you let me explain the situation to Paige tonight, try to get some sleep, then discuss it with you over breakfast?"

"Yes, of course," Benicio said. "What time do you need to be in court tomorrow?"

"Noon."

"Then let's reschedule our breakfast from seven to eight, to give you time to sleep. I'll have the jet fly you to Chicago afterward."

Lucas hesitated, then nodded. "Thank you."

He turned toward the door.

"One last thing," Benicio said.

Lucas paused, still facing the door, one hand on the knob, lips parting in a silent sigh. "Yes, Papá?"

"In light of this latest tragedy, I think we must assume that the killer's intent is to hurt the Cabals where they expect it least and will feel it most. Given that, we have to also assume that the ultimate prize for him would be a member of a CEO's family."

"Yes, of course, but we can discuss this—"

"I'm not talking generalities, Lucas. I'm bringing this to your attention because it obviously affects you and Paige, and you need to consider that immediately."

"He's targeting teenagers. I'm not a teen—"

"I'm not referring to you. This killer is obviously smart enough to attack the edges, pluck from the herd the most vulnerable, those children farthest removed from Cabal protection. If he wanted a teenager from a Cabal CEO's immediate family, there is only one who doesn't live with a Cabal and who isn't under twenty-four-hour guard."

"Oh, God," I said. "Savannah."

The Most Endangered
Kid on the Planet

EARLIER THIS YEAR, WHEN KRISTOF NAST SUED FOR CUS-
tody of Savannah, he'd done so by claiming to be her father. At first, I hadn't believed him. Savannah, as the
daughter of a notoriously powerful woman who was both
a witch and a half-demon, showed every sign of matching
or surpassing her mother's powers, and as such she'd be a
prize acquisition for any Cabal.

As for Kristof being her father, it was preposterous. No
witch would ever get involved with a sorcerer, much less
a high-ranking Cabal sorcerer. Then I'd met Kristof, seen
Savannah's eyes staring back at me, and knew there was
no question of paternity.

Even if I'd still doubted it, his actions proved he wasn't
trying to recruit a potential employee. Kristof hadn't just
made a halfhearted attempt to kidnap Savannah. He'd
put his all into getting custody, and he'd died trying
to stop Savannah from hurting herself. A sorcerer like
Kristof Nast would never do that for a witch who wasn't
his daughter.

This story had been churning in the Cabal gossip mill
for months now. Anyone looking for Cabal children
would know about Savannah. They'd also know that, un-

like every other child and grandchild of a Cabal CEO, she wasn't ferried to and from a private school in an armored car filled with half-demon bodyguards. She had only Lucas and me, and right now, she didn't even have us.

I will say, with some modicum of pride, that I did not panic. Okay, I did have a few moments of heart palpitations and rapid breathing, but I managed to pull myself together before hitting the clinical anxiety stage.

It took only a few minutes for Lucas and his father to come up with a plan that kept me from barreling out the door and grabbing the next plane home. Benicio had already dispatched the corporate jet to Portland. By the time he mentioned the possible danger to Savannah, Cabal guards were en route to pick her up. I will admit to a brief moment of "What if this is all a setup and he's going to snatch Savannah" anxiety, but I managed to stifle it before I blurted out any wild accusations. Lucas trusted his father to bring Savannah here, so I trusted him.

Lucas made the call to Michelle's parents, apologized for waking them, and tossed together a plausible story to explain why several huge men would be arriving at their door to collect Savannah. Or I assume he came up with a plausible story. I heard none of it. I knew enough about Lucas, though, to know he was capable of manufacturing the most convincing lies at a moment's notice—yet another birthright from his father.

At my request, Lucas also talked to Savannah. What did he tell her? The truth. I'm sure of that. If it was me on that phone, I'd have sugarcoated it for her. I couldn't help it. The urge to make her life easier was too great. So I'd have given her a watered-down version, and she'd have listened, then asked to speak to Lucas to get the truth.

Once Benicio was gone, Lucas walked to the sofa, sat down beside me, and took my hand.

"You okay?" he murmured.

I squeezed his hand and managed a wan smile. "I'll be better when she's here, but I'm okay."

"About this case," he said. "Am I correct in assuming you want it?"

"I want it, but—"

"After what happened tonight, we've moved beyond the luxury of worrying about conflict of interest. Someone needs to investigate this."

"You don't think the Cabals can handle it?"

"Individually, I'd say the Cabals are quite capable of handling the situation. But together? Together they work at a fraction of their capacity."

"Infighting?"

He nodded. "Precisely. It's like two warring countries teaming up against a common enemy. Each will want to lead the attack. Each won't share their information for fear of divulging contacts and techniques. Each will want the other to put *their* men at risk. A plan of action won't be decided so much as negotiated."

"And in the meantime, more kids will be hurt."

"Collateral damage. I won't say the Cabals don't care; they aren't monsters. But they are structured around profit-making and self-preservation. Those priorities will always come first, intentionally or not."

"But obviously your father foresees this or he wouldn't still be asking you to take the case. Why doesn't he tell the other Cabals, 'Thanks for the offer, but we'll go it alone'?"

Lucas leaned back into the sofa. "Politics. At this level, even my father's hands are tied. If he refuses to cooperate, it'll not only affect his standing with the other Cabals but also cause internal dissent. Understandably, his employees will question why he'd refuse extra help."

"So it's down to us. In that case, then, I definitely want to—" I stopped. "Wait. What about Savannah? I certainly can't let her tag along and—"

"I have a thought on that. Someone who could look after her."

I shook my head. "You know how I am. Either I look after her myself, or I'll go crazy worrying. I don't trust anyone—"

He told me who he had in mind.

"Oh," I said. "That might work."

Benicio called to say that Savannah was on the jet and would arrive in Miami just after six. Lucas told him our decision, that I would take the case, starting immediately. As for Lucas's role, we'd decided on honesty over subterfuge. Of course he'd help me. Yes, this meant working alongside the Cabals, but the cause was right, and he wouldn't cheapen that by hiding his involvement. If Benicio felt he'd won a victory, we had to let him have that satisfaction. Our only defense was that we wouldn't accept a Cabal paycheck for the job. We were doing this on our own, for our own reasons.

With securing Savannah's safety now our top priority, Lucas asked his father for a rain check on breakfast. Instead, Benicio would bring a copy of the case files for me later in the morning, after Lucas was gone and I'd had time to settle Savannah in at the hotel. Benicio promised Lucas that he would help with protection arrangements for Savannah, and Lucas wisely refrained from telling him we'd already done so. While we appreciated Benicio's help, neither of us wanted Savannah in his custody for long, in case he hoped to use the opportunity to pitch to her as a future employee.

We met Savannah at the airport. By "we," I mean Lucas, myself, and Troy. Yes, Troy was still with us, though I had every intention of handing him back to his boss after lunch. Nothing against Troy, but there was something unsettling about a huge half-demon dogging your every step. Savannah, however, took our new shadow in stride, as if there was nothing at all unusual about having a bodyguard/chauffeur—further proof that Cabal royal blood flowed in her veins.

Over breakfast, we answered Savannah's questions about the attacks. She listened with more curiosity than concern. Altruism isn't Savannah's strong suit. I tell myself it's part of being a teenager, but I suspect there's more to it than that.

"Just as long as I don't get kidnapped again," she said. "Twice in one year is enough for anyone. I swear, I must be the most endangered kid on the planet."

"You're special."

She snorted. "Yeah, well, special never seems to bring anything but trouble. Now I know why my mom moved us around so much." She looked up sharply. "We don't have to move again, do we?"

"It's not that kind of problem. All we need to do is find you a safe place to stay while I look for this guy."

"What?" She looked from me to Lucas. "No way. You're kidding, right?"

"Paige can't investigate while worrying about you, Savannah."

Her eyes swung to meet mine. "You wouldn't do this. You wouldn't send me away."

I opened my mouth, but guilt zapped my voice.

"Savannah . . ." Lucas warned.

Her gaze clung to mine. "Remember the last time? You said you wouldn't leave. Not ever."

"Savannah—" Lucas's voice sharpened.

"We can work the case together. You've got all those new spells. You can protect me better than anyone. I trust you, Paige."

A right hook below the belt. I managed a strangled, "I—we—"

Lucas told her who'd be looking after her.

Savannah blinked, then eased back in her chair. "Well, why didn't you say so?" She took a swig of orange juice. "Hey, does this mean I get to skip school?"

After breakfast we returned to the airport to see Lucas off. As Savannah chatted with Troy, Lucas and I discussed my next steps in the case.

"The boy who was attacked first, Holden," I said. "He called the emergency line, too. Don't you think that's odd? That almost every victim had time to call for help before they were attacked? Jacob, I can see, because he had a cell phone. But the others?"

"I'd strongly consider the possibility that they were

permitted to make the call, perhaps by prolonging the chase so they could reach a phone."

"But why?"

"It was already too late for help to arrive, so the killer was probably ensuring that the case remained under Cabal jurisdiction, and the victims weren't found by humans first. However, we should concentrate on facts, rather than interpretation. It's too early for that."

"Speaking of facts, I wish Holden saw his attacker." A thought struck me. "What we need is the eyewitness report of someone who *wasn't* supposed to escape. We need a necromancer."

Lucas shook his head. "A good idea, but murder victims are very difficult to communicate with so soon after they pass over, and on the rare occasion when a necromancer manages to make contact, the spirits are almost always too traumatized to recall details surrounding their death."

"I don't mean Jacob. I mean Dana. A good necromancer can make contact with someone in a coma."

"You're right, I'd forgotten that. Excellent idea. I have several necromancer contacts, all of whom owe me considerable favors. On the flight, I'll place some calls and see which of them could get to Miami quickest."

Visiting Hour

BEFORE TAKING SAVANNAH TO THE AIRPORT, THE CABAL guards had escorted her to our apartment to get more clothing. Benicio had also asked her to pack suitcases for Lucas and me, since we'd arrived in Miami with only one change of clothing. Considerate of him, I'll admit. I'd been too worried about Savannah to think of that myself. The only downside was that this meant Savannah picked out what *she* thought we should wear.

Lucas had taken his suitcase straight onto the jet without opening it, probably fearing that the look on his face when he glanced inside might make Savannah feel her efforts were underappreciated. Though Lucas owned very little in the way of casual clothing, I suspected every piece of it was in that bag, and not a single item suitable for court. I only hoped she'd thought to grab him some socks and underwear.

When I unpacked my bag, I saw that lack of undergarments wouldn't be a problem for me.

"What did you do, empty my entire lingerie drawer into the bag?" I said, untangling a web of bras.

"Course not. I don't think they make suitcases that

big." She tugged a pair of garter straps from the bra-knot. "Do you actually wear these? Or are they just for sex?"

I grabbed the garters. "I wear them."

Of course, when I did wear them it was only because they improved a certain sexual advantage of wearing skirts, one that was very awkward to accomplish with full nylons. That, however, wasn't a tidbit I was sharing with anyone—well, other than Lucas, but he already knew.

"You promised me I'd get stuff like this when I went to high school," she said, lifting a pair of green silk panties.

"I promised no such thing."

"I mentioned it, and you didn't say no. That's the same as promising. Do you know how embarrassing it is changing in a locker room, having the girls see me wearing cotton grannies?"

"All the more reason to keep you wearing them. If it embarrasses you to have *girls* see them, it'd be even more embarrassing to have guys see them. Like a modern-day chastity belt."

"I hate you." She fell back, spread-eagled onto the bed, then lifted her head. "You know, if you won't get them for me, I might sneak behind your back and buy my own. That'd be bad."

"You gonna start doing laundry, too?"

"As if!"

"Then I'm not worried."

Someone knocked at the door. Savannah vaulted from the bed and was out of the room before I could stuff my handful of lingerie into a drawer. I heard Savannah's shout of greeting and knew who it was.

"Paige is in the bedroom putting away her underwear," Savannah said. "It'll take a while."

I grabbed another handful.

"Shit," said a voice behind me. "She's not kidding. What'd you do, rob a lingerie store?"

There stood the world's only female werewolf, a title that sounds more like it should describe a circus freak show than the blond woman in the doorway. Tall and lean, Elena Michaels had a werewolf's typically athletic build, and the kind of wholesome good looks that cause men to say things like, "Wow, if she dolled herself up, she could be a knockout." Those who dared say such things, though, were more likely to find themselves knocked out.

Today Elena wore a T-shirt, cutoff jean shorts, and sneakers, with her long silver-blond hair tied back in an elastic band and maybe, just maybe, lip gloss... and looked a helluva lot better than I did after hours of grooming. Not that I'm envious or anything. Oh, did I mention she was thirty-two and looked mid-twenties? Or that she can eat a sixteen-ounce porterhouse steak and not gain an ounce? Werewolves get all the goodies: extended youth, extreme metabolism, sharpened senses, and superstrength. And, yeah, I'm envious.

Still, if I can't have a werewolf's gifts, I'll take a werewolf as a friend. Being part wolf makes them extremely loyal and protective... which made Elena the only person to whom I'd entrust Savannah.

Elena surveyed the mess of lingerie scattered across the bed. "I'm not even sure where half that stuff goes."

Savannah zoomed past Elena, jumped on the bed, grabbed a bra, and held it up to her chest.

"This one's mine," Savannah said, grinning. "Can't you tell?"

Elena laughed. "Maybe in a few years."

Savannah snorted. "At the rate I'm going, it'll take a few years plus a few pairs of socks. I'm the only girl in the ninth grade who still wears a training bra."

"I was still wearing one in tenth grade, so I've got you beat." Elena bent down to pick up a negligee I'd dropped. "Expecting to spend a lot of time alone with Lucas, I see."

"I wish," I said. "He's already headed back to Chicago. Savannah packed my clothes, and I do hope there *are* clothes in this bag somewhere."

"At the bottom," Savannah said.

I shoved the last of the lingerie into a drawer, then stuffed the half-packed suitcase into the closet and turned to Elena. I resisted the urge to hug her. Elena wasn't the hugs-and-kisses type. Even fleeting physical contact, like handshakes, made her vaguely uncomfortable, though nowhere near as uncomfortable as they made someone else . . . which made me realize someone was missing from this reunion.

"Where's Clay?" I said. "Waiting in the car? Hoping he can avoid saying hello to me?"

"Hello, Paige," came a Southern drawl from the living room.

"Hello, Clayton."

I popped my head around the bedroom door. Elena's partner, Clayton Danvers, was standing by the window, his back to me, likely not an unconscious gesture. Like Elena, Clay was blond-haired, blue-eyed, and well built. While Elena was attractive, Clay was traffic-stopping gorgeous . . . and had all the charm of a pit viper.

The first time we met, Clay had tossed me a bag containing a severed human head, and things went downhill from there. I don't understand him, he doesn't understand me, and the only thing we have in common is Elena, which causes more problems than it solves.

He finally deigned to face me. "You said Lucas isn't here?"

"He had to zip back to Chicago for his court case."

Clay nodded, clearly disappointed. One could argue that he simply hoped for someone else to talk with, to avoid having to make conversation with me, but the truth was that Clay seemed to genuinely like Lucas, which shocked the hell out of me. Not that Lucas wasn't likable. Just that Clay, well, he didn't much like anybody. His usual reaction to anyone outside his Pack ranged from near-tolerance to outright loathing. I'd landed on the farthest possible end of that scale, though I was slowly inching away from the brink.

"Ready to go?" Clay said, looking behind me at Elena.

"I just got here," she said.

"We have a long drive—"

"And all the time in the world to drive it." Elena walked from the bedroom and looked at me. "We rented a car so we can drive back to New York, take our time, see the sights, make a vacation out of it. If anyone is after Savannah, Jeremy thought it might be wise if we keep on the move for a few days, rather than rush home."

"Good idea. Thank him for me."

She grinned. "Having us out of his hair for a few days is all the thanks he needs."

"Can we stop in Orlando?" Savannah asked.

"You want to go to Disney World?" Elena said.

Savannah rolled her eyes. "Not likely."

I mouthed something to Elena. She grinned.

"Ah, Universal Studios. Sorry. I thought Disney World sounded kind of cool myself, but we could go to Universal, if that's okay with Paige."

"Have fun," I said. "I transferred some money into Savannah's account, so make sure she pays her own way."

From Elena's brief nod, I knew Savannah's money wouldn't be spent on anything but junk food and souvenirs, as it had when I'd given her money for her week with them this summer. I knew better than to argue. Their Alpha, Jeremy Danvers, was very well off, and the three of them shared everything, including bank accounts. If I insisted on paying, I'd insult Jeremy. If he had his way, Savannah wouldn't even be using her own money for candy bars and T-shirts.

"Got your bag packed?" Clay asked Savannah.

"Never unpacked it."

"Good. Grab it and we'll go."

"You two have a nice trip," Elena said, plunking onto the sofa. "I'm visiting Paige."

Clay made a noise in his throat.

"Stop growling," Elena said. "I'm here, and I want to spend some time with Paige before I leave. Unless you'd prefer I *stayed* here. You know, that might not be such a bad idea. I could stick around, help her out—"

"No."

"Is that an order?"

"Savannah?" I cut in. "There's a Starbucks a few blocks over. Why don't you show Clay where it is, grab us some coffees?" I looked at Clay. "When you get back, you should probably take off. Benicio's stopping by soon, and he made some noises about taking Savannah into protective custody, so I'd rather she wasn't here when he arrives."

Clay nodded, then walked to the door and held it open for Savannah. When it closed behind them, Elena looked at me.

"Taking mediation lessons from Lucas, I see. Sorry about that. I know you have better things to do than listen to us bicker." She shook her head. "We've worked out a lot of things, but he still has trouble with the idea that I need to keep a corner of my life for myself, a corner that doesn't include him."

I sat in the chair across from her. "He doesn't like me. I understand that."

"No, it's not you." She caught my skeptical look. "Seriously. He just doesn't like me having friends. God, that sounds bad, doesn't it? Sometimes I hear myself saying things like that, and they make perfect sense to me, but then I think of how they must sound to others—" She stopped. "So tell me about this case."

"Ouch. You have to work on your 'steering clear of personal issues' segues."

She laughed. "That obvious, eh?"

"As for Clay not wanting you to have friends, I know he's like that, and I know why, so you don't need to worry about it. I'm not going to mail you brochures for women's shelters. I'll admit, at one time, I was a little concerned. Not that I thought he was abusive or anything, but he's, uh, extremely committed—"

"Obsessive."

"I wasn't going to say it."

She laughed and shifted to recline on the sofa, feet on the coffee table. "Don't worry, I say it all the time. Usually to him. Sometimes shouted. Occasionally accompanied by a flying object. We're working on it, though. He's learning to give me some space, and I'm learning that he's never going to be happy about it. Oh, I told him about that idea we had, for the ski trip this winter? He flipped. Then I said it'd be the four of us, not just you and me, and he simmered down, actually said that sounded okay. That's the trick, I think. Suggest something he'll hate, then offer a less painful alternative."

"If that doesn't work, next time you argue about me, remind him you could befriend Cassandra instead."

Elena whooped a laugh. "Oh, that'd put the fear into

him . . . though he probably wouldn't believe it. Speaking of believing, would you believe she's still calling me?"

"Are you serious?"

"She somehow got my cell phone number."

"I didn't—"

"I know you didn't, that's why I didn't ask. Problem is, now I have to talk to her, at least long enough to say I don't want to talk to her. When she called the house line, Jeremy would say I wasn't home, and Clay—well, Clay never let her get past hello." Elena swung her legs down and twisted around to sit at the opposite end of the sofa, facing me. "I hate to admit this, but I'm spooked. I mean, she can't want us to be buddies, not after what she did, so what does she *really* want?"

"Honestly? She probably doesn't have an ulterior motive. I think she really wants to get to know you better, and she doesn't see any conflict between that and trying to steal your lover or convince the council to leave you for dead." I shrugged. "She's a vampire. They're different. What can I say?"

"Two words. Serious psychotherapy."

I grinned. "We'll go halfsies and get her a gift certificate for Christmas."

Elena was about to reply when the door opened. Savannah walked in, carrying my key card in one hand and a steaming coffee cup in the other. I was sure that whatever was in that cup, it wasn't hot chocolate, and probably wasn't even decaf, but I said nothing. I doubted Clay realized she was too young for coffee. I only hoped Elena would step in when the wine and whiskey came out.

Savannah held the door open for Clay, who walked through carrying a cardboard cup holder with three cups.

"That was fast," Elena said. "Too fast. What'd you do? Run all the way there? Or drive?"

"It was only half a block."

"Uh-huh."

"He's right," Savannah said. "It was closer than Paige thought, but we're just dropping off your drinks, then we're going to check out the marina while you guys talk."

Elena glanced at Clay, tensed, as if waiting for him to refute this. When his mouth opened, her fingers tightened on the sofa cushion.

"First, we're taking your suitcase down to the car," he said to Savannah. He turned to Elena and handed her a coffee cup. "When you're done here, just come and get us."

She smiled up at him. "Thanks. I won't be long."

He nodded and passed me a cup.

"Tea," he said, then glanced at Savannah. "Right?"

"Chai," she said.

I took the cup with thanks, then laid it down and helped Savannah get ready.

A Fortuitous Collision of Circumstances

SAVANNAH WAS, AS SHE'D SAID, ALREADY PACKED, BUT I wasn't letting her go without an armful of instructions, most of which were some variation on "be good" or "be careful."

Handing Savannah over to anyone, even to people I knew would protect her with their lives, wasn't easy for me. Elena made it easier, though, by arranging a twice-daily check-in time of eleven in the morning and eleven at night. If either of us would be busy at the designated time, we'd forewarn the other, so no one would be left worrying about a call not made or not answered. Yes, it bordered on obsessive-compulsive, but neither Elena nor Clay made me feel I was overreacting, and I truly appreciated that.

I planned to walk down with Elena and see them off, so Savannah and I didn't bother with good-byes. As the door swung shut behind them, I turned to Elena.

"Clay's really good with Savannah," I said.

"Uh-huh."

"You don't think so?"

She plunked down onto the sofa. "No, I'm just waiting for part two of that comment."

"You mean the part that goes 'You know, he'd probably make a pretty good—'"

She held up a hand to stop me. "Yep, that part."

I laughed and plunked into my chair. "Any progress on that front?"

"He's moved from hints disguised as jokes to outright hints. That took a year, so I figure I have another year before he insists on progressing to actual discussion. He's being pretty good about it, though. Taking his time, getting me used to the idea before he pops the question."

"He knows you're not ready."

"Problem is, I'm not sure I'll ever be. I want kids. I really do. I always assumed I'd grow up, marry a nice guy, live in the suburbs, and raise a houseful of kids. But with Clay, well, I always thought a life with him meant giving up all of that. Even the 'growing up' part."

"Highly overrated."

"I think so." She grinned and stretched her legs along the sofa. "Kids, though, well, it's a big step, and not just for the normal reasons. Clay knows I'm not going anywhere, so it isn't a question of commitment. It's the werewolf issue. Two werewolves having a baby? Never been done. Who knows what—" She rubbed her hands over her arms. "Well, I'm just not ready, and right now, I don't have time to worry about it, not with all these recruitment problems."

I put down my Chai. "That's right. You met that new recruit this week. How did—"

Two raps at the door cut me off.

"Guess Clay's getting antsy," I said. "At least he tried."

Elena shook her head. "That's far too polite a knock for Clay."

"And it's the wrong door," I said, following the sound. "That'd be our bodyguard."

Elena laughed. I opened the door that joined the two suites and she saw Troy.

"Shit," she murmured. "You weren't kidding."

"I just saw Mr. Cortez's car pull into the lot," Troy said. "Figured you might like some advance warning. I thought I heard"—he leaned into the room and saw Elena—"voices. Hello."

He leaned farther into the room for a better look, and it was obvious he wasn't going anywhere without an introduction.

"Troy, this is Elena; Elena, this is Troy Morgan, Benicio's bodyguard, temporarily on loan."

Elena stood and extended her hand. Troy nearly tripped over his feet to take it. As usual, I don't think Elena noticed the attention, and certainly didn't reciprocate.

"You're a, uh, friend of Paige's?" he said.

"A fellow council member," I said. "She just stopped in for a visit . . . with her husband."

"Hus—" He looked down at Elena's hand and saw her engagement ring. "Oh." He stepped back, reluctantly. "The interracial council, huh? So you're a supernatural. Let me guess—"

"Sorry," I said. "But if Benicio's coming up, we'd better get Elena gone."

Another rap at the door, this time the hall one.

"Come on," Troy said to Elena. "We'll duck out through my room."

"Say good-bye to Savannah for me," I said. "I'll call you tonight."

Elena let Troy usher her into his room. I paused, then opened the hall door and invited Benicio in. His new bodyguard stayed in the corridor. Before I'd even closed that door, the adjoining door reopened and Elena popped her head through. She motioned toward the hall, mouthing "guard." I discreetly waved her inside. Better for her to go out the main door, and arouse Benicio's suspicions a bit, than have the guard see her sneak from Troy's room and raise Benicio's suspicions a lot. I doubted Troy usually had women spend the night while he was on duty.

"Is Savannah here?" Benicio asked, looking around. He saw Elena.

"She was just leaving," I said.

Elena brushed past Benicio with a small smile and a nod. I held the door open, then closed it behind her and turned to Benicio.

"Now, where were we?" I said. "Oh, you brought the case files. Thanks."

I took the files. Benicio glanced at the half-open bedroom door, trying to see through it.

"Is Savannah—"

"Did Lucas get to Chicago okay?" I asked. "He was worried about being late. He cut it pretty close this morning."

"The plane landed at eleven."

"Time to spare, then. Good."

Benicio slipped a look through the bedroom doorway. "I assume Savannah—"

"Is everything in this?" I said, hoisting the file.

Before he could answer, I walked to the window and spread the file on the wide sill, pretending to look through it as I surveyed the parking lot below. I saw Clay and Elena's blond heads bobbing through the scattering of cars, moving fast, Savannah's dark head between them.

"Let's see. Incident reports . . ." Elena, Clay, and Savannah stopped at a car. A convertible, of course. A moment's pause, then Clay tossed Elena the keys and they climbed inside. "Scene photos, medical reports . . ." The car peeled from the lot. "Looks like everything's here. Now, you were saying . . . ?"

"Savannah," he said. "I don't see her here, Paige, and I certainly hope you wouldn't be foolish enough to let her wander around the hotel unaccompanied."

"Of course not. She's staying with friends while I investigate this."

"Friends?" He paused. "The woman who just left, I presume. Perhaps you don't realize how serious this is. You cannot turn Paige over to a human—"

"She's a supernatural. Someone who will take very good care of Savannah."

Benicio paused, only for a moment, processing everything he knew about my supernatural contacts in less time it would take most people to name the capital of France.

"The werewolf," he said. "Elena Michaels."

I'll admit to a moment of disconcertion. The werewolves valued their privacy, which was why I hadn't told Troy who Elena was. When Benicio did his homework, he didn't miss anything.

"Werewolf?" Troy murmured behind us. "She was a werewolf? Shit. Now there's a story that'll buy me a few rounds at the club."

"No," Benicio said. "You won't tell anyone."

Troy straightened. "Yes, sir."

"As a matter of interracial courtesy, we must respect the werewolves' privacy. You may, however, take a few drinks on my club tab, to compensate."

Troy grinned. "Yes, sir."

"I don't mean to criticize, Paige," Benicio said. "And I

don't wish to insult your friends, but I must point out that the Cabal is far better equipped to protect Savannah. You lack experience in such matters, and what may seem like a good idea to you is not necessarily the wisest option."

"It wasn't my idea."

"Then who—?" He stopped, realizing the only possible answer. Then he nodded. "If Lucas thinks this is best, we'll leave the girl with them . . . for now. If the situation worsens, though, we may need to reconsider our options."

"Understood," I said. "Now, what can you tell me about this case?"

Benicio ordered a room-service lunch for us, which we ate in the hotel room while discussing the case. If Benicio had any problem discussing Cabal problems with a witch, he gave no sign of it, but was as generous with his information and offers of assistance as I could want. More generous than I wanted, to be honest. I was uncomfortable enough taking a case Benicio had brought to us. I didn't want to work with him any closer than necessary.

There were a few strategic moves I could make that made me feel less like I'd been suckered into working for Benicio. Earlier, I'd notified the hotel that I'd be staying on, and asked them to change the billing to my credit card. They were less than a third full, with no hope of major bookings soon, so after some dickering, we'd agreed on an affordable rate. I didn't tell Benicio that I'd switched the billing. By the time he found out, it'd be too late for him to argue.

I also gave Benicio back his bodyguard. When he protested I argued that with Griffin on grief-leave, Benicio

needed one of his regular guards, and my own investigating would be less conspicuous without a half-demon
shadow.

Benicio left at one. Lucas still hadn't called about the
necromancer. While I waited, I read through the files. I
kept my cell phone on the desk, checked for messages
twice, and adjusted the ring volume once. A bit anxious
for Lucas's call? Nah.

When the phone finally rang, I checked caller ID, and
answered with "You found someone?"

"I apologize for taking so long. Two of my contacts
were slow in phoning back, then I had to wait for court to
recess."

"But you found someone?"

"A fortuitous collision of circumstances. A first-rate
necromancer who just happens to be on business in
Miami this week." His voice sounded oddly strained, as if
forcing cheerfulness. Must have been the connection.

"Perfect," I said. "When can he meet me? Or is it she?"

"Early this evening, as a matter of fact. Very fortunate.
The only other possibility couldn't make it until Monday,
so this is quite the lucky break."

Did it sound as if he was trying to convince me? Or
himself?

"Okay, so tell me about—"

"Hold on." A muffled word or two to someone else. "It
appears the recess ended sooner than I expected. Do you
have a pen?" He gave me the address and directions.
"Now, everything's been arranged. Someone will meet
you there. They're expecting you between six-thirty and
seven. It's a reasonably good section of town, but I'd still

advise that you ask the cab driver to wait until you're inside. Go to the rear door, knock, and give your name."

"Speaking of names, what's this necro—"

"They're calling me in now. I have to go, but I'll phone you tonight. Oh, and Paige?"

"Yes?"

"Trust me on this one. However things may appear, please trust me."

And with that, he was gone.

The Meridian Theater
Proudly Presents...

"IS THIS IT?" THE DRIVER ASKED.

I leaned forward and read the sign: PARKING FOR EM-
PLOYEES AND GUESTS OF THE MERIDIAN. ALL UNAUTHO-
RIZED VEHICLES WILL BE TOWED AT OWNER'S RISK AND
EXPENSE. Was I a guest of the Meridian? What was the
Meridian? Damn Lucas. I'd left a message on his cell,
asking him to call me back with more information, but
obviously court was running late today.

The directions he'd provided had taken the cab on a
convoluted path through an industrial area when, according to my new Miami map, I could have accessed
the same street off a major thoroughfare. Of course, the
driver hadn't suggested a shorter route, though I had
caught him smiling at the meter once or twice.

The address Lucas gave me was right here. The parking lot. What exactly had he said? There'd be a rear door.
To my left was a block-long wall dotted with air vents and
barred windows, plus two entrances: a loading dock, and
a double set of gray-painted metal doors.

I asked the driver to wait, got out, and walked to the
doors. They were indeed solid, with no handles or locks.

Beside them was a doorbell marked DELIVERIES. I double-checked the address, and rang the bell.

Thirty seconds later, the door swung open, letting out a blast of shouting voices, rock music, and power tools. A young woman squinted out into the sunlight. She wore cat's-eye glasses, red leather pants, and an ID badge with an obscenity in the name space.

"Hi, I'm—" I raised my voice. "I'm Paige Winterbourne. I was supposed to meet—"

The woman shrieked over her shoulder. "J.D!" She looked back at me. "Well, come in, girl. You're letting out all our air-conditioning."

I excused myself while I paid the cab driver, then hurried back to the building. As I stepped inside, a fresh song started, volume cranked. At first wail, I winced.

"Isn't that god-awful?" the young woman said, slamming the door behind me. "It's Jaime's warm-up song. 'My Way.'"

"Tell me that's not Frank Sinatra."

"Nah, some dead Brit."

"Recorded as he was dying a long, painful death."

The woman laughed. "You got that right, girl."

A fortyish man appeared, slight, balding, carrying a clipboard, and looking harried to the point of exhaustion. "Oh, thank God. I thought you weren't going to make it."

He grabbed me by the elbow, tugged me into the room, and propelled me through a mob of drill-wielding men working on what looked like a scaffold.

"You *are* Paige, right?" he asked, moving us along at warp speed.

"Uh, right."

"J.D. I'm Jaime's production manager. They didn't send you around the front, did they?"

I shook my head.

"Thank God. It is a zoo out there. We've been sold out since last week, but some moron at WKLT has been announcing all day that we still have seats available, and now we have a line from here to Cuba of very unhappy folks."

A pink-haired woman appeared from behind a heavy velvet curtain. "J.D., there's a problem with the sound levels. The acoustics in here are shit, and—"

"Just do your best, Kat. We'll take it up with the booking agent later."

He pushed me past the woman, then through the curtain. We stepped out onto a side stage, in front of a rapidly filling auditorium. I stopped to gape, but J.D. tugged me along, crossing the stage to the opposite side.

"What kind of—" I began.

J.D. stopped in mid-stride and I nearly bashed into him.

"I don't believe this," he said. "I don't fucking believe it. Tara! Tara!"

A woman scurried up the steps. She could have been J.D.'s twin, carrying a matching clipboard, just as slight and harried, not balding but looking ready to tear out her own hair.

"Front row," J.D. said. "Second seat right of the aisle. Is that not reserved for Jaime's guest?"

Tara consulted her clipboard. "A Ms. Winterbourne. Paige Winterbourne."

"This is Ms. Winterbourne," J.D. said, jerking a finger at me. Then he jabbed the same finger at the sixty-year-old platinum blond in the second seat. "That is not Ms. Winterbourne."

"I'll get security."

Tara disappeared behind the curtain. J.D. surveyed the

theater, now nearly three-quarters full, with a steady stream flowing in.

"I hope they didn't overbook. Houston overbooked and it was an absolute nightmare." He stopped. "Oh, my god. Take a look at what's coming through the door now. Do you see what she's wearing? I didn't think those came in purple. Some people will do anything to catch Jaime's attention. In Buffalo last month—Oh, good. Your seat is clear. Follow me."

He kept his hand on my elbow, as if I might otherwise be swallowed by the crowd. A security guard escorted the platinum-haired grandmother down the aisle. She turned and shot a lethal glare at me. J.D. quick-marched us down the steps.

"Is front row okay? Not too close for you?"

"Uh, no. It's fine. This, uh, Jamey, is it? Is he around? Maybe I could—"

J.D. didn't seem to hear me. His gaze was darting over the crowd, like a sheepdog surveying an unruly mob of ewes.

"We needed more ushers. Ten minutes to show time. I told Jaime—" A watch check. "Oh, God, make that eight minutes. How the hell are they going to get everyone in here in eight minutes? Go ahead, sit down and get comfortable. I'll be out to see you at intermission. Enjoy the show."

He darted into a group of people and disappeared.

"Okay," I muttered. "Enjoy the show . . . whatever it is."

As I sat, I glanced at the people on either side of me, hoping one of them might be this Jaime guy, who I assumed was the necromancer I'd come to meet. To my left was a teenage girl with piercings in every imaginable location . . . and a few I would have preferred not to imagine. On my other side was an elderly woman in widow's weeds with her head bowed over a rosary. Talk about audience diversity. Now I was stumped. I couldn't imagine what kind of show would interest both of these people.

I looked around, trying to pick up some clues about the show from the theater, but the walls were covered in plain black velvet. Whatever the show was, I hoped I wasn't expected to sit through it before I spoke to this Jaime. Maybe after it started, he'd come out and get me. I guessed he was the theater owner or manager. Someone important, from what J.D. said. An odd profession for a necromancer. Unless this Jaime wasn't the necromancer. Maybe he was only the guy who would take me to the necromancer. Damn it! I didn't have time for this. I pulled out my cell phone, called Lucas's number again, but only got his voice mail.

I left a message. "I'm sitting in a theater right now, with absolutely no idea why I'm here, what's going on, or who I'm supposed to talk to. This better be good, Cortez, or I'm going to need a necromancer to contact *you*."

I hung up, and glanced at my neighbors again. Not about to disturb the rosary-widow, I turned to the teen and offered my brightest smile.

"Packed house tonight, huh?" I said.

She glowered at me.

"Should be a great show," I said. "Are you a . . . fan?"

"Listen, bitch, if you raise your hand and get picked instead of me, I'll pop out your eyeballs."

I turned my endangered orbs back to the stage and inched closer to the rosary-widow. She glared at me and said something in what sounded like Portuguese. Now, I don't know a single word of Portuguese, but something in her voice made me suspect that, whatever she said, the translation would sound roughly like what pierced-girl beside me had said. I sunk into my seat and vowed to avoid eye contact for the rest of the show.

Music started, a soft, symphonic tune, far removed from the caterwauling rock backstage. The lights dimmed as the music swelled. A scuffle of activity as the last people scurried to their seats. The lights continued to fade until the auditorium was immersed in darkness.

More sounds of activity, this time coming from the aisle beside me. The music ebbed. A few lights appeared, tiny, twinkling lights on the walls and ceiling, followed by more, then more, until the room was lit with thousands, all casting the soft glow of starlight against the inky velvet.

A choral murmur of oohs and ahhs surged, and fell to silence. Absolute silence. No music. No chatter. Not so much as a throat-clearing cough.

Then, a woman's voice, in a microphone-amplified whisper.

"This is their world. A world of peace, and beauty, and joy. A world we all wish to enter."

The rosary-widow beside me murmured an "Amen," her voice joining a quiet wave of others. In the near-dark, I noticed a dim figure appear on stage. It glided out to the edge, and kept going, as if levitating down the center aisle. When I squinted, I could detect the dark form of a catwalk that had been quickly erected in the aisle while the lights were out. The woman's voice continued, barely above a whisper, as soothing as a lullaby.

"Between our world and theirs is a heavy veil. A veil most cannot lift. But I can. Come with me now and let me take you into their world. The world of the spirits."

The lights flickered and went bright. Standing midway down the raised catwalk was a red-haired woman, her back to those of us in the front rows.

The woman turned. Late thirties. Gorgeous. Bright red hair pinned up, with tendrils tumbling down around her neck. A shimmery emerald green silk dress, modestly cut, but tight enough not to leave any curve to the imagination. Dowdy wire-rimmed glasses completed the faux-professional ensemble. The old Hollywood "sex-goddess disguised as Miss Prim-and-Proper" routine. As the thought pinged through my brain, it triggered a wave of déjà vu. I'd seen this woman before, and thought exactly the same thing. Where . . . ?

A sonorous male voice filled the room.

"The Meridian Theater proudly presents, for one night only, Jaime Vegas."

Jaime Vegas. Savannah's favorite television spiritualist. Well, I'd found my necromancer.

Diva of the Dead

"I'M SENSING A MALE PRESENCE," JAIME MURMURED, somehow managing to walk and talk with her eyes closed. She headed toward the back of the theater. "A man in his fifties, maybe early sixties, late forties. His name starts with an M. He's related to someone in this corner."

She swept her arm, encompassing the rear left third of the room, and at least a hundred people. I bit my tongue to keep from groaning. In the last hour, I'd bitten it so often I probably wouldn't be able to taste food for a week. Over a dozen people in the "corner" Jaime had indicated started waving their arms, and five leapt to their feet, spot-dancing with excitement. Hell, I was sure if *anyone* in this audience searched their memories hard enough they could find a Mark or a Mike or a Miguel in their family who'd died in middle age.

Jaime turned to the section with the highest concentration of hand-wavers. "His name is Michael, but he says no one ever called him that. He was always Mike, except when he was a little boy, and some people called him Mikey."

An elderly woman suddenly wailed, and bowed forward, sucker punched by grief. "Mikey. That's my Mikey. My little boy. I always called him that."

I tore my gaze away, my own eyes filling with angry tears as Jaime bore down on her like a shark scenting blood.

"Is it my Mikey?" the old woman said, barely intelligible through her tears.

"I think it is," Jaime said softly. "Wait . . . yes. He says he's your son. He's asking you to stop crying. He's in a good place and he's happy. He wants you to know that."

The woman mopped her streaming tears and tried to smile.

"There," Jaime said. "Now he wants me to mention the picture. He says you have a photograph of him on display. Is that right?"

"I—I have a few," she said.

"Ah, but he's talking about a certain one. He says it's the one he always hated. Do you know which one he means?"

The old woman smiled and nodded.

"He's laughing," Jaime said. "He wants me to give you heck for putting up that photo. He wants you to take that down and put up the one of him at the wedding. Does that make sense?"

"He probably means his niece's wedding," the woman said. "She got married right before he died."

Jaime looked off into space, eyes unfocused, head slightly tilted, as if hearing something no one else could. Then she shook her head. "No, it's another wedding picture. An older one. He says to look through the album and you'll find it. Now, speaking of weddings . . ."

And on it went, from person to person, as Jaime worked

the crowd, throwing out "personal" information that could apply to almost any life—What parent doesn't display pictures of their kids? What person doesn't have photos they hate? Who doesn't have wedding photos in their albums?

Even when she misjudged, she was perceptive enough to read confusion on the recipient's face before they could say anything, backtrack, and "correct" herself. On the very few occasions that she completely struck out, she'd tell the person to "go home and think about it, and it'll come to you," as if their memory was to blame, not her.

This Jaime might really be a necromancer, but she wasn't using her skills here. As I'd told Savannah, no one—not even a necro—could "dial up the dead" like this. What Jaime Vegas did was a psychological con job, not far removed from psychics who tell young girls "I see wedding bells in your future." Having lost my mother the year before, I understood why these people were here, the void they ached to fill. For a necromancer to profit from that grief with false tidings from the other side . . . well, it didn't make Jaime Vegas someone I wanted to work with.

The dressing room smelled like a funeral parlor. Appropriate, I suppose. I looked for chairs, and found one under a bouquet of two dozen black roses. I didn't know roses came in black.

J.D. had escorted me here before being dragged off by his assistant, who'd been muttering something about a man refusing to leave his seat until Jaime summoned his dead mother.

After clearing the chair of roses, I tried calling Lucas again. Still no answer. Avoiding my calls, I suspected. Damn call display. I was phoning home for messages when the door opened and Jaime wheeled in.

"Paige, right?" she said, gulping air. The glasses were gone, and the loosened tendrils of hair that had looked so artfully arranged on stage now clung, sweat-sodden, to her neck and face. "Please tell me it's Paige."

"Uh, yes. I—"

"Oh, thank God. I was running back here and suddenly thought, what if that wasn't her? and I was winking at some strange girl and inviting her to join me backstage, which is exactly what I do not need. My place in the tabloids is ensured without that. So, Paige—"

She stopped and looked around, then opened the door and shouted. "Hello! Did I ask—?"

A tray appeared from behind the door, floating in mid-air. Presumably there was some flunky behind the door holding it. Or so I hoped. With necromancers, one can never be sure.

She grabbed the tray, then lifted the bottle of single-malt Scotch. "What are you people trying to do to me? I said no booze tonight. I have an engagement. No booze, no caffeine. Like I'm not bouncing off the walls enough as it is." She eyed the bottle longingly, then shut her eyes and thrust it out. "Take it, please."

The bottle vanished behind the door.

"And bring more Gatorade. The blue stuff. None of that orange shit." She closed the door, grabbed a towel, and mopped her face. "Okay, so where were we?"

"I—"

"Oh, right. So I was thinking, what if that's not her? I was expecting the witch. Well, maybe not expecting, but hoping, you know? Lucas called and told me he was sending someone—a female someone—and I thought, oh, my God, maybe it's the witch."

"The—?"

"Have you heard that story?" Jaime continued, her voice muffled as she tugged her dress off over her head. "About Lucas and the witch? Personally, I can't see it."

"You mean, Lucas dating a witch? Well—"

"No, Lucas dating. Period." Jaime shrugged off her bra. "No offense to the guy, really. He's great. But he's one of those people you just can't imagine having a social life. Like your teachers. You see them outside the classroom and it freaks you out."

Now stripped to her panties, Jaime proceeded to slather cold cream on her face, still talking.

"I heard she's a computer geek. Probably some skinny kid with big glasses and an overbite, scared of her own shadow. Typical witch. I can see Lucas hooking up with a girl like—"

"I'm the witch," I said.

Jaime stopped cleaning her face and looked at me. "Wha—?"

"The witch. Lucas's girlfriend. That'd be me."

She winced. "Oh, shit."

The door cracked open and J.D.'s voice floated through. "Got a fire to put out, Jaime. Needs your special touch."

"Just hold on, okay?" she said to me, throwing on a robe. "I'll be right back."

"Hey, it's me," I said, shifting the cell phone to my other ear. "Is your dad there?"

"Paige, nice to hear from you," Adam said. "I'm fine. Midterms went well. Thanks for asking."

"Sorry," I said. "But I'm kind of in a hur—"

A drill screeched outside the dressing room.

"Holy shit, what are you killing?"

"I think they're dismantling the stage," I said. "Is Robert—"

"He's out with Mom. What stage? Where are you?"

"Miami. And, before you ask, I'm here looking for a necromancer. I've found one but she's not quite . . . right, so I was hoping Robert could put me in touch with another one in the area."

"What do you want a necromancer for?" A pause, then his voice dropped. "You're not thinking of . . . you know . . . with your mom? You don't want to go there, Paige. I know you're still—"

"Give me credit. I'm not trying to call up my mother. It's for a case."

"You're working a case and you didn't call me?"

"I just did."

Another earsplitting mechanical yowl, followed by shouts and catcalls.

"Sounds like a party," Adam said. "You said something about a stage? Where are you? A strip club?"

"Pretty close, actually. I just got to see a strip act. Wrong gender, though. Now, tell—"

"Oh-ho, you aren't tossing out that teaser without an explanation. What the hell are you doing looking for a necromancer in a strip club?"

"It's not a strip club. It's a theater. Ever heard of Jaime Vegas?"

"The—" He whooped a laugh. "Are you serious? Jaime Vegas is a necromancer? I can't believe people watch that shit. So she's for real?"

"In a . . . manner of speaking."

"Oh, God, how bad is she?"

"Let's just say showbiz suits her well."

"Hey, now, don't go playing nice. This isn't Lucas you're talking to. What's she like?"

"Flakier than puff pastry."

Another whooped laugh. "Oh, man, I wish I was there. So about this case . . . you changed your mind about working with Lucas?"

"I never said I wouldn't work—"

"Sure you did. When I was up in Portland last month. Lucas was talking about that Igneus case, and I said maybe you could help, and you said—"

"This is just temporary. He's busy, so I'm filling in."

Jaime slid into the room. I lifted a finger. She nodded, grabbed a Gatorade, and perched on the edge of the vanity counter.

Adam continued, "If he's busy, that means you need a partner. I could—"

"I'm fine. You have school."

"Not for the next four days, I don't," Adam said. "No classes until Tuesday. I'll just hop—"

"Stay. If I need you, I'll call. In the meantime, can you ask Robert about nec—" I glanced at Jaime. "—that list? It's kind of urgent."

"I will if you promise to call back with *all* the details."

"I'll call you first thing tomorrow. As soon as you wake up. Say, noon?"

"Very funny. I'm up by ten. Call me back tonight. It's only seven o'clock here, remember."

I agreed, then hung up and turned to Jaime.

"Sorry about that. I wasn't sure how long you'd be." I put my cell into my purse and hefted it to my shoulder. "Look, I'm sure this is a bad time for you, right after

124 Kelley Armstrong

a busy show and all. I appreciate you taking the time to see me, and the show was...great. But you don't need me bugging you with this. Whatever favor you owe Lucas, consider it squared." I stepped backward toward the door and grasped the handle. "Anyway, it's been great meeting you, Jaime, and I wish you all the best—"

"I'm sorry about what I said. I stuck my foot in it so far I'm kicking myself in the stomach right now. After a show, I'm so wired, I just—I don't think."

"That's okay. I—"

"I mean, shit, I can't believe I didn't figure out who you were the minute Lucas told me your name. I knew your mom. Not personally, but I knew who she was, and then I heard about you and Eve's daughter last spring, so I really should have put two and two together, but when I do a show, my brain goes on hold and—" A wry twist of a smile. "And I babble and blather, and make no sense at all, not that you noticed or anything, right?"

"It's okay. Obviously you're busy and you don't need this, so don't worry about it. I have other necromancers I can contact."

She began brushing her hair. "Better necromancers."

"I have no idea whether they're better. I've never worked with you."

She looked up, as if surprised that I hadn't paid her a false compliment.

I continued, "I'm just saying this is probably a bad time—"

"You need me to contact a girl in a coma. Simple. It's ten o'clock and you're not going to get anyone else to do it tonight. Might as well give me a shot, let me repay Lucas."

What could I say to that? Spending the next couple of

hours with the Diva of the Dead wasn't exactly my idea of fun, but she seemed calmer now, as the high from her performance wore off. Maybe this wouldn't be so bad after all. Or so I kept telling myself as she dropped her robe and started searching for clothing.

Gone

FOLLOWING THE ADDRESS I GAVE, THE CAB STOPPED IN front of a square block of brick squeezed between a restaurant and a small accounting firm. Unlike its neighbors, this storefront had no obvious signage. It took a minute of searching to see the near-microscopic sign in the window: THE MARSH MEMORIAL CLINIC.

"Jesus," Jaime said as I rang the after-hours bell. "What is this? A rehab center?"

"A private hospital," I said.

"Shit. Who do you have to kill to get in here?" She caught my expression. "Ah, not *who*, but how many. A Cabal hospital."

A blond woman in her forties opened the door. "Ms. Winterbourne. Hello. Mr. Cortez said you'd be by this evening. Come in, please. And I presume this is Jaime Vegas?"

Jaime nodded.

"Has there been any change in Dana's condition?" I asked.

A brief flutter of emotion rippled the nurse's composure. "I'm afraid not. You're welcome to stay as long as you like. Mr. Cortez asked that this be a private visit, so if you need me, please buzz. Otherwise, I won't bother you. She's in room three."

I thanked her and followed her directions into a side hall. As we walked, Jaime looked around, taking in everything.

"And just think," she said. "This is for the employees. They've probably got a place in the Swiss Alps for the execs. And the family? God only knows. Can you imagine having this kind of money?"

"Remember where it comes from," I said, quoting Lucas.

"I try, but you know, sometimes, you see what a Cabal can do and you think, hmmm, maybe tormenting a few souls now and then wouldn't be such a bad gig. You're dating the guy who's supposed to own all this one day. I'm sure you think about that."

"Not in a good way."

"More power to you, then. I'd be tempted. Hell, I've *been* tempted. Ever met Carlos?"

"Carlos Cortez? No."

"He's the youngest. Well, you know, the youngest of the legit—uh, of Delores's kids. Carlos is the hunk of the litter. Takes after his mother, who's gorgeous . . . and as vicious as a rabid dog. Carlos got the vicious genes too, but seems to have missed out on Benicio's brains, so he's not very dangerous. Anyway, I met Carlos at a club a couple years back, and he showed some definite interest. There were a few moments there when I was tempted. I mean, here's a guy with money and power, wrapped in a damn near perfect gift box. What more could a girl want? Okay, maybe someone who doesn't have a reputation for nasty bedroom games, but everyone's got their hang-ups, right? Honest to God, that's what I thought. I'm standing there, looking at this guy and thinking, hmmm, maybe I could change him."

"Probably not."

"No shit, huh? I don't learn my lessons well, but that's one I've committed to heart. Take it or leave it, 'cause you ain't gonna change it. But that still didn't keep me from thinking about Carlos. Power and money—if Calvin Klein could bottle the scent, he'd make a fortune." She tossed a grin my way. "Just think, we could've been sisters-in-law. We'd certainly have livened up family reunions."

I pushed open a door marked with a small 3. "They're probably lively enough as it is."

Jaime laughed. "I bet. Can you imagine—"

She stopped as we stepped into the room. It was twice the size of my apartment bedroom. A leather couch and two matching recliners were grouped around a coffee table just inside the door. Past that was a king-size bed. A girl with long blond hair lay in the middle of it, a sunflower-patterned quilt pulled up across her chest. Her eyes were closed. Bandages encircled her neck. To one side, machines bleeped discreetly, as if trying not to wake her.

My breath hitched. How could anyone—? How could her mother—? Goddamn it! Why, why, why? I closed my eyes, swallowed, walked to Dana's bedside, and took her hand.

"Holy shit," Jaime whispered. "She's a kid."

"Fif—" My throat dried up. I tried again. "She's fifteen. But she looks small for her age."

"Fifteen? Jesus Christ. When Lucas said 'girl,' I thought, you know, he meant a woman. I should have known better. He says girl, he means girl."

"Is that a problem?"

Jaime inhaled, gaze glued to Dana. "Tougher, yes. Not to

communicate. I mean"—she tapped a manicured nail against her forehead—"up here. What do the doctors say?"

"She's stable. As to whether she'll regain consciousness, they don't know."

"Well, we might find that out tonight. If she's crossed over, I'll know it."

Jaime rolled her shoulders, approached the bed, and gripped the side rail. She stared down at Dana, then shook her head, opened her oversize purse, and pulled out what looked like a jumbo makeup bag.

"I'll call you in when I'm ready," she said, not looking up.

"I'm an old hand at this," I said. "Well, not exactly an old hand, but I've helped out at a few summonings. Here, pass me the censer and herbs and I'll set them up while you—"

"No."

The word came out sharp enough to make me jump. Jaime clutched her tool bag closed, as if I might pry it from her hands.

"I'd rather you waited in the hall," she said.

"Uh, sure. Okay. Call me then."

I walked to the door, then glanced back to see her still holding the bag closed, waiting. I pushed open the door and stepped into the hall.

Well, I said necromancers were queer beasts. Jaime might look a far cry from your typical spacey-eyed necro, but you have to wonder about a woman who'll strip in front of a stranger, yet draws the line at letting the same person watch her perform a summoning ceremony. Not that I minded being relegated to the sidelines. I knew what was in that Gucci makeup bag, and it wasn't designer lip-liner.

To summon the dead you needed artifacts of death. In

that kit, there'd be everything from grave dirt to scraps of moldy grave clothes to, well, dead things . . . or, at least, travel-size pieces of them. The tools-in-trade of a necromancer. Made me really happy to be a witch, casting spells surrounded by sweet-smelling herbs, pretty gemstones, and antique filigreed chalices.

About ten minutes later, Jaime called me in. When I entered, she was sitting beside the bed, holding Dana's hand. Most necromancers leave their tools out during a summoning, but Jaime's makeup bag had vanished, along with its contents. Only the censer remained, burning vervain, which necromancers used when contacting either traumatized souls, such as murder victims, or the souls of those who didn't realize they were spirits.

"It didn't work?" I asked.

"It worked." Jamie's voice had faded to a strained whisper and her face was pale. "She's here. I haven't—" Her voice strengthened. "I haven't made contact yet. I think it'd be easiest on her if I used channeling. Do you know how that works?"

I nodded. "You let Dana speak through you."

"Right."

"So I'll ask her the questions and—"

"No, no," Jamie said. "Well, yes, you'll ask the questions, but I'll relay them to her, and let her speak through me. She doesn't take over my body. That's full channeling, and if a necro ever suggests that, find someone else. No necro in her right mind ever gives herself completely over to a spirit."

"Got it."

"Now, for the first part, making contact, I'll do that on my own. It's easier that way. I'll establish contact and . . . explain things." She swallowed. "I'll tell her what hap-

pened, where she is. She may know, but . . . with kids . . .
there can be some resistance to the truth."

Damn it, I hadn't thought of this. We weren't just asking Jaime to contact Dana. We were asking her to tell the
girl that she was lying in a hospital bed, comatose.

"I'm sorry," I said. "If you don't want to do this, I totally
understand—"

"I'm fine. She'll figure it out sooner or later, right? Now,
she's almost certainly not going to remember a play-by-
play."

"Trauma amnesia," I said. "Lucas told me about it."

"Good. I'll make contact now. This may take a while."

Twenty minutes ticked by. During that time, Jaime sat
ramrod straight, eyes closed, hand clutching Dana's, the
occasional twitch of her cheek the only sign that something was happening.

"Okay," Jaime said finally, in a cheerful chirp. "Now
there's someone here who's going to help us catch the
guy who did this to you, okay, kiddo?"

"Good." The response was pitched an octave higher
than Jaime's voice.

"Her name is Paige, and she's a witch, just like you. Do
you know what the Coven is?"

"I . . . I've heard of it . . . I think."

"It's a group for witches. Paige used to be in the Coven,
helping witches there, but now she works outside the
Coven, so she can help all witches." That was a nice way
of putting it. I mentally thanked Jaime for the positive
spin. "What I want you to do is tell her everything you remember, then she'll ask you some questions, and we'll
catch this guy before you wake up."

So Dana was okay. Thank God. I relaxed for the first
time since walking into the room.

Dana asked when she'd be waking up.

"Any day now," Jaime said. "Your dad is supposed to be here soon—"

"My dad? I knew he'd come. Is my mom there?"

"She's been in and out," Jaime said. "Taking care of you."

"And they'll be there? When I wake up?"

"Sure will. Now, can you tell Paige what you saw?"

"Sure. Hi, Paige."

I opened my mouth, but Jaime answered for me. "You won't be able to hear Paige, hon. I'll have to relay her messages. But you'll get to see her when you wake up. She's been pretty worried about you."

Dana smiled through Jaime, the smile of a kid who wasn't used to people giving a damn. I'd make sure her dad knew about Dana's situation with her mother and, if he was the kind of father Benicio said he was, Dana would never have to spend another night on the streets. If he didn't, well, then I'd see to it myself.

"I'll try," Dana said. "But . . . I don't remember it so well. It's all jumbled up, like something I saw on television a long time ago and can't really remember."

"That's okay, Dana," Jaime said. "We know you won't remember much, so if you don't, we understand, but if you do remember something, anything at all, that'll be great."

"Well, it was Sunday night. I was coming home from a party. I wasn't loaded or anything. I'd had a joint, but that's it, just one joint I shared with this guy I knew. So I was walking home through the park—I know that sounds dumb, but around there, the park seemed safer than the roads, you know? I was being careful, staying on the path, looking, listening. And then . . ."

Her voice trailed off.

"Then what, Dana?" Jaime prompted.

"Then . . . I think I must forget what happens next because all I remember is this guy was suddenly standing right behind me. I must have heard him coming, maybe I tried to run, but I don't remember."

"Ask her—" I began.

Dana continued. "I know you're going to want to know what the guy looked like, but I didn't really see him. I know I should have . . ."

"Hey, if it was me," Jaime said, "I'd have been freaking so bad, I wouldn't remember a damn thing. You're doing fine, kiddo. Just take it slow and give us what you can."

"He grabbed me, and next thing I know, I'm on the ground, way off the path, in this forest. I was kind of awake, but not really, and I was so tired. I just wanted to sleep."

"Drugged?" I asked.

Jaime relayed the question.

"I—I guess so. Only, it didn't feel . . . I just remember being tired. I don't even think he had me tied up, but I didn't move. I didn't want to move. I just wanted to sleep. Then he put this rope around my neck, and I blacked out, then I was here."

"I want to talk about the phone call you made," I said.

"I made a phone call?"

"To the emergency line," I said. "The Cabal—the place where your dad works."

"I know what you mean, but I don't remember. Dad made my sister and me memorize it, and I know I'm supposed to call them first, so I must have."

I prompted her with a few questions about her attacker's voice, regional accent, word usage, anything that might have stuck in her mind more than a physical description, but she could tell me little more than that he didn't sound like he came from "around here."

"Oh, there was one thing he did say that seemed

weird. When he started choking me. It seemed like he was talking to someone, but there wasn't anyone there. Like he was talking to himself, only he used a name."

I perked up. "Do you remember it?"

"I think it was Nasha," Dana said. "That's what it sounded like."

"Ask her what exactly he said," I said, and Jaime did.

"He said he was doing this for this person, this Nasha," Dana said.

"Ritual sacrifice," I said.

Jaime nodded. We continued to prod Dana's memory, but she'd obviously been only partially conscious when she'd heard her attacker speak. Next we moved back to her attacker. He was likely supernatural, and may have done something to indicate his race, but Dana couldn't re-call anything. As the daughter of a witch and a half-demon, she was familiar with both spell-casting and demonic shows of power, but her attacker had demon-strated neither.

"That's great, hon," Jaime said when I indicated that I'd run out of questions. "You've been a big help. Thank you very much."

Dana smiled through Jaime. "I should be thanking you. And I will, when I wake up. I'll take you guys out for lunch. On me. Well, on me and my dad."

"Su—sure, kiddo," Jaime said, gaze flicking away. "We'll do that." She glanced at me. "Can I send her back now?"

I nodded, and capped my pen. "Tell her I'll see her when she wakes up."

A few minutes later, Jaime stood and rubbed her shoul-ders.

"You okay?" I asked.

She made a noncommittal noise and reached for her

handbag. I stifled a yawn, then stepped into the bathroom to splash cold water on my face.

"So, do you have any idea when she'll regain consciousness?" I said as I came out.

"She won't."

I stopped and turned slowly. Jaime was fussing with something in her purse.

"What?" I said.

Jaime didn't look up. "She's crossed over. She's gone."

"But you—you said—"

"I know what I said."

"You told her she was fine. How could you—?"

Jaime's gaze snapped to mine. "And what was I supposed to say? Sorry, kid, you're dead, you just don't know it yet?"

"Oh, my god." I sunk into the nearest chair. "I'm sorry. We didn't mean—I didn't mean—putting you through that—"

"Comes with the territory. If not me, then someone else, right? You need to catch this bastard, and this was the best way to get information, so . . ." She rubbed her hand over her face. "I could really use a drink. And some company. If you don't mind."

I scrambled from the chair. "Sure."

Two-for-One Special

THOUGH I WAS STILL IN SHOCK OVER DANA'S FATE, MY feelings had to take a backseat to Jaime's. She was the one who needed support, and I was happy to provide it.

I'd seen a jazz bar down the road, the kind of place with big plush booths you could get lost in and a live band that never played loud enough to challenge conversation. We could go there, have a few drinks, and talk through our difficult evening, maybe come to a better understanding of one another.

"No, I am so serious!" Jaime shrieked, waving her Cosmopolitan and sending a tidal wave over the glass. "This guy was sitting in his seat, with his pants undone, dick sticking out, hoping that'd get my attention."

The blond guy on Jaime's left leaned into her. "And did it?"

"Hell, no. A four-inch dick? I don't even slow down for that. Zipped right past him . . . and hoped he zipped up before the old lady beside him had a stroke."

"Would eight inches do it?" asked the dark-haired guy on her right.

"Depends on the face that goes with it. Now ten . . . ten and we'd be talking. Twelve, and I'd summon his fucking dog if he asked me."

A roar of laughter. I stared into my Mojito and wished I'd made it a double Scotch, neat. I didn't drink Scotch, but suddenly, it seemed like a really good idea.

Around us, music pulsed so loud it rippled Jaime's Cosmo puddle. I thought of wiping it up, but decided to wait until another stoned dancer stumbled off the floor and fell onto our table. It'd happened twice so far and was bound to happen again. I only hoped he or she would be wearing enough to soak up Jaime's spilled drink.

We'd been here nearly two hours, having never come within half a block of the jazz club. Jaime had heard the thumping music from outside and dragged me in for "just one drink." I'd had two. She was on number six. For the first two, she'd ignored all attention from the bar's male patrons. By the third, she'd begun sizing up the interested parties. When number five arrived, she'd made her selection from a quintet of stockbroker types who'd been watching us from the bar, and had waved over the two cutest and offered them seats on either side of her, squashing three into a bench made for two.

Though I'd kept my gaze on my drink, sending clear "I am so not interested" vibes, one of the remaining trio had decided the leftovers didn't look too unappetizing and slid in beside me. I wanted nothing more than to return to my quiet hotel room and mourn for Dana by planning my next step in finding her killer. Yet here I was, trapped against the booth wall, listening to Jaime's war stories, nursing my second Mojito, and fending off the wandering hands of my unwanted companion. And I was starting to get a little pissed.

The guy beside me, Dale—or was it Chip?—wriggled

closer, though we were already closer than I liked getting to anyone I wasn't sleeping with.

"You have really nice eyes," he said.

"Those aren't my eyes," I said. "Look up. Way up."

He chuckled and lifted his gaze to my face. "No, I'm serious. You have beautiful eyes."

"What color are they?"

"Uh . . ." He squinted in the darkness. "Blue?"

They were green, but I wasn't helping him out. I'd already repeated the "I'm seeing someone" line until it sounded like a challenge. Nearly as often I'd told Jaime that I really should be going, but she pretended not to hear me. When I tried again, she launched into another ribald story.

Nice to see she'd recovered from her traumatic experience at the hospital. I'd begun to suspect "traumatic" was an overstatement. Mildly disturbing maybe, on a par with realizing you'd left the house wearing brown shoes with a black dress. Nothing that couldn't be cured with a few Cosmopolitans and some wicked thumping bass.

"Excuse me," I said. "I need to—"

"Use the little girls' room?" he said, and laughed as he slid from the booth.

"Hold on, boys," Jaime said. "The ladies need to freshen up."

"Uh, no," I said as she extricated herself from the booth. "I'm leaving."

"Leaving? Already? I haven't finished my drink."

"That's okay. You stay, have fun."

She clutched my arm, more for balance, I think, than to keep me from going. "You're abandoning me? With these three?"

She cast a leering grin at the men. Dale blinked, then staggered to his feet.

"Hey, no, babe," he said, bleary eyes fixed in my general direction. "I'll drive you."

"Oh, I bet you'd like to," Jaime said. "But Paige already has a guy. A friend of mine. And you don't want to mess with him." She leaned into Dale's ear. "He's connected."

Dale frowned. "Connected?"

"Like the Kennedys," Jaime said.

"More like the Sopranos," I said.

Dale sat down.

"You stay and enjoy yourself," I said to Jaime.

"No can do. I told Lucas I'd look after you in the big bad city."

"Uh-huh. Well, I appreciate that, but—"

"No buts. My prodco got me a room way the hell out in the burbs and I am not going all that way tonight. I'm getting a room at your hotel. So come on, girl."

She started to steer me from the table. One of her companions leapt up.

"Can we give you a lift—?"

"Ooops, sorry about that. I might not get to finish my drink, but I can't forget my nightcap." She turned and sized up the two men. "Decisions, decisions."

The blonde grinned. "Two-for-one special."

"Tempting, but I'm too old for that shit. One per night." She looked them over. "Hmmm, this is tough. Only one way to do it." She pointed at the dark-haired one. "Eenie-meenie . . ."

Once out of the taxi, and away from Jaime and her "date," I called Lucas, but only got a cellular service recording saying he was out of range. Odd. I left a "call me" message, then phoned Adam and filled him in on the case. By that time, it was nearly midnight even in

California, and Robert had gone to bed. It didn't matter. Getting that list of necromancers was no longer high priority. Whatever Jaime's personal shortcomings, she'd done her job with Dana.

I hadn't slept since arriving in Miami, and my brain seemed to protest this lack of rest by making sure my sleep that night wasn't sound. I dreamed of being back in the hospital room, watching Jaime release Dana back to the realm of the dead. She dropped the hand she'd been holding, letting it fall back to the sheets. I stared at that hand, expecting to see chewed fingernails and a frayed braided bracelet. Instead the hand was plump and wrinkled, and bore a familiar gold watch.

"Mom?"

"She doesn't want to talk to you," Jaime said. "You lost the Coven. She handed it to you on a silver platter, and you still screwed up."

"No!"

I shot from my chair, stumbled, and fell into a bed smelling of hotel laundry soap. I pushed into the pillow and moaned. Suddenly, the bed tilted and I grabbed with both hands, struggling to stay on. I saw Lucas sitting on the edge. He had his back to me, and was peeling the label from an empty champagne bottle.

"One month," he said. "You knew what I meant."

He stood and the bed tumbled into a yawning pit of black. I started to scream, but the sound turned to a happy shriek.

"Cortez! You're getting champagne—get that bottle away from the bed!"

The scene cleared. Another hotel room. Three months ago. We were crossing the country at a snail's pace, with nowhere to go, nothing to do but enjoy the trip. The day before, Maria had wired Lucas the insurance money from his stolen motorcycle, and tonight he'd insisted on using part of it to get us a room with a Jacuzzi tub, a fireplace, and an adjoining suite for Savannah.

We were in bed, where we'd been since arriving late that afternoon. Room-service plates littered the floor and, from somewhere in the mess, Lucas had pulled out a bottle of champagne, which was now frothing onto the sheets...and me. As I laughed, he shook the last bits of foam onto me, then grabbed glasses, filled them, and handed me one.

"To one month," he said.

"A month?" I sat up. "Oh, right. One month since we beat the Nast Cabal and saved Savannah, an act which we may live to regret. Technically, though, you're a few days early."

Lucas hesitated, face clouding for a split second before he nodded. "I suppose I am."

The memory fast-forwarded a few hours. I was nestled in bed, champagne still singing in my head. Lucas's warmth pressed against my back. He stirred, mumbled something, and slid his hand between my legs. I shifted and rubbed against his fingers. A drowsy laugh, then his finger slipped inside me, a slow, soft probe. I moaned, my flesh tender from the long night but the slight ache only accentuating another deeper ache. He pulled his finger out and tickled a fingertip across the top of my clitoris. I moaned again and shifted my legs apart. He started a slow, teasing exploration that made me clutch the pillow.

"Lucas," I whispered.

Another laugh, but this one clear, no signs of sleepiness. I forced myself to shift from sleep to waking, and still felt a warm hand stroking me from behind.

"Lucas?"

A low laugh. "I should hope so."

I started to flip over, felt his hand disengage, and reached down to grab it.

"Don't stop," I said.

"I won't." He leaned over my shoulder, and slid his finger back inside me. "Better?"

"God, yes." I arched my back against him. "How—how'd you get here?"

"Magic."

"Mmmm."

"A good surprise?"

"The best."

He laughed softly. "Go back to sleep, then. I have everything under control."

"Mmmm."

As for falling back to sleep, naturally I did no such thing. Afterward, I propped myself up on Lucas's chest and grinned.

"These surprise visits are getting better all the time."

He returned a crooked smile. "I take it my unexpected arrival isn't completely objectionable, even if I did disturb your sleep?"

"Disturb away. It is a surprise, though. What happened with your case?"

"It ended this afternoon. Once the prosecution confirmed that its new witness resided in a cemetery, they decided to move straight to closing arguments."

"A definite advantage to working in a human court. They never subpoena dead witnesses."

"This is true. So, I'm here to help, if you want me."

"Hell, yes," I said, grinning. "In every possible way. So you're staying?"

"If that's all right with—"

"It's great. I can't even remember the last time we spent more than a weekend together."

"It *has* been a while," Lucas said softly, then cleared his throat. "My schedule lately has been busier than I anticipated, and I realize this isn't an ideal arrangement for a relationship—"

"It's fine," I said.

"It's not what you expected."

"I didn't expect anything." I flipped off him and sat up. "No expectations, remember? Take it one day at a time. That's what we agreed."

"Yes, I know that's what you said, but—"

"It's what I meant. No expectations, no pressure. You stay for as long as you like."

Lucas pulled himself up. "That's not what—" He paused. "We need to talk, Paige."

"Sure."

I felt Lucas watching me in the darkness, but he said nothing.

"What do you want to talk about?" I asked after a few moments.

"About—" He held my gaze for a moment, then looked away. "About the case. What happened tonight?"

"Oh, God." I thumped onto the pillow. "You have some strange friends, Cortez."

A quarter-smile. "I wouldn't classify Jaime as a friend but, yes, that's one way of putting it. So tell me what happened."

I did.

A Theory

AT SEVEN, STILL TALKING, WE MOVED THE CONVERSATION from the bed to the restaurant downstairs. Dining that early meant we got the best seats, a table in the corner of the atrium.

By nine, the tiny restaurant was full, with a line at the door. We were on our third cup of coffee, breakfast long since done, which earned us plenty of glares from those waiting at the hostess station, but not so much as an impatient glance from our server, probably owing to the size of the tip Lucas had tacked onto the bill.

"Nasha?" Lucas said when I told him the name Dana's attacker had invoked. "It doesn't sound familiar."

"I passed it on through Adam to Robert, to get his opinion. I'd called him yesterday to ask—uh, about some council stuff."

"And a list of alternate necromancers, I presume?"

"I—uh—" I inhaled. "I'm sorry. I know you said to trust you, and I really tried . . ."

A smile tickled his lips. "But gave up somewhere between Sid Vicious and the private strip show. Either of which, understandably, would strain the bounds of the deepest trust."

"Actually, it was *after* the striptease."

His smile broadened. "Ah, well, in that case, you out-lasted any reasonable expectation of faith. I'm flattered. Thank you."

"Still, I should have listened to you. You were right. Jaime did just fine."

"She is very good, though sometimes I think she'd pre-fer otherwise. Have you ever heard of Molly O'Casey?"

"Of course. Top-notch necro. Died a few years back, didn't she?"

Lucas nodded. "She was Jaime's paternal grand-mother. Vegas is Jaime's stage name."

"I thought it might be. She doesn't look Hispanic."

"She isn't. Her mother chose the name when she started Jaime in show business, as a child. As Jaime tells it, her mother was a flaming racist, and had no idea Vegas was Spanish. To her, 'Vegas' meant 'Las Vegas,' a good omen for a child with a stage career. Years later, when she found out the name's origin, she almost had a heart at-tack. Demanded Jaime change it. But, by then, Jaime was eighteen, and could do as she liked. The more her mother hated the name, she more determined she was to keep it."

"There's a story there," I said softly.

"Yes, I imagine there is."

We sipped our coffee.

"I thought you were in Chicago," said a voice above my head.

I turned to see Jaime pulling an empty chair from a table behind us. The trio at the table looked up in sur-prise, but she ignored them and clattered the chair down beside me, then dropped into it. She was wearing a silk wrapper and, I suspected, little else.

"Isn't this romantic," she said, snarling a yawn. "The

happy couple, all brushed, scrubbed, and chipper." She dropped her head onto the table. "Someone get me a coffee. Stat."

Lucas swept a lock of her hair off his muffin plate, then gestured to the server, who stopped mid-order and hurried over with the pot. Jaime stayed facedown on the table.

"Is your, uh, guest joining us?" I asked Jaime.

She rolled onto her cheek to look up at me. "Guest?"

"The guy? From last night?"

"Guy?"

"The one you took back to your room."

She lifted her head. "I took a—?" She groaned. "Oh, shit. Hold on. I'll be right back."

She stood, took three steps, then turned.

"Uh, Paige? Did I get a name?"

"Mark—no, Mike. Oh, wait. That was the blonde. Craig . . . or Greg. The music was pretty loud."

She pressed her fingers to her temples. "It still is. Greg, then. I'll mumble."

She staggered across the atrium.

I turned to Lucas. "Interesting lady."

"That's one way of putting it."

Jaime got rid of her "guest," and joined us for the rest of her coffee, then went back to her room for more sleep. She had a show in Orlando that night, so, in case we didn't see her again, we thanked her for her help.

Lucas unpacked while I phoned Robert about the "Nasha" connection. After four rings, the machine picked up.

"That's probably one clue that's not going to help us

much anyway," I said once I'd left a message. "I'd really hoped to get more from Dana."

"She's probably blocked what little she did see. We may want to shift our focus to ascertaining how the killer selected his victims."

"Damn, of course. He obviously targeted runaways with Cabal parents, but how would he find out something like that? Maybe the parents had a connection, because of their shared circumstances. Like a support group. Do the Cabals offer stuff like that?"

"They do, but separately. They strongly discourage interaction with the employees of other Cabals."

"What about therapists or social workers? Would they share them?"

Lucas shook his head. "What I believe we're looking for is someone who has obtained access to employee files at the Cortez, Nast, and St. Cloud Cabals."

I looked across the room at my laptop. "They're all computerized, aren't they? So someone hacked into the system . . . and I cannot *believe* I didn't think of that."

"You wouldn't because you aren't familiar with Cabal record-keeping procedures, and the amount of personal detail they keep. You won't find many corporations who keep records of their staff's personal situations. Nothing in a Cabal employee's life is sacred. If someone's mother-in-law has a gambling problem, the Cabal knows about it."

"For leverage."

"Not just leverage, but security. If that mother-in-law gets in trouble with a loan shark, her half-demon son-in-law may use his powers to permanently solve the problem. Likewise, a runaway Cabal child could be a potential security threat, so they keep track of them, and probably know more about their whereabouts than their

parents do. As for hacking into the system, while it's possible, Cabal security *is* top of the line."

"Everyone thinks their security is top of the line," I
said. "Until someone like me slips in the back door."

"True, but the systems are protected by both technical
and supernatural means. To hack them would require a
supernatural with an inside knowledge of Cabal security
systems."

"Someone who worked in the computer or security departments. Probably someone who was fired in the past
year or so. The old 'disgruntled employee' theory."

Lucas nodded "Let me phone my father. See whether
we can find anyone who'd fit that theory."

Lucas had no trouble getting the Cortez Cabal employee
list. Benicio knew that while Lucas might love to keep a
copy of that list for his own investigations against the
Cabals, he would do the honorable thing and destroy it
as soon as it had served its stated purpose. Getting the
other Cabal HR departments to cooperate wasn't nearly
so easy. Benicio didn't tell them Lucas would be access-
ing the list, but they didn't want *any* Cortez getting his
hands on their staff records. It took two hours just to get
a list of dismissed employees' names and positions.

Those lists were surprisingly short. I thought the
Cabals were holding out on us, but Lucas assured me
they looked accurate. When you hire only supernaturals,
and you find ones who work out, you bend over backward
to keep them. If they don't work out, it's better to make
them disappear rather than hand them a pink slip . . . and
not just to avoid paying severance. A pissed-off supernatural employee is a lot more dangerous than your average
disgruntled postal worker.

Once we narrowed the list down to employees in the computer and security departments, we had two names from the Cortez list, three from the Nasts, and one from the St. Clouds. Put those together and we had five possibilities. And no, there was nothing wrong with my math skills. Two plus three plus one should equal six. So why did we have a list of five names? Because one appeared on two rosters. Everett Weber, computer programmer.

According to the Cortez files, Everett Weber was a druid who'd worked as a programmer in their Human Resources department from June 2000 to December 2000, on a six-month contract. That didn't qualify as a dismissal, but people often take contract jobs expecting them to turn into permanent positions. We needed to find out how amicable Weber's leaving had been. And we needed details of his employment with the Nasts. Lucas phoned Benicio again. Seventy minutes later, Benicio called back.

"Well?" I said as Lucas hung up.

"Preliminary reports from the Human Resources department indicate that Weber's contract ended without rancor, but my father will investigate further. It's not uncommon for managers to be less than forthcoming when confronted with a potentially unreported employee problem. As for the Nasts, Weber worked in their IT department from January of this year until August, in a contract position."

"Another six-month contract?"

"No, a one-year contract that ended after seven months, but the Nasts refuse to elaborate."

I slammed my laptop shut. "Damn it! Do they want this guy caught or not?"

"I suspect the problem is coming from both sides. My father would be reluctant to let the Nasts know we're raising questions about someone in particular. Otherwise Weber may disappear into Nast custody before we can question him, a definite possibility considering he's currently residing in California."

"And the Nast Cabal is based in Los Angeles, meaning they'd beat us to him."

"Precisely. My father's suggestion, and one I would second, is that we proceed to California ourselves and investigate Everett further, before we press the Nasts for details."

"Sounds good, but—"

The ring of my cell phone cut me off. I checked the call display.

"Adam," I said. "Before I answer, what part of California are we heading to?"

"Close enough to Santa Cruz that you can ask him to join us."

I nodded and clicked on the phone.

An hour later we were back at the airport, picking up tickets purchased for us by the Cortez Corporation. This was, of course, Benicio's doing, though it was one step down from what he'd really wanted, which was for us to use the corporate jet. When Benicio offered the tickets instead, Lucas—eager to stop arguing and start investigating—had accepted. Neither of us was happy about the obvious manipulation, but the truth was that we could ill afford to be crisscrossing the country like this. Dana and Jacob deserved better than a low-budget investigation, and we'd make sure they got it, even if it meant accepting transportation expenses from the Cabal.

*   *   *

Of course, Adam didn't mind playing host and tour guide, not when it came with the opportunity for excitement. I've known Adam for half my life, long enough to accept that he's the kind of guy who does as little as he can get away with—unless the "doing" involves straight-up ass-kicking action. Today, with the prospect of some less-than-legal adventuring, he was keen enough to actually meet our plane on time.

Adam was twenty-four, and good-looking in a wholesome California way with a perpetual tan, light brown hair sun-streaked blond, and the well-built body of a surfer. Like his stepfather, he was a half-demon. Robert had long since suspected Adam was the most powerful subtype of fire demon—an Exustio—but it had only been last year that he'd finally incinerated something and proved Robert right. That marked the culmination of seventeen years of increasing powers, dating back to childhood, when Talia had gone seeking answers for Adam's early displays of power, not content to accept a psychiatrist's explanation that Adam's literally hot temper was only adolescent acting-out. Her search had led her to Robert Vasic, who'd eventually given her the answers she sought . . . and fallen in love with her.

"So what's the plan?" Adam said as we climbed into his Jeep.

"We're starting right at the source," I said. "A home invasion, if we're lucky."

"Sweet."

"I thought you'd think so."

Less-than-Legal Adventuring

EVERETT WEBER LIVED OUTSIDE MODESTO, IN A SMALL farmhouse, an ugly cinder block with a freshly mowed lawn and tidy yard, but with woodwork years overdue for a paint job. Probably a rental, owned by whoever owned the surrounding vineyards. Like most renters, Weber was quite willing to keep the place neat but wasn't about to dip into his own pockets for repairs.

Weber worked at a place in Silicon Valley, so we hoped that at one P.M. on a Friday, that's where he'd be. From Lucas's preliminary background check, Weber appeared to live alone. Add in the fact that his house was on a dirt road, with no neighbors for a half-mile in any direction, and a daytime break-and-enter wasn't as risky as it sounded.

The remote location made it perfect for a B&E but more difficult to get up close and check for occupancy. We called the house from the road, and no one answered the phone, but that didn't necessarily mean Everett wasn't there. After some skulking around, Lucas proclaimed the house empty, and we met at the back door, whereupon we discovered that every window came complete with bars and security decals. After a quick check,

Lucas declared the decals legit. Weber had a security system, and it was activated.

"No disarming spells in your repertoires, I suppose?" Adam whispered as we huddled near the back door.

Lucas pulled a small kit from under his leather jacket. "No, but I do have this."

"Cool." Adam crouched beside Lucas as he worked. "Now this you didn't learn in law school."

"You'd be surprised," Lucas murmured. "No, this comes from having Cabal contract employees as clients. As you might expect, the Cabals don't contract them for their typing skills. In some cases, an exchange of skills proves more valuable than financial remuneration." He fiddled with a mess of wires. "There. Now comes the difficult part. I need to cut these three at the same time or I'll set it off. However, if I do cut them, it's easily discovered, and Weber will know his system was breached. This may take a few minutes." He reached into his kit. "First, I need to—"

Adam reached down and grasped the mess of wires. A spark, then they disintegrated to ash.

"Or we could just do that," Lucas said.

"Damn those spontaneous electrical fires," Adam said.

"Been practicing, I see," I said.

Adam grinned and wiped the ash from his hand. He grabbed the door handle.

"Wait," I said.

I cast an unlock spell. Adam opened the door. We paused, but no alarm sounded. Lucas finished replacing the wires, then waved us inside.

We soon understood why Weber put a security system on a rented farmhouse. Any money he'd saved on rent, he'd invested in electronics, with multiple computers, a plasma TV, and a hi-fi system that I'm sure rocked the neighbors even a mile away.

While Adam and Lucas started searching, I headed for my area of expertise: the computer. I quickly discovered that Weber applied the same standard of security to his hard drive as he did to his house. Although he was the only person living there, he had the computer password-protected. It took nearly thirty minutes to crack that, only to find that all his data—even his e-mail—was encrypted. I burned the files onto a CD for later.

Since Lucas and Adam were still searching, I returned to Weber's computer to search for a specific piece of information: a credit card number. Seeing how careful Weber was with his files, I assumed this search would be futile. Well, I was wrong. Five minutes of hunting and I found a cookie containing an unencrypted credit card number. Later I could hack into the credit card company system and search his records, in hopes that if he was our killer, he'd used his card for traveling.

After another hour, we declared the house thoroughly searched. Lucas and Adam hadn't found anything. We could only hope that decrypting Weber's files and checking his credit card records would prove more fruitful.

We retreated to Santa Cruz, where Adam lived with his parents. I was eager to get Weber's credit card records, but Adam's mother, Talia, insisted that we have dinner first and, having been on food-free mental superdrive since breakfast, I had to agree that my brain needed nourishment before I did something as dangerous as hack into credit card companies.

We had fettuccine Alfredo alfresco, on the multilevel

deck that covered half the backyard. Talia and Robert ate with us to hear about the case. As usual, Adam's initial recitation had left out half the details and mangled the rest, so they'd waited to hear the real story from the source.

Talia was one of the few humans who lived within the supernatural world. That was her choice, to accept the dangers of that knowledge in order to better understand her son and husband, and play a full role in their lives. Over the last few years, Robert's health had begun to fail, and Talia had been picking up the slack. Robert was only sixty-eight, but his physical condition had never been what one would call robust, forcing him even from an early age to take the scholarly approach to helping other half-demons, acting as a resource and a confidant. Talia, who was twenty-seven years younger, had embraced the midlife career change. As for Adam taking over Robert's work, well, let's just say no one expected him to be sitting behind a desk, reading demonology texts, anytime soon.

Adam bit off a chunk of bread and chewed it as he talked. "So that's it. We broke, we entered, we found zip."

"I hope you were careful—" Talia began, then stopped. "Yes, I'm sure you were. If there's anything Robert and I can do . . ."

"Lend us your Miata?" Adam said. "The Jeep's been making a funny noise."

"The Jeep's been making funny noises since you bought it, and the last time you drove my car, you buggered up the convertible roof, but if there's anything *else* we can do . . ."

"You asked about a demon named Nasha," Robert said, speaking for the first time since the meal had begun.

"Oh, that's right," I said. "I completely forgot."

"Well, I would have relayed an answer through Adam, but I was stalling to give myself more time, and possibly find a better answer. There's no mention in any text of a demon named Nasha. It's quite likely the poor girl misheard, but I can't even find a name that phonetically resembles Nasha. The closest is Nakashar."

"Nakashar's an eudemon, isn't he?" Adam said as he peeled an orange. "Very minor. Outside of the Babylonian archive journals, he's not even mentioned."

I looked up, surprised Adam knew this.

Adam continued. "So it's not likely to be Nakashar. Eudemons can be summoned, but they won't interfere in our world. Sacrificing to them is like bribing a meter maid to get out of a speeding ticket. We're talking about a druid, though, right? So we should be looking at Celtic deities. What about Macha?"

"Of course," Robert said. "That would make sense, wouldn't it?"

"I know zilch about the Celtic pantheon," I said.

"Not surprising. Although they are often classified as demons, they aren't included in demonology texts because only druids can communicate with them. They don't fit the classic definition of either eudemon or cacodemon. If you ask them, they'll tell you they're gods, but most demonographers are uncomfortable with that appellation, and prefer to label them 'minor deities.' The study of Celtic deities—"

"—is fascinating," Talia cut in with a smile. "And I'm sure everyone would love to hear about it...another time."

Robert chuckled. "Thank you, Lia. Let's just say that

Macha is a likely suspect. She's one of the three Valkyrie aspects of the Morrigan, and she certainly does accept human sacrifices. That's one piece of evidence to support your theory, then. Now, I know you want to get back to work. Adam? If you can help your mother with the dishes—"

"Oh, don't torture him," Talia said. "I'm sure he wants to help Pa—" She caught a look from Robert. "Or perhaps first he can show Lucas that motorcycle."

"That's right." Adam turned to Lucas. "Remember I was telling you about that guy my friend knows? Bought an Indian, took it apart, and couldn't figure out how to put it back together? Well, his wife's making him sell it, so I had him e-mail me some pics. Looks like a big metal jigsaw puzzle, but I thought you might like to take a look. You could probably get it cheap, store it here until you guys get a place."

"You boys go on, then," Robert said. As they left, he motioned for me to stay behind.

"Okay," I said when they were gone. "Since when does Adam know about minor eudemons and Celtic deities?"

"Surprised?" Robert smiled. "I think that was the idea. He's been studying for a few months now, but probably didn't mention it because he wanted to astound you with his sudden brilliance."

I moved to the chair beside Robert's.

"It's never been easy for him," Robert continued. "Hearing everyone talk about your accomplishments. I'll admit, I've been guilty of lauding your achievements in the past few years, hoping it would encourage him to take on a more active role in the council."

"He's talked about it," I said. "But it's never gone beyond talk. With added power comes added responsibility."

Robert smiled. "And added work, both of which lack a certain appeal for Adam. In the last few years, though, he's been looking at where you were, and where he was—a college dropout, tending bar—and it bothered him enough to re-enroll at college, but I think he was still able to justify it, tell himself you're an anomaly and no one else can be measured along the same yardstick. Then he met Lucas, and saw what he's doing with his life. I think he's realized that if he continues down this route, he'll be left behind, the friend who watches from the sidelines, buys the beer, and listens to the war stories."

"So boning up on demonology is step one in a bigger plan."

"I wouldn't say a 'plan' per se. Adam has ambitions, but he hasn't figured out where to channel them." As Talia returned for another armload of dishes, Robert smiled up at her. "Now, his mother knows how she'd like to see them channeled. Into book-reading and studying, hands-off work like his old man."

"Nothing wrong with that," Talia said. "Unfortunately, for Adam, it would require heavy sedation and fireproof chains. Being involved means being *involved*, the more dangerous the better."

"It's not that dangerous," I said. "Not really."

Talia laughed and patted my shoulder. "You don't need to whitewash it for me, Paige. I knew my son was never going to lead a quiet life working in an office. In some cases, biology really is destiny. He has power. Better he should use it for good. Or, at least, that's what I keep telling myself."

"He's got a first-rate defense system," I said.

"Exactly. He'll be fine." She exhaled and nodded. "He'll be fine. Now, Paige, go find what you need to stop this guy, and if you need our help, just ask."

* * *

I'd hacked into this credit card company's files before—
the last time being only a few weeks ago when Lucas
needed information for a case. They hadn't changed any
of their security parameters since then, so I popped into
the system easily. Within twenty minutes I had Weber's
credit card transaction records. Nothing on them indicated that he'd visited any of the target cities in the last
six months. That, however, might only mean that he was
smart enough not to make hotel reservations or dinner
purchases with his credit card. Or he might have used a
different card.

Lucas slipped into the study as I finished. When I told
him I'd struck out, he decided to make some phone calls
and see whether we could find another way to place
Weber out of town on the days of the attacks. These calls
were best made from a pay phone, so he took Adam and
left. Did he really need Adam to chauffeur him around
Santa Cruz? No, but if he'd left him, I'd have spent the
next hour with Adam breathing down my neck as I tried
to crack Weber's data files. So Lucas took him along.

It took me about thirty minutes to determine the en-
cryption program Weber had used on his files. Once I
knew what he'd used, I downloaded a cracking program
and translated them into text. For the hour I waded
through the boring detritus of an average life: e-mail
jokes, online dating postings, bill payment confirmations,
Christmas card address labels, and a hundred other
mundane bits of data raised to the value of top-secret information by a paranoid mind and a shareware encryp-
tion program.

At ten-fifty, my watch alarm went off. Time to check
in with Elena. I phoned her, talked to Savannah, then

returned to my work. The rest of the files on the disk appeared to be work-related. Like most professionals, Weber's day didn't end when the clock struck five, and for contract employees, the drive to translate that contract into a full-time job often means bringing work home to impress the company with your throughput. He had plenty of data files on his computer, and a folder filled with programs in SAS, COBOL, and RPG. The mind-numbing side of programming: data manipulation and extraction.

I looked at the lists of data files. There were over a hundred on the disk and I really didn't want to skim through each one. Yet I couldn't just put them aside based on assumptions about the content. So I whipped up a simple program to open each file and write a random sampling of the data into a single new file. Then I scanned the new file. Most of it looked like financial data, not surprising given that Weber worked in the accounting division of a Silicon Valley company. Then, a third of the way down the file, I found this:

```
Tracy Edith
McIntyre       03/12/86   shaman      NY5N34414

Race Mark
Trenton        11/02/88   sorcerer    YY8N27453

Morgan Anita
Lui-Delancy    23/01/85   half-demon  NY6Y18923
```

Now, Silicon Valley companies may employ some pretty young people, and some pretty strange people, but I don't think teenage supernaturals made up a significant proportion of their staff. I found two other similar lists farther down. Three files with information on the teenage children of supernaturals. Three Cabals had been the victims of a killer targeting their youth. Definitely not a coincidence.

My sampling program had pulled off only the first eighty characters in each record, but the information in those records extended well over that. As with most data files, though, all you saw were strings of numbers and Y/N indicators, meaningless without a context. To read and understand these files, you needed a program that extracted the data using a record key.

Ten minutes later, I'd found the program that read the Cabal files. I ran it, then opened the file it created.

```
Criteria A: age<17; living with parent(s)
= N; current location city NOT blank, cur-
rent location country = USA
```

ID	Name	Age	Cabal	P.Race	State
01-645-1	Holden Wyngaard	16	Cortez	shaman	LA
01-398-04	Max Diego	14	Cortez	Vodoun	NY
01-452-1	Dana MacArthur	15	Cortez	hd/witch	GA
02-0598-3	Colby Washington	13	Nast	half-demon	SC
02-1232-3	Brandy Moya	14	Nast	half-demon	AL
02-1378-2	Sarah Dermack	15	Nast	necro	TN
03-083-2	Michael Shane	16	StC	half-demon	CA
03-601-2	Ian Villani	14	StC	shaman	NY

```
Criteria B: living with parent(s) = Y;
parental marital status IN [D,W,S]; em-
ployee is custodial parent = Y; parental
occupation = bodyguard, department = CEO
```

ID	Name	Age	Cabal	P. Marital Stat.
01-821-1	Jacob Sorenson	16	Cortez	Widowed
03-987-1	Reese Tettington	14	St. Cloud	Divorced

At my elbow was a piece of paper with three names on it—the names of the teens killed from the other Cabals, the only information we had about them. I'd already memorized that list, but still looked over now, needing to be sure I wasn't imagining things. I read the names.

Colby Washington.

Sarah Dermack.

Michael Shane.

I grabbed my cell phone and called Lucas.

A Message of Hope

"HOLY SHIT," ADAM SAID AFTER I'D EXPLAINED WHAT I'D found. "Well, the Cabals can fire up their electric chair. Case closed."

"An economically efficient solution," Lucas said. "But I believe, in a case with such a potentially life-altering—or life-ending—conclusion, it's not unfair for the accused to expect a few luxuries, such as a trial."

"The guy made lists of teenage Cabal kids, and half the kids on those lists are now dead. Screw due process. Hell, I'll fry him myself, save the Cabals the cost of electricity."

"While we appreciate your enthusiasm, I believe we'll begin by talking to Weber—"

"Interrogate him? Hey, I picked up some good torture tips from Clay. I could—"

"We'll begin by *talking* to him," Lucas said. "Without the added incentive of physical, mental, or parapsychological duress. We'll mention the files—"

"And say what? Do you have a reasonable explanation as to why we found lists of dead kids on your computer? Lists created *before* they died? Oh, yeah, I'm sure there's a logical—"

I clapped a hand over Adam's mouth. "So, we'll talk to Weber. Tonight?"

Lucas checked his watch. "It's past midnight. I don't want to frighten him—"

Adam yanked my hand down. "Frighten him? The guy's a serial killer! I say we scare the living shit out of him, and—"

I cast a binding spell. Adam froze in mid-sentence.

"We'll confront him in the morning," Lucas said. "To be certain, however, that nothing happens in the mean-time, I'd suggest we return to his house, confirm that he's still there, and keep watch until morning."

I agreed, then broke the binding spell, and closed my laptop. As Adam recovered, he glared at me. I cut him off before he could complain.

"Are you coming with us? Or will our lack of murder-ous activity be too great for you to handle?"

"I'm coming. But if you use another binding spell on me—"

"Don't give me any reason to and I won't."

"Remember who you're talking to, Sabrina. One touch of my fingers and I could stop you from ever using a bind-ing spell on anyone ever again."

I snorted and opened my mouth to reply, but Lucas cut me off.

"One other small matter, before we leave," Lucas said. "My father has left over a half-dozen messages on my phone, looking for updates. Should I provide one?"

"Do you think it's safe?" I asked.

Lucas hesitated, then nodded. "My father may be overprotective, but he does trust my judgment and my ability to defend myself. If I tell him we wish to speak to Weber before taking him into custody, he'll accept that. I'll ask him to assemble an apprehension team."

"What?" Adam said. "We don't even get to take the guy down?"

"The Cabal team is trained to handle that, and I'll let them do their job."

Adam sighed. "Well, I guess a stakeout is still pretty cool."

"Jesus," Adam said, slumping into the driver's seat. "How long have we been sitting here? Why isn't it light out yet?"

"Because it's only five A.M." I said.

"No way. Your watch must have stopped."

"Didn't Lucas suggest you bring a magazine? He said it'd be boring."

"He said tedious."

"Which means boring."

"Then he should have said boring." Adam shot a mock glare at Lucas, who sat beside him, watching Weber's house through binoculars.

"Boring means something which is dull," Lucas said. "Tedious implies both long and very dull, which, I believe you'll agree, this is."

"Yeah? Well, remind me to pack my pocket dictionary next time you two drag me along on one of these 'tedious' adventures."

"Drag?" Lucas said, arching an eyebrow. "I don't recall any arm-twisting involved."

"Hey, brain-flash," Adam said. "Why don't I slip out for a closer look? Make sure he's still there."

"He is," Lucas said. "Paige cast perimeter spells at both doors."

"Yeah, well, no offense to Paige, but—"

"Don't say it," I said.

Adam opened the driver's door. "I'll go check."

"No," Lucas and I said in unison. When Adam hesitated, door still open, I added, "Close the door or we'll put my spell-casting ability to the test."

He grumbled, but closed it. Another two hours passed. Two hours during which I had cause at least every ten minutes to wish we'd left Adam behind. Finally, at seven-thirty, a light went on in Weber's bedroom. Adam lunged for the door handle. Lucas put out a hand to stop him.

"We're not jumping him the moment he gets out of bed," I said. "There's no rush."

Adam groaned and sank into his seat.

We'd prepared our plan of action before leaving the Vasics. I'd remembered what the gang punks in the alley had said on seeing us, which also reminded me of my own impression the first time Lucas showed up on my doorstep, clean-cut and funereally earnest in his department-store suit. With the right choice of clothes and a couple of books from Robert's library, we were set.

Lucas and I gave Adam time to sneak around and cover the rear door, then we climbed the front steps. Lucas rang Weber's doorbell. Two minutes later, a thin, dark-haired man answered. Weber matched his Cortez Cabal employee photograph, right down to the black shirt.

"Good morning," Lucas said. "Do you know where you'll be spending eternity?"

Weber's gaze dropped to our Bibles. He mumbled something and tried to shut the door. Lucas grabbed the edge and held it fast.

"Please," I said. "We have an important message for you. A message of hope."

Now, we really didn't expect Weber to let us in. My

religio-babble was only intended to give Lucas time to ready his knock-back spell, which would send Weber reeling away from the door so we could get inside. But as the words left my mouth, Weber's eyes widened.

"You're the ones," he said. "The ones Esus said would come."

I blinked, but Lucas nodded and murmured an affirmation. Weber ushered us inside, then cast a nervous glance out the front door before closing it.

"Go on in," he said, wiping his palms against his pants. "Sit down. Oh, wait, let me clear that chair. I'm sorry the place is such a mess. I've been—"

"Busy," Lucas finished.

Weber nodded, head bouncing like a bobble dog's. "Busy, yes. Very busy. When Esus told me . . . well, I wanted to run, but he said I shouldn't, that it would only make things worse."

"He's right," Lucas said.

"He's always right." Weber cast a nervous glance around. "He said it's not safe here. He said you'd take me someplace safe."

My gaze shot to Lucas, trying to gauge his reaction, but he gave none.

"That's right," Lucas said. "Just let me call our driver."

Lucas reached into his breast pocket for his cell phone, to call the extraction team. Obviously Weber wouldn't be comfortable talking here, so there was no use trying. Time to skip to the next phase and take him in for questioning.

Lucas only had time to press the first button when a sharp crack rang out, followed by a tremendous crash. A metal canister hit the floor between us. Lucas lunged, grabbing me by the shoulders and throwing us both to the ground. The canister began to smoke.

"Cover your—" Lucas began, but the sound of breaking wood drowned him out.

I turned to see the front door slam open and three men dressed in black barrel through. All three turned their guns on us, then disappeared as smoke filled the room.

They Always Grab the Girl

SOMEONE STARTED SHOUTING ORDERS, BUT I WAS DOU-
bled over, hacking my lungs up, unable to hear anything
but my own coughing. I pulled my shirt over my nose, but
it didn't help. My eyes teared up from the gas; between
that and the smoke, I was blinded. Fingers grabbed my
arm and tugged me forward. Trust Lucas to keep his calm,
whatever the situation.

I stumbled behind Lucas's dark shape. A doorway
loomed before us. As we moved through it, the smoke
lessened, but my eyes still streamed tears. I wiped my
free arm across them. Lucas kept pulling me, presumably toward the back door and clean air.

"Paige!" Adam's voice. Through the smoke I could
make out his outline running toward us.

"Get outside," I rasped. "It's—"

He charged. The hand on my arm wrenched me backward. I tripped and spun to see that it wasn't Lucas holding me. It was Weber.

I punched at Weber, but my fist glanced off his shoulder. His other hand sheared down. I felt something hit me
between the ribs. Heard Adam's bellow of rage. Lucas

lunged through the door and cut Adam off in mid-charge. The stink of sulfur and burned flesh overwhelmed the fading smell of the gas. Lucas gasped in pain. I tried to wrench myself from Weber's grip, but he held me fast.

"Nobody move!" Weber screeched, his voice shrill with panic. "I've got the girl."

A split second of clear, if near-hysterical, thought. Of course he'd grab the girl. They always grabbed the girl. But why did I have to be the girl?

Then cool steel pressed against my throat, and I stopped thinking. The blade pressed into my throat, and blood trickled down my neck. In that moment, it seemed that even to breathe might be fatal, that with the slightest movement some vital artery would be severed. As I held my breath, I became aware of another pain, sharper and lower. My rib cage. I pressed the spot. Blood seeped through my fingers. I'd been stabbed. The thought hit me so hard I rocked, and in rocking felt the knife nick my throat again. I closed my eyes and began to count, fighting against panic.

"Move the knife away from her throat," Lucas said, his voice even but strained.

"She—she's my hostage."

"Yes, I know," Lucas said slowly. "But if you wish her to remain a viable hostage, you cannot take the chance of accidentally wounding her, so please lower that—"

A loud scuffle cut him off, as the men from the other room barreled into the kitchen. I didn't dare look to confirm that, could only stare at the empty space in front of me. Weber tensed, and the blade dug into my throat again.

"Stand down!" Lucas shouted over the clamor. "He has a hostage. Put your weapons down!"

"Everyone against the wall," a man barked.

"Don't pretend you don't know who I am," Lucas barked back. "I gave you an order. Lower your weapons!"

"I take my orders from the Nast—"

"You'll take your goddamned orders from me or you'll be regretting it into the next life! Now stand down."

A moment of silence, then the pressure on my throat lessened.

"I want a helicopter," Weber said. "I want—"

"You want to get out of here alive," Lucas said, his voice returned to its usual soft, reasonable tones. "The house is surrounded by professional snipers. The moment you step into their line of sight, they will shoot."

"I—I have a hostage."

"And they are trained to handle that. You'll be dead before you have time to hurt her."

Weber hesitated, knife trembling against my throat. Adam tensed, but Lucas kept a restraining hand on his shirt. Lucas's lips moved in an incantation. Then he stopped as Weber lowered the knife.

"Good," Lucas said. "Now you need to—"

"Esus, god of water's great gift!" Weber shouted, sliding his fingers along the knife's blade and flicking my blood to the floor. "Esus, hear me!"

"You don't want to do this," Lucas said.

Weber's eyes rolled back and he started speaking in another language. I counted to three, then threw myself forward. He caught me, one arm going around my neck. My feet flew out as he yanked me back. Adam lunged at Weber. The knife shot to my throat. Weber yelled a warning, but Adam kept coming. The knife bit through my skin. Then Adam stumbled, thrown off balance by Lucas, who'd this time had the presence of mind to use a knock-back spell rather than touch Adam.

"Everybody stay back!" Weber shrieked.

"We will," Lucas said, motioning Adam to move behind him. "Now, lower that knife—"

"Esus!" Weber shouted. He wiped the dripping blood from my neck and flung it to the kitchen floor. "Take this offering and deliver your loyal servant!"

Weber paused, but nothing happened. I looked at Lucas. He met my eyes and I could see his fear, but he motioned for me to stay calm and wait. Weber ran through his supplication twice. Then he waited. We all waited, the hum of the refrigerator the only sound.

"He's not answering," Lucas said softly. "He won't interfere. Now, if you want to negotiate, you need to lower that knife. I won't talk to you while you have a knife at her throat."

Weber looked at the ceiling one last time, then lowered his gaze to Lucas. "If I lower the knife, they'll shoot me."

"No, they won't. They have their weapons down, and they won't take the chance that you can get your knife back to her throat before they aim and fire. Lower the knife . . ."

As Lucas continued reasoning with Weber, the knife blade quavered against my throat. One slip, one push too hard against the skin, and . . . oh, God, it hurt to breathe. Blood now soaked the front of my shirt, wet and clammy against my skin. Where had I been stabbed? Beneath the heart, I knew, but what was there? What organs?

And then I thought: Goddamn it, you're standing here sniveling and hoping your boyfriend saves you before you bleed out. Typical witch.

I closed my eyes and whispered a spell. Though the words of the two men covered mine, every syllable pressed my throat against the knife blade. I ignored the pricks of pain and kept casting. As the last words left my mouth, the knife went still. I swallowed and prayed it wasn't a coincidence. I counted to five, waiting for the knife to resume shaking. It didn't. Another swallow, then I concentrated my all on holding the binding spell and very slowly eased sideways, away from the knife.

"Don't—" Weber started, then realized he couldn't move his hand. "What the—?"

Weber's other hand shot forward to grab me as I side-lunged out of his reach. The spell snapped. I saw the knife blade swing down. As I twisted and dove for the floor, the knife slashed through the side of my stomach. Then Lucas grabbed me, knocking the knife away, as Adam launched himself at Weber. Weber screamed. The stink of scorched flesh filled the tiny kitchen. The Cabal SWAT team leapt into action. And it was all over.

Laying the Blame

OF THE NEXT HOUR I REMEMBER ONLY IMAGES AND SNIP-
pets that whizzed past at MTV speed. Lucas stanching
my wounds. Adam pacing behind us. The SWAT team
leader barking orders. A man examining my wounds.
Adam snapping questions. Lucas reassuring me. A weight
on my chest, slowly bearing down. Gasping for air. Lucas
shouting orders. A door slamming. Road rumbling beneath tires.

The next time I came to, I was lying on some kind of
bed that vibrated and swayed. I struggled to open my
eyes, but could only pry them open a slit. When I inhaled, the air was sharp, metallic. I felt a light pressure
around my mouth. An oxygen mask. A surge of panic
made my head hurt. I dipped toward unconsciousness
again and fought my way back.

A soft jolt and the vibrations ceased.

"Finally."

Lucas's voice, distant and muffled. A squeeze on my
forearm. I felt the warmth of his fingers, resting on my
arm. Then his breath tickled my ear.

"We're here," he said, still sounding as if he was a

room-length away. I had to concentrate to make out the words. ": . . . you hear me?"

A clang, then the whoosh of an opening door and the dim light turned midday bright. Lucas's grip on my arm tightened.

"What are you doing here?" he said, voice cold.

Another voice answered. Familiar . . . Benicio. "I came in with the team. Our team. The one you requested. How is she?"

A clatter, and the low murmur of other voices. My bed jerked. Lucas's fingers brushed my forehead as my bed lifted. A jolt, a murmured apology, and I was tugged into the sunlight. A few bumps, then the squeak of wheels and the rush of air. Lucas's hand found mine and gripped it as we moved.

"You're upset," Benicio said, his voice low.

I managed to open my eyes enough to see Lucas at my side, walking fast, Benicio beside him, leaning in for privacy.

"And that surprises you?" Lucas clipped his words, voice colder than I'd ever heard it.

"I don't blame you for being angry, but you know I had nothing to do with this."

"It was all a misunderstanding. Or a coincidence. Have you decided yet? If not, may I suggest you choose misunderstanding? It provides more opportunity for prevarication."

Benicio reached for Lucas's free arm. "Lucas, I—"

Lucas swiped at his father's hand, catching it and knocking him back. Benicio's eyes went wide. Lucas's face twisted as he spun to say something, but as he wheeled around, he noticed my eyes were half open and stopped in mid-turn. He bent over me, nearly tripping as he tried to keep pace alongside the stretcher.

"Paige? Can you hear me?"

I tried to nod, but had to settle for fluttering my eyelids. He squeezed my hand.

"You're okay," he said. "You're in a hospital—a private hospital. Robert arranged it. They need to . . ."

I slid back into unconsciousness.

The cuts on my neck proved the least of my injuries. The blade had left only shallow gashes that required no more than a quick cleaning and small bandages. I'd sustained two other injuries—one serious but relatively painless, the other minor but painful as hell. The chest wound had cut my lung, collapsing it. The doctors had inserted a chest tube, cleared out the blood, and reinflated my lung, which now seemed fine, although they had to keep the chest tube in for a day or two. The abdomen cut had sliced only through muscle—well, okay, undoubtedly more fat than muscle, but the doctors said "muscle" so I'm sticking to their version. Though the wound was superficial, every time I moved, it was like getting stabbed all over again.

The next morning I opened my eyes to see Adam hunched over a psychology textbook, highlighter in hand. I reached up to rub my face and nearly toppled the IV onto the bed. Adam grabbed it just in time.

"Shit," he said. "I finally convince Lucas it's safe to leave for a few minutes and you decide to wake up. If he comes back, close your eyes, okay?"

I managed a weak smile and opened my mouth to speak, then made a face. I pointed to the water. Adam poured me a glass. He started to put in the straw, but I grabbed the glass and took a gulp. The water hit my parched throat and bounced back, dribbling out my mouth.

"That's attractive," he said, reaching for a tissue.

I snatched it before he could do anything as humiliating as wipe my face. He picked up something from the dresser.

"Brought you something." He handed me a stuffed beanbag bear dressed in a black witch's hat and dress. "Remember these?"

"Hmmm." I struggled to focus, still woozy. "Right. The dolls." A small smile, as the memory surfaced. "You—" I wet my lips and tried again. "You used to buy them for me. Gifts."

He grinned. "Every ugly wart-faced witch doll I could find. Because I knew how much you loved them."

"Hated them. And you knew it. Used to lecture you on sensitivity and stereotyping." I shook my head. "God, I was insufferable sometimes."

"Sometimes?"

I swatted him and laughed, then gasped as pain shot through my stomach. Adam grabbed for the call button, but I lifted my hand to stop him.

"I'm okay," I said.

He nodded and sat down on the side of the bed. "You had us pretty worried. At the house everything seemed okay, but then, boom, you blacked out and your blood pressure dropped—" He shook his head. "Not a good scene. I was freaked, and Lucas was freaked, which only freaked me out even more, 'cause I figured this guy doesn't scare easy and if this scares him, there must be reason to be scared and—" Another shake of the head. "It wasn't good."

"Paige."

I looked up to see a figure in the doorway. The voice

told me it was Lucas, but I had to blink to double-check. Pale and unshaven, he was still dressed in the suit he'd worn for the missionary ruse at Weber's house, but the jacket and tie were gone. His shirt was wrinkled and splattered with coffee stains. One sleeve of his shirt was charred at the forearm, with bandages peeking through the gaping hole. That was the drawback to working with Adam—when he got mad, you had to stay out of his way, or you paid the price in second-degree burns.

"I'll be outside," Adam said, shifting off the bed.

He slipped out the door. As Lucas approached I saw that the stains on his shirt weren't coffee brown, but rust red. Blood. My blood. He followed my gaze.

"Oh, I should change. I—"

"Later," I said.

"Do you want to call Savannah? I can—"

"Later."

I held out my hand. He took it, then reached down to hug me.

An hour later, I was still awake, having persuaded the nurse to hold off on my pain medication. First I needed answers.

"Are they holding Weber in L.A.?" I asked.

Lucas shook his head. "My father won that battle. Weber is in Miami, with a trial date set for Friday."

"I don't get that," Adam said. "Why bother? They know the guy's guilty. What are they going to do, say 'Whoops, we didn't issue a proper warrant' and let him walk?"

"He's entitled to a trial," Lucas said. "It's Cabal law."

"But is it a *real* trial?" I asked.

"A Cabal trial mirrors a human law trial at its most basic level. Lawyers present the case to judges who determine guilt or innocence and impose sentence. As for Weber being released on a technicality, it's unlikely to the point of impossible. The concept of civil rights is much more narrowly defined in a Cabal court."

"You don't need to worry about this guy, Paige," Adam said. "He's not coming back out."

"That's not—" I turned to Lucas. "Has he confessed?"

Lucas shook his head. His gaze slipped to the side, just barely, but I'd been with him long enough to know what this meant.

"There's something else, isn't there?" I said. "Something's happened."

He hesitated, then nodded. "Another Cabal teen died Friday night."

I bolted upright, sending shock waves of pain through me. Lucas and Adam both sprang to their feet, but I waved them down.

"I'm sorry," Lucas said. "I shouldn't have blurted it out like that. Let me explain. Matthew Tucker was the nineteen-year-old son of Lionel St. Cloud's personal assistant. When Lionel came to Miami for the meeting Thursday, Matthew came along with his mother. On Friday night, while we were watching Weber's house, a group of the younger Cabal employees decided to go clubbing, and Matthew joined them. After a few drinks, they wandered out of a nightclub district and into a less savory neighborhood. The group split up, and everyone thought Matthew was with someone else. When they returned without him, the Cabals sent out search teams. They found him shot to death in an alley."

"Shot?" Adam said. "Then it's not our guy. Stabbing and strangulation. That's his MO."

"The Nast Cabal has since confirmed that their second victim, Sarah Dermack, was shot."

"Did this Matthew call the emergency number?" Adam asked.

Lucas shook his head. "But neither did Micahel Shane, the St. Cloud victim."

"Was Matthew on Weber's list?" Adam asked.

"No," I said. "And if he lives with his mother, who's not a bodyguard, he doesn't seem to satisfy the criteria. He's also older than the others. But still, it does seem—"

"Like something completely different," Adam cut in. "The guy was in the wrong place at the wrong time and got shot."

"What are the Cabals saying?" I asked Lucas.

"Almost to the word, exactly what Adam just said."

Our eyes met and I saw my own doubts reflected back.

"So we have questions, then," I said. "If the Cabals aren't going to ask them, we need to do it ourselves. That means we need to go to Miami and talk to Weber."

Lucas went quiet. Adam looked from him to me.

"My opinion?" Adam said. "You both take this 'protecting the innocent' thing way too far, but if you've got questions, then you'd better get them answered before it's too late. Yeah, I know you don't want to take Paige to Miami, and I can totally understand that, but Weber's locked up. He's not going to hurt her."

"It's not Weber he's worried about." I turned to Lucas. "How does your father explain what happened?"

At first, Lucas didn't respond, seeming reluctant to give his father's rationales a voice. Then he took off his glasses and rubbed the bridge of his nose. "His explanation is that he has no explanation. He assumes that, in mentioning Weber's name to the Nasts, he inadvertently provided them with the impetus to begin their own investigation, which culminated in the SWAT raid."

"I suppose that makes sense," I said. "I know you think

your father did this intentionally, but you were in that house, too. He'd never put you in danger like that."

"Paige is right," Adam said. "I don't know your dad, but from the way he was acting yesterday, this was as much a shock to him as it was to you."

"So it's settled," I said. "We're going to Miami."

"On one condition."

The hospital I was in was a small private clinic, far less opulent than the Marsh Clinic in Miami, but serving a similar purpose. This one was run not by a Cabal, but by half-demons. Doctors, nurses, lab techs, even the cook and janitor were half-demon.

San Francisco, like several other big American cities, had a sizable half-demon enclave. Half-demons had no central body like the witch Coven or werewolf Pack. As with most distinct groups in a larger society, though, they recognized the comfort and advantages of community, and many who didn't work for a Cabal gravitated toward one of these half-demon cities.

One of the major advantages to living near other supernaturals is medical care. All the major races avoid human doctors and hospitals. Of course, supernaturals can be and have been treated in hospitals. If you get hit in a head-on collision, you can't tell the paramedics you want to be flown to a private clinic hundreds of miles away. In most cases, such hospital stays are uneventful. But sometimes they aren't, and we do what we can to avoid taking this chance.

Lucas's condition was that, since I needed ongoing medical care, I must transfer to another hospital. Therein lay the problem. Miami was Cortez Cabal territory. The nearest non-Cabal supernatural-run hospital was in Jacksonville. Not only was that a six-hour drive from Miami, but it was run by sorcerers. If a witch was injured in Jacksonville, she'd stand a better chance of recovery by going home and treating herself than by showing up at a clinic staffed by sorcerers.

Benicio wanted me to recuperate at the high-security condo/hospital reserved for family, but Lucas refused. Instead I'd go to the Marsh Clinic and Lucas would stay with me. He'd order all my meals from restaurants and he'd administer my medication, which the San Francisco clinic would provide. The Marsh Clinic would give me a bed and nothing more. If my recuperation hit a speed bump, an outside doctor would be flown in.

Adam switched the phone to his other ear. "Elena's letting you stay up how late? Does Paige know this, 'cause, as a friend, I should tell her." He shot me a grin. "Uh-huh, well, I don't know . . . Bribery works, though." He paused. "Oh, no. No way. This calls for a T-shirt, at least. And none of those cheap three-for-ten-dollars tourist shirts, either."

I'd made my morning call to Elena early today. At eleven we'd be in the air, and I didn't want to worry her by not phoning. On Saturday morning, Lucas had been an hour late phoning because I'd been in surgery, and Elena had been ready to pack her bags and fly out to find us.

I finished brushing my hair and surveyed the results in the mirror on my hospital bed table. After two days in a hospital bed, it wasn't good. A hair clip was my only hope. And maybe a hat.

We were leaving within the hour. Lucas was in a conference with my doctor, getting last-minute nursing instructions and medication.

On the phone, Adam continued to tease Savannah and, although I couldn't hear her end of the conversation, I knew she was lapping it up. From the moment Savannah met Adam, he'd been the subject of a serious girlhood crush. I thought it would wear off after a few months, as adolescent crushes usually do, but a year later Savannah showed no signs of wavering in her affections, which were displayed through endless teasing and insults. Adam handled the situation admirably, acting as if he had no idea that she saw him as anything more than a pesky substitute big brother. Lucas and I did the same, never saying or doing anything that would embarrass her. She'd outgrow it soon enough. In the meantime, well, there were worse guys she could have a crush on.

"Uh-oh," Adam said. "I hear Paige coming back. Last chance. T-shirt or I tattle. No?" He turned from the phone. "Hey, Paige—!" He paused. "Medium? Not likely. I'm a large." Pause. "Ouch. Nasty. Hanging up now." Another pause. "Yeah, okay. Say hi to Elena and Clay for me. And get to bed early."

He hung up my cell phone, then thumped onto the edge of the bed, making my hand bounce and brush mascara on my forehead. I glared at him, grabbed a tissue, and erased the damage.

"You're doing okay, aren't you?" he said. "After everything . . . you're doing pretty good."

"Better than I was a few weeks ago, you mean, right? I know. I just needed a kick in the pants, and this case did it."

"Not just that," he said. "I mean, in general, you're doing good. You had a rough couple months settling in, but now, and this summer when you guys stopped by, I thought, she's happy. Really happy."

"I've still got a few things to figure out, but yes, I'm pretty darn happy."

"Good."

As I zipped up my makeup bag, Adam slid off the bed, walked to the window, and looked out. I watched him for a moment.

"Still mad about Miami?" I said.

He turned. "Nah. Sure, I'd love to help and, yeah, I'm a bit pissed at being left behind, but Lucas is right. His dad already made a point of introducing himself to me and dropping hints about post-college 'employment opportunities.' I'm probably better off avoiding the Cabals until I get my shit together. Which reminds me . . . you were saying last month that we need to do something about Arthur."

"Definitely. We need a necromancer on the council, and it does no good to anyone to have one who's never around. That whole fiasco with Tyrone Winsloe? Arthur didn't even return our calls until it was over. I've been hinting that he should find a replacement, but he ignores me."

"Guy's a miso—what do they call it? Doesn't like women? Not gay, I mean, but . . ."

"Misogynist."

"Yeah, that's it." Adam perched on my bed. "So I was thinking, maybe I should talk to him instead. What do you want me to do?"

Advice flew to my lips, but I bit it back. "What do you think?"

"Maybe if he's ignoring us, we should ignore him. Just get a replacement and let him find out about it whenever he bothers showing up at a meeting. How's that?"

I stifled the urge to give my opinion. Difficult border-
ing on painful. "We—*you* could do that. Maybe ask your
dad if he has any suggestions for a replacement."

I noticed Lucas walk past the door—for the second
time. God forbid he should interrupt a conversation.
When I called out to him, he popped his head in.

"Ready if you are," I said.

He disappeared, then returned, pushing a wheelchair.

"That better not be for me," I said.

"You're quite welcome to attempt walking. However, if
you pass out halfway to the front door, you may wake up
back in this bed, recuperating, while I interview Weber
in Miami."

I glared at him and waved the chair over. Adam
laughed.

"Oh, hey," Adam said. "Before I forget, what do you
want to do about that motorcycle?"

Lucas helped me into the wheelchair. "I should wait.
It's hardly a necessary expenditure—"

"Tell your friend yes," I said to Adam. I looked up at
Lucas. "You want it. I know you do. Take the bike and if
you don't want to use your insurance money, consider it
an early Christmas gift from me. I know you don't have a
place to work on it yet, but you will sooner or later."

"Probably sooner," Adam said, grinning. Then he
looked over my shoulder at Lucas and the grin vanished.
"The, uh, housing market's good right now, I mean. It's
always slow in fall, so maybe you'll find a place."

"No rush," I said. "We're still settling in."

Adam looked at Lucas again and I craned my neck,
trying to intercept the look that passed between them,
but it vanished before I could catch it. Lucas reached for
his satchel.

"Here, let me take that," Adam said. "You get the girl,

I'll carry the bags." A quick grin. "Not exactly fair, but I won't be doing the grunt work forever. You just wait." He looked at me. "As soon as I get home, I'm asking Dad about those necro replacements for Arthur. I'll have that all set up by the next meeting."

I smiled. "Great. I'll leave you to it, then."

Adam accompanied us to the airport, where we thanked him for all his help, and I promised to keep him updated on the case. Then we said our good-byes and boarded the plane.

Highly Inappropriate

WE TOOK THE CORTEZ JET BACK TO MIAMI. LIKE STAYING in their hospital, using their jet was a question of safety versus, well, safety. Was I in greater danger on their plane or on a commercial flight? I'd have been happy taking my chances on a regular plane. Not that I expected to be attacked in mid-flight by Cortez hitmen, but because it was in my nature not to make a fuss where my own health was concerned. Lucas disagreed and, considering I couldn't yet sit upright for longer than a few minutes, he was probably right.

Back in Miami, Benicio was scrambling to make peace with Lucas in the only way he could—by arranging for us to see Weber. Although Weber was being held in Cortez custody, each Cabal had assigned a guard. Such cooperation would be heartwarming, if they hadn't done so only to safeguard their own interests in the prisoner. No one, not even the son of a CEO, was getting near Weber without approval from every Cabal.

I thought our request was simple enough. We'd promised to comply with any security precautions. We were on the same side. Moreover, without us, they wouldn't have Weber. Yet, as quickly became obvious, that was

probably more a deterrent than an asset. The Cortez
Cabal had scored a major coup when we found Weber,
and the other Cabals seemed to be refusing our request
out of pure spite.

We spent the next day at the clinic, working through the
case details while Benicio lobbied the Cabals on our behalf. Lucas had managed to track down the ingredients
for a healing poultice and a healing tea. I prepared them
myself, and he didn't argue—both were witch magic, requiring witch incantations, and although he knew the
procedures, I was better at them. That's not ego talking—witches are better at witch magic, just as sorcerers
are better at sorcerer magic. This was also my first field
test of a stronger healing spell that I'd learned from the
tertiary-level grimoires I'd found that spring. I cast it on
the poultice, where it was supposed to not only speed
healing, but act as a moderate-strength topical analgesic.
To my delight, it worked even better than I expected. By
the end of the second day, I was out of bed, dressed in
my normal clothes, and feeling more like someone under
house arrest than a patient.

Dana's father hadn't yet arrived. Getting word to
Randy MacArthur was proving nearly impossible. As for
Dana's mother, well, the less I thought about her, the
better, or I'd pop stitches. While I was at the clinic, I assumed the role of surrogate visitor. Dana was beyond
knowing or caring, but I did it anyway.

That night I persuaded Lucas that I was well enough to
go out for dinner. To stretch the excursion out as long as

possible, I'd ordered dessert. Afterward, we lingered over coffee.

"Your dad seems to be really pushing for us on this," I said. "You don't still think he had something to do with the raid, do you?"

Lucas sipped his coffee. "Let's just say that, while I don't discount the possibility of his involvement, I admit I overreacted. You were hurt, I was frightened, and I lashed out at the most convenient target. It's just . . . I have some serious trust issues with my father."

I slipped him a tiny grin. "Really? Go figure."

Before Lucas could continue, his cell rang. After two nos, one thank-you, and one "We'll be there," he hung up.

"Speak of the devil?" I said.

He nodded. "The answer is still no. Worse yet, it seems likely to be a permanent no. They've moved the trial to tomorrow."

"What?"

"They say they've rescheduled because both sides are ready earlier than expected, but I suspect our sustained efforts to obtain an audience helped sway their decision."

"So they're blocking us by bumping up the trial." I leaned back in my chair, hiding a grimace as the movement pulled at my torn stomach muscles. "That's it, then. We're screwed."

"Not yet. As my father pointed out, if Weber is found guilty, there's always the option of appeal. At least this will give us the opportunity to hear the entire case. If the prosecution presents concrete evidence linking Weber to the attacks, we may deem an appeal unnecessary."

"And save everyone, including ourselves, a lot of grief."

"Precisely. Likewise, if they've found nothing new and they fail to address alternate possibilities—that Weber was working with the real killer, or unwittingly obtained the information for him—then we have grounds for appeal." He sipped his coffee. "How are you feeling?"

"Well enough to go to the trial, if that's what you're asking."

The session was set to begin promptly at eight; Lucas assured me this was normal for a Cabal trial. Unlike human murder trials, a Cabal session never stretched for weeks or months. Their court days ran from eight A.M. to eight P.M. and every effort was made to finish within a day or two.

We arrived by cab just past seven. The court and holding cells were almost exactly what I'd first expected the corporate offices to be, a renovated warehouse hidden deep in an industrial ghetto. Lucas had the driver drop us at the sidewalk behind one of the shabbier buildings.

Normally, I'd have insisted on paying the driver, but today I let Lucas. The last thing he needed was a squabble over cab fare. Every stress of the past few days was etched on his face. As he turned from paying the driver, I noticed his tie was crooked. I had to do a double take, certain I was mistaken.

"Hmm?" he said, catching my look.

"Your tie's crooked."

His hands flew up to adjust it.

"Here, let me." I stood on tiptoes to fix it. "You need to get some sleep tonight. In a real bed. We're moving to a hotel."

"Not until you're better."

"I am better," I said. "I look better, don't I?"

A small smile. "Better than better."

"Well, then—"

"Oh, look," a voice said behind me. "If it isn't the geek crusader."

Lucas stiffened. I stifled the urge to sling a fireball over my shoulder. Lucas didn't need this. A fireball would be justified. Inappropriate, but justified.

I turned to see a slim, well-built man in his early thirties, his model-caliber face marred by a sneer. Behind him stood William Cortez, which led me to hazard a guess at the identity of the younger man: Carlos.

"There must be a protest march going on somewhere," William said. "I'm sure they'd be more appreciative of your talents, Lucas. Leave the real work to the grown-ups."

I clenched my jaw to keep from reminding him who'd done the "real work" of bringing in the killer, and risked their lives to do so.

"Paige, you've met William," Lucas said. "And this is Carlos. Carlos, Paige. Now, if you'll excuse us—"

"Not bad, little brother," Carlos said as he checked me out. "Got to hand it to you. Better than I expected. You must have some hidden assets after all."

"Oh, Lucas has hidden assets," William said. "About five million of them, and that's just the guarantee. Hold out for the big gamble, and he has a half-billion more."

Carlos laughed. "No shit. That kind of dough, any loser can get laid, huh? A few blow jobs is a small price to pay for a shot at Cortez cash."

"Not necessarily," I said. "From what I hear, it can be too high a price." I met Carlos's gaze and smiled. "At least with some of the Cortezes."

His eyes hardened. "Like hell."

"If you say so."

I let Lucas lead me away. We'd gone about five steps when he leaned down.

"Dare I ask?" he whispered.

"Jaime."

He started to laugh, but choked it back. "Jaime and Carlos?"

"No," I said. "Jaime and *not* Carlos. She decided five million wasn't enough."

His laugh escaped then, a burst of laughter that made me grin and squeeze his hand. I glanced back to see Carlos glaring after us. Guess I hadn't made a new friend. Too bad.

"To be honest, I suspect it's far less than five million by now," Lucas said as we walked. "At the rate he goes through money, I'd say Carlos is down to about five dollars. He'll have to hold out for the inheritance."

"I thought five million *was* the inheritance."

"No, the trust fund." His lips curved. "Silence falls, as she refrains from stating the obvious, namely that her impoverished boyfriend is not as impoverished as she believed. Remember that next time you challenge me for paying cab fare."

Lucas pulled open the back door to the warehouse, and we stepped through into a lobby that would be the envy of any small-town courthouse. A few people milled about, but Lucas looked neither left nor right, just led me toward a set of interior double doors.

"Somehow I suspect you're no more able to pay the cab fare now than you were ten minutes ago," I said. "No trust-fund-dipping from this Cortez. You could be kidnapped by demon guerillas and still refuse to use any of it for the ransom."

"True." He smiled down at me. "But if you're ever kidnapped, I'll make an exception."

A swarthy young man in a suit and cap appeared at Lucas's side. "Mr. Cortez, sir?"

"Yes?" Lucas said.

"I work for the St. Clouds. Mr. St. Cloud's driver."

"Rick, isn't it?"

The man smiled. "Yes, thank you, sir. I just wanted to say we appreciate it, what you did, catching this guy. Griffin's inside. He'll speak to you himself, but I wanted to add my thanks. And, uh—" His gaze flicked to the double doors. "To say there's a back way in there, if you'd rather take that."

"Back way?" I said.

"Uh, yes, miss. Past the others. The Nasts and a few of the St. Clouds are in the waiting area. There's another way into the courtroom. You and Mr. Cortez might be more comfortable using it."

"Thank you," Lucas said. "But we'll be fine."

"Yes, sir."

The man backed away and slipped into a side hall. I glanced up at Lucas's taut face. All the tension he'd expelled on our walk into the building had returned double-strength. Once we walked through those doors, it was only going to get worse.

Lucas needed a distraction. As I glanced down the two side halls, I had an idea. Highly inappropriate but, sometimes, a little impropriety is exactly what you need.

"Nearly forty-five minutes left," I said. "We'll be sitting all day. No need to rush in there."

"Do you feel well enough to take a short walk?"

"Not what I had in mind."

I tugged him toward the nearest side hallway. His brows lifted, but when I didn't answer, he followed. I turned at the first branch, walked to the third door and opened it. An office. I tried the fourth. Locked. A quick unlock spell and the door opened into a large storage closet.

I flicked on the light. "Perfect."

"Dare I ask?"

"If you have to ask, you really *are* tired this morning."

He hesitated, then smiled.

"Well?" I said, backing into the closet.

He strode through the door, kicked it shut behind him, and cast a lock spell. I stepped back, but he grabbed me and pulled me to him in a deep kiss.

"Damn," I said, gasping as I pulled back. "I've missed that, Cortez. Last night I was wondering how much weight my hospital bed held. Should've conducted a test."

"Perhaps tonight."

"Uh-uh. Tonight we're springing for a hotel and a bed for two."

"Are you sure you feel up to it?"

I showed him how up to it I felt. After a few minutes of kissing, I slid my hands between us, unbuttoned his shirt, and ran my hands down his bare chest.

"You know, Carlos got me thinking," I said. "If I'm going to be become a CEO wife—"

"Co-CEO, wasn't it?"

"Sorry. Co-CEO. It's going to cost me a lot of blow jobs, isn't it?"

Lucas laughed. "Yes, a lot, I'm afraid."

"Then these few days in the hospital have put me behind on my quota. I have some serious catching up to do." I traced a finger down his chest and slipped it under his waistband. "The doctor said no bending, but he didn't say anything about kneeling."

Lucas's breath caught.

I grinned up at him. "Well?"

"As loath as I am to refuse, you *are* still recovering." He reached down and hiked my skirt up to my hips, lips going to my ear. "May I suggest something less taxing for now?"

I pushed my skirt down. "Uh-uh. It's a blow job or nothing." I stepped backward toward the door. "Of course if you're not interested..."

He pulled me to him, then pressed my hand to his crotch. "Interested enough?"

"I'm not sure," I said, tracing my fingertips across the bulge in his pants. "It's a bit hard—"

"A bit?"

"—a bit *difficult* to tell." I undid his belt, then his slacks, and slid my hand inside. "Umm, let's see. Yes, I'd say that's interested enough."

I lowered myself to my knees and set about distracting him.

Afterward, we talked quietly, delaying our exit from the room. At 7:45, I pulled away.

"Fifteen minutes," I said. "We should get inside."

"In a moment." He kissed me. "I love you."

"Of course you do. You have to. It's the law."

A smile. "Law?"

"Any girl who gives a guy a blow job in a broom closet is entitled to at least one 'I love you.' Whether you mean it or not, you're morally and legally obligated to say it."

He laughed, then kissed the top of my head. "Well, I do mean it. You know that."

"I do. And I also know that if we don't get into that courtroom before the session starts, they'll have an excuse to not let us in at all."

Signed, Sealed, Delivered

AS LUCAS PUSHED OPEN THE DOOR INTO THE WAITING area, a wave of appropriately somber conversation rolled out. Then it stopped and every head turned to watch us enter. There were at least a dozen men, ranging in age from mid-teens to postretirement, all in suits that would have paid our rent for three months, and all of them sorcerers. It reminded me of the day I'd joined the previously all-male computer club in high school. One step through that door and the icy stares nearly froze me in my tracks.

Lucas, now feeling more himself, simply gazed about the room, nodded once or twice, then put his hand against the small of my back and propelled me through the crowd.

A straight-backed, silver-haired man in his seventies stepped into our path. My gaze snagged on the black band around his suit jacket arm.

"What do you think you're doing?" he hissed. "How dare you bring her here?"

"Paige, this is Thomas Nast, CEO of the Nast Cabal. Thomas, this is Paige Winterbourne."

Thomas Nast. My eyes returned to the black band on

his arm. For his son, Kristof. This was Savannah's grand-father.

"I know perfectly well who she is, you—" He bit the word off with an audible click of his teeth. "This is a slap in the face to my family and I won't stand for it."

Lucas met the old man's glare with a level gaze. "If you are referring to the events leading to your son's demise, may I point out that your family was the instigator in the matter. By pursuing custody in such an unconventional manner, Kristof contravened intra-Cabal policy."

"My son is dead. Don't you dare imply—"

"I'm not implying anything. I'm stating fact. The escalation of events leading to Kristof's death was entirely of his own devising. As for his death itself, Paige played no role in it. If there had been any evidence to the contrary, you would have brought it forward at the inquiry this summer. Now, if you'll excuse us . . ."

"She is not going to sit in our courtroom—"

"If it weren't for her, none of us would be sitting in that courtroom. Good day, sir."

Lucas led me around Nast and through the next set of doors.

The courtroom seated maybe fifty people, tops, and was half-full when we entered. As Lucas looked around for good seats, a door at the front of the room opened and Benicio walked through. His timing was too perfect to be coincidental. He'd been waiting for us. Why, then, wouldn't he meet us in the other room and escort us past the Cabal gauntlet? Because he knew better. Lucas would not have appreciated his father protecting him from Thomas Nast and the others, for the same reason that Lucas refused to slip in the back door. Lucas chose his path, quite literally, and accepted the consequences of it.

Benicio caught Lucas's eye and waved him to an empty row right behind the prosecution bench. When Lucas nodded, a glimmer of surprise crossed Benicio's face. He hovered at the end of the aisle, as if not quite sure Lucas really intended to join him. We walked to the front and I slid in first, letting Lucas follow so he could sit beside his father.

"Good to see you, Paige," Benicio said, leaning over Lucas as we sat. "I'm glad you could join us. You seem to be making a speedy recovery."

"Not as speedy as she'd like," Lucas said. "But she's doing well."

"It may be a long day," Benicio said, and I steeled myself for a considerate "suggestion" that I forgo the trial. "If you need anything—a cushion, a cold drink—just let me know."

As I nodded my thanks, the front doors opened again and Griffin walked in, accompanied by Troy and a man I didn't recognize but could guess, by his size, was a fellow guard. Troy led Griffin to our row, where Benicio stood and ushered him in to sit with us. Troy and the other guard took seats on opposite ends of our row.

While Lucas and I talked to Griffin, both front doors opened almost simultaneously. Through one, Weber stumbled in, blinking at the sight of the crowded courtroom. He was dressed in a regular shirt and trousers. Although he wasn't handcuffed or chained, there was a gag across his mouth. That might seem cruel, but a druid's power is the ability to call upon his deities, so the gag was an understandable precaution.

As the guards led Weber to his seat, three sixtyish men walked through the other front door. The judges. Last night Lucas had explained the basics of the Cabal justice system. Cases are presented not to a single judge or a jury, but to a panel of three judges, and the majority vote carries. The judges work a five-year term and the same three are used by all four Cabals, in a circuit-court arrangement. The men—always sorcerers, therefore always male—are selected by an intra-Cabal committee. They are lawyers nearing the end of their careers, and are paid very handsomely for their term, meaning they can retire at the end of it, so they are not beholden to the Cabals for later employment. Fifty percent of their payment is withheld until after the term is completed, and any judge found guilty of accepting bribes or otherwise compromising his position forfeits that portion. All this is intended to make the judges as impartial as possible. Is it perfect? Of course not. But to give the Cabals their due, they'd taken reasonable steps to ensure a fair justice system.

To keep the trials short, they are a bare-bones affair in every respect. Opening and closing arguments are limited to ten minutes each. The lack of a jury means there's less need to explain every step in detail. Expert witnesses are allowed only when necessary—no Ph.D.-whores being paid to claim that DNA identification is a faulty science. Even regular witnesses don't always need to take the stand. Noncritical ones, like Jaime, have their statements taken beforehand and answer questions posed by each side.

Breaks were as basic as the session itself, with a single fifteen-minute morning recess. By then I was already feeling the effects of my rushed recuperation. Lucas insisted I take painkillers, and I had to agree. Without them, I'd have been done by lunch. As it was, let's just say it wasn't the most comfortable morning I'd ever spent. To get through it, I concentrated on paying attention and taking copious notes. Lucas and I shared a steno pad, which we passed back and forth, marking down pertinent points, elaborating on one another's notes, and exchanging written comments on the progress of the trial.

For lunch, a caterer delivered sandwich trays and we had thirty minutes to eat while standing in the lobby. Benicio ate with us, and the three of us managed to carry on a reasonably normal conversation. Benicio only slipped up once, suggesting that we join him for dinner the next night . . . a dinner that would also include three prominent foreign shareholders who just happened to be in town. Lucas handled it with a gentle reminder that, with the way the trial was progressing, we'd likely be busy preparing Weber's appeal.

After lunch, Lucas called the hotel where we'd stayed earlier. Our former room was still unoccupied and the manager offered it to us at the same rate. When Benicio heard our plans, he phoned the Marsh Clinic and arranged to have all our belongings moved to the hotel, so I could go directly there and rest after the trial. A considerate move, and only the latest of many, which prompted me to admit that perhaps Lucas had inherited more from Benicio than his "natural talent for lying."

The trial did not go well. Weber had retained his own counsel. When I'd first learned this, I'd been relieved. As the trial progressed, though, I found myself wishing he'd let the Cabals assign him a lawyer. As much as I hated to give them credit, I saw nothing grievously unjust in their system and, had they provided Weber's counsel, I'm sure he would have had competent representation, which was more than he had now.

There were two ways to play this case. One: stress the circumstantial nature of the evidence. Two: plead insanity. Weber's lawyer chose both. And that presented a problem. The first says Weber didn't do it. The second says he did, but he can't be held responsible. Using both says he did kill those teens, but you can't prove it and anyway, he was crazy, but not crazy enough to leave any hard evidence.

At six o'clock, the lawyers presented their closing arguments. At six-twenty, the judges retired to council. At six-thirty they returned with a verdict.

Guilty.

The sentence: death.

Weber, not surprisingly, panicked, and had to be forcibly escorted from the room, screaming muffled invocations from behind his gag.

As one of the judges said some final words, I took the notepad and drew a question mark, to which Lucas wrote "no change." We'd heard no further evidence to damn or acquit Weber, and none of our concerns had even been raised. So we would proceed with his appeal.

The judge thanked the witnesses and counsel, and court was adjourned. Benicio leaned over and whispered that he'd be right back, and asked us to wait. Then he escorted Griffin to the front of the courtroom. The other guard followed, but Troy stayed at his post in our row. Benicio, Griffin, and the other guard walked to the door through which Weber had just been taken. Before Griffin stepped through, he turned, caught our attention, and mouthed a thank-you. Then they were gone.

"You must be exhausted," Lucas said, handing me my purse from the floor.

"I'm okay," I said. "Do we need to launch the appeal today?"

Lucas shook his head. "I'll tell my father that we plan to go ahead and he'll relay the message to the Cabals. Tonight we rest and try to put it out of our minds."

I glanced up to see Benicio slip back into the courtroom, accompanied by his new guard.

"There he is," I said. "That was fast."

"Good," Lucas said. "Earlier, he offered to drive us to the hotel and, if you don't mind, I'd like to accept. Then we can tell him our appeal plans on the way, rather than delay our departure by doing so now."

"If it gets me to a bed sooner, I'm not arguing."

Lucas looked up as Benicio eased into our aisle. "Paige and I would like—" He stopped. "What's wrong, Papá?"

Benicio shook his head. "Nothing. You were saying?"

Lucas studied his father's face. At first, I could see no sign of anything wrong. Then I noticed it, the slightest tilt to Benicio's head, not quite meeting Lucas's eyes as he spoke to him.

"I'm sure Paige can't wait to get out of here," Benicio said. "Why don't we—"

A cough. We looked up to see William and Carlos standing on my other side.

"Thomas Nast wants to speak to you, Father," William said.

Benicio waved him away. William's lips tightened.

"We'll wait for you in the car, Papá," Lucas said. "We can discuss the appeal on the drive."

"Appeal?" Carlos said. "For who?"

"Everett Weber, of course."

Carlos laughed. "Hell, little brother, I didn't know you'd taken up necromancy."

Lucas's eyes cut to his father. Benicio rubbed his hand across his mouth.

"He doesn't know, does he?" William said, lips twitching in a smug smile.

"Know what?" Lucas said, gaze never leaving Benicio's.

"That execution sentence?" Carlos said. "Signed, sealed, and delivered."

I blinked. "You mean...?"

"Everett Weber is dead," William said. "If justice was done, it would be done swiftly. Father and the other CEOs agreed on that before the trial began."

Lucas turned to Benicio. "Before the trial began...?"

"Of course," William said. "Do you think he'd let you embarrass us by trying to set a child murderer free? Can't ever leave well enough alone, can you, Lucas? Saving the innocent, saving the guilty, it doesn't really matter, as long as you stick it to the Cabals. Thank God Father didn't tell them you wanted an audience before the trial or who knows what kind of hornet's nest you'd have stirred up."

Lucas stared at his father, waiting for him to deny any of this. Benicio only dropped his gaze. I stood. Lucas looked at Benicio one last time, then followed me into the aisle.

We weaved around clusters of sorcerers and headed into the parking lot. More Cabal clusters out here, having a smoke or getting a dose of Miami sun before jetting home. As we passed one group, a young man caught my gaze. I glanced into a pair of big blue eyes and felt a jolt of recognition. I paused, but Lucas didn't, his attention elsewhere, and I hurried to keep up.

We continued through the packed parking lot in silence. As we walked, I tried to push past my shock and think clearly. Weber was very likely guilty, so his execution, while unnecessarily swift, was probably not unjustified. It might still be possible to speak to him, through a necromancer, and reassure ourselves that he was indeed the killer. As I was wondering whether I should mention this to Lucas yet, a voice hailed us.

"Lucas? Hold up a sec."

I tensed and turned to see a young man striding toward us. Tall and lanky, a year or two younger than me, blond hair tied back in a ponytail, gorgeous big blue eyes. As I saw those eyes my heart skipped. He was a sorcerer, of course, but it was more than that. This was the same young man whose gaze I'd met just a moment ago, whom I now realized I didn't recognize, but felt like I should. Then I noticed the black armband and the recognition clicked. He reminded me of Kristof Nast. Kristof's eyes. Savannah's eyes.

A few paces behind him was another young man, late teens, also wearing an armband. He met my glance with a scowl, then looked away.

"Hey, Lucas." The first young man stopped and extended his hand. "Good to see you."

"Sean, hello," Lucas said, distractedly, his gaze wandering.

"Good work you did, catching that freak. Course, no one's going to send you a thank-you card, but most of us do appreciate it."

"Yes, well . . ."

Lucas turned toward the road, clearly eager to go, but the young man didn't move. His eyes flicked to me, then dipped back to Lucas. Lucas followed the path of his gaze, then blinked.

"Oh, yes, of course. Paige, this is Sean Nast. Kristof's son."

"And that's—" Sean turned to his reluctant companion and waved him over, but the younger man scowled and scuffed his shoe against the pavement. "That's my brother, Bryce."

These were Savannah's half-brothers. I quickly extended my hand. Sean shook it.

"This isn't a good place," he said. "And I know you guys are busy, but we're staying in town for a few more days, and we thought maybe—"

"Sean?"

Sean shot a glare in his brother's direction. "Okay, okay, I thought maybe—"

"Sean!"

"What?" Sean spun on his heel, then his eyes went wide.

As I turned, I saw a suit jacket thrown on the hood of a car. Someone eager to shed his formal trappings. Then I saw pants, and shoes, and a hand protruding from the jacket sleeve. Red drops dripped from the outstretched fingers and over the car's left headlight, leaving a glistening trail before plinking into the small pool of blood below.

Pointing Fingers

WE RAN TO THE BODY. I REMEMBER THAT FIRST VIEW AS A series of close-up snapshots, as if my brain couldn't comprehend the whole. The hand splayed palm-up, a rivulet of blood trickling down the index finger. A black band around the biceps of his suit coat. His eyes closed, long blond eyelashes resting on a smooth cheek, a cheek still too young for shaving. Tie loosened and stained red, merging with the wet stain on his white dress shirt, the stain growing. The stain growing . . . blood still flowing . . . heart still pumping.

"He's alive!" I said.

"Grab his other arm," Lucas said to Sean. "Get him on the ground."

The two lowered the boy off the car hood and onto the pavement. Lucas and I dropped to our knees on either side. Lucas checked for signs of breathing while I felt his pulse.

"He's not breathing," Lucas said.

Lucas started CPR. I ripped off the boy's shirt and used it to mop up the blood, trying to see the source so I could staunch the bleeding. I cleared away enough blood to see three, four, maybe five stab wounds, at least two pumping blood. The wet shirt quickly turned sodden. I looked up at Sean and Bryce.

"Give me your shirts," I said.

They stared at me, uncomprehending. I was about to ask again when I saw the shock in their eyes and realized they hadn't budged since we'd begun.

"Have you called for help?" I said.

"Call—?" Sean's voice was distant, confused.

"Nine-one-one or whoever. Somebody, anybody, just call!"

"I have it," Lucas said. "Take over here."

We switched places. I put my hands over the boy's chest and leaned forward to pump, but his skin was so slick with blood that my hands slid off. I stabilized my balance and pushed his chest, counting fifteen repetitions.

I pinched the boy's nose, bent over his mouth, and exhaled twice. Lucas gave instructions to the dispatcher. I pumped the boy's chest again. The blood seemed to have stopped flowing. I told myself I was mistaken. I had to be.

As I swiveled back to his mouth, Lucas took over chest compressions. I leaned over the boy. As my lips touched his, something hit me, a full-bodied smack like an airbag going off. For a second, I was airborne. Then I crashed backward to the pavement. Pain ripped the breath from my lungs in a ragged gasp and everything went black for a split second.

I recovered just in time to see a blond man dive at me, face twisted with rage. Before he could reach me, Lucas slammed into him, knocking him to the ground. As I scrambled away, the blond man's hand shot up, fingers outstretched toward me, but Lucas pinned both his arms down, which for a sorcerer was as effective a power-buster as gagging was to a druid. The man struggled but, as he quickly learned, Lucas was a lot stronger than he looked.

"My son—she was—"

"Trying to save his life," Lucas said. "We've called an ambulance. Unless you know CPR, let us—"

The screech of tires cut him off. An unmarked mini-van whipped into the parking lot. Before it even stopped, two paramedics leapt out. I tried to stand, but the force of the blow had set my stomach wound ablaze. Lucas knelt beside me.

"Can you get up?" he asked.

"I'm trying," I said. "Doesn't look like it, I know, but I am trying."

He put his arms around me and lifted me gingerly. "We can't do anything here. Let's get you inside."

As Lucas stooped to put my arm around his neck, I saw the blond man kneeling beside the boy, gripping his hand. The crowd around him parted and Thomas Nast walked through. The old man stopped. He swayed. Two or three men lunged to steady him, but he pushed them away, walked over, looked down at his bloodied grand-child, and dropped his face into his hands.

With the scene unfolding outside, the courthouse was empty and still. Lucas led me to a sofa in a back room and helped me lie down. Once I was comfortable, he slipped out, spell-locking the door behind him. Moments later, he returned with a paramedic. The man examined me. He found my stitches strained but not burst, and advised bed rest, painkillers, and a formal checkup in the morning.

When the man left, I forced myself to acknowledge the obvious. If the paramedic had time to look after my minor injuries, that could only mean one thing.

"He didn't make it, did he?" I whispered.

Lucas shook his head.

"If we'd called sooner—"

"It didn't matter. By the time we got to him, it was already too late."

I thought of the boy. Savannah's cousin. Yet another member of her family she'd never met, didn't even know existed. And now, he didn't.

A commotion in the hall cut my thoughts short, the thunder of footsteps and angry voices. Lucas started a lock spell, but before he could finish, the door banged open and Thomas Nast strode through, Sean at his heels, eyes red.

"You did this," he said, bearing down on Lucas. "Don't tell me you didn't."

Lucas's hand shot out and waved a circle as he murmured the words to a barrier spell. Nast hit it and stopped short. Sean caught his grandfather's arm and tugged him back.

"He didn't do anything, Granddad," Sean said. "We told you that. Lucas was doing CPR on Joey, then had to call for help, so Paige took over."

Nast's face contorted. "This witch touched my grandson?"

"To help him," Sean said. "Bryce and I didn't know how. They were there and—"

"Of course they were there. They killed him."

"No, Granddad, they didn't. Bryce and I followed them from the courthouse. We were right behind them the whole time. They didn't do anything."

The door opened again and two men came in. The first

waved a notepad—our notepad—dropped in the parking lot.

"This is yours, isn't it?" he said to Lucas. "I saw you writing in it during the trial."

Lucas murmured an affirmation and reached for the pad, but the man snapped it out of his reach. Sean Nast snatched the pad from behind and peered at it, then glanced up at us.

"You were preparing an appeal," Sean said. "You didn't think Weber did it."

By then all the Cabal CEOs, including Benicio, had crowded into the small room, and Lucas had to admit we had questions about Weber's guilt, which led to the obvious question of why no one had been apprised of our suspicions. Lucas would never lower himself to "I told you so" even when so richly deserved. I might have filled in the blank had Benicio not done so himself. His admission won him no brownie points for honesty, and the other Cabals jumped on him, accusations flying.

That only opened the floodgates to more finger-pointing. Within minutes, everyone had a theory on who was behind the murders, and they all involved another Cabal. The Cortezes had covered up Weber's innocence because the real killer was one of their own. The Nasts lived nearest to Weber, so they'd planted evidence and launched the SWAT attack, again to hide the real killer in their midst. The Boyds were the only Cabal the killer hadn't attacked, so they were obviously behind it. And the St. Cloud Cabal? Well, no evidence pointed to them as the culprits, which was only proof that they were.

In the midst of all this, Lucas quietly retrieved our notepad and helped me sneak out the door. My incision still felt as if it had been ripped open and stuffed with hot coals, so I had to lean heavily on Lucas, and our

progress was slow. Once again we made it halfway across
the parking lot before someone hailed us.

"Where do you think you're going?" William called.

"Don't stop," I murmured to Lucas.

"I wasn't going to."

William strode around and blocked our path. "You
can't just run out on this."

"Sadly, no," I said. "But I can hobble, and believe me,
I'm hobbling as fast as I can."

Lucas started to skirt his brother, but William stepped
in front of us.

"Move," I said. "Now."

William glared at me. "Don't you—"

"Don't *you*," I snarled back. "I just saw a boy die because you people executed the wrong man. I'm mad as
hell and my pain medication ran out hours ago, so get out
of my way or I'll blast your ass back into that courtroom."

A whoop of laughter, and Carlos sauntered over to us.
"Whoo-hoo. You've got a real spitfire there, Lucas. I gotta
hand it to you. You done good."

"She's had a difficult day, William," Lucas said. "I'd get
out of her way."

William strode toward me. "No little witch is going to—"

I flicked my fingers and he stumbled backward.

Carlos laughed. "The girl knows sorcerer magic. Maybe
you should listen to her, Will."

"Maybe Lucas shouldn't be teaching her tricks,"
William said, bearing down on me again. "Sorcerer magic
is for sorcerers."

"And witch magic is for witches," I said.

I recited an incantation and William inhaled sharply as
the air was sucked from his lungs. His mouth opened
and closed, struggling to breathe. I mentally counted to
twenty, then ended the spell. He doubled over, gasping.

"Shit," Carlos said. "Never seen witch magic like that."

"And, on that note, we'll take our leave," Lucas said. "Good night."

He led me around William and out of the courthouse parking lot.

"We need to stay on this case," I said as Lucas lowered me onto the hotel room bed. "Now more than ever. If the Cabals keep bickering, the killer will have a heyday."

"Um-hmm."

Lucas bent to tug off my pumps. I pulled my leg back to do it myself, but he waved me away and removed them, then folded back the covers. I started unbuttoning my blouse. He nudged my hands aside and did it for me.

"Weber didn't just coincidentally create that list of potential victims," I said. "He did it for someone. He had access to the files and knew how to extract the data. If we can contact his spirit, he should be able to lead us to the killer . . . or point us in the right direction."

"Um-hmm." Lucas tugged off my skirt and folded it.

"I know a few good necros. We can call one in the morning."

Lucas tucked my legs under the covers. "Um-hmm."

"First thing we need to do is—"

I crashed into sleep.

I was in a forest, doing a ceremony with Lucas. Someone banged on a door, which, of course, seemed odd under the circumstances, but my brain, perhaps recognizing I was asleep, overlooked the illogic, and my dream-self yelled at the intruder to leave us alone.

Another triple knock, louder this time. The forest

evaporated and I clawed up from bed. Lucas's arms went around me, gently restraining.

"Shhh," he whispered. "Go back to sleep."

Another knock. I jumped, but he ignored it.

"They'll go away," he said.

And they did. I snuggled against his bare chest. Sleep tugged at me. I surrendered and felt myself drifting under again when the bedside phone buzzed.

"Ignore it," Lucas whispered.

Five rings. Then silence. I relaxed again, stretched out—*Da-da-di. Da-da-di.*

"Isn't that . . ." I mumbled into a yawn.

"My cell phone." A sigh rippled through him. "I should have turned it off. I'll answer it and get rid of him. Perhaps I can reach—" He twisted and sighed again. "Of course not."

He slid from the bed and retrieved the cell phone from his suit coat. When his tone changed, I knew it wasn't Benicio. I propped myself up on the pillow. His gaze shunted to me, brows knitting. I mouthed, "Who is it?"

"Yes, well, your timing is . . . interesting," he said into the phone. "Just a moment, please." He covered the mouthpiece. "It's Jaime."

"Did you call her?"

He shook his head. "She heard what happened today and thinks she might be able to help. She's outside."

I pushed back the covers and swung out my feet. "Perfect. Not my first choice, but the sooner we can contact Weber, the better."

He opened his mouth, as if to argue, then snapped it shut, and told Jaime he'd be right there.

Waking the Dead

SINCE WE'D MISSED DINNER AND IT LOOKED AS IF WE weren't going back to bed any time soon, Lucas went to get us something to eat. He was gone before I finished dressing. A quick hair-brushing and face wash and I was presentable, but nothing more. When I saw Jaime pacing the living-area carpet, my first thought was "Geez, she looks almost as bad as I do."

Dressed in jeans and a T-shirt, no makeup, Jaime was hardly the picture of showbiz celebrity. Though I'd originally guessed her age at late thirties, Lucas said she'd passed forty a couple of years ago. Today, she looked it. Maybe this dressing-down was intentional, a disguise to avoid recognition . . . although she hadn't struck me as the type who *would* try to avoid recognition.

I walked into the room, trying not to stagger.

"Jesus, are you okay?" she said.

She hurried to help me, but I waved her back.

"Of course you're not okay," she continued. "I heard what happened in California. I should have thought—I can talk to Lucas if you want to go back to sleep."

"I'm fine." I considered the sofa, but the recliner seemed

as if it would offer more support. "So you heard about the trial?"

Jaime hovered until I was seated, then dropped onto the sofa. "Cabal gossip flies faster than a spooked spirit. I asked the guy who took my deposition to call me when a verdict came in, but I still haven't heard from him. Probably never will. I'm necromancer non grata with the Cabals."

"Really? With your grandmother, you should be prime recruitment material and, God knows, they hate to offend anyone they can use."

Jaime twisted her rings. "Well, I'm not quite the necro my nan was. And, of course, my high profile doesn't sit well with the Cabals. When I started hitting the big time, they wanted me to shut up and shut down. Lucas helped me with that. They leave me alone now."

The door lock clicked. Lucas pushed the door open with his foot, both hands occupied with a tray of food. Jaime watched him struggle for a moment, then jumped up and went over to help.

"Mmm, that smells great," I said. "Soup?"

"Seafood chowder. Not quite the caliber you're accustomed to, but it was this or split-pea."

"Good choice." I picked up a crystal glass of ruby red liquid. "Wine?"

"Not when you're taking these," he said, plunking my medication bottle on the tray. "It's cranberry juice. Dessert is crème brûlée—a more appetizing alternative to pudding."

I grinned up at him. "You're the best."

"No shit," Jaime said. "Last time I was sick, the guy I was seeing brought me a bottle of ginger ale . . . and expected me to pay him back for it."

Lucas took a mug and a second crème brûlée from my

tray and laid them in front of Jaime. "If you'd prefer something else, the kitchen is open for a few more minutes." He placed cream and sugar containers beside the coffee. "And, no, you don't have to pay me back for it."

"I am definitely dating the wrong guys."

Lucas started unwrapping his sandwich, then paused. "Should we eat on the road?"

"Ten minutes isn't going to make a difference. Eat your sandwich, then we'll go."

"Go where?" Jaime said.

I explained the evidence against Weber, and how we were certain he'd obtained those lists for the killer. "The only way we're going to find out who wanted those lists is to talk to Weber. So you can help us by doing that, if that's okay."

"Well, umm, sure. Anything I can do. I thought we'd start by contacting Dana again but, well, I guess contacting this Weber guy makes more sense. We know where he's buried, right?"

"Oh, I'm sure they haven't buried him yet," I said.

"They have," Lucas said. "Cabal policy. They inter their dead immediately."

Jaime nodded. "Otherwise, it's like propping open the door to Tiffany's and going home for the night."

Lucas caught my confused look. "Supernatural remains are considered extremely valuable necromantic relics."

"Yep," Jaime said. "Other people go to the black market for DVDs and diamonds. Us necros get to buy decomposing body parts. Another reason why I give thanks every day for this incredible gift I've been given." She scraped the last bit of custard from the ramekin and licked the spoon. "Okay, this wasn't quite what I had in

mind for my evening, but let's do it. Time to wake the recently deceased."

Jaime had just finished her final Orlando show when she
heard the news about Weber. She'd then rented a car for
the two-hundred-mile trip to Miami, so we now had a vehicle. Lucas drove because he was the only one who
knew where to find the cemetery. But, as I soon discovered, that wasn't the only reason. When we hit the out-
skirts of Miami, Jaime put on a sleeping mask. At first, I
thought she was taking a catnap. Then I realized that allowing a necromancer to know where the Cabal buried
their dead would be a serious security breach. Not that I
could imagine Jaime skulking around a moonlit cemetery
with a shovel, but I gave her bonus points for blindfold-
ing herself rather than put Lucas in an awkward position.
    The Cabal didn't bury their dead in a municipal ceme-
tery . . . or any recognizable cemetery at all. Lucas drove
past the city limits, then made so many turns that I was
lost even without a blindfold. Finally he pulled off the
road and headed down a thin strip of land flanked on
both sides by swamp. A mile later, the road ended. I
squinted out the window.
    "This is the cemetery?" I said.
    Lucas nodded. "It's hardly conducive to graveside vis-
its, but the alligators tend to discourage trespassers."
    "Alligators?" Jamie tugged down her blindfold. "Jesus,
we're in the middle of the fucking Everglades!"
    "The periphery, to be precise. The Everglades are com-
prised primarily of saw-grass plains, not swampland as
you see here. This would be Big Cyprus Swamp, which
is technically located outside the Everglades National
Park."

"Okay, let me rephrase that, then. Jesus, we're in the middle of a fucking swamp!"

"Actually—"

"Don't say it," Jaime said. "We're not in the middle of a swamp, we're at the edge, right?"

"Yes, but we will be going into the middle, if that makes you feel better."

"Oh, believe me, it does." She peered out into the dark tangle of trees, hanging moss, and stagnant water. "How the hell are we going to get to the middle?"

"We need to take the airboat." He glanced at me. "If you do see an alligator, your new shock spell should be ample deterrent."

"Great," Jaime muttered. "And what are us nonspell-casters supposed to do? Run for our lives?"

"I wouldn't advise it. The average alligator can outrun the average human. Now, Paige, if you could cast a light spell, we'll work our way down to the boat."

Sorry, No Virgins Here

AFTER HOT-WIRING THE AIRBOAT, LUCAS PERSUADED US IT was safe to come aboard, and we set off for the cemetery. The trip reminded me of a Tunnel o' Horrors ride I'd taken once, the kind where you're traveling along in pitch black. Nothing jumps out at you, but that doesn't make it any less terrifying, because you spend the whole time tensed, waiting for the big boo. I've never much seen the attraction of intentionally scaring yourself silly, but at least with those rides, you know nothing in there can hurt you. Not so with the Everglades. It's dark and it stinks, and you're zooming under tree branches hanging with moss and vines that tickle across the back of your neck like ghost fingers. Everywhere you look, you see trees and water, miles of them in all directions. Of course, there's not much danger of drowning. The gators'll get you first.

Don't ask me how Lucas knew where he was going. Even the combination of my light spell and the boat's headlight illuminated no more than a dozen feet in front of us. Yet, despite the lack of obvious markers, Lucas expertly guided the boat through twists and turns. After about twenty minutes, he eased off the throttle.

"What's wrong?" I asked.

"We're here."

"Where the hell is here?" Jaime said, leaning over the side of the boat. "All I see is water."

Lucas steered another few yards, inched the boat sideways, then hoisted up a tie line. I directed my light-ball over his head and saw grass leading up onto a hillock that rose from the water like the back of a sleeping brontosaurus.

"Can we get out?" I said.

He nodded. "Stick to the path, though. And try to avoid stepping in the shallow water."

"Let me guess," Jaime said. "Piranha?"

"Not this far north. There are, however, water moccasins, coral snakes, and cottonmouths."

"Let me guess: They're all poisonous."

"Very."

"Anything else we should know about? Lions and tigers and bears, maybe?"

"There are, I believe, still a few black bears in the swamp, but not in this immediate area. As for feline predators, while I've heard of bobcat sightings, I've personally only seen a panther."

Fortunately, we didn't encounter any alligators, water moccasins, bears, or panthers. I heard a splash now and then, but it was probably a large fish. If not, well, sound carried at night, so it was likely miles away . . . or so I told myself.

The path wound through a few acres of soil just dry enough to walk on, like ground after spring thaw, when you can't decide whether to switch to shoes or stick with boots. The perimeter was ringed with cypress trees, those gnarled, drooping, moss-festooned specters that characterized the Everglades. As the ground rose and dried, the plant life gave way to grasses, hardwoods, and the occasional cluster of white orchids.

Lucas pushed back a curtain of willow branches and ushered us into a semicleared patch.

"Cabal cemetery number two," he said. "Reserved for executed criminals and the unfortunate victims of what the Cabal likes to call 'collateral damage.'"

"I see they saved a few bucks on headstones," I said, peering over at the unmarked ground. "How the heck are we going to find—No, hold on, there's some freshly turned earth, so that must be where they buried Weber. Oh, wait, there's another new grave over there . . . and that stuff looks pretty fresh, too. Damn. They must employ full-time gravediggers."

"The ground here dries very slowly, so most of these aren't as new as they look, though I suspect all three have been dug this month. As for finding Weber's grave, it isn't really necessary. In communicating with the recently deceased, relative proximity is as satisfactory as absolute."

"'Close enough' counts in horseshoes *and* raising the dead." Jaime wiped her palms against her jeans. "Okay, time for the gross stuff. Can you guys take a walk while I set up?"

We wandered over to the opposite side of the graveyard. For the next twenty minutes, we sat in the darkness, doing battle with swarms of mosquitos and near-invisible biting gnats that Lucas said were called, quite appropriately, no-see-ums.

Finally Jaime called us back.

Although we were within a few yards of Weber's assumed burial site, we had no intention of actually doing anything with his body. Communicating with the dead, fortunately, did not require raising the dead. Necromancers could indeed return a spirit to its physical body but, having seen it done once, I never wanted to witness it again. Instead, most necromancers communicated with the spirit world in other ways. Earlier Jaime had decided she'd use channeling again, as she'd done with Dana. Channeling was more difficult than other forms of communication, but it would allow us to communicate directly with Weber.

Again, Jaime lit a censer of vervain, since Weber probably fell into the category of a traumatized spirit. Beside the censer of vervain was another of dogwood bark and dried maté. This was a banishing mixture, used to drive away party-crashing spirits. When you summon in a graveyard, uninvited ghosts are a definite possibility. For now, this mixture would be kept unlit, but Jaime had an open book of matches right below it, ready to use.

Once we were ready, Jaime closed her eyes and invited Weber's spirit to join us. It wasn't a simple "Hey, come on out." Inviting a spirit required long inducements, and we settled back, knowing this could take a while.

After about two minutes, the ground vibrated. Jaime stopped mid-invocation, hands raised.

"Uh, tell me no one else felt that," she said.

"The ground out here can be a little unstable," Lucas said.

I glanced at him. "Like 'eroding into the swamp at any moment' unstable?"

"No, the Cabal has taken precautions to ensure the cemetery won't sink into the Everglades until it reaches full capacity. Minor shifts, though, are not to be unexpected. Please continue."

Before she could, the earth rumbled again. I pressed my hand to the ground, which vibrated like a twanged piano tuner. Jaime grabbed her matchbook and lit the censer holding the repelling herbs. The ground gave a tremendous shake, so violent I would have toppled sideways if Lucas hadn't caught me. Behind Jaime, an oak seedling quavered, then vaulted into the air. The ground ripped open, clods of dirt spewing like volcanic lava.

"Jesus fucking Christ!" Jaime said, scuttling toward us. "I *know* I didn't do that."

A strip of turf ripped back, like a peeled sardine can, opening a deep rectangular pit. From the bottom of the pit came scratching, scrabbling sounds.

"I would strongly suggest we don't wait to see what that is," Lucas said.

We all scooped up a handful of Jaime's equipment. As we turned to run, the thing in the pit rose to the top and, despite Lucas's advice, even he stopped to look. A body levitated over the grave. It was an old woman with long gray hair, dressed in a hospital gown. Her flesh had desiccated rather than decayed, reminding me of those bog mummies from England.

The body rotated ninety degrees, until its feet pointed at us. For a moment, it hovered there. Then, suddenly it sat upright, eyes flying open.

"Who dares disturb my eternal rest?" boomed a deep male voice with a Scottish burr.

Jaime backpedaled past us. I started to follow, then noticed Lucas hadn't moved. I tugged his jacket.

"Hey, Cortez, I think that's our signal to run."

"While I have no aversion to the general concept, it may not be warranted."

"Dinnae whisper, mortal!" the corpse rumbled. "I asked you a question. Who dares—"

"Yes, yes, I heard that part," Lucas said. "However, considering that we did not disturb you, but rather you have answered an invitation extended to another, I believe it is you who must identify yourself."

"Are you crazy?" Jaime hissed. "Leave it alone!"

"I repeat," Lucas said. "Please identify yourself."

The corpse's head snapped back with a sickening crack, then twisted in a full circle, the flesh around its neck splitting, banshee wail ripping through the Everglades.

"Ah, *The Exorcist,* if I'm not mistaken," Lucas murmured. "One must admire an entity with a full appreciation of contemporary pop culture." He raised his voice to be heard above the wailing. "Your name, please."

"My name is war! My name is pestilence! My name is misery and pain and everlasting torment!"

"Perhaps, but as a form of address, it is rather unwieldy. What do your friends call you?"

The thing stopped its head-spinning and glowered at Lucas. "I have nae friends. I have worshipers. I have devotees. And, thanks to you, today I have one fewer of those."

"Esus," I said.

The corpse turned toward me and sat up straighter. "Aye, thank you." It glared at Lucas. "The witch knows who I am."

"And, apparently, you know who we are," Lucas said.

"I am Esus. I know all. I know you, and I know the witch, and I know the necromancer." He peered over at Jaime. "Caught your show. Nae bad, but it could use a wee oomph."

Esus's voice had lost its orator boom and settled into an odd blend of Scottish and American idiom—the speech of an ancient spirit who liked to keep up with the times.

Jaime eased up beside us. "So you're a . . ."

"A druid deity," I said. "Esus, god of woodland and water."

"I like the witch," Esus said. "I'll talk to the witch."

"And we'll talk to Everett Weber," Lucas said.

"No, you willnae. I gave you a chance to speak to Everett and what did you do? Nearly got the poor bastard shot by a bunch of Cabal cowboys. But did I interfere? Nae. I stood down and let my acolyte be taken into custody, because I trusted you to get him out of there." The corpse threw up its hands. "But, och, he's out of there now. After he's dead!"

"That's true." I sidled as close to the reanimated corpse as I dared. "But, being all-knowing, you also know that wasn't our fault. We did our best with the information we had."

Esus's sigh blew bits of withered flesh out the corpse's torn neck. "I know. But I still cannae let you talk to Everett. He's a wee bit traumatized right now, being suddenly dead and all."

"Understandable," I said. "But we really do need to speak to him, and now is the best time."

"Nae can do, lassie. Ask all you want, but I'm nae changing my mind. Of course, whatever Everett knows, I know, so you could ask me. It'll cost you, thocht."

"Nuh-uh," Jaime said. "No deals with the devil. I've learned my lesson on that one."

The corpse glowered at her. "I am nae the devil. Or a demon. Or some skittering spook. I am . . . ." Esus crossed his arms. "A god."

"Very well, then," Lucas said. "What would you like?"

"What do you think I'd like? What do all gods like? Sacrifice, of course."

"I'll give up booze for a week," Jaime said.

"Ha-ha. You could use a wee bit of that humor in your show. Far too much of that touchy-feely stuff for me. A good corpse joke now and then would liven things up. As

a druid god, I demand true sacrifice. Human sacrifice."
He looked at Lucas. "You'd do."

"I'm sure I would. No human sacrifices."

"A goat, then. I'll take a goat."

Jaime looked around. "Would you settle for a gator?"

"No live sacrifices," Lucas said. "Of any kind. In return
for clear and comprehensible answers to our questions, I
will offer you a half-pint of blood."

"Yours?"

"Of course."

Esus pursed his lips. "A full pint."

"Half before and half after."

"Agreed."

Esus dictated instructions for setting up the sacrificial
circle. Then I helped Lucas draw the blood. Not for the
squeamish. I'd put in plenty of volunteer hours at blood
donor clinics, but our methods that night were, shall we
say, a tad more primitive, involving a penknife and a bra.
As a tourniquet, there's no better suited item of clothing,
nor one that is less likely to be missed. And if it got
bloodstained, well, I never turn down an opportunity to
freshen my lingerie wardrobe.

Once the blood was drawn, I untied the makeshift
tourniquet and repositioned it over the wound. Lucas
held his arm up to slow the flow, then turned to Esus.

"Sufficient?" Lucas said.

"Red silk," Esus said. "Bonny. Dare I assume there are
matching panties?" His gaze slid down me, grin turning
to a leer, which, considering he was in the shriveled
corpse of an old woman, was less than flattering. "Maybe
I asked for the wrong sacrifice."

"Sorry, no virgins here," I said.

"Ne'er been that keen on virgins myself. And I'll take red silk over white lace any day. Tell you what, dump sorcerer-laddie here, and you and I—"

Lucas cleared his throat. "What can you tell us about the killer?"

"Afraid of a wee competition, señor?"

Lucas raked a pointed look over Esus's current corporeal form. "No, not really."

"Och, I'll find a better body, of course." Esus turned to me. "Blond or brunette?"

"I kinda like what I've got," I said. "Sorry."

"Oh, I can do that, too. Dinnae see the attraction, but—"

"We had a deal," Lucas said. "Now, we found records of Cabal children on Everett's computer and a program that selected potential victims. What we want to know is—"

"Who bought the data," Esus said. He closed his eyes and intoned a low hum, dragging the note out for a few seconds. "That which you seek can be found in a land inhabited by neither the dead nor the ever-living. Like you, yet nae like you. A hunter, a stalker, an animal heart in a—"

Lucas cleared his throat. "Perhaps we should define clear and comprehensible."

"Perhaps we should define dull and boring." When Lucas only stared at him, Esus sighed. "Have it your way. He's earthbound. Human. Now that's information that Everett himself couldnae give you because he ne'er saw the man. I caught a glimpse of him at the courthouse, when he killed that bairn. Damned Cabal shamans put up a barrier to keep me outside, so I couldnae help Everett. I was trying to find a kink in the armor when the dobber grabbed the bairn. Didnae get a good look at him, thocht."

"Why not?" Jaime said. "I thought you were all-seeing."

"All-knowing, nae all-seeing," he snapped. "I'm a god, nae Santa Claus."

"But if you're all-knowing—" she began.

I elbowed her to silence. I doubted gods, even minor Celtic deities, appreciated having their shortcomings pointed out.

"What *can* you tell us about him?" I asked. "From the glimpse you got?"

"Male, corporeal human form, light hair, average size, and fast as Thor's thunderbolt. Stabbed that poor bairn so fast he didnae have time to scream. Your man has killing experience, and lots of it. In the auld days, priests made a dozen sacrifices to me every spring, and none of them was as good at it as this fellow."

"Back to the files, then. How did that come about?"

"The way most jobs come about. Networking. After the Nasts fired Everett—oh, and do you know why they fired him? Because some sorcerer's laddie wanted the job for his co-op. Obviously, Everett wasnae happy. He was looking for a wee bit of revenge, maybe shooting his gob off too much. This guy found out, called and asked Everett if he wanted to make some cash hacking into Cabal employee files. Everett figured the guy was looking to recruit Cabal employees. Happens all the time."

I nodded. "Then he asked for employee files for the Cortez, Nast, and St. Cloud Cabals."

"Nae, he wanted all four. The Cortez and Nast ones Everett could get easily enough, having worked for them. He knew a fellow in the St. Cloud computer department, so he could buy those files. But he had nae idea how to get the Boyd file. This guy didnae care. He said the other three would be good enough; he'd take care of the Boyds later."

"Everett gets the three files, and then . . ."

"Then he wants Everett to extract the information on employees' bairns. And that's when he knew the guy was nae recruiting."

"No kidding," Jaime muttered.

"Look, I'm nae defending Everett. He fucked up. But he's nae saint and he's nae hero. He got greedy and he got scared and between the two, he convinced himself that there could be some innocent reason why a bodie would want a list of runaway Cabal bairns. When those bairns started dying, we both knew he was in trouble. If the Cabals didnae get him, the killer would, tidying up his loose ends. When I saw you were heading in Everett's direction, I told him to go quietly, because I knew your reputations, and figured you would hunt down the truth."

"Sorry," I murmured.

"Och, couldnae be helped. Once the Cabals had a suspect, they were nae letting anything as inconvenient as the truth get in their way. I should have foreseen that."

"How did he get the list to this guy?" I asked.

"Very cloak-and-dagger. The dobber isnae stupid. He communicated by phone, gave nae way to contact him, told Everett where to leave the printouts. When Everett dropped off the lists, there was cash waiting for him."

"So there were two lists," I said. "One of Cabal runaways—the easy marks. Then one of personal bodyguards' kids, to prove that if he could get that close to the bodyguards, he could get that close to the CEOs themselves. From there he jumped straight to the families—"

"Nae, there was a third list. Everett did it separately. After the guy found out there were only two names on the second list, he wanted the bairns of the CEO's personal staff."

"Then Matthew Tucker *was* a victim," I said. "But, still, to jump from a secretary's son to a CEO's grandson seems a megaleap."

"It's likely his original intention was to remain with the third list," Lucas said. "However, the convergence of Cabal families for the trial provided him with the perfect opportunity to escalate faster."

"And now that he's hit the top, that's where he'll bide," Esus said. "Going back to killing the kids of mere employees now would be admitting he bit off more than he can chew. Here on in, it's a CEO family or nothing. You'd better watch your back, señor."

"I doubt he'll jump to an adult while he still has a decent pool of teenage victims to choose from. He's striking at young people for a reason, and not just because they're easier targets."

"He wants it to hurt," Esus said. "Your man is hurting because of something the Cabals did, and he wants to hurt them back."

Lucas prodded Esus with more specific questions about the date and times of phone calls, et cetera, then we gave him his final half-pint, and bade him farewell.

Go-between

IF ESUS HADN'T INSISTED ON LUCAS'S BLOOD, I'D HAVE gladly given the second half-pint, for reasons both personal and practical. On the practical side, we had no food or drink to boost Lucas's blood sugar after his "donation," and he had to navigate the boat back to the dock. Though I couldn't drive a boat, I could drive a car, and insisted on doing so from the dock to the edge of Miami, where Jaime removed her blindfold and took over. We managed to stay awake until about two seconds after we collapsed into bed at a little past four.

Since it was so late when we'd returned to the hotel, Jaime slept on our hotel room sofa. When I awoke late the next morning, I found a note from Lucas. He hoped to find some tangible evidence connecting Weber to the killer, either in his phone records or personal effects, the latter of which had been shipped by the crateload to Miami for pretrial searching.

Beside the note, Lucas had left a glass of water, two painkillers, and the ingredients for a fresh poultice for my stomach. Though I hated to admit it, I needed that...

otherwise, I don't think I'd have been able to climb out of bed that morning. As it was, I still had to lie in bed for twenty minutes, waiting for the pills and the tertiary healing spell to take effect. Once I could move, I showered, dressed, then slipped into the sitting area of our suite, expecting Jaime to still be asleep. Instead, she was reading a magazine on the sofa.

"Good, you're up," she said. "Let's go grab something to eat."

"Fuel up before you head back on the road? Good idea."

"Uh, right." She grabbed her brush, leaned over, and began sweeping it through the underside of her hair. "You like Cuban?"

"Not sure I've ever had it."

"You can't leave Miami without trying some. I saw this funky little place near the clinic."

"The clinic?"

"You know, where Dana is."

Jaime continued to brush her hair from the bottom, which effectively covered her face and any untoward gleam in her eye. She started to work on a nonexistent tangle. I waited. I gave her ten seconds. She only took four.

"Oh, and since we'll be in the neighborhood, we can stop in and see how Dana's doing. Maybe try contacting her again."

Jaime tossed her hair back and brushed the top, allowing her to slant a glance my way, and gauge my reaction. I'd wondered what had driven her back to us. Somehow I doubted she'd really heard the news about Weber and thought "Oh, I should rush back to Miami and help out." Last night she'd mentioned wanting to contact Dana, and now I realized this was probably the real reason she'd returned, that she felt guilty over having misled Dana and wanted to talk to her again. This couldn't help the case, but if it would help put Dana's—and Jaime's—soul at peace, well, there was little I could do here until Lucas came back. So I placed my eleven o'clock phone call to Elena, then left with Jaime.

"She's not there," Jaime said, tossing down her amulet beside Dana's still form. "Goddamn orientation training."

"Orientation?" I said.

"That's what I call it. Other necros have fancier terms. Gotta make it sound all mystical, you know." Jaime rubbed the back of her neck. "After a spirit crosses over, you have a day or two, sometimes three, to contact them, then the ghost Welcome Wagon snatches them up and shows them the ropes. During that period, the spirit is on hiatus. Some kind of psychic door slams and you can scream your lungs out, but they can't hear you."

"I've heard of that," I said. "Then, afterward, you can contact them, but it's harder than it would be in the first couple of days."

"Because they've learned how to 'just say no' to pesky necros. After that, we're as welcome as encyclopedia salesmen. You have to pester them until they listen just to get rid of you. Unless *they* want something, and then they'll drive *us* nuts until we listen." Jaime raked her hands through her hair. "This makes no sense. If she's in training, then why—" She twisted her hair into a pony-tail. "You wouldn't have a clip, would you?"

"Always," I said, digging in my purse. "With this hair, it pays to be prepared. A drizzle of rain or shot of humidity and it's ponytail time."

"So the curl's natural?"

"God, yes. I wouldn't pay for this."

She laughed and fixed the clip in her hair. "See, now, *I* would. That's the irony, isn't it? Girls with curly hair want straight and girls with straight hair want curly. No one's ever happy." She glanced in her compact. "Decent enough. Ready for lunch?"

I returned my chair to its place across the room. "What were you saying earlier? About something not making sense?"

"Hmm? Oh, don't mind me. I never make sense. Don't forget, you wanted to check in with the nurse before we leave."

According to the nurse, Randy MacArthur was expected in two days. That made me feel better. Dana might not be coming back, but it would help her to know that her father had been there for her. We hadn't told anyone that Dana was gone. If keeping quiet meant she'd be on the respirator long enough for her father to see her "alive" one last time, then she deserved that much.

As we walked from the clinic, I noticed a balding man across the road on a bench, reading the newspaper. As we headed down the road, he watched us over his paper. Nothing unusual about that—I'm sure Jaime got more than her share of lingering looks. When we'd gone half a block, though, I happened to glance over my shoulder and saw the man strolling on the other side of the road, keeping pace with us thirty feet or so behind. When we turned the corner, he did the same. I mentioned it to Jaime.

She glanced back at the guy. "Yeah, I get that sometimes, usually from guys who look like that. They recognize me, hang around a bit, work up the courage to say something. There was a time, I'd have killed for the attention. Now, some days, it's just—" She shrugged off the sentence.

"More than you bargained for."

She nodded. "That's the bitch of celebrity. You spend years chasing it, dreaming of it, starving for it. Then it happens and the next thing you know, you hear yourself whining about the lack of privacy and you think, 'You ungrateful bitch. You got what you wanted, and you're still not happy.' That's where the therapists come in. Either that or you self-medicate your way into Betty Ford."

"I can imagine."

Her gaze flicked toward me and she nodded. We walked in silence for a minute, then she checked over her shoulder.

"Let's, uh, skip the Cuban place, if you don't mind," she said. "We'll drive someplace else, lose the admirer."

"Sure. Does this happen a lot?"

"Is three or four times a week a lot?"

"Are you serious?"

She nodded. "Now, I have to admit, most aren't middle-aged admirers, just folks who want me to contact someone for them. I don't do private consultations, but people don't believe me. They think they just aren't offering enough money. There was this woman once, a friend of Nancy Reagan's. You remember Nancy . . . or are you too young for that?"

"She had a thing for psychics." I'd read this somewhere, having been in preschool during the Reagan administration, but I doubted Jaime would appreciate a reminder of our age difference.

"Well, Nancy had this friend— Is this where we're parked?"

"Next lot."

"Jesus, my memory lately . . . I swear, the holes are getting bigger."

We walked into the parking lot. Though it was midday, tall buildings surrounded the tiny strip of land, wrapping it in shadow.

"What? Buggers too cheap for electricity?" Jaime said, squinting into the half-filled lot. "Hey, our city has only the second-highest crime rate in the nation. When we hit number one, we'll celebrate by springing for security lights."

"I'd cast a light spell," I murmured. "But I hear footsteps."

As Jaime shoulder-checked, a car door slammed. We both jumped.

"I didn't see a car turn in here, did you?" I said.

She shook her head. I glanced around, but saw no one.

"Let's just—" Jaime began.

The slam of a second door cut her off. She followed the noise and swore under her breath.

"Walk fast and don't look," she whispered. "Two very big guys bearing down fast."

"How big?"

"Huge."

I stopped and turned around. "Hey, Troy."

Troy lifted his sunglasses onto his head. "Hey, Paige. Morris, this is Paige."

The temp bodyguard was the same one who'd been at the courthouse yesterday. He was several inches shorter than Troy, broader in the shoulders, and black, which ruined the whole bookend-bodyguard effect. Morris did, however, share Griffin's stone-faced demeanor, responding to the introduction with a nod so abrupt I thought it might be a hiccup.

Across the lot, our middle-aged stalker headed for a Mercedes. Troy lifted a hand in greeting. The man waved back, confirming what I'd only just suspected, that he was a Cabal employee sent to follow not Jaime, but me.

I completed the introductions by identifying Jaime. Troy smiled and shook her hand.

"The celebrity necro," he said. "Pleased to meet you."

"Uh, thanks," Jaime said, surreptitiously tucking in the back of her T-shirt. "So I'm guessing you guys are Cabal security?"

"Benicio's bodyguards," I said. "And I'm guessing the boss is in the SUV waiting for me."

"Yeah, different city, same plan. I told you, he likes routine."

"Benicio Cortez? Here?" Jaime glanced at the Cadillac SUV. "Oh, shit."

"It's more like 'aww, shit,'" I said. "Now comes the boring part. I have to send Troy back to say I want Benicio to come here, then he'll insist I come there, and poor Troy will get his daily dose of jogging running between us."

Troy grinned. "True, but the good part is that it's definitely not routine. Most times, when I say Mr. Cortez wants to speak to someone, they trip over me running to get to him."

"It's getting late, so let me make this easy on you. Wait here and I'll see what he wants."

I walked to the SUV, tapped the rear window, and motioned for the driver to lower it. Instead, Benicio opened the door.

"Come around the other side and get in please, Paige."

"No, thanks." I held the door open and stepped into the gap. "Let me guess: The clinic called you when I showed up, then you had one of your security guys hang around outside and follow me when I left."

"I wanted to speak—"

"I'm not done. My point was that you knew the moment you got that call that Lucas wasn't with me, and he'd already told you he wasn't happy about your approaching me in Portland. So now, when he's probably never been more pissed off with you, you decide this is a good time to follow me into an empty parking lot, corner me, and strong-arm me into talking to you."

"I would like to speak—"

"Am I talking to myself? Did you hear anything I just said? No, forget it. You go ahead and talk, and then Lucas will find out about it, and you can save yourself one place setting at Christmas dinner for the next umpteen years." I tried to stop there, but couldn't help adding, "Do you have any idea how upset he is right now?"

"Having my phone calls automatically blocked was a good clue. I want to explain myself, but I can't do that if he won't speak to me. So I hoped perhaps I could speak to you instead."

I shook my head. "I won't be your go-between."

"I'm not asking for that. What I'm saying is that I recognize you're a full partner in Lucas's life and in this investigation, and I'm speaking to you as such. You're an intelligent young—"

"Don't," I said. "Don't insult me and don't play me. You have something to say? Fine. But you'll say it to both of us. You'll follow me back to the hotel and I'll take you to Lucas. We'll tell him you met up with us outside the clinic and, seeing he wasn't with me, you asked if you could speak to us both at the hotel."

"Thank you."

"I'm not doing it for you."

The Usual Suspects

INSTEAD OF HAVING BENICIO FOLLOW US, I DECIDED TO ride with him and let Jaime follow us in her rental car. I had questions, not about why he'd betrayed Lucas, but about the investigation. When Lucas saw his father he'd be too upset to ask about the case, so I'd do it for him.

Benicio confirmed that the Cabals had resumed their investigation. After Joey Nast's death, they'd changed tactics. No longer content to follow the clues, they'd rounded up the usual suspects—anyone known to have a beef with the Cabals—and were trying to "extract" clues.

"Extract?" I said, the blood draining from my face. "You mean torture."

Benicio paused. "The Cabals do employ intense inter-rogation techniques. I would hesitate to use the word torture . . . But you must understand, Paige, the pressure that the Cabals are under. Not just the pressure, but the fear, the feelings of impotence. Do I think this is the best way to proceed? No. But I'd be hard-pressed to find members of my board who agree. The Nasts are in charge of the investigation now."

"Because of Joey."

"Correct." He gazed out the side window for a moment,

then turned to me. "Until last month, the Nasts' New York office was in the World Trade Center."

"Did they lose—?"

"Twenty-seven people, out of a staff of thirty-five. The Cabals—we place ourselves above such things. We may kill one another but, as supernaturals, we have little to fear from the outside world. If we are attacked, we have the resources to strike back. But what happened last month..." He shook his head. "There's no revenge for that, and the Nasts are damned if they're going to be victimized again." He looked at me. "You can't concern yourself with our side of the investigation, Paige, because you can't stop it."

"I can if I find the killer."

He looked at me, then nodded.

I didn't lie to Lucas. As he so often reminds me, I'm horrible at it. The best I could do was omit damning details about my encounter with Benicio, and slant the story so he'd draw the conclusion that his father had expected Lucas and me to be together. Did he buy it? Probably not, but since I was obviously intent on brokering peace, Lucas decided not to stall the negotiations with a fresh injury complaint.

Once I'd secured Lucas's approval, I phoned down to Benicio in the lobby and invited him up. Since this was family business, I suggested Jaime take Troy and Morris to the hotel restaurant for coffee. Troy agreed, but Morris decided to wait in the hall.

Less than a minute after I hung up, Benicio rapped at the door. Lucas opened it. Before he could get in so much as a greeting, Lucas cut him short.

"Having renewed the investigation, Paige and I are

committed to using all available resources. If you agree to communicate only for the purpose of sharing our findings, I will accept your calls. I trust that whatever leak led to the raid on Everett Weber's house has been repaired."

"You have my word—"

"Right now, I could have your blood oath and still not believe you. Perhaps instead you will take my word. If you lie to me again and another person dies because of it, we are through."

"Lucas, I want to explain—"

"Yes, I know you do, which leads me to my next request. I don't want to hear your explanation. I know perfectly well what happened. You made an executive decision. To your mind, Weber was obviously guilty and I was questioning that simply because it is my nature to question. Therefore, given the choice between indulging your son's quixotic whims and saving the Cabal from embarrassment, you chose the Cabal."

He paused. Benicio opened his mouth, but nothing came out.

Lucas continued. "I would like copies of the crime-scene reports for Matthew Tucker and Joey Nast."

"Uh, yes, certainly. I'll courier them over right away."

"Thank you." Lucas walked to the door and opened it. "Good day."

"Are you angry with me?" I asked after Benicio left.

He blinked, his surprise at the question answering. "For what?"

"Bringing your father here."

Lucas shook his head and put his arms around my

waist. "I needed to get those case files, but I have been, I'm afraid, avoiding making the call."

"How are you holding up?" I asked.

"Besides feeling like an idiot? After twenty-five years of experience, I consider myself a reasonably good judge of my father's capacity for deception, and yet I never once suspected he wasn't lobbying to get us an audience with Weber. I can't believe I was that stupid."

"Well, I certainly don't know him anywhere near as well as you do, but I never doubted his intentions, either. He knew you were upset about the raid, so naturally he'd want to get back in your good books by going to bat for you on Weber. It made sense to me."

"Thank you," he said, kissing the top of my head.

"I'm not just saying that to make you feel better."

A crooked smile. "I know. That's one thing I can count on, that you always tell me the truth. With my father, I know he's not the most trustworthy of men, but I—" He paused. "I can't help wanting a closer relationship, like we had when I was young. I feel like we *should* have that again and, somehow, that the onus for reestablishing it falls to me."

"It shouldn't."

"I know that. Yet sometimes . . . I know it must be difficult for him, being who he is. He doesn't have anyone he can trust, not even his family. He can barely stand to be in the same room as his wife. His relationship with their sons is almost as bad. I know that's at least partly, if not primarily, his own fault, yet sometimes, when I'm with him, I want to compensate for that."

He eased us down onto the sofa. "My father called me when I was on the plane to Chicago. We talked. Really talked. He didn't make a single reference to the Cabal or my future in it. He just wanted to talk about me, and about you and me, how we were doing, how happy he was to see me happy, and I thought—" Lucas shook his head. "I was an idiot."

"He's the idiot," I said, leaning over to kiss him. "And if he doesn't see what he's missing out on, then I'll take his share."

Someone rapped at the door.

"Whoops," I said. "Forgot Jaime. She probably wants to grab her stuff and take off."

I opened the door.

"So what's next on the agenda?" Jaime said as she walked in. "Lunch is out, I guess, but maybe I can grab take-out for us."

"That would be . . . very nice," I said. "But what about you? When's your next show?"

"Show? Oh, the tour. Right." She opened her purse, pulled out lipstick, and walked to the mirror. "Next stop Graceland. Well, Memphis actually, but I might as well just hold it at Graceland, 'cause half the people in the au-dience are going to ask me to summon Elvis. I just give them some song-and-dance about how he's up in heaven enjoying fried peanut-butter-and-banana sandwiches and singing for God. Pisses him off to no end, but you gotta give the folks what they want, and no one cares what he's really doing."

"What *is* he really doing?" I asked.

"Sorry, kids, that's the X-rated show. Let's just say he's happy. Where was I? Right, Memphis. I don't do my Elvis schtick until Halloween, which means I have six days to myself. I'm supposed to be rehearsing but, hell, like I couldn't do that shit in my sleep."

"So instead, you're . . . ?"

"Taking some much-needed downtime and building up good karma credits helping you guys. I figure I'll hang around here, and if you need a necro, I'm ready and willing."

"That's very generous," Lucas said. "But we probably won't need—"

"Sure you will," Jaime cut in. "Every murder case needs a necro. And if you want someone to make phone calls or run errands, I'm your gal Friday."

Lucas and I exchanged a look. I could understand Jaime wanting a few days off. She'd looked exhausted yesterday, and although she'd bounced back, these spurts of energy seemed forced, as if she was running in high gear to keep from collapsing.

"So, what are you guys—" Jaime began, then she caught a glimpse of herself in the mirror and stopped mid-sentence. She yanked the clip from her hair and tried gathering it again, but her hands trembled so badly she couldn't keep it together long enough to get the hair clip on. She crammed the clip into her pocket. "Can I borrow your brush, Paige?"

"Um, sure, it's right—"

She was already in the bathroom. Lucas lowered his head to whisper something to me, but Jaime popped out of the bathroom, wielding the hairbrush with harsh strokes.

"So where are we at? Any fresh leads?"

Lucas glanced at me. I shrugged discreetly. If Jaime was offering to help with the investigation, I saw no reason to refuse, and no reason not to fill her in.

"Lucas was checking Weber's phone records. Since that's how Esus said he was making contact with the killer, it seemed a good place to start." I looked at Lucas. "Please, tell me it was a good place to start."

"It wasn't a bad place to start, though I'd hesitate to call my findings overwhelmingly encouraging. Once I ap-

plied the approximate time range, I came up with a reasonably definitive list of five phone calls. The last two
took place in the past week, presumably after the killer
took a hard look at the second list and decided to expand
his criteria. Both calls came after the killings began. The
first, received on the eighth, came from Louisiana, where
he was likely preparing for his attack on Holden. The
second came the following day, from California, presumably arranging to pick up the final list. Both calls were
made from pay phones."

"And the earlier calls? Before the attacks? Tell me they
all came from the same place."

"From the same region, though, again, all from pay
phones. The first was made in Dayton, Ohio, the second
in Covington, Kentucky, and the third near Columbus,
Indiana. Triangulate those points on a map and in the
middle you'll find Cincinnati."

"So he's from Cincinnati?" Jaime said.

"It's reasonable to assume he was residing there, at
least briefly, before the killings began. By making the
calls from three smaller cities, it would appear he was
avoiding a deliberate link with Cincinnati."

"So should we head up to Cincinnati? Start asking
around the supernatural community?"

"There isn't a supernatural community in Cincinnati."
I glanced at Lucas. "Is there?"

"While there may be a few supernaturals living in the
region, there is no 'community' to speak of. The Nasts
recently considered locating a satellite office there for
that very reason." He caught my frown and explained.
"Cabals prefer to expand into virgin territory, where they
don't have many resident supernaturals to contend with."

"So there's nobody in Cincinnati to ask." Jaime sighed.
"Shit. It couldn't be that easy, could it?"

"There's still the motivation lead," I said. "Esus thinks we're looking for a supernatural with a vendetta against the Cabals. The only other reasonable motivation is money. Pay me a billion bucks and I'll stop killing your kids. But the Cabals haven't received any blackmail notes." I paused. "Unless they have and they're just not telling us. Damn, I hate this."

"I feel reasonably safe in saying that no extortion attempts have been made," Lucas said. "Now that one of Thomas Nast's grandsons is dead, a killer with any knowledge of Cabals would know he can't buy his way out of this. As Esus said, it's personal."

"Then, when you put the clues together, we have a serious lead here. Adult male, living in the Cincinnati area, has reason to want revenge on the Cabals—not one, but all the Cabals. There can't be many supernaturals who fulfill that criteria."

"So we just ask the Cabals—" Jaime looked over at Lucas. "It's not that easy, either, is it?"

"Probably not," he said. "I'm afraid that if I give the Cabals too much information, we'll have a repeat of the Weber incident."

"Or a sudden epidemic afflicting male supernaturals living in Ohio," I said.

"Precisely. We'll start instead by canvasing my contacts. If a supernatural has reason to be this angry at the Cabals, someone must have heard of it."

"There's nothing we outsiders like better than gossip about the big bad Cabals," Jaime said. "I could make a few calls of my own."

"Excellent idea," Lucas said. "First, though, let me talk to a local contact. He publishes an underground anti-Cabal newsletter, and he's always my best source of Cabal rumor."

"He lives in Miami and puts out an anti-Cabal newsletter?" I said. "He'd better hope your father never finds out."

"My father knows all about Raoul. In such matters he follows Sun Tzu's maxim about keeping your friends close and your enemies closer."

"Uh-huh," I said. "Okay, well, is this Raoul someone I can meet?"

"He's a shaman, not a sorcerer, so he'll have no aversion to discussing matters with a witch. In addition, we may be able to find some, uh, interesting reading material in his bookstore."

"Spells?"

A tiny smile. "Yes, spells. Remember, though, that by bringing you to the source of the spells, any that you care to acquire must be purchased by me, and therefore count toward my accumulated total option choices."

I grinned. "You got it."

"Spells don't help me," Jaime said. "But I could use a book to read. Mind if I tag along?"

That was fine with us, so we grabbed our things and left.

Literary Haunts

RAOUL WAS ON VACATION. ACCORDING TO HIS ASSISTANT, he hadn't taken so much as two consecutive days off in five years but now, when we needed him, he'd decided it was time for a monthlong European holiday. I suspected this wasn't coincidence—he'd probably heard of the Cabals' latest "investigative" tactics, and feared he'd be next on their list.

Although Raoul was gone, he wasn't out of contact. That's the life of the self-employed—you can never really be away, or you might come home to find your business in shambles. Even lying in my hospital bed, I'd checked my e-mail and followed up on anything critical—well, anything my customers considered critical. Raoul hadn't left a phone number, but he was available by e-mail. His assistant sent off an immediate "Call Lucas Cortez" message for us.

"Can we check out the grimoires?" I said. "Wait, let me guess. He keeps those locked up, meaning they aren't available until he comes back."

"I'm afraid so."

I sighed. "Strike two. Well, let's go find Jaime."

Although the building was larger than most used bookstores, every available inch of space was in use, leaving a maze of narrow, serpentine aisles flanked by ten-foot-high shelves. The occasional murmur or shoe squeak indicated other shoppers, but they were lost among the stacks.

"Guess we should split up," I said. "Should we lay a trail of bread crumbs?"

"Perhaps, though I may suggest a more prosaic solution. Do you have your cell phone?"

I nodded. "Whoever finds her first, calls. Got it."

I tracked Jaime to the horror section and told her about Raoul.

"Shit," she said. "There's no luck like bad luck, huh? Guess we should get back to the hotel then, and Lucas and I can tap into the gossipmonger circuit."

I looked at her empty hands. "You didn't find anything?"

"Not what I was looking for."

She turned to leave, but I put a hand on her arm.

"We can spare a minute. What were you looking for?"

"Stephen King. Now, every bookstore *must* have him. But he's not here."

I scanned the shelf, which appeared to be arranged alphabetically by author. "You're right. That's strange. Did you want his latest? Maybe it's in general fiction."

"I'm actually looking for *Christine,* which should be under horror."

"Let's check the map up front, maybe ask the clerk." I started walking. "Isn't *Christine* the one about the possessed car?"

"That's it. I've been wanting to reread it ever since this show I did a couple months ago. A guy had this car that he swore was possessed, just like in the book. I don't do private consultations, but my prodco was filming the show, and they thought it'd be cool if we checked out his car in the parking lot. Oh, here's the map."

I scanned the map. "Aha. Here's our problem. King gets his own shelf in the Popular Authors section."

As we walked to the section, Jamie continued her story. "So this kid—he's maybe your age—has this gorgeous 1967 Mustang convertible. First thought: 'Uh-oh, call DEA.' The kid didn't look like any trust-fund brat, so where'd he get a car like that? When I ask him, he gets all nervous. Says his grandpa left it to him. And sure enough, it really is haunted. Guess who by?"

"The grandfather," I said.

"Bingo. The old guy jumped me the second I got within sensing distance, so spitting mad he could barely communicate. Seems he *did* leave the car to the kid. But on one condition. He wanted to be buried in it. No one else in the family would listen, but the kid promised to do it."

"And then he stiffed him."

Jaime laughed. "Yeah, the kid stiffed the stiff. Took the car, took the money, and plopped Gramps into the cheapest casket he could buy."

"So what'd you do?"

"Told the kid the truth. Either he buried Gramps in the car or he had to live with a permanent pissed-off hitch-hiker. Oh, here it is."

The King section took up two eight-foot-long shelves, and the books weren't alphabetized. As I skimmed the titles, I glanced at my watch.

"We can skip this," Jaime said. "No biggie."

"Another minute or two won't matter. Oh, I forgot to call Lucas. He can help."

"Why don't I just grab something else."

As if one cue, a book tumbled from the top shelf and landed between us. Jaime picked it up.

"*Salem's Lot.*" She shook her head. "Not one of my faves. You ever read it?"

"I started to, because I thought it was about witches. When I found out it was vampires, I stopped. Not keen on the vamps myself."

"Who is? Damned parasites." Jaime stood on tiptoes to put the book back. The moment she released it, it jolted out and fell to the floor.

"I think it's lonely," I said with a laugh. "Looks like it's gathering some dust up there."

Again, Jaime put the book back. This time, before she could let go, the book slammed into her palm hard enough to make her yelp. Then it tumbled to the floor.

"Maybe there's some kind of catch up there," I said. "Here, I'll find a new place for it."

As I bent for the book, it spun out of my reach. Jaime grabbed my arm.

"Let's go," she said.

A book flew from the shelf, hitting her side. Another book sailed from a lower shelf, then another and another, pelting Jaime. She doubled over, arms wrapped over her head.

"Leave me alone!" she said. "Damn you—"

I grabbed her arm and propelled her out from the hailstorm of books. As we moved, I looked down at the novels strewn across the aisle. They were all copies of *Salem's Lot.*

The moment we were out of the Stephen King section, the books stopped flying. I speed-dialed Lucas and told him to meet us at the door.

"Ghost?" I whispered to Jaime as I hung up.

She nodded, gaze tripping from side to side, as if ready to duck.

"I think it's over," I murmured. "But we'd better scram, before someone notices the mess."

Again, Jaime only nodded. I rounded a corner, and looked down the unfamiliar aisle.

"Classics," I said. "Wrong turn. Let's back up—"

A book shot straight out from the shelf and clipped Jaime in the ear. More flew out, pummeling her from all sides. I shoved her out of the way, catching a few books myself, each striking harder than one would think possible for a slender paperback. One hit me in the knee. As I pitched forward, the book flopped to the floor. *The Iliad* . . . the same as every other book flying from the shelves.

I righted myself and kept propelling Jaime forward until we reached the front door. Lucas took one look at my expression and hurried over.

"What happened?" he whispered.

I motioned that we'd tell him outside.

On the way to the car, I told Lucas what had happened. Jaime stayed silent. Strangely silent, not chiming in with so much as an "uh-huh."

"Seems the bookstore had a resident ghost," I said. "I've heard of things like that happening. A necromancer is sitting in a bar, having a drink, minding his own business, and all of a sudden a spirit realizes there's a necro in the house and goes wild, trying to make contact. Like a shipwreck survivor spotting a rescue boat."

Jaime nodded, but kept her gaze straight forward, walking so fast I could barely keep up.

"It certainly does happen," Lucas said. "But I suspect

that's not what we had here"—he shot a pointed look at Jaime—"is it?"

She nibbled her lower lip and kept walking. Lucas tugged my arm, indicating for me to slow down. When Jaime got about twenty feet ahead of us, she glanced over each shoulder, realized we weren't with her, then turned to wait.

For a minute we just stood there, looking at each other. Then Lucas cleared his throat.

"You have a problem," he said to Jaime. "I presume you came to us for help with that problem. But we aren't going to drag it out of you."

"You have more important things to do. I know that. But I think it . . . it might be related."

"And I assume you are going to explain what 'it' is as soon as we get back to the hotel?"

She nodded.

Undelivered Message

THE HOTEL ROOM DOOR WAS STILL SHUTTING BEHIND US when Jaime started talking.

"I've got a haunter," she said. "And it's a strange one. I was going to tell you guys, but I know you're busy and I wasn't sure what was going on—I'm still not." She perched on the arm of the armchair, still talking. "It started Wednesday afternoon, before my Orlando show. At first I figured it was Dana, that she knew she was dead and wanted to pay me back for lying to her." Jaime twisted her rings. "I shouldn't have done that . . . not that I could have told her she was dead—it's not my place, right? But I went overboard with the reassurances. They just came out automatically, like I was doing a show."

She glanced from Lucas to me. When neither of us spoke, she continued.

"That's what I do with my shows, in case you haven't guessed. I make it up. No one wants to hear the truth. Fanny Mae wants to make contact with her dead hubby, and the guy's standing beside me screaming, 'Worried about me? You fucking whore, you weren't worried about me when you hopped into bed with my brother an hour after my funeral!' You think I'm going to tell her that? I tell her the same thing I tell everyone else. He misses you, but he's happy and he's in a good place. And you'd think, you'd really think, that after I've given the same damned message for the thousandth time, that people would wise up, but they don't. Tell them what they want to hear and they never complain."

She inhaled and shifted down onto the seat. "When this spook came knocking, I figured it was Dana, so I came back here to talk to her. But she was gone, and my haunter wasn't, so obviously it isn't her."

"Can't you contact it?" I said.

Jaime shook her head. "That's what's so weird. I can't make contact. Not only that, but it's behaving . . . well, it's just not following ghost-necro protocol." She looked at me. "Do you know how this works? How a spirit contacts a necro?"

"Vaguely," I said. "Most necromancers I know don't really talk about it."

"Typical. They act like it's some big trade secret. Way I figure it, my friends—the supernaturals, at least—*should* know how it works. Otherwise, they see me mumbling to myself and staring at blank walls, they're going to figure I've lost it. There are two main ways a spook says hi. If he knows the proper procedures, he can manifest, and I get sight and sound. If he doesn't know the tricks, then all I get is audio—the old voices-in-my-head. Any ghost should be able to do the latter. But this one can't."

"So it's throwing things instead?"

"It is now. Up until today, it's just been hanging around, like a mental stalker. I know it's there. I sense it all the time, as if someone is looking over my shoulder, and it's"—she lifted a hand to show her trembling fingers—"making me nervous. Then to start poltergeisting? That's just—well, I'm spooked, and I'll admit it."

"True poltergeist activity is rare, isn't it?" I said.

"Extremely rare. When I was younger, I did some ghost-buster work to pay the bills. Number one haunted-homeowner complaint? Poltergeists. I went out on dozens, if not hundreds of calls. I found exactly three real poltergeists. The rest of the time, it was clever kiddies looking for attention. I'd tell the people some cock-and-bull about the ghosts wanting to see the family spend more time together, and that usually fixed the problem. Real poltergeist activity, though, means a ghost has found a way to move things in our dimension, and that's a very special talent."

Lucas frowned. "So how does a ghost who can't even contact a necromancer manage to manipulate objects cross-dimensionally? I see the problem. Have you considered the possibility that this isn't a human-based entity at all?"

"Maybe a minor demon," I said. "Or a nature spirit."

"Could be, I guess," Jaime said. "But I'm a necro. I talk to the dead, like my title says. If it ain't dead, why's it bugging me? You guys are the spell-casters—the conjurers—so it should be trying to talk to *you*. And I'm pretty sure the message is for you, anyway. Until the bookstore, it backed off whenever you two were around."

"Because it thought you were going to convey the message," I said. "But maybe the message is to tell us to start conjuring, so it can communicate. When it realized you didn't understand, it bumped it up a level in the bookstore. So let's try some group conjuring. Among the three of us, it has to find someone it can talk to."

Jaime looked up at the ceiling. "You hear that, Casper? We're going to try making contact, so you can back off now."

After a moment of silence, I asked. "Did it stop?"

Jaime shook her head. "I think the contact problem

goes both ways. I can't hear it and it can't hear me. Let me grab my kit and see if we can fix that."

As Jaime opened her suitcase, Lucas's cell phone rang.

"Yes, I'm certainly interested," he said after an exchange of greetings. "However, it may be another week or so before we can see it. Will that be a problem?" He paused. "Good. Thank you." Another pause. "No, I haven't had a chance yet and, ultimately, it is her decision, but I would very much like to see it." Pause. "Yes, I'll let you know as soon as we return to Portland."

He signed off, then pulled out his Day-Timer from his satchel and made a note as Jaime set up her implements on the floor. This time, she didn't bother asking us to leave.

"A real séance," she said as she finished. "Now all we need is sleeping bags and a pillow fight. When I was young, I was never allowed to go to sleepovers, in case the kids tried a séance. Might have given them more than they expected."

We settled onto the floor.

"I'll be casting a general summoning spell," Lucas said. "A mild one, I should say, nothing likely to conjure up anything dangerous."

"I'll do my communication spell," I said. "It's for mental communication with the living, but it might help."

"Mental communication?" Jaime said. "Witches can do that? Cool."

"Not really. It only works if the other party is expecting it and only if they're some distance away, so really, what's the point? Save a few bucks on cell phone charges? The reception is crappier than the cheapest cell provider."

We all settled in, did our thing... and nothing happened.

"Hey!" Jaime yelled at the ceiling. "An hour ago you

were tearing apart a bookstore trying to get my attention, and now you can't be bothered to say hello? Do you know who you're talking to? The most famous necro in the U.S. of A. Not only that, but a former Coven Leader and the son of a Cabal CEO. Three powerful supernaturals, waiting with bated breath to talk to you."

Across the room, Lucas's Day-Timer fell from the table.

"I think that means it isn't impressed," I said.

The Day-Timer cover flipped open.

"I believe that's a sign," Lucas said. "Shall I . . . ?"

"Go stand by it and watch," I said. "We'll keep working."

Jaime did her invocation while I cast.

"Nothing," Lucas said before I could ask. "Perhaps—"

The pages started to flip.

"Seems we have a time delay from the ghost world," I said.

"It's turned to the first *D* page in my address book," Lucas said. "If the spirit is referring to a specific person on this page, I'm not making the connection. My supernatural contacts are coded in another section. These are all humans."

My purse slid off the chair by the door, unzipping as it fell and scattering the contents on the carpet. A moment later, my PalmPilot spun.

"A techno-savvy spook," Jaime said. "Maybe it wants to communicate by text messaging."

"Or, more likely," Lucas said, "it's *not* techno-savvy or, at least, can't operate an electronic organizer. I believe the message we're supposed to receive is that the correct name is located, not in my address book, but in Paige's."

"How would it know what's in there?" I said, crossing the floor to pick up my Palm.

"Perhaps it doesn't know, so much as assume. Who

might you know whose last name starts with a *D*? Presumably a supernatural."

"That could be a dozen people, maybe more. There's—Wait, we've had other clues. The bookstore. Of all the books in one section, it only knocked down copies of *Salem's Lot*."

"Witches?" Lucas asked.

Jaime shook her head. "Vampires—but if the spook doesn't know its pop culture, it might think witches."

"It was also knocking down copies of Homer's *Iliad,*" I said.

"Oh, great," Jaime said. "We move from *Who Wants to be a Millionaire* to 'Final Jeopardy.' Where are we going to find an egghead who's read the *Iliad*?"

"Uh, right here," I said. "Well, I had to. Required reading for college English."

"It was on my curriculum as well," Lucas said.

"Okay, the high school dropout reveals herself again," Jaime said. "Hey, I knew the Stephen King answer. That oughtta get me a nice parting gift. So what's the *Iliad* about?"

"The Trojan War," I said.

"With the horse," Jaime said. "I knew that. Any supernaturals in the story?"

"There's an enchantress, Circe—no, that's the *Odyssey*."

"Unless, again, the spirit is mistaken about its literary references," Lucas said. "If it believed *Salem's Lot* was about witches, and the sorceress was from the *Iliad* . . ."

"Let's start there, then," Jaime said. "Witches whose last names start with *D*. You're a witch, so the ghost might assume you know—"

"Cassandra," I said, thumping my Palm down. "Cassandra the Prophetess, from the *Iliad*. Cassandra DuCharme, from the interracial council."

"Let me guess," Jaime said. "This Cassandra is a witch."

"Vampire."

"Even better." Jaime looked to the ceiling. "Is that it? Do we win?"

No response.

"If it can't hear us, it'll need some other prompt," I said. "Hold on."

I grabbed my pen and notepad from the spilled contents of my purse, tore a sheet from the pad, and wrote CASSANDRA. I laid the sheet on the table. Again, the spirit gave no response.

"Well," Jaime said. "Three possibilities. One, we're flat-out wrong. Two, the spook has simmered down because we finally got the message. Three, it's illiterate."

"If the message *is* Cassandra, I still don't know what that means," I said.

"Why don't you call her," Lucas said. "See whether she can shed some light on this."

Paddling Upstream During a Hurricane

I USED OUR HOTEL ROOM PHONE TO CALL CASSANDRA. THIS was moderately indiscreet, and normally I'd have been more cautious, but the truth was, phoning from the hotel was the best way to ensure she'd answer. Cassandra was a call-screener, and not one who just ignored calls from strangers. She almost always let her machine pick up, then phoned back at her leisure. The only way to persuade her to answer was to pique her curiosity. A call from a Miami hotel just might do that.

Cassandra answered on the second ring.

"It's Paige," I said.

The line went silent and I could fairly hear Cassandra's annoyance buzzing down it. Short of "accidentally" pulling out the phone cord, though, there was little she could do. Well, she could hang up, but that would be crass, and Cassandra would never be crass.

"What is the problem, Paige?" she asked, voice dripping icicles.

"I had a question—"

"Oh, of course you do. Why else would you call? Just to chat, say hello? Hardly. Very presumptuous of you,

Paige, to come asking for favors after what you've done to me with Elena."

"I haven't done—"

"I don't know what you've been telling her about me but, let me assure you, I will set her straight. I understand you feel threatened in your friendship with her, but—"

"Cassandra," I said sharply. "I haven't said anything to Elena about you. Why would I? If she's not taking your calls, then I'd suggest you ask her why not. Or better yet, ask yourself."

"What's that supposed to—"

"It has nothing to do with me, that's all I'm saying. Believe me, I have better things to do than sabotage your friendships. No one else's world revolves around you, Cassandra."

"Did you call me to insult me, Paige?"

"No, I called to see how you're doing."

"Very funny."

"No, I'm serious. I'm in the midst of a murder investigation and your name came up—"

"Oh, and you suspect me, do you? How . . . thoughtful."

"No, I don't suspect you," I said through gritted teeth. Sometimes, carrying on a conversation with Cassandra was like paddling upstream during a hurricane. "The victims had all their blood and I'm sure you wouldn't waste a free meal. I'm calling because your name came up, so I was concerned. Has everything been okay there?"

"Are you saying I'm in danger? How long did you know this before you deigned to call?"

"About two minutes."

A pause, as her brain whirred to think up some way to turn my concern into a slight.

"What's going on there?" she asked.

"A murder investigation, like I said. There have been several deaths—"

"And you haven't notified the council?"

I counted to three. Across the room, Lucas pointed to the minibar. I rolled my eyes.

"It's not council business," I said. "It's Cabal—"

"Well, then, it can't concern me, can it? Cabals will have nothing to do with vampires. So obviously I'm neither a suspect nor a potential victim."

"Guess not," I said. "Must be a mistake. I'll see you at the next council—"

"Don't blow me off like that, Paige. If my name came up in this investigation, I want to know more about it. What's happening?"

I squeezed my eyes shut. I'd tweaked her curiosity and now she wouldn't let me off the phone without a full explanation. I didn't have time for that.

"Like you said, it must be a mistake—" I began.

"I didn't say that."

"Sorry for bothering you. If I hear anything else, I'll let you know. Thanks. Bye."

I dropped the phone into the cradle and collapsed onto the sofa.

"Jesus," Jaime said. "She sounds like a piece of work."

"Next time we have to make contact, I'll trade you," I said. "Your spook for my vamp."

"Think I'll stick with the spook. So it seems maybe my haunting isn't related to the case after all. This spirit saw me with you last week, you know Cassandra, and it wants to relay a message to her. Although, from what I heard, I can't imagine anyone *wanting* to talk to her."

"She's not that bad," I said. "We just don't get along."

"Maybe, but she *is* a vampire. Gotta be a whole passel of spooks in the next world because of her, just biding their time waiting for her to show up. Maybe that's the message: When you die, we're gonna kill you . . . or something like that. Course, they'll be waiting a long, long time."

"Not for Cassandra," I said. "She's an old one. Probably less than fifty years left on her quasi-immortality warranty."

"That doesn't matter, though, right? If anyone's waiting for her on the other side, they'll be disappointed, since vamps don't go there."

Both Lucas and I looked up. "They don't?"

"Hoo-ha, look at that. The necro knows something the whiz kids don't. Vamps are dead already, remember? So where do the dead go when they die? There's a stumper. All I know is there are no dead vampires in the ghost world. My opinion? *This* is their afterlife. When their time card runs out, poof, they're gone. And that's your undead lesson for today. Now it's time to get back to work. Or should I grab take-out first? We missed lunch and it's almost dinnertime."

"You have contact calls to make," I said. "My only contacts are council members, who know next to nothing about Cabal business. So I'll get dinner. What does everyone want?"

"What I want is for you to take a break," Lucas said. "You've been—"

"I'm fine."

"When I saw you dashing through the bookstore, Paige, you looked pale enough to *be* Jaime's ghost. And, as well as you might think you're hiding it, don't think I've failed to notice that you wince every time you sit or stand. As for dinner—" He lifted his cell phone. "Room service. Wonderful invention. Go lie down. Please."

"But I—"

"Paige . . ."

"The files on Joey and Matthew," I said. "We still haven't read them—"

He handed me the files. "Read them in bed, then."

I hesitated, then took the files and left them to their phone calls.

I fell asleep reading the files and didn't awake until after nine. Lucas, having suspected I'd drift off, had ordered me a sandwich and salad earlier. He'd also removed my clothing, probably assuming I was down for the night. When I got up, I thought of redressing, but it seemed a waste of effort, so I just pulled on my kimono. Decent enough. It wasn't like I hadn't seen Jaime in less.

Jaime had reserved the adjoining room, and was in it finishing her calls, but when I awoke, she came over to fill me in. Both she and Lucas had canvased their contacts and found no one who'd heard so much as the vaguest rumor about a supernatural living in Ohio who'd recently had contact or trouble with the Cabals. Even Raoul hadn't been able to help. Lucas was disappointed, but not surprised. When you lived so far off the Cabal grid, it was unlikely you'd have any opportunity to clash with them.

Knowing the Cincinnati connection might be a false lead, Lucas and Jaime had broadened their questions to include any supernatural targeted by the Cabals in the past two years. That led to a list of twenty names, plus half a dozen promises to call back with more information. Of those names, though, neither of us could see any whose beef against the Cabals was great enough to launch a murderous rampage. The most common complaints were being refused Cabal employment, or being harassed because *they* refused Cabal employment. No one would ever kill teenagers over something like that.

We hoped that when the other contacts called back with their lists, we'd see more likely possibilities.

"And until then?" I said. "I didn't see much in the crime-scene files, but we should probably go through them together. Let me grab—"

Lucas put a restraining hand on my knee. "Tomorrow. We've done enough today, and I believe we've earned ourselves an hour or two of respite."

"We could order in a movie," Jaime said.

I said nothing, but Lucas caught my underenthused look. He pushed to his feet, crossed the room, and tugged the scroll tube from his suitcase. When he glanced over at me, I grinned.

I turned to Jaime. "Would you mind if we skipped the movie? My brain's still whirring, and I really need a more active distraction. Lucas and I have this spell we've been dying to practice."

"Spell-casting practice?" she said. "Sounds like work to me."

I grinned. "Never, especially not when it's a new spell. You can never have too many spells."

She laughed. "You kids are such keeners. You're so cute. So what does your new spell do?"

"Lowers a target's core body temperature five or six degrees, inducing moderate hypothermia."

Jaime looked from Lucas to me. "Uh-huh. Okay, I gotta ask: What the hell do you guys need a spell like that for?"

"We both have a limited range of lethal spells."

"And . . . that's a bad thing?"

"It can be. Don't worry. We're both very responsible spell-casters. We'd never misuse our power. Oh, hey, if you don't mind sticking around though, we could use a target."

"Target?"

"Well, we can't know for sure whether the spell works without a target."

Jaime stood. "I hear my television calling. You kids have fun."

"We will."

Lucas waited for Jaime to leave, then plunked down beside me.

"Alone at last," he murmured.

I snatched the scroll from him, unwound and read it. "So how are we doing this? Straight-up spell-casting? Or fun and games?"

"Do you need to ask? The decision, though, should really be yours. If you're too tired, or too sore—"

"Oh, I feel fine." I grinned. "Fine enough, anyway. Strip spell-casting okay?"

"Better than okay." He looked down at my kimono. "Although you would appear to be at an initial disadvantage."

"You arguing?"

A slow grin as he pulled me to him. "No, not at all."

We didn't get the spell working, having exhausted our— or my—store of energy before a successful cast. It didn't matter. It *used* to matter. Success or failure at spell-casting practice used to matter a lot, to both of us, and we'd both admitted to hours or even days of frustration following a failure. But now that we almost always practiced together, it had become a game rather than a test. And, no matter whether we cast a new spell successfully or not, practicing together did have one definite advantage—it meant we never left a session feeling frustrated.

I'm Not Dead Yet

WE AWOKE AT SEVEN. JAIME POPPED OVER MINUTES LATER, and from the looks of things, hadn't slept more than an hour or two. While Lucas picked up breakfast, I took a quick shower. I'd just stepped out when someone rapped at our door. Lucas probably, with his hands full again.

"Could you grab that?" I called to Jaime.

I dressed, then opened the bathroom door to find Jaime standing there.

"Vampire at the door," she said.

"Seriously?"

"Seriously."

I sighed. "Please tell me it's not Cassandra."

"Short auburn hair? Looks about my age? Perfect makeup? Designer outfit?"

"Shit," I said, leaning against the wall.

"How about I don't invite her in?"

"Unfortunately, that doesn't work. Cassandra goes where she pleases, invited or not, wanted or not. Crosses, holy water, icy glares, nothing keeps her out."

"I heard that, Paige," Cassandra called from the main room. "Stop hiding in the bathroom and tell me what this is all about."

I walked through the bedroom into the living area. Cassandra was lounging by the window, taking in the sunlight and, sadly, not bursting into flame.

I turned to Jaime. "Cassandra, this is—"

"I know who she is," Cassandra said. "I have a television."

"Oh, but you two had already introduced yourselves— No, wait..." I looked at Jaime. "You didn't know her name. So how'd you know she was a vampire?"

"Easy. It's like you witches and sorcerers can recognize one another. I'm a necro. She's dead. So I can tell. Only dead things walking around are vamps. Well, there are zombies, but they don't smell like French perfume."

"Don't be ridiculous," Cassandra said, fixing Jaime with a glower. "I'm not dead."

"Of course you are. So you came all this way—?"

"I am *not* dead."

Jaime slanted me an eye-roll. "Sure, whatever. Now—"

The hall door opened. Lucas walked through, then stopped. He looked at Cassandra, then down at his tray of breakfast for three.

"Don't worry," Jaime said. "She doesn't eat. Well, she does, but even you aren't that hospitable."

"Ah, Cassandra, I presume," he said, laying the tray on the dinette table.

"Cassandra, this is Lucas Cortez," I said. "Lucas, Cassandra DuCharme."

Cassandra's gaze skimmed over Lucas, assessing and dismissing him in a millisecond. Anger darted through me, not so much at the insult as at the coolly confident way she did it, with a look that said, if she had wanted him, she could have him. Now I knew how Elena felt.

"Cassandra's just leaving," I said. "Seems she took a wrong turn on her way somewhere else."

"I'm not leaving until I get an explanation."

"First, we don't owe you an explanation. Second, if I thought you'd leave once we gave it, I'd tell you in a heartbeat. We're very busy, and as much as I appreciate your interest—"

"You said my name came up in reference to this case. I want to know who, how, and why."

"Don't know, don't know, and don't know," Jaime said. "It didn't tell us."

"It?"

"The spook."

Cassandra crossed her arms. "Spook?"

"Ghost," I said. "Or maybe not—we haven't determined that yet. A spiritual entity of some kind has been pestering Jaime and it has something to do with you. That's all we know."

"Me? Why on earth would a ghost want to communicate with me?"

"Maybe because you put him there," Jaime said. "Dinner coming back to haunt you. Literally."

Before Cassandra could answer, our room phone rang.

"Jesus," Jaime muttered. "Grand Central Station."

Lucas picked up the extension from the side table. He announced himself, then waited. His gaze flicked to me, a slight frown on his lips.

"Yes, of course, perhaps we—" He paused. "Oh, well, certainly then. Come up." Lucas hung up and turned to me. "That was Sean Nast."

"Savannah's—Kristof's son?"

"Yes, he has something to tell us, about the case. He was phoning from the lobby."

"You want me to skedaddle?" Jaime said.

"No need. He knows from the trial that you've been working with us. But perhaps . . ."

He looked at Cassandra.

"I'm not going anywhere until I get some answers," she said.

"Yes, I understand, but given the animosity between the Cabals and vampires—"

"It's not animosity," Cassandra said. "To have animosity, you have to acknowledge that the other party exists. You needn't worry. I will be as the Cabals wish me to be: invisible. Since no one can outwardly recognize vampires"—she shot a pointed look at Jaime—"there's no need for him to know what I am."

A knock at the door. Lucas opened it. Sean Nast walked in, followed by a man who could only be a Cabal bodyguard. Sean turned to his guard.

"Wait outside," he murmured.

"Mr. Nast said—" the guard began.

"Please," Sean said.

The guard nodded and retreated into the hall. Lucas closed the door behind him.

"Granddad's getting paranoid," Sean said. "I feel like I'm twelve again."

"Sean, this is Jaime Vegas," Lucas said. "Jaime, Sean Nast, Thomas Nast's grandson."

Sean grinned. "Hey, my frat watches you on *The Keni Bales Show* every month."

As they shook hands, Sean's gaze flicked to Cassandra.

"Sean, this is Cassandra," Lucas said. "Cassandra, Sean Nast."

If Sean noticed the lack of a surname for Cassandra, he gave no sign of it, only shook her hand with a "Pleased to meet you," then turned to us.

"Tyler Boyd is missing." He glanced at me and added, "That's the Boyd CEO's youngest son. He's seventeen."

"He's missing? Since when?"

"We aren't sure. Tyler went to his hotel room around eleven last night. When he didn't show up for breakfast, his dad sent someone to get him. His bodyguard was in the room, dead, and Tyler was gone. Mr. Boyd called Granddad and the Cabals have been out searching ever since."

"Good," Lucas said. "My father has excellent shaman trackers."

"That's the problem. They didn't call your dad, or anyone in your Ca—your family's Cabal."

"What?" I said. "But he went missing here, right? In Miami?"

"And the Cortezes have all the resources here, I know. It's crazy. I am so fucking—" He glanced at Jaime and Cassandra. "Sorry. I'm just fed up with their crap. Joey's dead and now Tyler's missing and all the Cabals can do is bicker about who's to blame and who's trying to take control of the investigation. Without your dad's trackers and CSIs, all we have is a bunch of VPs and bodyguards milling around the city, hoping to bump into Tyler."

"So you want me to call my father."

Sean rubbed his hand over his chin. "Yeah, I know you're on the outs with him, and I hate to ask, but I don't know what else to do. I tried phoning his company switchboard but, of course, they just kept routing me to some junior, junior assistant who won't even relay a message. If you have your father's direct number, I'll make the call."

"Your family wouldn't appreciate that. Better let me handle it."

"I'm not worried about what my family thinks. You can tell your dad I'm the one who told you to call."

"I'll call him, because he has the resources to process the scene and search for Tyler. I won't, however, tell him it was at your instigation. You're angry, with good reason, but that's not a decision you want to make right now."

"I don't care—"

"Lucas is right," I said. "Not only don't you want to start a rift with your family, but you don't want to widen the one between your Cabals. It'll only make things worse."

Sean nodded. "Okay, but after you make the call, will you come to the Boyds' hotel with me? I came here because I wanted to get your dad involved, but also because I wanted to get you two involved. So far you've done a hell of a lot more than the Cabals."

"We'll certainly go," Lucas said. "But I believe it would be best if we arrived independently. Why don't you give Paige the hotel address while I phone my father?"

When Lucas was gone, Sean glanced at Jaime and Cassandra, neither of whom was making any attempt to pretend they weren't listening. He obviously had something else to say to me, so I offered to walk him down to his car. The bodyguard followed us to the elevator. While we waited, Sean gave me the address for the Boyds' hotel.

"So, you, uh . . . ." Sean said as we stepped onto the elevator, "you've got someone with Savannah, right? She's someplace safe?"

"With friends," I said. When I saw him hesitate, I added, "Supernaturals."

"Good, good. I figured that. I tried mentioning it to my uncle, that someone should ask whether she's being protected, since she's a potential target. I can't mention it to Granddad. After . . . after what happened with my dad, he . . . well, we aren't allowed to talk about Savannah. My uncle wouldn't ask Benicio about her, either. I think they . . ."

"Would rather pretend she doesn't exist? After last spring, I'm just as happy if they do."

He shoved his hands in his pockets and rocked on his heels. I should have kept my mouth shut. Nothing stops a conversation deader than reminding someone that his family is responsible for sending your life swirling down the gutter.

The elevator doors opened. I motioned for Sean to wait as I jotted down an e-mail address.

"This is Savannah's," I said. "If you ever want to say hi, introduce yourself, this might be the easiest way to do it. If you'd rather not, I understand."

He took the paper. "I'll do that. I'd like to . . . make contact. It's not right, ignoring her." He folded the sheet into quarters and tucked it into his wallet. As he did, he looked down at a tattered photograph in his ID holder. "You wouldn't have a picture of her, would you?"

"Sure do." I took out my wallet, and flipped through my card holder, which was filled with photos. "Someday I need to break down and buy a purse-size photo album, like those little old ladies who show you all their grandchildren while you're waiting in line at the bank."

I took out two. One was Savannah on her first-ever horseback ride that summer; the other was Savannah, Lucas, and Adam shooting hoops near our place last month.

"Cute kid," he said, smiling. "Definitely got Dad's eyes."

"You can keep that one," I said, pointing to the horseback photo. "I have it on file at home."

He thanked me and we said our good-byes.

I returned to our room to find Cassandra and Jaime sitting at opposite ends of the sofa, Jaime reading her latest magazine, Cassandra coiled to pounce the moment I walked in.

"So the killer is targeting Cabal families?" she said. "The Nasts first, and now the Boyds?"

I gave her a very brief rundown of the events to date.

"The grandson of a CEO?" Her frown deepened. "So it's a revenge crime."

"Uh, yes. That's what we—"

Lucas opened the bedroom door.

"Did you get hold of your father?" I asked.

Lucas nodded. "He's on his way to the hotel with a team. I told him we'll be arriving shortly, and he's promised to clear the way for us. That should be simple enough. I suspect anyone with the authority to challenge him will already be out searching for Tyler. Shall we go?"

Cassandra stood and picked up her purse.

"Uh-uh," I said. "This is very serious—"

"I realize that, Paige. You're looking for a missing person. A vampire is a far better tracker than a shaman."

I hesitated and glanced at Lucas. He nodded.

"Good," Cassandra said. "You can explain the rest of this matter on the way."

Predatory Insight

LUCAS HAD RENTED A CAR THE MORNING BEFORE, SO WE no longer needed to borrow Jaime's. She stayed behind in the hotel room and promised to call if anyone else showed up. Now, normally, if we have a guest in the car, I'll sit in the backseat. It's only polite. But Cassandra brings out the rude in me, so I slipped into the front passenger seat and left her to wrinkle her Donna Karan in the cramped rear.

It took us an infuriating forty-five minutes to reach the Boyds' hotel. Not only was it on the other side of the city, but we hit gridlock in a construction zone and might have been even later if Lucas hadn't navigated an alternate route down back roads.

On the way, I gave Cassandra a fuller overview. When we pulled into the hotel parking lot, she was still asking questions.

"I'm sorry to interrupt," Lucas said. "At the risk of offending you, Cassandra, I must ask that you, again, not reveal—"

"I have no intention of letting them know what I am."

"Thank you."

"It might be even better if Cassandra waited here," I said. "Until we start searching."

"Good idea. Cassandra, if you—"

The door banged shut. She was already striding toward the building.

"Or maybe not," I said.

"If we don't impede her involvement, perhaps she'll satisfy her curiosity faster."

"And go home faster?"

He gave a small smile. "That would be the idea."

Troy met us in the parking lot, then escorted us into the hotel, which looked more like a luxury condo complex than any temporary lodgings I'd ever seen.

From the outside of Tyler Boyd's second-floor suite, one would never guess a murder had recently been committed there or that a crime-scene team was ripping the room apart. Only when the door opened did the noise within escape.

Two men were working in the living area, one taking photos and the other running a handheld vacuum over the sofa. A third man appeared from a back room, carrying what looked like a laptop case. He exchanged a hasty hello with Lucas, then hurried out the door.

The murdered half-demon guard lay sprawled across the remains of the coffee table, covered in glass shards and wood splinters. His head was twisted to the side, face fixed in a grimace. I fought the urge to look away from that dead stare. Beside me, Cassandra leaned over the corpse, eyes studying it with detachment. I tried to emulate her, to see this body not as a person but as a piece of evidence.

At first I thought the guard's throat had been cut. Then

I saw a length of wire draped over his neck and realized he'd been strangled with it.

"Our coroner believes that was done postmortem."

Benicio's voice came from behind us. He looked at Cassandra. His gaze passed over her with curiosity, and perhaps a little interest, but when we didn't introduce her, he didn't ask. Maybe he trusted Lucas's judgment. Or maybe, knowing his son's eclectic collection of contacts, he didn't want to ask.

"Dennis has already made some preliminary observations." Benicio called the security chief from another room. "Dennis? Would you please share your findings with Lucas and Paige? And answer any questions they might have?"

"Of course, sir." Dennis motioned to the dead guard. "We think he was approached from behind and possibly injected with something. That would explain why he didn't fight back."

"Didn't fight?" I looked at the shattered table. "Oh, I see. The damage is from him falling."

"Falling very hard." Lucas knelt and prodded a black chunk by the guard's hand.

As I crouched I caught a familiar scent, one that brought back memories of Girl Scout summer camp. Burnt firewood. Pieces of charred wood surrounded the guard's clenched hands.

"An Aduro," I said. "He grabbed for the table as he fell and burned it, meaning he wasn't dead when he collapsed."

Cassandra examined the wire embedded in the guard's neck. "No blood."

"Which indicates it was done postmortem," Dennis said. "Plus the fact that it's unlikely anyone could have garroted a man his size, with his powers."

"What about Tyler?" I said. "Did he escape or was he taken?"

Dennis waved us to the bathroom. We stepped inside. Benicio stayed in the doorway, looking on. Across the room, a slight, red-haired man examined the window ledge with some kind of electronic scanner. The window itself was broken. There were a few bits of glass on the inside, but most presumably had fallen out.

Lucas turned around to look at the broken door jamb. "So either Tyler was in here when the killer arrived, or he managed to get in here before being attacked. Then the killer broke into the bathroom, but—" Lucas turned to the window. "Tyler was already gone, out that window. Simon? Any indication that the killer staged the window break?"

The red-haired man shook his head. "No, sir. There are blood smears on one shard. I'll need a sample from the Boyds' lab to match it, but the DNA is definitely from their family, so I'm assuming it's Tyler's. There are no signs of struggle or blood in the bathroom. I found Nike prints on the ground below, imprinted hard, indicating someone jumped from this window."

"So we're assuming Tyler fled," Lucas said. "That's logical. I doubt the killer would take him out of the hotel. Too risky. He's always killed on-site before. He's not likely to change his methods now."

Benicio's cell phone rang. After a few clipped words, he hung up. "Tyler's been found." He saw my expression and added, "He's alive."

"Was he chased?" I said. "If he was, then the killer could still be in the area—"

"He's not," Cassandra said. "He's moved on."

"What?"

The barest eye-roll, as if her conclusion was so simple

it shouldn't require an explanation. "He's a hunter. He strikes at the easy targets. When they're no longer easy, he finds another."

"So you think he chased Tyler—" I began.

"The moment the boy escaped, your killer abandoned him. As Lucas said, he kills on-site. He'll hang a girl in a tree or drape a boy over a car, but that's only for outrage value. He's a hunter. He kills them where he finds them, and he kills efficiently. When that other attack was interrupted, he left the boy alive rather than risk discovery. He's not about to chase this young man through the streets of Miami."

"By moved on, you mean—" I looked at Lucas. "To another member of a central family. That's what Esus said. With Joey Nast, he reached the top level, and he'll stay there now."

Cassandra nodded. "Anything else would be a regression. However, with each step he takes, he makes it more difficult for himself. He'll need to take advantage of every possible moment when security might be lax, such as—"

"Such as when the Cabals believe the killer is stalking another victim. When they're all out searching for him. Lucas? Who are the other teens? Are there any in your family? Nephews—"

"I have an eleven- and a twelve-year-old grandson," Benicio said. "Hector's boys. I tripled their guard as soon as Griffin's son was killed, and I've moved them to a secure location outside of Miami. As for others, Lionel St. Cloud has one boy, Stephen. He's eighteen. Then there are a few more teenage Nast grandsons, and Frank Boyd has several nephews around Tyler's age."

"Stephen St. Cloud," Lucas said. "He's already hit the Nasts. If he can't get to a Cortez, he'll go for a St. Cloud."

"I'll call Lionel—"

"Where are they staying?" Lucas asked.

Benicio hesitated, finger poised over his phone key-pad. "The Fairfield over in South Beach. Just wait while I—"

We were already out the door.

"Why the hell didn't you tell us what you were thinking?" I said, twisting in my seat to glare at Cassandra as Lucas pulled away from the hotel parking lot.

"But I did."

"You knew the killer had moved on the moment you saw that Tyler had escaped, but you said nothing. Then, when you did bother to tell us he'd moved on, you had to be prodded to explain what you meant by that. This isn't a game, Cassandra."

"Isn't it?" she said. "Your killer might disagree."

"You know what I mean. You should have told us immediately, warned us—"

"So you'd have left a few minutes earlier? I intended to explain myself, Paige. I simply didn't see the need to rush."

"You—"

Lucas glanced over, telling me to ignore Cassandra, but I couldn't.

"A young man might be dead and you didn't see the need to rush!"

Her green eyes met mine, sculpted eyebrows arching. "Well, if he's dead, there's certainly no reason to hurry, is there? If you mean that you might have saved him had I told you sooner, I can hardly imagine that sixty seconds would make a difference one way or the other. Yes, a young man is in danger. Yes, he might die. Tragic, but certainly nothing that doesn't happen every hour of every day."

"Oh, well, then that makes it okay."

"I didn't say it did, Paige. I was merely pointing out that death is a tragedy but, ultimately, an unavoidable one. You can't save everyone, as difficult as that may be for you to accept."

"I'm not—" I snapped my jaw shut, swallowed the rest of the sentence, and forced myself to face the windshield again.

Lucas's cell phone rang. He handed it to me.

"Paige Winterbourne," I answered.

A slight pause. Then Benicio asked, "Is Lucas there?"

"He's driving. Did you get in touch with Lionel St. Cloud?"

Another pause, as if considering whether to insist I pass him over to his son. "Yes, I called him, and he tried to call Stephen, but there's been no answer. Both of Stephen's uncles came to search for Tyler, but we did manage to find a cousin still at the hotel. He reports that Stephen's room is locked and no one's answering the door. Now, Paige, I've dispatched my search team to the Fairfield. They may be a few minutes behind you, but they will be there quickly. I—" He paused. "The killer may still be at that hotel. I don't want Lucas going in-side."

"I understand that," I said. "I can ask him to stay out while I go in, but—"

"I mean for you to both stay out, at least until you're accompanied by the search team. An extra minute or two isn't going to make much difference."

"So I've heard," I said. "But I'm not willing to take that chance. Just tell your team to hurry and meet us inside."

I pressed the disconnect button. As I was passing the

phone back to Lucas, it rang. He reached over and turned it off.

After another minute, we moved into the center lane. To our left stood a large Spanish-style villa. A discreet sign near the palm-flanked drive announced we'd arrived at the Fairfield.

Unnatural-Born Killer

THE FAIRFIELD WASN'T NEARLY AS OPULENT AS THE BOYDS' hotel, though I suspected the price was still at least double what we were paying. It had that kind of graciously understated atmosphere that doesn't come at an understated price. Stephen St. Cloud's room was on the third floor. When the elevator was slow in coming, we took the stairs.

We emerged at the far end of a quiet corridor. At the opposite end, a dark-haired man in his twenties lounged by the elevators. He didn't glance over until we stopped outside Stephen's room. Then he did a double take, and strode toward us, glowering.

"Good morning, Tony," Lucas said.

"What the hell are you doing—"

"My father sent me. Have you been able to get into Stephen's room yet?"

"Not unless I can walk through walls. We need a locksmith."

"No," I said. "You just need a witch."

I cast my top-level unlock spell. The last words were still leaving my mouth as Cassandra reached for the door handle. When I finished, she pushed it open and walked inside, leaving us in the hall.

"No deadbolt or chain," I said, checking the lock mechanism as I walked through. "Gotta love these card-locks. Any witch could walk right in."

Cassandra strode from the living area into the bed-room. We'd barely made it out of the front hall when Cassandra walked from the bedroom and brushed past us on her way to the door again.

"I have it," she said. "Let's go."

"Guess that means he's not here," I said. "I don't see any signs of a struggle, so he seems to have left on his own. Tony? Any idea where he might have gone?"

Tony glanced at me, then turned to Lucas.

"What?" I said. "Is my voice pitched outside a sor-cerer's range? Lucas, please, interpret."

"Do you know where Stephen might be?" Lucas asked.

"Out grabbing breakfast, I guess. Everyone else left to search for Tyler, and Step was bitching about being left behind. He hates being treated like a child."

"So he pulled a snit fit and took off," I said. "Very ma-ture. Please tell me he has a bodyguard with him."

"Does he have a bodyguard?" Lucas interpreted for the invisible witch.

"Uh, yeah," Tony said. "Me."

We stared at him.

Tony shrugged. "Well, his dad needed Step's regular guard to help in the search, so he told me to watch him, make sure he stayed in his room."

"Which you did admirably," I said.

Tony glared at me. "He's eighteen, an adult. I don't know what all the fuss is about. If you'll excuse me, I have work to do."

"Don't worry," I called after him as he stalked off. "We'll

find Stephen ourselves. But thanks for offering to help us look."

Cassandra popped her head back through the doorway. "Are you two coming?"

In the few seconds it took us to reach the door, she'd made it to the elevator and pushed the button. A minute later we were heading for the main lobby. Cassandra paused partway there, head turning from side to side, eyes narrowing. I don't understand how vampires track people, and I've never dared ask Cassandra. All I know is that it's not by scent, yet it's like tracking by scent in that they pick it up at the source and the trail fades over time.

Cassandra wheeled and strode back down the hall. I looked at Lucas, shrugged, and hurried to catch up. As she shoved past a middle-aged couple, the man muttered an epithet after her. Not stopping, she glanced over her shoulder, eyes meeting his. The man looked away fast, his arm going around his wife's waist as he picked up their pace.

Cassandra veered into a side hall. I turned the corner as she pushed a door clearly marked EMERGENCY EXIT. Before I could call a warning, she flung the door open. Sunlight flooded in, momentarily blinding me. I braced for the alarms, but none came.

Cassandra walked though, letting the door swing shut behind her. Lucas grabbed it before it hit me. We stepped outside. When the sun-blindness cleared, I found myself at the edge of a half-filled parking lot.

"Damn," I murmured. "You can't track him if he took a car."

Ignoring me, Cassandra marched into the parking lot. From the front of the building came the squeal of tires peeling into the lot.

"The search team?" I asked Lucas.

"I doubt they'd make their arrival so obvious, but they should be here by now. I should fill them in. Will you be all right?"

"I'll get a speed-walk workout," I said. "But I'll be fine. You go on."

I went after Cassandra. She'd stopped about twenty feet from the door.

"Can you—?" I began.

She started off again, darting between two minivans. I sighed and broke into a jog. She moved fast, taking a roughly diagonal path across the parking lot, weaving around cars. When I stepped behind her, she wheeled so fast I jumped back. Her eyes narrowed, and I was preparing a retort when I noticed her gaze was fixed somewhere behind me. I turned but saw nothing.

"Someone's here," she said.

In a hotel parking lot, that didn't strike me as strange, but before I could say so, she strode past me and backtracked a row. Then she stopped and surveyed the lot.

"Maybe we should—" I began.

She disappeared between two cars. I looked around. Beyond the distant road noise, the lot was still and quiet. I cast a sensing spell. Nothing. Not even Cassandra, who should have been within range. Damned spell. I really needed more practice.

I stood on tiptoes. Sunlight glinted off Cassandra's auburn hair as it bobbed between the cars. As I headed toward her, I heard the soft fall of footsteps behind me. I slowed, but didn't turn. Instead I glanced at my reflection in the side of an SUV. The gap behind me was empty.

I was turning my attention back to Cassandra when a shadow flickered past, the metal side of the SUV darkening for a split second. I whirled, casting my sensing spell as I turned. This time the spell caught something, but farther off, to my left. At the same moment I heard the clack of women's shoes to my right and the equally purposeful footfalls of the person approaching from my left. On my right, the footsteps stopped as Cassandra emerged from between two cars.

"There you are," she said. "You have to keep up, Paige. I can't be—"

I turned left. Again, it was who I expected. Lucas covered the distance between us, expression blocked by the sun.

"Strange," I said to Cassandra. "I sensed Lucas, but not you."

She frowned.

"With my spell, I mean. It didn't pick you up."

"Yes, well, your spells aren't exactly foolproof, Paige."

"Or it could be the whole undead thing, I guess."

Her lips tightened. "Now, don't you start on that, too. I am not. . ."

As she spoke, I saw Lucas's face and my gut tightened. I didn't hear the rest of what Cassandra said.

"They found him, didn't they?" I said.

Lucas nodded, and I knew they hadn't found Stephen alive.

Stephen had been killed in his car, shot in the temple, then placed in the reclined driver's seat, with sunglasses on and a ball cap pulled down to cover his wound. To anyone walking past, it would look as if he was dozing in his car. Odd, but not alarming.

I told Lucas that I'd had the feeling I was being followed. Cassandra concurred, and Lucas deployed the team to search the lot while we stayed with the body. If I hadn't said anything, would Cassandra have mentioned her suspicions? I doubted it, yet not because I thought she'd intentionally prevent us from finding the killer. Why would she? She didn't care. And that, really, was the crux to understanding Cassandra. She didn't care.

An hour later, the team concluded that the killer was gone. I'd have liked to stay, to hear their findings, but it's difficult enough to conduct a clandestine crime-scene investigation in a hotel parking lot without having on-lookers.

"You've been quiet," Lucas murmured as we headed for our car.

"Thinking."

When I didn't go on, he said, "Share?"

I motioned that I'd discuss it in the car. I waited until we were on the highway before speaking. I told myself I was collecting my thoughts, but I think I was waiting to see whether Cassandra would speak first. She didn't.

"He's a hunter," I said. "He strikes fast, leaves the bodies where he killed them, uses the most convenient method, and changes plans if things get complicated. An experienced killer."

"Yes, as Esus said—" Lucas began.

He noticed I'd directed my comment to Cassandra, and stopped. She continued staring out the side window. Either she was ignoring me, which wouldn't be surprising, or I'd drawn the wrong conclusion, which, given my track record of late, wouldn't be surprising either.

"He's an expert stalker, too," I said. "Dana never heard him coming. Joey didn't have any warning. Even a druid god didn't hear him attack. I'm sure he was following me in the parking lot, but I only heard the odd footfall, saw one flash of movement. And I couldn't pick him up with my sensing spell."

Lucas glanced across his shoulder at me. "So you're suggesting that Esus may have been mistaken, that our killer may indeed be noncorporeal, a demon or another entity."

"I wouldn't call it a demon," I said. "Though some may argue the point. The kind of entity I'm thinking of lives right here in our world. The killer took down a two-hundred-plus-pound trained bodyguard. Felled him like a tree. That doesn't happen by jabbing him in the back with a hypodermic. He'd still have had a moment or two to fight. This kind of killer has a special way to incapacitate his victims. But so far, he's only used it twice—on Dana and this guard. That's why both had neck injuries. To cover the marks. Marks that are very difficult to detect, but ones that I'm sure every Cabal autopsy looks for."

"A vampire bite," Lucas said.

Cassandra nodded. "That would be my interpretation as well."

I bit back the urge to scream, "And when the hell were you going to say so?"

Lucas turned into our hotel parking lot. "The only problem with that scenario is that I can't imagine what grudge a vampire could possibly bear against a Cabal."

"I'm sure you couldn't," Cassandra murmured.

Lucas's eyes flickered to the rearview mirror. "No, Cassandra, I can't. But if you can, perhaps you could tell us."

For a moment, she said nothing. Then she sighed, as if put upon once again to explain the obvious.

"Cabals will have nothing to do with vampires," she said.

"Precisely," Lucas said. "They have a strict policy against dealing with either werewolves or vampires, which is why I can't imagine..." He stopped, then looked through the mirror at Cassandra. "Or, perhaps, that is not so much the argument *against* such a possibility as *for* it."

"For money and power, the Cabals are the biggest game in town," I said. "Maybe someone's tired of being kept off the playing field."

Stand-in Mother-in-law

WE RETURNED TO OUR HOTEL ROOM. JAIME HEARD US COME in and zipped over for an update.

"So my spook wasn't trying to get you to contact Cassandra," Jaime said, popping the top off a Diet Pepsi. "It just wanted to tell us that we're looking for a vampire."

"Probably," I said. "*Salem's Lot* is about vampires, and Cassandra would be the vampire I know best. So that fits the theory. This does change the possible motivation, though. It doesn't take nearly as much to send a vamp on a killing spree. They're already expert killers—it's not as big a deal for them. I'd say we now have two more likely motivations. One, a vampire tried signing up with the Cabals or cutting a deal with them, got rebuffed, and decided to show them why you don't mess with the undead. Two, a vampire is just pissed off in general at the Cabal no-vampire policy and is making a statement."

"A crusading vampire?" Jaime said. "The only vamps I've ever met aren't exactly the altruistic type." She glanced at Cassandra. "Exhibit one."

Cassandra gave her a cool stare. "Ah, yes. And remind me again why you're here? More to do with a nagging spirit than a nagging conscience, if I recall correctly."

Jaime flushed. "Well, I've solved that problem and I'm still here, aren't I?"

"So your ghost is still being quiet?" I asked.

"So far, so good."

"Cassandra," Lucas said. "If we are dealing with a vampire, then this is your area of expertise. Given Paige's two possible motivations, should we consider both equally or concentrate on a revenge scenario?"

"Vampires are capable of crusading for a cause," she said, easing onto the sofa. "Though typically only one that benefits vampires, as this one would. You'd be looking for a young vampire. As with any race, the youngest are the most idealistic, the most likely to work for change. The older ones know their energies are better spent pursuing more realistic, individualistic causes." She slanted a look at Lucas and me. "You'll learn that soon enough."

"Not if I can help it," I murmured.

"The pursuit of righteousness is romantic, immature, and, ultimately, self-destructive, Paige. One would think you'd have learned that lesson this spring with Samantha."

"Savannah," I said. "And the only thing I learned was that the purest form of evil isn't something like a Cabal. It's the person who's willing to sacrifice another to save herself."

Jaime's gaze followed our exchange with interest. Before she could comment, Lucas spoke.

"So, having decided that both avenues are equally likely, may I suggest we pursue both? The fact that we are likely now dealing with a vampire explains why none of my contacts heard of such a situation, since vampires have little contact with other supernaturals. That means I'll have to go directly to the Cabals for information or, more accurately, through my father, who can ask about specific instances where a vampire may have had Cabal contact.

Meanwhile, perhaps Cassandra could help Paige contact the vampire community, assess the general mood and any Cabal-related rumors."

"I don't believe I offered to help," Cassandra said. "This isn't my problem."

"No?" Jaime said. "Isn't that why you serve on the inter-racial council? So if a vamp goes rogue, you can take him out? Every race does it, monitors their own. We have to."

"This isn't the same. You're asking me to *betray* my own. To sneak Paige into their midst and gather information to be used against us."

"No," I said. "We're asking you to sneak me in to gather info that can be used to help you—all of you. Cabals don't like vamps now. How do you think they're going to react when they find out it's a vampire who has been killing their kids?"

"I'm not concerned about retaliation."

"Good. Then you can go home, Cassandra. I can get what Lucas wants without you."

Cassandra's lips curved as she reclined against the cushions. "You need to work on your bluffing, Paige. Your technique is far too obvious."

I grabbed my purse and headed for the bedroom.

"It won't work, Paige," Cassandra called after me. "Your only other vampire contact is Lawrence and he's been in Europe for two years. You'll be lucky if he remembers your name. He certainly won't rush back here to help you."

As my fingers grazed the bedroom door handle, I stopped. I knew I should take the high road, phone my contact, and ignore her taunts. But I couldn't, not with Cassandra. I flipped open my Palm, clicked on my phone book, found an entry, strode back, and held it up for Cassandra.

She read it and blinked. And, in that small reaction, I took more pleasure than I liked to admit.

"Aaron?" she said. "When did he give you—"

"After we rescued him from the compound. He told Jeremy and me that anytime we needed something vampire-related, we could call him."

"Jeremy might not appreciate your calling in a joint favor that doesn't benefit werewolves."

"Which is why I'll phone him first. But we both know he'll tell me to go ahead."

"Werewolves rescuing vampires?" Jaime murmured. "Someday, you have got to tell me this story. Well, Cass, looks like she's trumped you. Time to lay down your cards and go home."

"Is she here for a reason?" Cassandra said.

"I don't want to bicker with you, Cassandra," I said. "I appreciate what you did this morning, helping us hunt for Stephen, but please, go on home. We can handle this."

As my tone softened, the fire leached from her eyes. She sighed and reached for my Palm.

"Let me call Aaron," she said. "Save your marker for another time."

I hesitated. "Maybe that's not such a good idea. Unless I seriously misread things, Aaron seemed pretty miffed with you back at the compound."

"It was a misunderstanding."

"The last time he saw you, you turned him over to an angry Romanian mob and fled for your life. Call me crazy, but I don't think there's much wiggle room for mis-understanding there."

Across the room, Jaime snorted a laugh. Cassandra glared at her, then turned back to me.

"I didn't hand him over to the mob," she said. "I simply

left him there. I knew he could handle himself. Anyway, none of that matters now. We're back on good terms."

"Such good terms that you don't have his phone number?"

She plucked the Palm from my hand, marched into the bedroom, and closed the door.

Two hours later I was boarding a plane for Atlanta, to meet with Aaron. Unfortunately, I was not alone, having been unable to convince Cassandra that she had better things to do. I tried to be gracious by saying I'd understand if she preferred to fly first class. My kindness, though, only provoked a similar outpouring of generosity, and she treated me to a first-class seat next to hers.

I'd brought my laptop and, as soon as we were seated, set to work catching up on my business e-mail. Cassandra stayed quiet until the plane lifted off.

"I hear from Kenneth that you're trying to start a new Coven," she began.

"Not really," I mumbled, and typed faster.

"Well, that's good."

I stopped, fingers poised above the keyboard. Then, with great effort, I forced them back to the keys and resumed typing. Do not rise to the bait. Do not rise—

"I told him I couldn't imagine you'd do anything so foolish."

Type faster. Harder. Do not stop.

"I can understand why you'd want to. It must be very hard on your ego. Getting kicked out of your Coven. And as Leader, no less."

I willed my fingers back to the keyboard, but they ignored my brain's command, and kept clenching into fists instead.

"I suppose it was very satisfying for you, those few months as Coven Leader. You'd obviously want to recapture that sense of importance."

"It was never about being important. I just wanted to—"

I stopped and resumed typing.

"You just wanted to do what, Paige?"

The flight attendant stopped by. I ordered a coffee. Cassandra took wine.

"You wanted to do what, Paige?" Cassandra repeated when the server was gone.

I turned to look at her. "Don't needle me. You always do this. You're like one of those sitcom mothers-in-law, poking and prodding, feigning interest, but only looking for a soft spot, someplace to sneak in an insinuation, an insult."

"Isn't it possible that I'm not feigning interest? That I really do want to know more about you?"

"You've never been interested in me before."

"You've never been interesting before. But you're finally growing up, and I don't just mean getting older. In the last year or so, you've matured into an intriguing individual. Not necessarily someone I'd choose to be stranded on a desert island with, but conflict of opinion can make for more interesting relationships than common interests. If I challenge your opinions, it's because I'm curious to hear how you defend them."

"I don't want to defend them," I said. "Not now. Your questions feel like insults, Cassandra, and I don't want to deal with them."

To my surprise, she didn't say another word. Just sipped her wine, reclined her seat, and rested for the remainder of the flight.

Disconnected

VAMPIRES ARE A RACE OF CITY DWELLERS. THAT MAY SEEM obvious, since it's far easier to kill undetected in a city with hundreds of annual unsolved murders, rather than in a small town that might see a single homicide a year. In truth, though, that's not a major factor in their choice.

Real vampires aren't the marauding bloodsuckers you see on late-night TV, racking up a dozen victims every night. A real vampire only needs to kill once a year, though they must feed more often than that. Feeding is easy enough—if you ever pass out in a bar and wake up the next morning with a hangover that seems worse than normal, I'd suggest you check your neck. You may not find the marks, though. Unless you know what you're looking for, vampire bites are nearly impossible to see, and the aftereffects are no more debilitating than donating blood on an empty stomach.

Since a vampire bite is rarely fatal, it would be easy enough for vamps to live outside the city and commute for their annual kill. It might even be safer. The problem is that pesky semi-immortality. When you don't age, people notice. It may take a while, but they eventually start to ask what brand of moisturizer you're using. The smaller the town, the more people pay attention, and the more they talk. In a big city, a vampire could stay in one spot for fifteen to twenty years, and never hear more than a few snide Botox comments. Plus, there's the whole boredom issue. Small towns are great for raising a family, but if you're single and childless, Saturday nights on the front porch swing get a little dull after the first hundred years.

So, vampires like the city life. In North America, they also prefer the sunshine belt, with over half of the continent's vampires living below the Mason-Dixon line. Northern winters probably lose their appeal pretty quickly when you realize you could lie on the beach all day and never risk so much as a sunburn. And it's much easier to bite someone in a tank top than to gnaw through a parka.

Cassandra had arranged to meet Aaron in a bar on the south side of Atlanta. I'd never been to Atlanta, and our quick taxi ride from the airport to the bar didn't provide much opportunity for sightseeing. What I noticed most was how modern it was. It looked, well, it looked like a northern city, very high-tech, very efficient, very unsouthern. I'd expected something like Savannah or Charleston, but I saw little that reminded me of either. I suppose if I'd considered my history first, I'd have known better than to expect much Old South in Atlanta. General Sherman took care of that.

The taxi drove us to a neighborhood best described as working-class, with row houses, postage-stamp-size lawns, and streets lined with ten-year-old cars. The driver pulled up in front of a bar sandwiched between an auto-supply store and a Laundromat. The sign on the door read LUCKY

PETE'S BILLIARDS, but the BILLIARDS part had recently been stroked out.

Cassandra paid the driver, stepped from the car, looked at the bar, and shook her head. "Aaron, Aaron. Two hundred years old and you still haven't developed an iota of taste."

"Seems fine to me. Hey, look, the sign says Fridays are Ladies' Night. Cheap beer after four. Is it past four?"

"Unfortunately, yes."

I spotted Aaron on my first survey of the bar. I would say, with some certainty, most women would spot Aaron on their first survey of any bar. He's at least six feet two, broad-shouldered, and tanned, with sandy blond hair and a ruggedly handsome face. Aaron sat at the end of the bar, engrossed in a beer and a cigarette, and ignoring the glances of a secretarial quartet behind him. As Cassandra approached, she took in his muddy work boots, worn jeans, and mortar-dust-coated T-shirt.

"How nice of you to dress up for me, Aaron," she said.

"I just got off work. You're damned lucky I even agreed—" He saw me and blinked

"This is—" Cassandra began.

"Paige," Aaron said. "How're you doing?"

"Good." I slid onto the stool beside his. "How have you been?"

"Keeping out of trouble." A quick grin. "Mostly. And watching my back a little better. Still damn embarrassing, getting kidnapped like that. Beer?"

"Please."

He motioned to the bartender. "I won't ask you, Cass. There's nothing here you'd touch. Probably not even the patrons. Are you going to pull up a stool or just stand there?"

"This hardly seems the place for a private conversation," she said, then wheeled and headed for a booth near the back.

Aaron shook his head. I ordered my beer and he took a refill on his. As he pushed aside his empty glass, he noticed his cigarette in the ashtray and stubbed it out.

"It's not enough that I'm a vampire, I gotta kill people with secondhand smoke, too." He pushed the ashtray up beside the empty beer glass. "I heard a rumor about you hooking up with the Cortez boy. That true?"

I nodded, took my beer from the bartender, and laid down a five. Aaron waved it back and exchanged his fresh beer for a ten, with a murmured "no change."

"Thanks," I said.

"I owe you more than a cheap beer. Now, this Cortez, it's Lucas, right? The youngest? Doesn't work for the family?"

"That's right."

"Well, that's good, because someone was trying to tell me it was the next older one. You don't wanna get mixed up with those Cabal guys. But, now, Cassandra said she wanted to talk about a Cabal situation, and since you're here, I'm assuming you're involved. But if you're with Lucas, and he doesn't work for the Cabals ..."

"Let's go sit with Cassandra and I'll explain."

I told Aaron the story. When I finished, he leaned back and shook his head.

"Fucking unbelievable. We need that kinda trouble like we need a stake through the heart. You find this loser, you make sure the Cabals know the rest of us had nothing to do with it." He took a gulp of beer. "I guess you want to know whether I have any idea who might be behind it. I'm also guessing you've already checked out John and his gang."

"John?" I said.

"John, Hans, whatever he's calling himself today. You know who I mean, Cass."

"Oh," Cassandra said, lip curling. "Him."

"Well, you've told Paige about him, right? His little anti-Cabal crusade?"

My head snapped up. "Anti-Cabal crusade?"

She frowned. "When did he start this?"

"Oh, only about a decade or so ago."

"This is the first I've heard of it."

Aaron shook his head. "No, it's just the first time you've heard it and paid attention."

"What is that supposed to mean?"

Aaron turned to me. "Guy's name is John, but he calls himself Hans; thinks 'John' isn't a proper name for a vampire. He's one of the New Orleans vamps."

"Oh."

Aaron grinned. "That explains everything, doesn't it? John's got this burr about Cabals. It goes with the whole mentality of those guys. They're vampires, so they're 'special' and they should rule the frigging supernatural world. If it wasn't for that damned writer . . . It's gone straight to their heads. I wouldn't be surprised if they were behind this."

"Any idea where we can find them?" I asked.

"I can get John's address but it might take a day or two. He's not exactly on my Christmas card list. But if you're in a hurry, his posse hangs out at the Rampart in New Orleans." He looked at Cassandra. "But you check it out for her, Cass. Don't be taking Paige in there."

"Vamps only?" I said.

"Nah, just not a very nice place. I'll put out some feelers, too, see if I can pick up any rumors."

I pulled out my notepad to give him my number.

"Hold on," he said, and took out his cell phone. "Safer this way. Every damned piece of paper I stuff into my pockets winds up in the washing machine. I can tell you where I was when I heard Lincoln had been shot, but do you think I can ever remember to empty my pockets before doing laundry? Not a chance."

I dictated my phone number and Lucas's, and Aaron entered them into his cell directory. Then he returned the phone to his jacket, lounged back in his seat, and cracked his knuckles.

Cassandra sighed. "What is it, Aaron?"

"Hmmm?"

"Whenever you do that"—she waved at his hands—"it means there's something on your mind. What is it?"

He paused, then looked over at me. "The Rampart. It's a problem, and it's been a problem for a while, which brings up something else. The interracial council. I know you have Cass, but maybe you'd consider taking another vamp—"

"Excuse me?" Cassandra said.

"Oh, get your back down. I mean a second vampire, someone who'll bring forward vampire concerns, like the Rampart. I'll do it, but if you know of someone better, that's cool. There aren't enough vamps to have our own governing body, and the council used to perform that role—"

"Used to?" Cassandra said. "If anyone has concerns, I'll take them to the council."

Aaron turned and met her gaze. "Cass, you stopped doing that years ago. Decades. You're not . . . You're not part of anything anymore. You're disconnected."

"Disconnected?"

"I'm not trying to give you a hard time. There have always been two vampire delegates for a reason, one as a resource and one as an ombudsman. Now that Lawrence is gone, you've taken over his old role and, well, someone needs to do yours."

When she didn't respond, he touched her elbow, but she yanked her arm back.

"I am *not* disconnected," she said.

Aaron sighed, and looked at me. "Think about it."

I nodded. We finished up and left.

The New Orleans Vampire Situation

I SWITCHED THE CELL PHONE TO MY OTHER EAR AND walked into a quieter corner of the airport. "We have a flight for New Orleans leaving in an hour, so I'll be stuck there overnight."

"Perhaps I should have come along," Lucas said. "I haven't accomplished much here. My father convened an intra-Cabal meeting this afternoon, and he says that no one recalls any dealings with vampires. That, of course, is preposterous. Even if no vampires have approached them, they must have encountered one or two in the course of business. Either they think I'm stupid or they just can't be bothered to lie more creatively."

I let out an oath.

"My sentiments exactly. Now, my father *has* admitted to one recent Cortez Cabal encounter with a vampire. Apparently one tried to arrange a private meeting with him in July. The request was denied, of course, and the matter ended there."

"What did this vampire want to speak to him about?"

"No one bothered to ask. As soon as they found out he was a vampire, they didn't care to hear anything else. Not a reason, not a name, nothing. And as much as I'm

predisposed to think my father is withholding information, I must admit that this is exactly how Cabal employees are trained to deal with vampires."

"Can I just say 'arghh!' When this is over, we don't ever
have to work with these nice people again, right?"

"You have my word on that. Perhaps then, one good
thing will come of this. It might persuade you to join me
in future *anti*-Cabal work."

"Hey, no one needed to convince me. I was always
willing to help. You just had to ask."

Silence buzzed down the line. Cassandra appeared at
my shoulder to say that the plane was boarding. I motioned that I'd be right there.

"I have to go," I said to Lucas.

"I heard. About working together, I was always under
the impression—that is to say—" He paused. "You need
to run, but I'd like to discuss this later. And don't forget to
call me when you get to New Orleans."

"I won't."

Cassandra had said little since we'd left Aaron. Again,
she bought me a first-class ticket. I knew Cassandra had
money, lots of it, and I doubted she ever flew coach, but
it was still a nice gesture. She also offered me her in-
flight meal, which I refused, though I did accept her
package of cocktail nuts. By the time I finished dinner,
she was on her second wine, which told me something
was wrong. I'd never seen Cassandra drink more than
half a glass at a sitting.

When the flight attendant came by with dessert, I
looked at the gelatinous square they called lemon me-
ringue pie, and opted for a tea instead. Cassandra motioned to her wineglass for a refill.

"How long have you been attending council meetings, Paige?" Cassandra asked as the attendant left. "Five, six years?"

"Almost twelve."

"Twelve years, then." She fingered the stem of her glass. "You've always had a good memory, so perhaps you'll remember better than I can. When's the last time we investigated a vampire concern?"

"In '98. Dallas, Texas. We had a report of a killer draining his victims' blood. Turned out it was a human killer, though, so I suppose that doesn't really count as a vampire concern." I paused. "Let's see, before that it would have been '96. A vacationing Russian vampire was raising a ruckus—"

"Yes, yes, I remember that. I meant when did I last bring a *concern* before the council?"

"Like what Aaron was talking about? A situation that's worrying vampires in general?"

"Exactly."

I took my tea from the attendant and pulled out the bag. "You've never done that."

"Oh, come now, Paige. Of course I have." She leaned back in her seat. "Never mind. You were only a child, and you were always goofing off with Adam—"

"Hey, I never goofed off in a meeting. Don't you remember all those times Robert gave Adam shit for not paying attention like I did? Drove Adam crazy. Then he'd take it out on me afterward, teasing me about brown-nosing—" I stopped, noticing Cassandra's attention had wandered to her wineglass. "Point is, I paid attention. I took notes. Quiz me if you like. Dates, places, I can name them. In twelve years, you've never brought a vampire concern to the council."

"That didn't strike you as odd?"

I shrugged. "Numbers-wise, vampires are rare, and you're all pretty self-sufficient, so I figured you didn't have concerns. It never bothered anyone else, so it didn't bother me. Lawrence didn't bring up concerns when he was your codelegate."

"That's because Lawrence was so old, he didn't care about anyone but himself." She fluttered her hands over her table. "Took off to Europe and never even bothered to tell us he wasn't coming back. I may be self-centered, but I'd never do that."

I sipped my tea.

Cassandra looked at me sharply. "Well, I wouldn't."

"Okay. Sure. Now about this bar, the Rampart—"

"I must have brought a concern to the council in the past twelve years. What about the Gulf War draft? Several vampires had taken on the identity of American citizens and they were worried about being called for the draft—"

"There was no draft for the Gulf War. That must have been Vietnam."

She frowned. "When was Vietnam?"

"Before I was born."

Cassandra snatched up her napkin and folded it precisely. "Well, there's been something since then. I only remember *that* one because it was historically significant."

"Probably."

By the time we reached New Orleans, it wasn't yet eleven, still too early for bar-hopping. As I phoned Elena for my nightly check on Savannah, Cassandra directed the taxi to the Empire Hotel, her local favorite. After we checked in, I called Lucas, letting him know I'd arrived safely, then showered and got ready.

When we went downstairs, Cassandra had the door-man hail us a cab.

"This bar," I said. "The Rampart. Aaron has a problem with it?"

Cassandra sighed. "That's just Aaron. For a man who looks like he doesn't spend much time thinking, Aaron spends far too much time at it. Thinking and worrying. He can be the worst mother hen you can imagine."

"So he's overreacting about the Rampart? About it not being safe for me?"

"The Rampart is safe insofar as any bar is safe these days. It's a favored hangout for local vampires, nothing more."

"No offense, but if vamps like hanging out there, it doesn't sound like the safest place for anyone with a pulse."

"Don't be ridiculous, Paige. Dogs don't piss in their beds and vampires don't hunt where they live."

Cassandra strode toward a cab pulling to the curbside. I hurried after her.

Cassandra explained more about the Rampart on the drive. This might seem dangerous, having such conversations within earshot of humans, but supernaturals haven't needed to rabidly monitor their discussions since the nineteenth century. These days, we keep our voices down and watch what we say, but if the odd "demon" or "vampire" escapes, people jump to one of three logical conclusions. One, they misheard. Two, we're discussing a movie or book plot. Three, we're nuts. If our taxi driver overheard any of our conversation, the biggest danger we faced was that he'd ask where this "vampire bar" was located, not so he could alert the proper authorities to a nest of bloodsucking murderers, but so he'd have another destination to add to his list of recommendations for visiting Goths and Anne Rice fans. After all, this was New Orleans.

Speaking of Anne Rice, while I'm sure she's a lovely woman, there are many in the supernatural world who blame her for the New Orleans vampire situation. Roughly coinciding with the popularity of Ms. Rice's novels, the influx of vamps to the city rose astronomically. At one point in the late eighties there had been nine vampires in New Orleans ... in a country that historically sees a national average of fewer than two dozen. Some had emigrated from Europe just to move to New Orleans. Fortunately, three or four have since left, and the population has averaged five or six over the past decade.

The problem with the New Orleans vamps isn't overpopulation. It's that they all share a similar mind-set, the same mind-set that drew them to the city in the first place. For these vampires, seeing their cultural popularity skyrocket with Ms. Rice's books was like a rock singer seeing his face on the cover of *Rolling Stone,* the ultimate moment of self-affirmation, when they could say "See, I'm just as cool as I always thought I was." And for the vampires of New Orleans, life has never been the same since.

The Rampart wasn't just a vampire bar in the sense that it attracted vampires. It was actually owned by vampires. As Cassandra explained: John/Hans and two others had bought the place years ago. They'd kept it small and exclusive, a place they could make their own and amuse themselves playing bar owners.

The taxi driver stopped in an industrial district. Security lights dotted every building except the one beside us, which was swathed in a blackness that seemed almost artificial. As I opened the door, I saw that it was indeed artificial. The brickwork and the windows had been painted black. Even the lone street lamp had been wrapped in black crepe paper and the bulb broken or removed.

"Early Gothic Nightmare. How original," Cassandra said as she climbed from the car. "Last time I was here it looked like a perfectly normal bar. No wonder Aaron is getting his shorts in a twist. He can't stand this sort of thing."

"Well, their taste in decor may be criminal, but unfortunately they aren't violating any council statutes. At least they're keeping it low profile. I don't even see a sign."

"I don't even see a door," Cassandra muttered. "They've probably painted it black like everything else. Now where was it the last time . . . ?"

As her gaze traveled along the building, a limo pulled up and belched three giggle-wracked young women onto the curb. Two wore black leather miniskirts. The third was dressed in a long white dress that looked more suited for a wedding than girls' night out. A beefy bodyguard grabbed the bride's elbow to steady her and led the trio toward the building. As the limo reversed, its headlights illuminated the four. The "bride" turned into the lights and squinted.

"Hey," I said. "Isn't that—what's her name—she's a singer."

The quartet had just vanished around the building

when a Hummer pulled up and disgorged two young
men in undertaker suits. They followed the same path as
the bridal party.

"So much for keeping a low profile," Cassandra muttered.

"At least we found out where the door is," I said.

Cassandra shook her head and we circled the building
in search of an entrance.

Keeping Up with the Times

WHEN WE GOT TO THE OTHER SIDE, WE STILL COULDN'T find a door.

"This is ridiculous," Cassandra said, pacing along the building. "Are we blind?"

"I don't know about you," I said. "But I can't see in the dark. Should I risk a light spell?"

"Go ahead. From the looks of those fools going inside, I doubt they'd notice if you lit up the whole neighborhood."

Before I could begin the incantation, an ivy-covered trellis moved and a shadow emerged from behind it. A girl, no more than a teenager, stumbled out, her white face and hands floating, disembodied, through the air. I blinked, then saw that she was dressed in a long black gown; together with her black hair it blended into the backdrop of the building.

When she saw us, she swayed and mumbled something. As she staggered past, Cassandra's head whipped around to follow, eyes narrowing, the green irises glinting. Her lips parted, then snapped shut. Before she tore her gaze away, I followed it to the girl's arm. Black gauze encircled her bare forearm. Around the edges, blood smeared her pale skin.

"She's hurt," I said as the girl reeled onto the road. "Wait here. I'll see if she needs help."

"You do that. I think Aaron is right. You should wait outside."

I stopped. My gaze went to the girl, tottering along the side of the road. Drunk or stoned, but not mortally wounded. Whatever was going on inside might be worse, and I couldn't rely on Cassandra to handle it. I reached past her and tugged on the trellis.

"I meant it, Paige," Cassandra said. "See to the girl. You're not coming in."

I found the handle, pushed the door open, and squeezed past Cassandra. Inside, the place was as dark as its exterior. I touched walls on either side, so I knew I was in a hallway. Feeling my way along, I moved forward. I got about five steps before smacking into a wall of muscle. A beefy face glowered down at me. The man shone a flashlight over us, and smirked.

"Sorry, ladies," he said. "You got the wrong place. Bourbon Street is that way."

He lifted his flashlight to point, swinging it near Cassandra's face. She swatted it down.

"Who's in tonight?" she demanded. "Hans? Brigid? Ronald?"

"Uh, all three," the bouncer said, stepping back.

"Tell them Cassandra's here."

"Cassandra who?"

He shone the flashlight beam in her face. Cassandra snatched it from his hand.

"Just Cassandra. Now go."

He reached for his light. "Can I have my flash—?"

"No."

He hesitated, then turned, banged into the wall, cursed, and headed off into the darkness.

"Fools," Cassandra muttered. "What are they playing at here? When did they do all this?"

"Uh, when's the last time you visited?"

"It can't be more than a year—" She paused. "Maybe a few years. Not that long."

The door opened so fast that the man behind it nearly fell at our feet. Mid-forties, not much taller than my five-foot-two, he was pudgy with soft features and gray-flecked hair tied back with a velvet ribbon. He wore a puffy shirt straight out of *Seinfeld,* the top three buttons undone, revealing a hairless chest. His pants were ill-fitting black velvet, tucked into high-top boots. He looked like a middle-aged accountant heading off to a *Pirates of Penzance* audition.

He righted himself and blinked owlishly into Cassandra's flashlight beam. I gestured toward the exit. He didn't seem to see me, but stood gawking up at Cassandra.

"Cass—Cassandra. So—so good of you—"

"What the hell are you wearing, Ronald? Please tell me Fridays are Masquerade Night here."

Ronald looked down at his outfit and frowned.

"Where's John?" Cassandra said.

"J—John? You mean Hans? He's, uh, inside." When Cassandra turned toward the door, Ronald jumped in front of it. "We didn't expect—we're honored of course. Very honored."

"Get your tongue off my boots, Ronald, and get out of my way. I came to speak to John."

"Y—yes, of course. But it's been so long. I'm just so pleased to see you. There's a blues bar just a few blocks over. Very nice. We could go there, and Hans could join us—"

Cassandra shoved Ronald aside and reached for the door handle.

"W—wait," Ronald said. "We weren't ready for you, Cassandra. The place, it's a mess. You don't want to go in there."

She tugged open the door and walked through. I grabbed it before it closed. Ronald blinked at me, as if I'd materialized from nowhere.

"I'm with her," I said.

He grabbed the door edge, then paused, uncertain. I tugged it open enough to slip through into what looked like another, longer hallway. Ronald scurried after us. He passed me and jostled Cassandra's heels. At a glare from her, he backed off, but only a step.

"I—I think you'll like what we've done here, Cassandra," Ronald said. "It's a new age for us, and we're taking advantage of it. Adapting to the times. Refusal to change is the death knell of any civilization—that's what Hans says."

"Step on my heels again and you'll hear a death knell."

She stopped before another door, waved me forward. I slipped past Ronald.

"I want you to wait out here," Cassandra said.

I shook my head. "You go, I go."

"I won't be responsible for you, Paige."

"You aren't," I said, and pushed open the door.

Beyond the door was a cavernous room, just barely illuminated by a dull red glow. At first, I couldn't make out the source of the lighting, but then I noticed that the faux Grecian pillars were pieced with tiny holes, each letting out a thin ray of red light, like an infrared pointer.

One glance around and I knew the designation "bar" no longer applied to the Rampart. It was a club, probably a private one. The only furnishings were a half-dozen couches and divans, most of them occupied. Areas on either side of the room had been cordoned off with beaded curtains. Only the occasional murmur or muffled laugh broke the silence.

On the nearest sofa, two women were curled up together, one semireclined, holding her hand out, the other bending over whatever her companion held. Cocaine, maybe methamphetamine. If Hans and his bunch had opened an exclusive drug club, they were treading dangerous ground for people who had to stay below the radar. I wasn't sure whether this violated the council's statutes, but we'd need to look into it after this investigation was over.

One of the women on the divan leaned over her partner's arm. I tried to glance over discreetly, to see what kind of drugs they were using, but the woman wasn't holding anything. Instead, she stretched out her arm, empty palm up, forearm braced with her other hand. A dark line bisected the inside of her forearm. She clenched her fist and a rivulet of blood trickled down. Her companion lowered her mouth to the cut.

I stumbled back, hitting Cassandra. She turned sharply, mouth opening to snap at me, then followed my gaze. She wheeled on Ronald.

"Who is that woman? I don't know her."

"She's not—" Ronald lowered his voice. "—not a vampire."

"Not a—?" I said. "Then why is she . . . ?"

"Because she wants to," Ronald said. "Some like to give, some to receive. Hardly a new fetish, but they've become more open about it. We're simply taking advantage—"

Cassandra stomped off before he could finish. She strode to the nearest curtain and shoved it back, to the yelps of the surprised guests within. She swung around, letting the curtain fall, and headed for the next cubicle. Ronald scrambled after her. I stayed where I was. I'd seen enough.

"You're not seeing the beauty of it, Cassandra," Ronald whispered. "The opportunities. Hiding in plain sight, that's the ultimate goal, isn't it? Other races can do it. Why shouldn't we?"

Cassandra shoved back another beaded curtain. I looked away, but not fast enough. Inside was the singer, in her mock bridal ensemble, splayed across the center of the couch, arms outstretched, her two female companions each attached leechlike to an arm, her dress shoved up around her hips while her male bodyguard crouched before her, pants down . . . and I don't need to describe anymore. Suffice to say, I hoped to wipe the scene from my memory before it reappeared at an inopportune moment, and ruined a perfectly good round of bed games.

Cassandra whirled on Ronald. "Get these people out of here now."

"But—but—they're members. They've paid—"

"Get them out and consider yourself lucky if money is all you lose."

"M—maybe this wasn't such a good idea, maybe we made an error in judgment, but—"

Cassandra brought her face down to his. "Do you remember the Athenian problem? Do you remember the penalty for their 'error in judgment'?"

Ronald swallowed. "Give me a minute."

He hurried to the singer's cubicle and pushed his head through the beaded curtain. I caught the words "police," "raid," and "five minutes." The quartet came barreling out so fast, they were still pulling on their clothes as they raced past me.

A minute later, as the last stragglers stumbled for the exit, a door opened at the far end of the room. In strode a tall woman in her late twenties. Her face was too angular to be pretty, with features better suited to a man. She wore her blond hair long and straight, an uncomplimentary style that left one with the fleeting impression that she might be a guy in drag, yet her black silk baby-doll revealed enough to reassure any confused onlooker that she was indeed gender female. Even her feet were bare, toes painted bright red, as were her fingernails and her lips. It looked as if she'd put on her lipstick in the dark, and smeared it. As she moved into the semilit room, I saw that it wasn't lipstick at all, but blood.

"Wipe your mouth, Brigid," Cassandra snapped. "No one here is impressed."

"I thought I heard harping," Brigid said, gliding into the center of the room. "I should have known it was the queen bitch—" A tiny smile. "Whoops, I meant queen bee."

"We know what you meant, Brigid. Have the guts to admit it."

Cassandra's gaze slid from Brigid and riveted to a young man following Brigid so closely that he was almost hidden behind the statuesque vampire. He was no more than my age, slightly built and pretty, with huge brown eyes fixed in a look of bovine befuddlement. Blood dribbled down the side of his neck, but he seemed not to notice, and stood there, gaze fixed on the back of Brigid's head, lips curved in an inane little smile.

"Get him out of here," Cassandra said.

"You don't give me orders, Cassandra," Brigid said.

"I do if you're fool enough to need them. Send him home."

"Oh, but he is home." She reached down and stroked his crotch. "He likes it here."

"Don't be boorish," Cassandra said. "Find another dupe to charm when I'm gone."

"I don't need to charm him," Brigid said, hand still on the young man's crotch. He closed his eyes and began rocking. "He stays because he wants to stay."

Cassandra thrust the young man toward Ronald. "Get him out of here."

Brigid grabbed Cassandra's arm. When Cassandra glared at her, she dropped it and stepped away, lips drawn back. She saw me and her eyes glimmered. I tensed, binding spell at the ready.

"You bring your human along and I can't bring mine?" Brigid said, eyes fixed on mine.

"She's not human, which you'll discover if you continue what you're doing."

Brigid's blue eyes gleamed brighter. Charming me, or trying to. The power rarely worked on other supernaturals, but to be sure, I took the opportunity to field-test yet another of my new spells: an anticharm incantation. Brigid yelped.

"Stings, doesn't it?" Cassandra said. "Leave the girl alone or she'll move onto something even less comfortable."

Brigid turned to Cassandra. "What do you want, bitch?"

Cassandra smiled. "Undisguised hate. We're making progress. I want John."

"He's not here."

"That's not what your bouncer said."

Brigid flipped her hair off her shoulder. "Well, he's wrong. Hans isn't here."

Cassandra turned on Ronald, who backed up against the wall.

"He was in the back room, with Brigid and the boy," Ronald said.

"Let me guess," Cassandra said to Brigid. "He told you to come out here and create a diversion while he slipped out the back door. Come on then, Paige. Time to hunt a coward."

Never Underestimate the Power of Vampire Ego

THE BACK DOOR OF THE RAMPART OPENED INTO AN ALLEY.

"What about Ronald and Brigid?" I said, hovering in the doorway. "They might know something, and the moment we're out of sight, they're going to bolt, too. Two birds in the hand are definitely worth more than one in the bush."

Cassandra shook her head, gaze traveling along the alley. "They'd never betray John. Without him, they wouldn't survive." She turned left. "This way."

"You picked up his trail?"

"No, but I'd go this way."

We looped behind a body shop and came out into a warren of dilapidated row houses that looked as if they'd been boarded up since I was in grade school. At the end of the lane, Cassandra stopped and studied the houses. A bottle clinked. I jumped.

"If you hear someone, it's not him," she said.

"Someone else is out here?"

"Lots of someones, Paige. Abandoned doesn't mean empty."

As if to underscore this, a woman's laugh floated down the street. A bottle sailed from a second-story window and smashed on the road, adding to a puddle of broken glass.

Cassandra walked to the far sidewalk and traversed the row of houses, with me at her heels. I felt silly tagging along after her and, worse yet, useless, but there was nothing else I could do. My sensing spell wouldn't work for finding a vampire, and if he wasn't going to give himself away by making noise, there was no use searching on my own.

Two houses from the end, Cassandra peered up at the building. She grabbed the rusted railing and started climbing the steps to the front door. Halfway up, she stopped. She looked at the door, tilted her head, then wheeled. I ducked out of her way, but she stayed on the step and gazed out into the street. After a moment, she turned back to the house, studied it, then shook her head and marched down. At the road, she passed the last house with only the briefest glance and crossed the road. I jogged after her.

"Is there anything I can do?" I asked.

"Yes. Stay out of my way."

I threw up my hands, and walked back to the house she'd first approached.

"I didn't say wander off," she called after me.

"I'm not wandering. Something about this house caught your attention, so I'm checking it out while you search the others."

"He's not in there."

"Good. Then it won't hurt for me to check."

"The last thing I need is to be worrying about you stepping on someone's dirty needle."

"I'm not a child, Cassandra. If I do step on a needle or get mugged, I preabsolve you of all responsibility. You search that side of the road while I double-check your hunch back here."

Cassandra huffed something under her breath and stalked off. I climbed the steps to the row house. The front door was boarded over, but someone had kicked a large hole at the bottom. I crouched and crawled through.

The smell hit me first, triggering memories of a stint volunteering in a homeless shelter. Inhaling through my mouth, I looked around. I was in a front hall. Peeling wallpaper hung from the walls, mingling with strips of flypaper polka-dotted with mummified bug bodies. I cast a light spell and shone it along the hallway floor. The carpet had long since been torn up, leaving bare underlay. As I moved forward, I pushed the trash out of the way with my foot. Though there were no needles, there was enough broken glass and rat droppings to make me glad I'd changed out of my open-toed sandals before leaving Miami.

From the hall, I had three destination choices: upstairs, the living room, or the door at the end, which presumably led into the kitchen. I cast a sensing spell from the foot of the stairs. It might not work on vampires, but in a place like this, the living were of equal concern. When the spell came back negative, I headed for the living room. No sign of a vampire there, or anything large enough to hide one. Same with the combined dining/kitchen area. Even the closets were bare, all doors and shelves having been stripped off, presumably to feed the fire pit in the middle of the living-room floor.

As I headed for the stairs, something whispered across the upstairs floor. The sound was too soft for footsteps . . . unless the feet belonged to the large furry rodents who'd left their calling cards in the debris below. I walked halfway up the stairs and launched my sensing spell. It came back negative. Now that I thought about it, that was strange. Recent rat droppings meant recent rats, and my spell should have picked them up. I suspected I knew the reason for the sudden out-flux. Rats don't just flee a sinking ship—they flee stronger predators, too.

I prepped a knock-back spell and climbed to the top landing. The house was still and silent. Too still. Too silent. The preternatural stillness reminded me of earlier that day, when I'd thought the killer had been stalking me in the parking lot.

From the top of the stairs, I could see into all four rooms. I wanted to be at the front of the house, which narrowed my choices to two, one of which was the bathroom—too small for what I had in mind. I peeked in the front bedroom, making sure it was empty, then stepped inside and cast a perimeter spell across the doorway. Problem was, I'd never tried this spell with a vampire, so I couldn't rely on it now. When this was over, I'd have to test my whole array of sensory spells on Cassandra. Not that she'd ever offer herself up as a guinea pig, but there were ways around that.

Next I readied a fresh knock-back spell. "Readying a spell" means to start the incantation, so it can be launched with a few final words. Spells are wonderful weapons, but on a speed-of-use scale, they rank down there with bows and arrows. If the arrow isn't already in the bow when you get jumped, you're in trouble. The other problem, though, is that you can't pause mid-incantation indefinitely. Lucas and I had once spent a weekend experimenting with this, and concluded that you could ready a spell for about two minutes. After that, you had to prep it again. This being my first practical application of that research, I was re-readying my spell every sixty seconds, just to be sure.

I crossed to the front window. It was boarded up, but someone had pried loose the middle board to let in sunshine. I stood sideways, so I could see both the window and the doorway, then I redirected my light spell behind me, for backlighting.

Once my eyes adjusted to the darkness of the street below, I could make out Cassandra's figure walking down the empty road, Pradas clicking impatiently against the asphalt, Dolce & Gabbana coat snapping behind her. How many people were huddled behind other windows along this street, drawn there by our earlier noise and now watching as this impeccably dressed, attractive forty-year-old woman strode unaccompanied down their street? Talk about an easy mark. Yet no one came out. Maybe they didn't dare.

Judging by Cassandra's angle and purposeful stride, she was heading here, presumably having found nothing farther down. That meant my hunch about John's whereabouts was probably correct, and it meant I had to move fast.

I turned my back to the door and adjusted my lightball until I could see the reflection of the door in the window glass. Then I took out my cell phone. I readied a new spell, called our apartment, and started talking before the machine picked up.

"Hey, it's me. I'm still in New Orleans. Cassandra got a lead on a vamp and she's following him now. He was supposed to be at this bar, but he ducked out the back door. Can you believe that? Mr. I'm-an-Evil-Vampire running out the back." I paused, then laughed. "No kidding. Vamps, huh?"

Through the reflection in the window I saw a shape cross the doorway. I prepped a fresh spell and continued talking into the answering machine.

"I bet he is," I said as the shape crept closer. "Probably hiding in some cubbyhole hoping the rats don't get him. Guys like this, it's a wonder they haven't died out—"

I cast the rest of the binding spell, then whirled to see a man frozen in mid-lunge. Slender, early thirties, black hair slicked back into a ponytail, white linen shirt, flowing knee-length black leather coat, and matching leather pants. Mascara, maybe. Eyeliner, definitely.

"John, I presume," I said. "Forgot that vampires really do cast a reflection, didn't you?"

His brown eyes darkened with fury. Below, the front door clicked shut.

"Up here," I called. "I found him."

Cassandra's heels clicked double-time up the stairs. As she rounded the corner, she looked almost concerned. Then she saw John and slowed.

"Like my statue?" I said. "The not-so-cunning vampire swooping down on his not-so-unsuspecting prey."

"I see your binding spell has improved." She looked at John and sighed. "Let him go."

I released the spell. John fell on his face. Cassandra sighed again, louder. John scrambled to his feet and brushed off his pants.

"She trapped me," he said.

"No," I said. "Your ego trapped you."

John adjusted his coat, then scowled at a line of grease across his white shirt.

"This better come out," he said.

"Hey, I didn't do that," I said. "That's what you get crawling around dumps like this."

"I wasn't crawling. And I didn't duck out the back door. I—"

"Enough," Cassandra said. "Now, John—"

"I prefer Hans."

"And I prefer not to have to chase you through abandoned buildings, but it seems neither of us gets our wish tonight. I came to speak to you about—"

"The Rampart." John rolled his eyes and slouched against the wall, then noticed his shirt creased and adjusted his slouch. "Let me guess, you've been to see Saint Aaron. Such a waste of a gorgeous vampire. I could reform him, of course." He grinned, all teeth. "Show him the error of his ways, or the way to delicious errors. Show him what that perfect body—"

"You're not gay, John. Get over it. Now, I don't know what beef Aaron has with the Rampart, but I know nothing about it and I saw no cause for concern myself."

John straightened. "Oh?"

"The matter I came to discuss involves the Cabals."

"The Cabals?" John's brows knitted. "What about the Cabals?"

"This"—she flourished a hand at me—"is Paige Winterbourne. You've met her mother."

Recognition sparked in John's eyes, but he dowsed it and shrugged.

Cassandra continued, "Of course, I don't expect you to remember a nonvampire, but Paige's mother was the Leader of the American Coven. Though I'm sure you don't follow spell-caster gossip, Paige is involved with Lucas Cortez, Benicio Cortez's youngest son and heir."

From John's expression none of this was news to him, but he gave no sign of it and let Cassandra continue.

"Young Lucas has some ethical disputes with his father's organization and is actively involved in anti-Cabal activities. That's why Paige approached me. As a fellow council member, she's well aware of my strong anti-Cabal stance."

I nodded, though the thought of Cassandra taking a

strong stance on anything had me struggling to keep a straight face.

"Paige wanted me to join their little crusade, but I'm hardly about to join forces with spell-casters. She then told me that you and your . . . associates have formed your own anti-Cabal league. Naturally, I'm intrigued, though I cannot understand why you wouldn't have approached me about this yourself."

"I—we—didn't someone tell you? I asked Ronald—"

"For now, I'll accept that excuse, though I wouldn't suggest you try it again. As for this campaign, I hear that you've been quite busy. Busy and successful."

John hesitated, then shrugged. "Not surprising, really. They're such an easy target."

"But this latest assault? Truly inspired."

Again, John hesitated, and I saw by his expression that he had no idea what Cassandra was talking about. He coughed to cover his confusion, then pressed on. "Yes, well, it was a team effort. Months of planning. We were pleased with the results, though, and we hope to build on that success for our next effort."

"I'm sure you will."

Cassandra walked to the window and looked out, re-grouping and plotting her next move. I left her to it. That fake phone call had tested the limits of my deceptive abilities.

John shot up the sleeves on his coat. "We've let these Cabals go on too long. It was an amusing exercise to watch, but they've forgotten their place in the supernatural world. We should have taken a hand in the Cabals right from the start, demanded tribute, something to remind them who's in charge. Not that I blame you—"

Cassandra looked at John. He lifted his hands and stepped back.

"Not at all. You were misled, like the rest of us. When they said they didn't want vampires joining up, we didn't care. Why should we? Vampires certainly aren't going to punch time cards for spell-casters. We just didn't see where that would lead."

"Where that would lead..." Cassandra murmured. "Yes, of course. I'm assuming you're referring to the recent problems we've had with the Cabals."

"Sure. Right."

Cassandra glanced at me, my cue to play the clueless outsider.

"What problems?" I said.

Cassandra waved to John, as if to grant him the floor.

"Well, the, uh, general problems they have with vampires. They know we could rise against them at any time. Too long we've lain dormant, complacent with our place in the world—"

Cassandra strode to the door and disappeared into the hall. John hurried after her.

"Did you hear something?" he asked.

"No, I've heard enough. Paige? Come on."

I followed her from the house.

Understanding Cassandra

"I HOPE WE'RE LEAVING BECAUSE YOU HAVE AN IDEA," I said as we walked along the street.

"He doesn't know anything."

"How do you know? You barely prodded him."

"What was I supposed to do? Rip out his fingernails? I'm over three hundred years old, Paige. I have an excellent understanding of human and vampire behavior. John knows nothing."

I glanced back toward the row house.

"Don't you dare," Cassandra said. "Really, Paige, you can be such a child. An impetuous child with an overdeveloped sense of her own infallibility. You're lucky that binding spell held John or I would have had to rescue you yet again."

"When have you *ever* rescued me?" I shook my head, realizing I was being deftly led away from my goal. "Forget John, then. What about the other two? We should stop by the Rampart, see if you can pick up their trail—"

"If John doesn't know anything, they don't know anything."

"I'm still not convinced John doesn't know anything."

She muttered something and walked faster, leaving me

lagging behind. I took out my cell phone. She glanced over her shoulder.

"I'm not standing here waiting for a cab, Paige. There's a restaurant a few blocks over. We'll phone from there."

"I'm not calling for a cab. I'm phoning Aaron."

"It's three A.M. He will not appreciate—"

"He said to call him when we finished talking to John, whatever the hour, and see whether he's found any other leads."

Cassandra snatched the cell phone from my hand. "He hasn't. Aaron spent the last seventy years in Australia, Paige. He's barely been back for two years. How could he possibly know anything about us? About the vampires here?"

"He knew about John and the Rampart." I peered at her through the darkness. "You really don't want me asking other vampires for information, do you?"

"Don't be ridiculous. I took you to Aaron. I brought you here. I chased down John—"

"*I* chased down John. You walked right past him."

"John doesn't know anything."

"But you do."

"No," she said, meeting my eyes. "I don't."

I knew then that she was telling the truth. She didn't know anything... and that's why she was blocking and snapping at me, because these were her people, she represented them, and she should have known something. Known about the Rampart, known about John's anti-Cabal crusade, known who'd had run-ins with the Cabals. But she didn't. That was the problem.

"Lucas and I can handle this," I said, my tone softening. "You don't need to—"

"Yes, I do need to. You were right. As council delegate I need to help solve this before the situation gets worse for all involved." She handed me my cell phone. "Go ahead. Call Aaron."

I shook my head. "It can wait until morning. Let's go back to the hotel and get some sleep."

Of course, I didn't want to sleep. I wanted to plot my next move. I wanted to call Lucas and get his opinion. I wanted to call Aaron and see whether he'd uncovered anything. Most of all, though, I wanted to shake Cassandra until her fangs rattled.

I did none of this. I could hardly track fresh leads at this hour, so there was no reason not to phone Lucas and Aaron in the morning. As for Cassandra, well, let's just say I was having trouble working up a good dose of righteous indignation. For once in my life, I think I understood Cassandra, or some minuscule part of her.

Aaron was right: Cassandra was disconnecting. A modern term for an ancient vampire affliction. When a vampire begins to pull back from the world, it's a sure sign that she's coming to the end of her life. I'd always thought it was intentional. You know you don't have much time left, so you begin to withdraw, make peace with yourself.

I'll admit, if I knew my time was coming, I'd throw myself into the world like never before, and spend every minute with those I loved. Yet it made sense that vampires might be more reflective, might isolate themselves, as they saw the end coming and realized the full cost of their existence. Even if they killed only one person a year, that added up to hundreds of victims over a lifetime. Hundreds who'd died so they could live. As that life draws to an end, they must look back and question their choice.

Seeing Cassandra deny her disconnection, fight to pretend that she's just as much a part of the world as ever, I understood that the process must be as involuntary as any other part of aging. I've said that Cassandra didn't care about anyone but herself, and she'd been that way my entire life. Although I was sure she'd never been the most altruistic person, if she'd always been as self-centered as she was today, she'd never have been granted a seat on the council. Perhaps, as she grew older, she'd begun finding it more difficult to care, as the years and the faces blurred together, her own self and life the only constant. Yet she'd told herself she wasn't affected by it, that she was still as vibrant and vital as ever. Could I really blame her for that? Of course not.

What about my mother? Could I blame her? She must have seen the signs with Cassandra. Why didn't she say anything? When Cassandra's codelegate, Lawrence, had taken off for Europe, sinking into the final stages of his decline, my mother should have insisted on getting a second, younger vampire delegate. If she had, maybe none of this would have happened. We'd have known which vampires were having trouble with the Cabals. Yet my mother had done nothing. Why? Perhaps for the same reason I sat on the hotel bed, staring at the door, knowing I should go out there and confront Cassandra, yet unable to do so.

Fear glued me to that bed. Not fear of Cassandra herself, but fear of offending her. I've never been very good at respecting my elders. Everyone deserves my basic respect, but to earn extra requires more than just having lots of candles on your birthday cake. My mother raised me to be Coven Leader, meaning I grew up knowing that my "elders" would someday be my subordinates. Yet there's a big difference between kowtowing to a seventy-year-old witch and showing respect to a three-hundred-year-old vampire. I couldn't just walk out there and say, "Hey, Cass, I know you don't want to hear this, but you're dying, so get over it."

Something had to be done. It made my gut churn to admit that my mother may have made a mistake, but if she had, I couldn't perpetuate it simply to avoid disrespecting her memory. If Aaron wanted a place on the council, then he should have it. I wouldn't tell Cassandra that now—that would be kicking her when she was down. But we did need to talk.

Cassandra stood in the living area, staring out the window. She didn't turn when I walked in. As I watched her, my resolve faltered. This could wait until morning.

"Bathroom's all yours," I said. "You can have the bedroom, too. I'll pull out the sofa."

She shook her head, still not turning. "Take the bedroom. I don't sleep very much anymore."

Another sign of a dying vampire. I watched her stare out the window. She looked . . . not sad, really, but somehow smaller, dimmer; her presence was confined to that corner of the room instead of taking over the whole of it.

"Can we talk, then?" I said.

She nodded, and walked to the couch. I took the chair beside it.

"If you want to speak to John again, I'll help you," she said. "I will warn you, though, that he's likely to send us on a wild-goose chase." She paused. "Not intentionally. He simply puts too much credence in gossip."

"Well, maybe Aaron can help us sift through John's bullshit. Aaron seems to have a good network of contacts."

Cassandra stiffened, almost imperceptibly, then nodded. "Aaron was always very good at that, immersing himself in our world. Helping others. Keeping order. It's what he does best." A small smile. "I remember, we were in London when Peel began recruiting his bobbies, and I told him, 'Aaron, finally, a career for you.' He'd have been horrible at it, of course. If he caught a hungry child stealing a loaf of bread, he wouldn't have arrested him, he'd have helped him steal more. He's a good man. I—" She paused. "So we'll talk to John again, then. Aaron should be able to get an address for us later today."

"I can probably get it tonight. If he owns the Rampart with Brigid and Ronald, then one of them has to have their address in the public record system. I'll also call Lucas, tell him I won't be coming back to Miami just yet, see whether he wants to join us."

Finding John's address was even simpler than I'd hoped. It was in the phone book. Just to be sure, though, I hacked into public records and double-checked. It may seem that supernaturals, particularly vampires, would avoid leaving a paper trail and, in most cases, they do. Few supernaturals will list themselves in the local phone books, as John had. Yet when it comes to such highly regulated matters as the issuing of liquor licenses, it's more dangerous to provide false information. Vampires carry valid driver's licenses and file their taxes like everyone else, though the name on their paperwork may or may not be their true birth name, depending on how they prefer to keep their identity current. Some pick a victim in their age range and take over his identity for a while. Others pay supernatural forgers to create fresh documents every decade or so. Like Cassandra, John apparently chose the latter route.

Next I called Lucas. As I'd expected—and hoped—he did want to join us. We discussed whether Cassandra and I should wait for him before visiting John, but he didn't think his presence would help. He'd catch the next flight to New Orleans, and we'd meet up after lunch.

By this point, it was after six, so sleep was out of the question. I fixed a fresh poultice for my stomach and cast a fresh healing spell. It helped. A few hours of sleep might have helped more, but I didn't have time for that. The painkillers might have helped, too, but I'd left them back in Miami, and not by accident. This trip, I needed to be clearheaded.

At seven, we went to a bistro down the road, where I had beignets and café au lait while Cassandra drank black coffee. After breakfast, Cassandra tried calling Aaron, but he wasn't answering his cell, so she left a message. Then we hailed a cab and headed out to interview the vampire again.

Embracing One's
Cultural Heritage

WE STOOD ON THE SIDEWALK IN FRONT OF JOHN'S HOUSE.
Cassandra looked up at it and sighed.

"You weren't really expecting a brick bungalow, were
you?" I said. "At least it's not as bad as the Rampart." I
peered through the wrought-iron fence. "Oh, I didn't see
that . . . or that. Is that what I think—oooh." I pulled
back. "You may want to wait outside."

Cassandra sighed again, louder, deeper.

Now, I have nothing against Victorian architecture,
having grown up in a wonderful little house from that very
era, but John's place was everything that gives the style a
bad name, plus a good dose of southern Gothic. It looked
like the quintessential haunted house, covered in ivy and
peeling paint, windows darkened, spires rusting. On
closer inspection, the disrepair was only cosmetic—the
porch didn't sag, the wood wasn't rotting, even the crum-
bling walkway was crumbled artfully, the stones still solid
enough that you wouldn't trip walking over them. The
yard appeared overrun and neglected, yet even a novice
gardener would recognize that most of the "weeds" were
actually wild-looking perennials.

"This used to drive my mom crazy," I said, pointing at

the lawn. "People paying to make their yard look like an abandoned lot. No wonder the neighbors have high walls. He has some nice gargoyles, though. I must admit, I've never seen them anatomically correct."

Cassandra followed my gaze, and shuddered.

"It sure is dark in there," I said. "Or are those blackout blinds? No, wait. It's paint. He's blacked out all the windows. Can't be too careful with those fatal sunbeams."

"The man is an idiot, Paige. If you doubted that last night, this house should seal the matter. We're wasting our time."

"Oh, but it's so much fun. I've never seen a *real* vampire's house before. How come your fence doesn't have wrought-iron bats?" I grabbed the gate and swung it open, then stopped dead. "Hey, I missed those. Forget the bats. *That's* what you need outside your condo."

Cassandra stepped into the gate opening, looked inside, and swore.

"I didn't think that word was in your vocabulary," I said. "Guess now we really know why the neighbors put up high fences."

There, flanking either side of the walkway, were a pair of raised fountains. The base of each was a shell-shaped bowl filled with water and lily pads. Standing in each bowl was a masculine version of Botticelli's famous "Birth of Venus." The man stood in the same pose as Venus, left hand coyly drawn up to cover his chest, right hand down by his genitals, yet instead of covering them, he held his optimistically endowed penis, pointing it upward. Water jetted from each penis and over the path into the basin of the twin statue opposite. The water didn't flow in a smooth stream, though. It spurted.

"Please tell me there is something wrong with his water pressure," Cassandra said.

"No, I believe that's the desired effect." I followed the path of the water over the walkway. "So, are we supposed to duck or run through between spurts?"

Cassandra marched around behind the left-hand statue, following a path undoubtedly created by countless delivery men.

"Hey," I said as I ducked between the statues. "That looks familiar."

Cassandra fixed me with a look.

"No," I said. "Not *that*. The face. Check out the statue faces. It's John, isn't it? He had them modeled after himself."

Her gaze flicked down. "Not entirely."

I grinned. "Cassandra, you and John? Say it isn't so."

"May I never be so desperate. I meant that if he was that gifted, I'd certainly have heard about it. The vampire community isn't that big."

"And neither, apparently, is John."

We climbed onto the porch, then both stopped to stare at the door knocker, an iron Nosferatu-style vampire head, teeth bared.

"You know," I said. "We might not be giving John enough credit. All this could be a clever example of reverse psychology. No one would ever suspect a real vampire would be stupid enough to live like this."

"One would hope that *no* person would ever be stupid enough to live like this."

She lifted the door knocker.

"Hold on," I said, putting my hand out to stop her. "Is this really such a good idea?"

"No," she said, wheeling and heading down the steps. "It is not. I saw a nice little boutique on the corner. Why don't we do some shopping, wait for Aaron to phone back—"

"I meant it might not be wise to announce ourselves. If he bolted last night, he might do the same again."

"Only if we're lucky."

"I think we should break in."

"Quite possibly the only suggestion that would make this excursion even more unbearable. If this involves crawling through a broken basement window, may I mention now that these pants are dry-clean-only, I didn't bring another change of clothes, and I'm certainly not going to—"

I finished murmuring an unlock spell and opened the door. Inside, all was dark and silent.

"It's daytime," Cassandra murmured. "He'll be asleep."

Guess I should have known that. I needed to brush up on my vampire lore.

The house was cool, almost cold compared to the warm fall day outside. I could chalk up the drop in temperature to an otherworldly chill from stepping into the abode of the undead, but I suspected John just had his air conditioner cranked too high.

I cast a light spell and looked around. The walls were covered in crimson velvet-flocked wallpaper, and decorated with paintings that probably violated obscenity codes in a dozen states.

"I didn't know goats could do that," I said, casting my light over one picture. "And I'm not sure why they'd want to."

"Could you dim that thing?" Cassandra said. "Please?"

"Sorry, it's a single-wattage spell," I said. "But I could blindfold you. Hey, look, there's a leather hood right there on the coatrack. Oooh, check out the cat-o'-nine-tails. Think John would notice if I scooped it?"

"You're enjoying this far too much."

"It's just so refreshing to see a vampire who fully

embraces his cultural heritage." I waved my light-ball toward the stairs. "Shall we see whether we can wake the undead?"

Cassandra shot me a look that said she was seriously reconsidering her thirty-and-up policy. I grinned back and headed for the stairs.

Upstairs we found more red velvet wallpaper, more paintings of questionable artistic merit, more S&M-themed knickknacks, and no John. There were four bedrooms. Two were furnished as sleeping quarters, but seemed to be used only as dressing rooms. The third could best be described as a museum of vampire-fetish, and is best left undescribed in further detail. The fourth door was locked.

"This must be his," I whispered to Cassandra. "Either that, or the stuff in here is even worse than the stuff in the last room."

"I doubt that's possible." Cassandra's gaze darted toward the fetish room. "Perhaps, though, I should wait in the hall. In case John returns."

I grinned. "Good plan."

I cast a simple unlock spell, assuming it was a normal interior door lock, the type that could be sprung with a hairpin. When that failed, I moved to my next stronger spell, then to the strongest. Finally, the door opened.

"Damn," I murmured. "Whatever he's got in here, he really doesn't want anyone to see."

I eased open the door, guided my light-ball around the corner, and found myself looking into . . . an office. An ordinary, modern home office, with gray carpet, painted blue walls, fluorescent lighting, a metal desk, two computers, and a fax machine. A whiteboard on the far wall held John's to-do list: pick up dry-cleaning, pay property taxes, renew cleaning contract, hire new dishwasher. Not a single mention of sucking blood, raping the local virgins, or turning his neighbors into undead fiends. No wonder John didn't want anyone coming in here. One glance through that door and all his image-building would be for naught.

I stepped out and closed the door behind me.

"You don't want to go in there," I said.

"Bad?"

"The worst." I looked along the hall. "So he's not here, and it doesn't look like he's slept up here in a while. So where does a culturally faithful vamp sleep? You didn't see a mausoleum out back, did you?"

"Thank God, no. He seems to have had the sense to draw the line at that."

"Probably because he couldn't get the building permit. Okay, well..." I looked at her. "Help me out here. I'm not vamp-stereotype savvy."

She paused, as if it pained her to answer, then sighed. "The basement."

We stood in the center of the basement. My light-ball hung over the only object in the room, a massive, gleaming, ebony black, silver-trimmed coffin.

"Just when you thought it couldn't get any worse, huh?" I said. "At least it's not a mausoleum."

"He's sleeping in a box, Paige. It doesn't get any worse than that. A mausoleum, at least you could fix up, add some skylights, perhaps a nice feather bed with Egyptian cotton sheets..."

"He might have Egyptian cotton sheets in there," I said. "Oh, and you know, it might not be as bad as you think. Maybe he doesn't sleep in there. Maybe it's just for sex."

Cassandra fixed me with a look. "Thank you, Paige. If those pictures upstairs weren't enough to taint my sex life for weeks, that image will certainly do it."

"Well, at least we know he's not having sex in there right now. I think it'd need to be propped open for that. So what's the proper etiquette for rousing a vamp from his coffin? Should we knock first?"

Cassandra grabbed the side of the coffin and was about to swing it open when her head jerked up.

"Paige—!" she called.

That was all I heard before a body struck mine. As I pitched forward, pain shot through my torn stomach muscles. I twisted and caught a glimpse of a naked thigh and a swirl of long, blond hair. Then a hand grabbed me from behind and a head plunged toward my neck.

I reacted on instinct, not with a spell, but with a move from a barely remembered self-defense class. My elbow shot up into my attacker's chest and my other hand slammed, palm first, into the nose.

A shriek of pain and my attacker stumbled back. I scuttled around, binding spell at the ready, and saw Brigid huddled on the floor, naked, cupping her nose.

"You bitch! I think you broke my nose."

"Stop whining," Cassandra said, reaching down to help me up. "It'll heal in the time it takes you to get dressed." She shook her head. "Two vampires laid low in two days by a twenty-two-year-old witch. I am embarrassed for my race."

I could have pointed out that I was twenty-three, but it wouldn't have had the same alliteration. At least Cassandra had some vague idea of my age. Most times she was doing well if she bothered to remember names.

Behind us, the coffin creaked open.

"What the hell is—" John grumbled, yanking a sleep mask from his eyes. "Cassandra?" He groaned. "What did I do now?"

"They broke in, Hans," Brigid said. "They were prowling around, looking at everything—"

"We weren't prowling," Cassandra said. "And we were trying very hard *not* to look at anything. Now get out of that coffin, John. I can't speak to you when you're in that thing."

He sighed, grabbed both sides and pushed himself up. Unlike Brigid, he was, thankfully, not naked, or I'd have been unable to resist vocalizing comparisons with the statues out front. Though John was shirtless, he wore a pair of billowing black silk pants, cinched at the waist. I assumed they were supposed to look debonair, but I was having serious MC Hammer flashbacks.

"We need some information," Cassandra began. "Last night, we weren't entirely forthright with you for security reasons. But, after we spoke to you, it was obvious that I may have underestimated your . . . stature in the vampire world."

"It happens," John said.

"Yes, well, here's the situation. A vampire has been killing Cabal children—the children of Cabal employees."

"Since when?" John said, then coughed. "I mean, I heard about that, of course."

"Of course. As of yet, the Cabals don't realize that they're hunting for a vampire. The interracial council would like to keep it that way, to catch the perpetrator quietly. We know the Cabals don't like vampires. We don't need to give them an excuse to come after us."

"Let them," Brigid said, stepping forward. "They want a war, we'll give them a—"

John hushed her with a wave. As he watched us, I realized that, as I'd hoped, Cassandra had indeed underestimated him. Playing the fool didn't mean he was one.

"If you catch him, what are you going to do with him?"
John asked. "I'm not going to help you find a vampire so
you can kill him. I could argue he's doing us a favor."

"Not if the Cabals find out."

John paused, then nodded. "So I assume you want to
know who has a beef with the Cabals."

"Shouldn't she already know?" Brigid said, slanting a
look at Cassandra. "That's her job, as our representative
isn't it? To know who's been naughty and who's been
nice?"

Cassandra met Brigid's sneer with a solemn nod. "Yes,
it is, and if I have been remiss in performing my duties, I
apologize. As of now, expect me to do so, and if I do not,
you may petition the council to have me removed. As
well, I may consider seeking a codelegate."

"We'd appreciate that, Cassandra," John said. "We've
all talked about this. We'd like a second delegate on the
council. I'd be willing, of course."

"I . . . appreciate the offer," Cassandra said. "Right now,
though, we need to resolve the most pressing concern. If
you know anyone who has had a problem with the
Cabals—"

"First, I want your word that whoever is responsible
won't be executed."

"I can't do that. Council law—"

"Fuck council law."

Cassandra glanced at me. I shook my head. This we
couldn't do. We both knew that the killer had to go to the
Cabals. To do otherwise would be to risk having them
turn on both the vampires and the council. All we could
do now was negotiate with them to minimize the fallout.

"We can't promise absolution," Cassandra said. "But we'll make sure he's treated fairly—"

"No deal."

"Perhaps you fail to understand the importance of this. The more children this vampire kills, the uglier this will get. We need to stop him—"

"Then stop him," Brigid said. "You shouldn't need us. And I don't think you do. I think this is all a little act for your council buddies, so they don't find out the truth."

Cassandra's eyes narrowed. "What truth?"

"That you knew exactly what was going on. You knew how bad things were. You want us to tell your little witch friend here so you can claim you didn't know a thing about it. Well, you can't possibly be that out of touch—"

"I'm afraid she is," said a voice behind us.

We turned to see Aaron step into the basement, followed by Lucas.

"Cassandra doesn't know what's been going on," Aaron said. "But I do."

Edward and Natasha

"HELLO, AARON," BRIGID SAID, SLIDING UP TO HIM AND running a finger down his chest. "You're looking good... as always."

Aaron lifted her finger off his shirt and let it drop. "Put some clothing on, Brigid."

She smiled up at him. "Why? Tempted?"

"Yeah, to cover my eyes."

Brigid sniffed and swung to Lucas. "So this is the Cabal crown prince, is it?" She looked him up and down. "Nothing contact lenses and a better wardrobe couldn't fix."

She took a step toward him.

"No, thank you," Lucas murmured.

"Brigid?" John said. "Please, get dressed."

"Don't bother," Cassandra said. "If Aaron has what we need, then we'll leave you two to your immortal slumber."

She headed for the door.

"Hold on," John said. "I may have details Aaron doesn't. My deal still stands."

"Deal?" Aaron said.

I nodded. "He wants us to promise not to execute the killer or hand him over to the Cabals."

"Ah, fuck, Hans, you know we can't do that. They'll come after us, hunt us down."

Brigid laughed. "You think we're afraid of the Cabals? We're vampires. The gods of the supernatural world, impervious to harm—"

"Yeah, until someone chops off our heads, then we're worm food like everyone else. Hans, maybe you've got Brigid believing that vamp-superiority crap, but I know you're smarter than that."

"We don't need this," Cassandra said. "If you have a name—"

"I do, but Hans may know more. I want to find this guy before he kills another Cabal kid."

"Why?" Brigid said. "Who cares about another dead Cabal brat?"

"The Cabals do."

John hesitated, then nodded. "Let's talk."

At Cassandra's insistence, we moved out of the basement. John suggested the backyard, so we waited for him there. Like the front yard, the rear was surrounded by a high fence. Here, though, the fence had been erected by John, not his neighbors. The yard was almost as big a shock as the home office, which is probably why he kept it hidden.

It was small, no more than a few hundred square feet. Instead of grass, it had rock gardens and koi ponds surrounded by gravel paths. In the center of the yard was a pagoda with a teak table and chair set, where we waited for John.

Brigid had already made it clear that she wouldn't be joining us. Apparently, she took her role as a "true" vampire very seriously, never venturing outside during the day. I suspected this was why John chose to have the meeting outdoors, so he could speak without her interruptions.

As we waited, Lucas explained how they'd found us. Aaron had called him early this morning, thinking we'd be sleeping in after our night chasing John. They decided to hook up and come to New Orleans together. Lucas knew we were heading to John's house, but didn't have the address. Aaron had the address.

I was anxious to hear Aaron's findings, but before I could ask, John returned. He was dressed in black leather pants and a white linen shirt. Still pretty Goth, but not as theatrical as last night's attire. I suspected there was a lot of theatrics to John's image. Last night he'd gushed about Aaron, but when the man showed up in person, Brigid had been the only one vamping it up.

"It's Edward, isn't it?" Aaron said as John pulled out a chair.

"That would be my guess," John said. "I don't know him well enough to say for certain—"

"*No one* knows them well enough to say for certain," Aaron said.

"Them?" I asked.

"Edward and Natasha. They're a couple. Been together a very long time."

"I've heard those names," I said. "In the council minutes. They're immortality questers."

"Did the council investigate them?" Lucas asked.

"Investigated and exonerated, if I remember correctly," I said. "It was at least thirty, forty years ago. Another vampire expressed some concern about their questing—no outright allegations, just a bad feeling. Anyway, Edward and Natasha weren't breaking any codes, just searching for answers, like most questers."

"Well, it's gone beyond bad feelings," Aaron said. "Seems rumors have been circulating about them in the vamp community for a while, saying they've gotten into some nasty shit up in Ohio." Aaron caught my look. "Yeah, they've been living in Cincinnati. Lucas told me that's where you figure the killer's from. I'd say we've got ourselves a suspect."

"Is this connected to their questing?" I asked.

"Possible," Lucas said. "They may have uncovered a ritual requiring supernatural blood."

"Then where's the Cabal connection? Sure, it's a great way to find supernaturals—just hack into the Cabal employment records—but you think they'd stick to the periphery, with runaways like Dana. Attacking a CEO's family is only going to raise the stakes."

"That could be a side effect of the killing itself," Lucas said. "After Dana and Jacob, Edward saw the chaos he was creating and couldn't resist a bigger challenge."

"Or maybe the ritual wasn't working and they thought Cabal royal blood might help."

"Not they," John said. "Only Edward."

Cassandra shook her head. "Those two don't do anything alone."

"They do now," Aaron said. "No one's seen Natasha for months. Rumor is she'd finally had enough, that things got too bad, and she took off."

"I find that hard to believe," Cassandra said. "They'd been together for over a century. After that long, you don't just—" Her gaze flicked toward Aaron. "What I mean is, it seems unlikely that those two would separate."

"Well, one way or another, she *is* gone," John said. "And I doubt Edward's happy about it."

Quest for Immortality

NEXT STOP: CINCINNATI, OHIO. USING EDWARD AND NAT-asha's known aliases, as provided by Aaron, Lucas had found two Cincinnati area addresses for the vampires. There, we hoped to find either more evidence or some clue as to their current whereabouts. Aaron offered to come along, and Cassandra was in for the long haul, so all four of us were going, which seemed an expensive proposition . . . until Lucas led us to the private airstrip at the Lakefront Airport.

"I wondered how you two got to New Orleans so fast," I said as we approached the Cortez jet.

Lucas's gaze slid away and he shifted our bags to his other shoulder. "Yes, well, after I spoke to you, my father called and when I told him we were pursuing a lead, he offered the use of the jet. It seemed a wise idea, allowing us to bypass the schedules and restrictions of commercial flight." He shifted the bags again. "Perhaps I should have—"

"You did the right thing," I said. "The faster we can move, the better."

"I don't see what all the fuss is about," Cassandra said as the flight crew scrambled to lower the boarding ramp.

"This business about refusing to join your own Cabal makes absolutely no sense. If you want my opinion—"

"I'm pretty sure he doesn't, Cass," Aaron said.

"Well, I was just going to say—"

With impeccable timing, the pilot hailed Lucas to discuss last-minute flight details. A crew member took our overnight bags, then the attendant showed us to our seats. By the time Lucas returned, the plane was taxiing down the runway. The attendant followed him in and took beverage orders, then chatted with Lucas for a moment as the plane lifted off. And if you think this sidetracked Cassandra from voicing her opinion about Lucas's situation, then you don't know Cassandra.

"As I was saying," Cassandra said after the attendant delivered our drinks. "I really fail to understand this whole rebellion of yours—"

"Cass, please," Aaron said.

"No, that's fine," Lucas said. "Go ahead, Cassandra."

"One would think, if you are serious about this Cabal reformation business, then the best position from which to effect change is within the organization itself."

"Ah, the Michael Corleone strategy," I said.

Aaron grinned. "Hey, I hadn't thought of that one."

The light flashed, telling us we could remove our seat belts. After taking his off, Aaron stood and shucked his jacket. Underneath, he wore a T-shirt with the sleeves ripped off. Now, not every guy can pull off the sleeveless T-shirt look, but Aaron...well, Aaron could. And the sight temporarily diverted Cassandra from her course. As Aaron reached around the corner to hang his jacket, her gaze slid down his well-muscled arms, and came to rest on his backside. A look flitted through her eyes, more wistful than lustful. Then she jerked her gaze away with a sharp shake of her head.

"Michael Corleone," she said, honing in on her target again. "Do I know him?"

"From the *Godfather* movies," Aaron said as he lowered himself into his seat. "His father was a Mafia don. He didn't want any part of the family business, but finally decided to take over and mold it into a legitimate business. In the end, he became exactly what he'd rebelled against."

"Is that what you're afraid of?" Cassandra asked Lucas.

"No, but the basic premise holds. One man cannot reform an institution, not when everyone working for him is happy with the status quo. I'd face such serious opposition that my authority would be completely undermined and, if I continued, the board of directors would have me assassinated."

"So you pursue individual acts of injustice from outside the organization." Cassandra sipped her coffee, then nodded. "Yes, I suppose that makes sense."

"And I'm sure he's thrilled to hear that his life meets with your approval," Aaron said.

She glared at him. "I was simply clarifying matters for my own understanding."

"Okay, but why do you always have to be so damned antagonistic about it? You never just *ask* questions, Cass. You lob them like grenades."

"Aaron," I cut in. "You said you have two addresses. One in the city and one outside it. Is that an old one and a current one?"

"I'm not sure," Aaron said. "They're under separate aliases, an old one and a current one. According to Josie—"

"Josie?" Cassandra cut in. "Your source is Josie? Oh, Aaron. Really. The woman has porridge for brains. She—"

"I'm not sleeping with her."

"That's not—" Cassandra shot a glare around the cabin.

"Where is that girl? What, she serves coffee and disappears until the flight's over? Paige's cup is almost empty."

"Uh, that's okay, Cassandra," I said. "But thanks for thinking of me."

"If you need anything, just press the buzzer by your elbow," Lucas said. "Otherwise, I've asked Annette to stay up front so we can speak freely. Now, about these two addresses. The rural one is under an older alias, but we should check out both. It won't take long."

"It'd be even faster if we split up," Aaron said. "Lucas and I take one, you ladies take the other. That way, we each have a spell-caster for breaking in and a vampire for sneaking around."

"Good idea," I said. "We'll take the rural address, and leave the city one for Lucas, in case he needs to do more than peer in the windows. He's the break-in pro, not me."

Cassandra's brows arched. "And you admit it? That's a first. You really are growing up, aren't you?"

"Cassandra?" Aaron said. "Shut up."

"What? I was praising her—"

"Don't. Please." Aaron looked at me. "I wish I could say she hasn't always been like this, but she has. After a few decades, you get used to it."

"Get used to what?" Cassandra said.

"So," Aaron said. "How do you guys like living in Portland?"

Cassandra and I stood on the side of a country road, our rental car parked behind us. Through the thick brush and gnarled skeletons of dead trees, we could make out a tiny cabin that looked like it predated indoor plumbing.

"Uh, rustic getaway cottage?" I said, double-checking

the address Aaron had scribbled into my notepad. "Maybe they preferred life before electricity."

"This is ridiculous," Cassandra said. "I warned you, Paige. Aaron is far too trusting. He hates to believe anything negative about anyone, but that Josie is, bar none, the stupidest vampire ever to walk the earth. Probably gave him the names of her ex-boyfriends instead of Edward's aliases. She—"

My cell phone rang. Thankfully.

"It's Aaron," he said when I answered. "We have the house here. Lucas is scouting it out now, but I talked to the lady next door and she gave me a spot-on description of Edward and Natasha. Says they've been away a lot lately, and she hasn't seen Natasha in a few months, but Edward stops by now and then."

"Want us to come and help search?"

"If you could. Four pairs of eyes are better than two. If Cassandra squawks, tell her she can wait at a coffee shop instead. That'll make her pipe down. She hates to miss anything."

I signed off and relayed Aaron's message to Cassandra.

"So this isn't the right house?" she said. "What a surprise."

She headed for the car. I stayed where I was, peering through the trees at the cabin.

"Wait there," I called back to Cassandra. "I want to check this out first."

I headed for the cabin. Cassandra's sigh was loud enough to be heard from the roadway but, a moment later, without so much as a whisper of long grass, she was beside me.

"The only thing you're going to find here is Lyme disease," she said. "That's not a vampire's house, Paige. It never has been. It's too small, too far from the city—"

"Maybe that's the point," I said. "Immortality questers are notoriously paranoid about security. They need a place to conduct their experiments. Why not here?"

"Because it's a dump. And it's certainly not secure."

"Does it hurt to look?" I said. "It's probably five hundred square feet tops."

Cassandra sighed, then swung in front of me and marched to the cabin.

Ask people what they fear most in life and, if they answer honestly, they'll say "the end of it." Death. The great question mark. Is it surprising then, that people have pursued immortality with a relentlessness that surpasses the pursuit of wealth, sex, fame, or the satisfaction of any other worldly desire?

You might think that supernaturals wouldn't fall into this trap. After all, we know what comes next. Well, okay, we don't know *exactly*. Ghosts never tell us what's on the other side. One of the first lessons apprentice necromancers learn is "Don't ask about the afterlife." If they persist, eventually they'll be unable to contact the dead at all, as if they've been put on a ghost-world blacklist. So we don't know exactly what happens next, but we know this much: We go somewhere, and it's not such a bad place to be.

Yet even if we know that a decent afterlife awaits, that doesn't mean we're in any hurry to get there. The world we know, the people we know, the *life* we know, is here on earth. Faced with death, we kick and scream as hard as anyone else. Maybe harder. The supernatural world is rife with immortality questers. Why? Perhaps because we know, by our very existence, that magical things are possible. If a person can transform into a wolf, why can't a person live forever? Vampires live for centuries, which seems proof that semi-immortality is not a pipe dream. Then why not just become a vampire? Well, without getting too deeply into the nature of vampirism, let's just say it's extremely difficult, even harder than becoming a werewolf. For most supernaturals, finding the holy grail of immortality seems more feasible than becoming a vampire. And a quester needs only to look around to know that being a vampire doesn't cure the thirst for eternal life. If anything, it sharpens it.

I always assumed that vampires were such ardent immortality questers because, having enjoyed a taste of it, they can't help wanting the whole deal. Now, after Jaime told me she'd never heard of a necro contacting a dead vamp, I began to wonder how many vampires knew there was no proof of a vampire afterlife. I've never thought immortality sounded all that great, but if it was a choice between that and total annihilation, I'd take eternal life any day.

"Well," Cassandra said, standing in the cabin doorway. "I think we can safely say there's no secret lab in here."

I squeezed past her. Inside, the cabin was even smaller than it had appeared, a single room no more than three hundred square feet. The door had been secured with a lock good enough to require my strongest unlock spell and there were no windows, which had raised my hopes that something of interest was hidden within. From what I saw, though, the lock was only to keep out teens looking for a party place. There was nothing here worth stealing.

The cabin did appear to be in use, maybe as a retreat for an artist or a writer, someone who needed a distraction-free place to work. Distraction-free it certainly was. The only furnishings were a wooden desk, a pullout sofa, a bookcase, and a coffee table. The desk was empty, and the bookshelf held only cheap reference texts.

I surveyed the bookshelf's contents, then peered behind the unit.

"Please don't tell me you're looking for a secret passageway," Cassandra said.

I turned to the sofa, grabbed one end and pushed, but it was as heavy as most sofa beds.

"Could you—?" I said, gesturing at the far end. "Please."

"You can't be serious."

"Cassandra, please. Humor me. You know I'm not leaving until I move this sofa, so unless you want to be here a while—"

She grabbed the end and hoisted. We moved it forward just far enough for me to roll up the area rug and look underneath.

"I've always said you were practical, Paige. Whenever someone in the council questioned your ideas, I said 'Paige is a practical girl. She's not given to flights of fancy.'"

"Huh," I said, heaving up the carpet. "Don't remember hearing that."

"Well, you must not have been around. The point is that I have always given you credit for common sense. And now, here you are, searching for a secret room . . ."

The floor under the carpet was a checkerboard of wood panels, each roughly three feet square. The gap between most of the panels was less than a quarter inch, but one groove looked a shade wider. I ran my fingers along it.

Cassandra continued. "If Edward and Natasha were into alchemy, which I doubt, they would have rented storage space in the city for their experiments. They would not be digging secret rooms under a run-down cabin in—"

My fingertips struck a catch, and the door sprang open.

I peered into the darkness below. "Strange place for a root cellar, don't you think?"

I cast a light spell, then tossed the ball into the hole. Along one side was a ladder. As I shifted to step onto the first rung, Cassandra grasped my shoulder.

"You're not invulnerable, Paige. I am. It might be trapped. I'll go first."

I suspected this offer had more to do with curiosity than concern, but I stepped back and let her go through.

Appetite for Art

AS I STEPPED ONTO THE LADDER, MY VISION CLOUDED FOR a second, like a mental stutter.

"Someone's coming," I whispered into the hole. "My perimeter spell just went off. I cast one across the front of the property."

Cassandra blinked, as if shocked by this show of foresight. She motioned for me to come down and hide there, but I shook my head, hurried to the door, cracked it open and peeked out. A young man headed toward the cabin. He struggled to carry an armload of supplies, and could barely see where he was going, let alone see me. When Cassandra peered over my shoulder, I pointed out a path along the left side of the cabin, behind the overgrown bushes.

Cassandra took the lead, as usual. This time, though, it made sense. A vampire's stealth is partly preternatural and partly hunting experience. By following in her footsteps I could move almost as quietly as she could.

Behind the cabin, the land was a patchwork of forest and meadow. The forest alternated between stands of evergreens and deciduous trees. Even the meadow itself seemed uncertain what form it should take, with patches of long grass interspersed with brush and brambles.

"Should we wait it out or come back later?" I whispered when we'd walked far enough.

"Wait it out."

"I'll phone Lucas, then. He's probably wondering where we are."

It turned out that Lucas and Aaron didn't need our help. The house had required little more than a quick sweep, and revealed nothing. With the news of our find, Lucas promised to hurry over and help *us*.

As I hung up, Cassandra glided out from a stand of trees. I hadn't noticed she'd left.

"This isn't going to work," she said. "He'll be there for a while. He's an artist."

"Artist?"

"He's set up in front of the cabin with a half-finished painting of it, although why on earth anyone would want a picture of that in their living room is quite beyond me."

"Wonderful. Well, since it doesn't look as if he'll leave on his own, we'll have to give him a supernatural push. Think a hailstorm would persuade him to call it a day?"

"I'll handle this. Wait here."

Cassandra slipped away without waiting for an answer, which was a good thing because I had no intention of staying behind. As good as Cassandra was, everyone can use backup. So I waited until she was out of sight, then looped around the cabin the other way.

The obvious plan of action was to charm him. Like most vampire powers, charming is a functional skill, another adaptation that makes them expert hunters. At its most basic, charming is extreme charisma. It allows a vamp to walk up to the most street-savvy girl in a bar and, within minutes, have her saying, "Hmm, yes, I think I would like to follow you into that dark alley."

By the time I got close enough to see around the cabin,

Cassandra would probably be nearly done "persuading" the artist to leave. If anything went wrong, though, I'd be close enough to help out. When I reached the front corner of the cabin, I readied a cover spell, which would keep me hidden so long as I stayed motionless. When the spell was half cast, I leaned out and finished the incantation at the same time, so I could watch without being seen.

Cassandra wasn't there. I could see the artist, a balding man in his late twenties, sitting on a folding camp stool, his attention riveted to the canvas on his portable easel. A bush a few yards behind the man shimmered, as if ruffled by a sudden breeze. Cassandra? Why was she over there? Oh, probably approaching from the road so he wouldn't wonder where she'd come from.

Cassandra's green shirt flashed between two bushes, now less than a yard behind the artist. Okay, stop playing and come out before you give the poor guy a heart attack.

As if hearing me, Cassandra eased into the open. She stood between the bush and the artist, her narrowed eyes gleaming. She tilted her head, gaze fixed on the back of his head. Then she smiled. Her lips parted, and the tip of her tongue slid over her teeth.

Oh, shit.

I jerked back behind the cabin just as she pounced. There was an intake of breath, half sigh, half gasp. Then silence. I wrapped my arms around my chest and tried very hard not to think about what was happening just a scant ten feet away, which, of course, made me think about it all the more. She wouldn't kill him. I knew that. She was just . . . feeding.

I shivered and hugged myself tighter. It wasn't such a bad idea, I told myself. Beyond the obvious debilitating effect of blood-draining, a vampire's initial bite, if done properly, knocked its victim unconscious, so the blood would flow freely. Cassandra's bite would guarantee the artist would be out cold for a few hours. And she did need to eat. But still . . .

"I told you to stay where you were, Paige."

I turned to see Cassandra at the corner of the cabin. There wasn't so much as a blood smear on her lips, but her color was high and her eyes had lost their usual glitter, lids half closed with the lazy, sated look of someone who's just had a very good meal . . . or very good sex.

"I—backup—wanted—" I managed.

"Well, I appreciate the sentiment, but you should have listened to me. Now come on. We need to check out that basement."

Instead of marching off in the lead, she prodded me forward. When I turned the corner, I saw the artist slumped on the ground. I couldn't suppress a shiver.

"He'll be fine, Paige," Cassandra said, her tone gentler than usual.

"I know."

"You may not like it, but I could argue that some people would feel the same about the chicken you ate for dinner last night."

"I know."

A soft chuckle. "You aren't going to argue the point? *Quelle surprise.*" She patted my back. "Let's get to that secret room. I can't wait to see what they've stashed down there."

Before we went back into the cabin, I cast another perimeter spell. If anyone arrived before Lucas and Aaron, we needed enough advance warning to move the unconscious artist. It may have seemed wiser to move him immediately, but with a vampire bite, the safest way to hide what happened is not to hide it at all. Better for the artist to wake up on the ground by his chair, thinking he'd suffered a blackout.

With Cassandra following, I climbed down the ladder. Then I stood at the bottom and cast my light-ball around four walls, each with a floor-to-ceiling canning shelf. Every shelf was empty.

I slumped against the ladder. "It really is a cold cellar."

"Don't be so hasty," Cassandra said, moving her hands along the far shelving unit. "Here, this one seems looser than the others. Grab the other end."

I took hold of the shelf and, on the count of three, pulled. The shelf didn't move. I walked to the nearest shelf and began examining it, the first wave of disappointment having given way to resolution. Maybe I had been mistaken about this room, but I wasn't leaving until I was certain of that.

I poked and pried at the shelf but it didn't budge. On to the next one.

"That one's firmly fastened," Cassandra said as she inspected the remaining shelf. "It doesn't so much as quiver."

I stopped yanking on the shelf and instead ran my fingers along both sides, where the unit fastened to the wall. It was rammed so tight against the wall that I couldn't even squeeze a fingernail into the gap. I crouched to examine the underside of the lower shelves.

On the second-to-bottom shelf, I found a nail sticking out near the corner. I prodded it. The nail slid into the wood and the shelf snapped hard against my hands.

"A catch," Cassandra said. "Well done again."

Before I could pull it open, my vision clouded.

"Not again," I muttered. "My perimeter spell, with flawless timing."

Cassandra checked her watch. "Aaron and Lucas."

"Or so I hope. I'll check. You go on in."

I scooted up the ladder and out the cabin door. Lucas and Aaron were picking their way through the brambles. I hailed them with a shout.

"Hear you found Edward's hidey-hole," Aaron called as they drew closer. "Way to go."

"We haven't had a chance to look inside yet," I said. "We ran into a few complications."

When they caught up, Lucas's hand brushed mine, then gave it a squeeze.

"Oooh, would that be one of those complications?" Aaron said, jerking his chin toward the fallen artist. "Or just a late-afternoon snack?"

"Both, I think," I said.

"Is she in a better mood now?"

"Actually, now that I think about it, a much better mood."

Aaron's laugh rang out through the quiet meadow. "Oh, yeah, same old Cassandra. I thought that might be the problem. She gets pretty damned testy when she hasn't eaten. That's one big drawback to socializing with nonvamps. Nobody wants to hear you say, 'I'm just popping out for a bite.' If she ever gets bitchier than usual, that's a good time to send her out on a late-night coffee run. Best way to cheer her up." He grinned. "Well, there are other ways, but you don't want to hear about those."

We circled past the artist and headed into the cabin.

A Strange Place to Take a Bath

I LED LUCAS AND AARON TO THE SECRET ROOM. AS I looked around, my first thought was, "That makes sense, and that makes sense, and . . . what the hell is that for?"

The room was just slightly larger than the fake cold cellar, maybe eight feet square. Along one wall was a bookcase, filled with ancient reference books and experimentation journals. The shelves on the opposite wall held vials, beakers, jars, and other scientific equipment. All this was exactly what I expected to see in a quester's laboratory. What I couldn't understand, though, was the claw-footed bathtub that took up a quarter of the floor space.

"I like to read in the bath, too," I said. "But that seems a bit extreme."

"Especially with no running water," Aaron said.

"I would assume it's used as a mixing basin," Lucas said. "Though it seems rather large for the purpose and it would likely have required removing the cabin floor to get it down here. Perhaps it has a greater significance, a relic of some sort."

Cassandra looked up from the journal she'd been reading. "You're both right. It would be used for mixing a compound, then bathing in it. Ingestion is the most common way to take immortality potions, but immersion is also popular."

"Find anything?" Aaron said, looking down over her shoulder. "At least it's not in code."

"It would be better if it was," she said. "A code can be deciphered and broken. Instead, what they've done is put in only enough detail to remind themselves what they did."

"Huh?"

She lifted the book closer to my light-ball. "'March seventh, 2001. Tried variation B again with fresher source material type Hf. No change. April twelfth, 2001. Expanded variation A to include source material type Hm, subtype E. No change.'"

"Shit," Aaron muttered. "Is it all like that?"

Cassandra nodded.

"What's the date on the last entry?" Lucas asked.

"June of this year."

"A month or two before Natasha left him," I said. "Any idea what they were doing at the time? Maybe something changed, made her decide to leave?"

Cassandra handed me the journal. "It's exactly like the other entries. They talk about 'materials' and 'variations' and 'subtypes,' but nothing specific."

I moved beside Lucas and held the journal between us as we read the last half-dozen pages. Then I flipped to the start of the book, which dated back to 1996, and skimmed to the present.

"The only change I see is a gradual increase in ingredient Hf and Hm. It appears on and off in the earlier entries, then becomes a regular ingredient in the last year. Otherwise, the entries are pretty similar—variations A through E, methodologies A through K."

"Let's see what other goodies we have, then," Aaron said. He scanned the equipment shelf. "Lots and lots of unlabeled, half-filled bottles." He grabbed one, pulled out the stopper, sniffed it, and gagged. "I may be invulnerable, but please don't ask me to taste-test anything."

I took the bottle from him and sniffed. "Sulfur." He handed me another one. "Rosemary." I eyed the shelf and named three more from looks alone. "All fairly common potion ingredients. Same with the dried stuff. Half these things you could pick up in any New Age shop."

"Which could mean that this is all they use," Cassandra said. "Or it could mean that they've hidden the more damning ingredients."

"Time to start looking for more cubbyholes," Aaron said. "I'll get the top shelves."

He ran his hand over the highest shelf, which appeared empty. As he swept along it, he dislodged a bottle and sent it crashing into the tub. Cassandra reached into the tub and touched the bottom, beside the broken pieces.

"Dry," she said. "It was empty."

She started to stand, then stopped, and ran a finger along the inside of the tub. With a frown, she leaned farther in, then shook her head and straightened.

"See something?" I said.

She shook her head. "It's been scrubbed clean."

"I believe I've found something here," Lucas said.

He was crouched in front of the equipment shelf. I expected to see another doorway behind the shelf. Instead, he gestured at the shelf itself, which he'd cleared of bottles. When I looked, I saw not a wooden shelf, but a drawer. It seemed too shallow to hold anything. Then Lucas pulled back the velvet cloth that lay over the contents—a row of surgical instruments.

"They, uh, could be veterinary tools," Aaron said. "Some questers use animal sacrifice. It's discouraged, but it does happen."

I met Lucas's gaze. "Hm and Hf."

He gave a slow nod. "Human male and human female."

Cassandra said nothing. When we looked over at her, she was bent over a hole in the floor, where she'd taken off a section of board.

"What's that?" I said.

She slammed the board back into place. "More ingredients. They're . . . human."

Aaron squatted beside her and reached for the loose board, but she held it fast to the floor.

"You don't need to look, either," she said.

"I've lived through Jack the Ripper, Charles Manson, and Jeffrey Dahmer. Nothing under that board is going to shock me."

"It's not going to make you sleep any easier, either." She looked at us. "I'll draw up an inventory of what's in here, and package it if you'd like. For now, I can tell you that they were using body parts, from multiple humans, and they weren't retrieving them from graveyards."

Her gaze skittered toward the tub. She blinked hard and looked away.

"It smells of blood, doesn't it?" Lucas said.

"I caught a whiff of something, and I thought it might be blood, but I can't pick it up again."

Aaron ducked his head into the tub. He inhaled, then shook his head. "Nothing. That's one smell we can always pick up but I'm not—" He stopped. "Scratch that. I caught it. Very faint, but definitely human blood."

"So that's what the tub is for," I said. "They put them in

there to . . . harvest what they needed without making too big a mess."

"Could be," Lucas said.

I met his gaze. "But you don't think so."

He picked up the journal and turned to a page near the end. "There are several references this year to immersion in source material Hm and Hf."

"Elizabeth Báthory," Cassandra murmured.

My gut sank, as I understood what they meant.

Elizabeth Báthory was a Hungarian countess who lived in the sixteenth century. According to legend, she'd killed six hundred and fifty young women, most of them peasants, and bathed in their blood because she believed it would grant her eternal youth. After several decades of killing, Báthory was arrested, tried, convicted, and put into a room. Then the door was bricked over.

It has been argued that Elizabeth Báthory was at least part of Bram Stoker's inspiration for Dracula, perhaps even more than the equally sadistic and better known Vlad Dracul, from whom Stoker borrowed the name. In vampire society, it was generally believed that Elizabeth Báthory had been a vampire and that she'd been seeking, not eternal youth, but her youth for eternity—in other words, an immortality quester.

It was also rumored that her experiment had succeeded, that she had found eternal life and that the story of her death had been concocted, not by human officials, but by powerful elements within the vampire community. When they'd discovered her crimes—and, yes, killing six hundred humans *was* a crime even by vampire standards—they'd masterminded her arrest and trial. Then, the vampires themselves walled her up, where she remains to this day, having outlived every vampire who knew where she was imprisoned.

In covering up the success of her immortality experiments, her captors had tried to ensure such crimes would never be repeated. Yet the story, true or not, had been passed down through generations of immortality questers. Most didn't dare replicate Báthory's work but, about every hundred years or so, somebody tried.

"But to bathe in blood," I said. "That would—each time you did it, you'd need to kill how many people? Where would they bury all those—?" I stopped, remembering the strange patchwork terrain out back. I swallowed. "I think I might know."

After uncovering the fourth body, we stopped digging. All four corpses were drained of blood, and all in the ground less than a year, which meant they weren't Edward and Natasha's requisite annual kills. When we looked out over the patchwork of old-growth and new-growth meadow, we knew if we kept digging we'd find many more.

After ensuring that the artist was still unconscious, we returned to the cabin and took what we could for later examination. Then we drove to Edward and Natasha's house in the city and searched it again, now looking for hidden rooms and caches. We found nothing, which didn't surprise us; it was unlikely they'd go to all the trouble of secreting away their materials at the cabin, only to leave some in their house.

Throughout the searches, we'd all been pretty quiet, still shocked over what we'd found at the cabin. As Lucas drove us to the airport, though, my numbed brain finally began to churn through the facts . . . and found a gaping crater in the logic.

"Doesn't it punch a big hole in our theory about his motivation for killing Cabal kids?"

Lucas slanted a look my way, telling me to continue.

"Okay, if Edward's experiments with humans failed, then I can see him testing them out with supernaturals. But what's he taking? Not blood, that's for sure. Or, at least, not enough to bathe in. If he's taking something else, like the stuff that Cassandra found—" I glanced into the backseat at her. "Was it . . . material that wouldn't be missed?"

She shook her head. "Some of it is external, some internal, but everything would have been missed, if not in a visual examination, then at least in the most cursory autopsy. Perhaps he was taking something different, something small enough to be overlooked."

"I doubt that," Lucas said. "Joey Nast was still alive when we found him. I can't imagine the killer had time to excise anything from his body."

"But everything else fits," I said. "We're looking for a vampire killer, possibly from the Cincinnati area. Edward is a vampire from Cincinnati, with killing experience that goes well beyond feeding. According to his neighbors, he hasn't been home in over a week. His longtime lover has left him, which might have sent him over the edge, desperate to find the key to immortality so he can win her back. Even his physical description matches what little Esus saw of him. It all fits."

"All except that one piece," Lucas said. "Edward appears to be our man, so I'd suggest that we consider another theory regarding his motivation."

"Like what?" Aaron said.

"I have no idea," Lucas said. "But I'm open to suggestions."

We all looked at one another . . . and said nothing.

A Most Unwelcome Intrusion

WE BOARDED THE JET. OUR FIRST STOP WOULD BE Atlanta. Although tomorrow was Sunday, Aaron had to work. Well, he didn't *have* to, but he'd promised a friend he'd take his shift and, since it didn't look like we'd be hot on Edward's trail just yet, he didn't want to break that promise. When we had a line on Edward, Aaron wanted to come back and help out. Being a vampire meant he had a lot of unused sick days, so he didn't expect to have any trouble getting time off his bricklaying job.

When Lucas returned from conferring with the pilot, he suggested we all try to sleep.

"It's not the most comfortable environment," he said. "But I doubt anyone slept much last night, and these next few hours may be our only chance tonight."

Cassandra nodded. "You and Paige should definitely try to sleep. I'm not tired, though, so I'll sit in the rear cabin, if you don't mind."

Lucas escorted Cassandra into the tiny private cabin behind ours.

"Did she sleep at all last night?" Aaron whispered to me when they were out of earshot.

I shook my head. "She says . . . she says she's not sleeping much lately."

His eyes filled with quiet grief, as if this was the answer he'd been both expecting and dreading.

"I'll sit up with her," he said.

As I pulled pillows and a blanket from the closet, Lucas disappeared into the crew area. He returned a few minutes later carrying two mugs of tea. He slid my "forgotten" bottle of painkillers from his pocket. I opened my mouth to argue, then caught his look, nodded, and held out my hand. He shook two into it, then sat beside me.

"How are you doing?" he asked.

"Shaken, but okay. When we heard Edward and Natasha were into dark stuff, I steeled myself for what we thought was the worst—that they were experimenting with humans. But the scale . . . the number of people they must have—"

I gulped my tea and sputtered as the hot liquid burned my throat. Lucas took my mug with a rush of apologies.

"No, that's my fault," I said. "I always tell you to make it hot. I drank it too fast."

I took the mug from his hands. As I moved it to my side table, my hands shook so badly that tea sloshed over the side, nearly burning me again.

"Damn it," I muttered, then managed a small smile. "Guess I'm not so okay after all."

He squeezed my hand. "Completely understandable."

"I know I have to be able to handle this better," I said. "If I'm going to help you, I need to get over my squeamishness. I'm too—"

"You're fine," he said. "I'm not feeling too 'okay' myself.

I can guarantee, as a, uh, partner in my endeavors, you'd likely never see anything on this scale again."

"Partner?" I said, my smile turning genuine. "Don't think I didn't notice the hitch in your voice. Don't worry. I have no plans to shoehorn myself into your life that way. I'll be here to help when you need me, but that's it."

"That wasn't—That is to say, I certainly don't mind, if you're interested . . ."

"I'm not. Well, I am, but I can't be, right? Between the council and the new Coven, my plate's already full." I inhaled. "We screwed up. The council, I mean. We should have caught this."

"You can't keep tabs on every vampire—"

"Can't we?" I said. "The Pack does it with werewolves, and there are more of them to police and fewer people to do it. I don't mean we need to be breathing down every vampire's neck, but we need to be more proactive in general. There were rumors. We should have heard them. I can't blame Cassandra for that. It's everyone's responsibility. I want to change things, to start paying closer attention. But I also want to start this new Coven. I *need* to do that. It's what I'm supposed to do."

"Because your mother would have wanted it," he said softly.

"Not just that. I wanted—or I thought I wanted . . ." I rubbed my hands over my face. "I know rebuilding the Coven is important, but some days I feel like there are other things I should be doing, things I'd *rather* be doing, and the Coven . . . I'm not sure it's still my dream, or that it ever really was."

"You'll figure it out."

Lucas leaned over and kissed me, a slow, gentle kiss that calmed the confusion crashing about in my head. After a few minutes, we reclined our seats, curled up together, and let the soft drone of the plane lull us to sleep. When the plane landed in Atlanta, I woke up just enough to hear Aaron and Cassandra's whispered exchange of good-byes. A moment after the cabin door shut behind Aaron, I felt Cassandra tug the fallen blanket up over me. I sensed her standing there, watching me, but by the time I pried my eyes open, she was gone.

When I woke again, the plane had landed in Miami. I knew it had to be past dawn, but the cabin's blackout shades made it nearly pitch black inside. I snuggled in closer to Lucas and pulled up the blanket to ward off the chill of the air-conditioning.

"Cold nose," Lucas said with a sleepy laugh.

I tried pulling back, but he lifted my chin and kissed me.

"That's nice and warm," he said.

"Hmmm. Very nice."

"We're going to have to see my father today," he murmured between kisses.

"Hmmm, not so nice."

Another laugh. "Sorry."

"No, you're right. We need to tell him what we found . . . and we should thank him for the use of the jet." I caught Lucas's look. "You don't still regret taking it, do you?"

He sighed. "I don't know. I worry about how it will be interpreted. Then I worry about whether it's a sign of backsliding. And then I worry about worrying too much, what you must think of it." A quarter-smile. "Self-doubt is not a sexy trait in a lover."

"Depends on the lover. You can be almost scarily self-confident, Cortez. I like being the only one who gets to peek through the chinks in the armor. If you're still worried, though, I do know a good temporary cure."

A crooked grin. "Distraction?"

"Um-hmmm." I slid my hands under the blanket.

"Wait," he said. "I still owe you for the broom closet, and believe I can be adequately distracted by reciprocating that favor."

I grinned. "You never owe me. But I won't argue if you insist."

"I do."

As he shifted forward to kiss me, a seat squeaked... only it didn't sound like the seat we were lying on. I lifted my head to see Benicio tiptoeing for the cabin door. Lucas bolted upright and swore.

Benicio stopped, his back still to us. "My apologies. I came by for an update. I was waiting for you to wake up."

"We've been awake, quite obviously awake, for a few minutes," Lucas said.

"Yes, well..."

"You couldn't resist eavesdropping on a private conversation," Lucas said. "Until it threatened to become too private."

"I—"

"We're dressed," I said. "You might as well come in and say your piece."

Benicio turned, his gaze glancing off Lucas's glare before veering to rest on the far wall. I got up and stalked past him, out the cabin door and into the serving station, where I turned on the coffeemaker. By the time I returned, I'd had enough time to cool down. I was still pissed, but there was little danger I'd "accidentally" dump Benicio's coffee in his lap.

"I was just summing up our findings," Lucas said as I passed out the mugs.

"I can't believe it," Benicio said. "They wouldn't have gotten away with that here, but in Ohio . . ." He shook his head. "We need more offices in the Midwest. I've said it before."

Lucas stopped, mug halfway to his lips. "The Nasts were looking into a Cincinnati office, weren't they?"

Benicio nodded. "They still are, I believe, but they delayed their plans. They ran into a problem with the area that needed to be cleared up first."

I turned to Lucas. Our eyes met.

"When did they—" Lucas began.

The intercom buzzed on. "Sorry for the interruption, sir, but there's a red-haired woman here and she demands to speak to you. She says—"

"That's fine," Lucas cut in. "She's with us. Let her in."

I glanced back at the still-closed door between the rear cabins. "Guess she stepped out before we woke up."

The main door opened and I caught a glimpse of Benicio's stand-in bodyguard Morris. Then a woman barreled past, nearly knocking the big man flying. It was indeed a red-haired woman, but not Cassandra.

Justifiable Hysteria

JAIME STUMBLED PAST THE GUARD, HEAD BOWED, SHOULDERS hunched. As she staggered forward, my first thought was that she'd been drinking. Then I noticed her shoes—one sneaker, one pump with a two-inch heel, both pulled on over bare feet, the sneaker still untied, as if she'd grabbed the first two shoes she could find, yanked them on and ran. Her blouse was misbuttoned and stained with splotches of brown and dark red, and her hair hung in a snarled mess, a clip clinging to one side. She pushed back her hair, revealing a face streaked with makeup and tears.

"Oh, God," I said, rushing forward. "What happened?"

She turned. Four bloodred gouges raked her face from eye to jaw. I gasped.

"I'll call a medic," Lucas said as I guided Jaime to a chair.

"N—no," she said. "Don't, please. I—I'm okay."

She collapsed into the chair, bent her head down almost to her thighs, and gulped air, body shaking. After a moment, she convulsed in one final shudder, then lifted her head and brushed her hair from her eyes. She looked around, a slow, cautious gaze, shoulders tensed, as if expecting something to leap out at her.

"I'll call the medic," Benicio said, rising slowly.

"No!" she snapped. Then she saw who she was snapping at. Her eyes went wide and she dropped her face into her hands with a hiccupping laugh. "Oh, yeah, a fucking breakdown in front of Benicio Cortez. My day is now complete." She tilted her head to the ceiling. "Thank you very much!"

I dropped into the seat beside Jaime and took her hands. She squeezed mine so hard her nails drew blood. I murmured a calming spell. Jaime inhaled a long, shuddering breath, exhaled and relaxed her grip. After one last cautious look around, she sank back into the seat with a relieved sigh.

"Gone," she said. "I thought that might be the problem. Must have thought you two had abandoned us for good."

Lucas explained to Benicio what was going on.

"A ghost who can displace objects but can't contact a necromancer?" Benicio said, frowning. "I've never heard of such a thing."

"Join the club," Jaime muttered. "The poltergeisting was bad enough, but now this—" She pointed at her cheek. "Last time I had a spook reach out and touch me was twenty years ago, when I accidentally disturbed something very old, and very powerful. And, believe me, that one could talk back—in several languages. This one—" She shook her head. "Well, I don't know what this one's problem is, but it's not acting like any spook I've ever met."

"We think it might not be a ghost at all," I said to Benicio. Then I looked at Lucas. "I think it's time to consider exorcism."

He nodded. "Past time, by the look of things. We should—"

"No exorcism," Jaime said.

"Yes, I realize they're unpleasant," Lucas said. "Yet it can't be any worse than what you're enduring now. This has gone far enough—"

"No, it hasn't," she said firmly. "It hasn't gone far enough. Not yet. Whatever this thing is, it has a message it's eager—painfully eager—to deliver to you guys. It's a rough ride, but I'm prepared to tough it out if it'll help solve this case."

"What if it's not trying to help us?" I said. "Look at the way it's acting. That's not normal behavior for a helpful spirit."

"But it has helped, right? It gave us the vampire clue and led us to Cass—" She stopped, eyes going wide. "Oh, my god. Paige is right. It *is* evil."

"I heard that."

I twisted to see Cassandra in the open doorway between the cabins. She stifled a yawn.

I smiled. "Got some sleep?"

"A nap."

"Good."

She started forward, then blinked, seeing Benicio. She slanted a look my way, and I knew she wanted a proper introduction this time.

I gestured toward Cassandra. "Benicio, this is—"

"Cassandra DuCharme," Benicio said, standing and extending a hand. "Pleased to meet you."

Cassandra's brows arched.

Benicio smiled as he released her hand. "When Lucas first raised the possibility that we were dealing with a vampire, I suspected it might have been you I met at Tyler Boyd's apartment. The Cabal keeps very good records on all supernaturals of influence, so I only needed to check our dossiers for your photograph to be sure."

"One advantage to vampire mug shots," I said. "They're never out-of-date."

"I assume you're here to represent the vampires' interests in this matter?" Benicio said.

"Yes," Cassandra said. "Something which, I fear—" She stopped and her gaze swept across the other side of the cabin, her frown growing as she saw no one there. She gave her head a sharp shake. "Which I fear may become—"

She wheeled, one hand shooting up, palm out, as if to ward something off. She scowled at the empty space behind her.

"Huh," Jaime said. "Good to see I'm not the only skittish one this morning."

Cassandra's gaze shot to Jaime, getting a look at her for the first time. "What the hell happened to you?"

"Same thing I think is happening to you," Jaime said. "Without the clawing, bitch-slapping, hair-pulling, and all that fun psychic wounding stuff."

"Jaime's spirit is back," I explained. "It's probably here now. Is that what you're sensing?"

Cassandra cast another look around. "I'm not sure. What—"

Jaime flew forward, nearly onto Lucas's lap. He lunged to grab her, but before he could, she jerked back into her seat so hard she ricocheted off it and would have toppled to the floor if both Lucas and I hadn't caught her.

"What?" she shouted at the ceiling. "We aren't moving fast enough for you? Impatient bitch."

"It's a woman?" Benicio asked.

Jaime flourished a hand at the claw marks down her

face. "Either that or a demon with talons. Fights like a woman, I'll tell you that much." She fingered her scalp and winced for effect, then looked at me. "You don't see any bald spots, do you?"

I lifted up in my seat for a better look, then shook my head. "Nothing a good brushing won't fix."

"Thank God. Last thing I need is—"

Jaime's head whipped back so fast her vertebra crackled. Lucas, Benicio, and I all jumped from our chairs, and even Cassandra stepped forward. Twin indentations appeared on the side of Jaime's neck. Before anyone had time to react, the dents punctured through the skin and blood spurted.

Cassandra shouldered me aside. Jaime yelped, her hand going to her neck as she backed away from Cassandra. Blood gushed over her fingers. Lucas reached to grab Cassandra's arm, lips parting to cast a spell. Then he saw that I wasn't trying to stop Cassandra.

"It's okay," I said to Jaime. "Let her—"

Jaime's bloodied hands shot out to push Cassandra away.

"She can—" I began, but Jaime's scream cut me short.

Cassandra reached for Jaime, but Jaime kicked her back. Arterial blood continued to spurt from Jaime's neck. As Lucas dove to grab her, I cast a binding spell, but it failed. Benicio was on the phone, calling for help. By the time a medic arrived, it would be too late, but there was no time to tell him this. I cast the binding spell and, again, in my panic, fumbled it. Lucas grabbed Jaime's arm, but it was slick with blood and she yanked free easily. She was fighting blindly now, kicking and hitting at anything that came close.

"Jaime!" I shouted. "Let Cassandra—"

Lucas tackled Jaime. She fought, but he pinned her

down. Cassandra bent over Jaime. Blood sprayed Cassandra's face as she lowered her mouth to the wounds. Jaime screamed and bucked, throwing Cassandra off, but when she jerked upright, the wounds had closed, leaving the tiny punctures invisible from where I stood.

Jaime scrambled to her feet, then hesitated. Her fingers went to the side of her neck.

"Vampire saliva stops the bleeding," I said.

"Oh," Jaime said, face reddening.

She swayed. Lucas caught her before she fell and guided her over to the chair, which I reclined before she sat down. When she tried to sit upright, I gently restrained her.

"Lie down. You lost a lot of blood. Lucas, could you—"

He stepped through the cabin door bearing a large glass and a carton of juice.

"Perfect," I said. "Thanks."

As I helped Jaime drink some of the juice, Benicio asked whether we thought a blood transfusion should be arranged. Cassandra said it wasn't necessary, that the amount of blood Jaime lost would replace itself without intervention. She'd know, I guess, so we took her word for it. When Jaime finished the juice she lay down and closed her eyes.

"They aren't supposed to do that," she mumbled.

"Do what?" I asked.

She yawned. "Kill the messenger."

Another half-yawn, then Jaime's face went slack. I put my fingers to her neck. Her pulse was steady. I pulled the blanket up over her and turned to the others.

"She's right," I said, keeping my voice low. "No matter how upset the ghost might be, it makes no sense to try to kill Jaime. She's the only one it has any hope of communicating with."

"Unless it knew she wouldn't die," Lucas said. "If so, then one could construe it as a message of sorts, telling us that it not only knows *of* Cassandra, but recognizes her by sight and knows that a vampire can stop blood flow."

"It's a vampire," Cassandra said.

"Not necessarily," I said. "It knew that you could stop the bleeding—any supernatural who's studied vamps knows that. As for the bite marks, they were probably intentionally vampirelike, to drive home its point about you."

"They weren't vampire*like*. They were vampire."

"But—"

"I know the bite of a vampire, Paige. I also know that there is one in this room besides me. I've been around long enough that I can recognize my own kind faster than you can recognize a sorcerer."

"If our ghost is—or was—a vampire, that would explain why it can't make contact with Jaime," Lucas said. "It's trying to do the impossible."

I gave a slow nod. "Meaning that necromancers never hear from dead vampires, not because they don't exist, but because wherever they exist, they're beyond contact. So now we probably know one thing about our ghost. That's a start."

"Two things," Jaime murmured, her eyes still closed. "It's a vamp and it's a she."

Cassandra, Lucas, and I exchanged a look.

"Natasha," I whispered. "She's not missing. She's dead."

The Curse of Clear Vision

"WHEN EDWARD ATTACKED DANA, HE SAID HE WAS DOING it for someone," I said. "Someone she heard as 'Nasha.'" I looked at Benicio. "Something stopped the Nasts from putting an office in Cincinnati. A problem that needed to be cleared up first. Would a local pair of serial-killing vampire immortality questers count?"

He gave a slow nod. "A Cabal always investigates the local supernaturals before building a new office. If they have minor concerns, they usually persuade the offenders to relocate. But in a case such as this, on this scale, particularly one that involves vampires...the solution would be a permanent one."

"Kill them."

"Let me make some phone calls," Benicio said. "Before we jump to any conclusions."

"So now you think the Nasts will tell you the truth?"

"No, but with this much detail to prompt their memories, I know people who will."

A half-hour later Benicio confirmed our suspicions. The Nast Cabal had learned of Edward and Natasha's murderous hobby, and decided they wouldn't make good neighbors. According to Benicio's sources, the original plan had been to kill both, but the vampires had outwitted several assassins and fled the country. Unwilling to accept failure so easily, the Cabal sent out one last hit man, who'd managed to behead Natasha. The Nasts then made a mistake. They decided not to spend any more money chasing Edward around the globe. By killing his mate, they'd taught him a lesson he'd not soon forget. And he hadn't.

"They killed Natasha, and he wants revenge," I said. "Understandable . . . when it comes to attacking the Nasts. But what do the other Cabals have to do with it?"

Lucas looked at his father. "A vampire asked for a private meeting with you in July. The Nasts executed Natasha at the end of August. Presumably, if several assassination attempts had been made, the Nasts had been chasing the pair for at least a month. I would say that the timing of that request wasn't coincidental."

"Edward wanted to speak to the Cortez CEO?" I said. "But why?"

"Presumably to request sanctuary," Lucas said. "That's not uncommon. If you are pursued by one Cabal, the best place to go for help is to another Cabal. If the Boyds and St. Clouds were being honest with us, I suspect they'd admit to similar requests."

"In other words, he went to each of the Cabals for help, and they each turned him down, wouldn't even find out what he wanted. And that pissed him off enough to start killing their kids? This doesn't make sense."

"No," Cassandra said, her first words since we'd begun. "It wouldn't. Not to you."

She moved to the window and opened the blind. For a

moment, she just stared outside. Then she turned back toward us.

"You have to see this from a vampire's point of view. Do I think such a slight is grounds for killing someone's children? Of course not. But I can understand why Edward might. What is the life of those children to him? No more than those bodies in his field. A means to an end. Is he killing them because he wants them to die? No. He's killing them because he wants to cause pain, to hurt those who hurt him. They killed his life partner. I don't think you really understand what that means."

"They'd been together a long time," I said. "Obviously, they—"

"Obviously nothing. What do you consider a long marriage in your world? Twenty-five years is a cause for great celebration, isn't it? Edward became a vampire when Queen Victoria took the throne. He'd been one for less than a decade when he went to Russia and met Natasha, who had just become one herself. They have never been apart since. One hundred and fifty years together, with no one else: no parents, no siblings, no children, no friends. Nothing but each other."

"Now she's gone, and he wants revenge. He'll keep killing until he's repaid every Cabal for her death, by killing children from each."

"No, he'll keep killing until he's dead," Cassandra said. "Nothing else will stop him. I have no idea what his plan is, and he may very well have one, but he won't stop when he reaches the end, because he won't feel avenged. How could he? No hurt he inflicts on the Cabals will match his own."

"Okay," said a sleepy voice from the other seat. Jaime opened one eye. "I get the whole 'eternal love' thing and, as weird as it sounds, I think you're right that my spook is this Natasha chick, but that leaves one big question. Why the hell would she want to help us catch her man?"

"Does she?" Lucas said. "I'm not certain that would be a correct interpretation of her actions to date. The only clue she's given us is the vampire lead, which was undoubtedly meant not to tell us that our killer is a vampire, but that *she* is."

I nodded. "Maybe figuring that if Jaime knew she was a vampire, she'd know the right way to make contact."

"So what does she want?" Jaime asked.

We all looked at Cassandra.

"I don't know her well enough to answer that," Cassandra said. "The only thing I can say, with some certainty, is that she wasn't a passive or unwilling partner in anything Edward did."

"In other words," I said, "she's not suffering a sudden attack of conscience and wants to help us stop Edward before more kids die."

"Definitely not," Cassandra said. "She may be seeking the same thing they sought before her death: protection from a rival Cabal, offering to help you find Edward on the condition that the Cortezes protect him from the Nasts. Or she may be hoping to feed you false information and lead you away from him."

"Doesn't matter either way," Jaime said. "Unless she learns how to carve words in my flesh, she's not telling us anything. Wherever she is, it's out of necro calling range. She's trying her damnedest to change that, but it's not working."

"And where exactly is she?" I said. "Stuck in limbo? Or a demon dimension? Or some separate vampire afterlife? Maybe if we knew . . ."

"We can look into that," Lucas said. "But we may never

find the answer. The important question right now is not where is she, but where is *he*?"

We knew Edward was almost certainly in Miami. Why go elsewhere when all the Cabals were right here? But where to find him? At this point, we might as well grab a map of Miami, start tossing darts into it, and conduct our search that way.

Benicio left shortly after that to start working the Edward angle with the Cabals—or the Cabals that weren't already working it. Presumably, the moment the Nasts heard the words "vampire suspect" they'd known exactly who was killing their kids and had started searching for him. Of course, it would have been nice if they'd shared that information, but that would also mean sharing the glory when he was caught—and accepting full blame for letting him slide from their grasp in the first place.

"The only way you're going to catch him is when he goes for his next victim," Cassandra said as she settled onto our hotel sofa. "And the best way to do that is to set a trap."

"Not a bad idea," Jaime said. "One possible target—or two of them—are your nephews, Lucas. I'm sure your dad won't want us using them for bait, but he's got the firepower to make sure they're safe. If you're there, it wouldn't be too bad for the kids. They know you—"

Lucas shook his head. "They don't know me."

"Well, maybe not very well, but you're their uncle. They see you at Christmas, family picnics, whatever. They—"

"I mean, quite literally, they don't know me. We've

never met, and it's unlikely they know I exist. Not only do my nephews not know me from a stranger, they barely know my father—that's Hector's way of punishing him for his succession choice."

"Okay," Jaime said. "But, still, this guy's going to go after those kids sooner or later. Hector knows that. I'm sure he'd help if it meant his kids would be out of danger for good."

"Not if that help also meant helping me, or an investigation he considers mine."

Jaime shook her head. "Man, and I thought my family was looped. Well, maybe we can use someone else. What about the older Nast boy? The one who came here?"

"Sean?" I said.

"Right. Sure, he's a bit older than the rest, but I bet he'd be willing to do it. And Ed sure as hell wouldn't turn down the chance to knock off another Nast."

"Perhaps," Lucas said. "But I wouldn't know where to find Sean. Thomas removed him and Bryce from Miami the day Stephen was killed. Every Cabal family member under thirty has been evacuated."

"And it won't take long for Edward to figure that out," I said. "When he does, we won't just need to search Miami for him. We'll have a dozen possible victims, in a dozen different cities, to worry about."

"We need to move fast," Lucas said. "To that end, I do have an idea. An instrument of last resort. A clairvoyant."

"Great," Jaime said. "Only one problem. Finding one of those would be tougher than finding Ed himself."

"Not necessarily. I have one among my contacts."

"Seriously?" Jaime said. "Who?"

"Faye Ashton."

"She's still alive?" Cassandra shook her head. "I'm glad

to hear it, but I can't see how she'd be much help. Quite mad."

I shivered. "That's what usually happens, isn't it? To real clairvoyants. Their visions drive them insane. Like the really good nec—" I stopped myself.

"Necromancers," Jaime said. "Don't worry, Paige, you're not telling me anything I don't already know. By the time my Nan died, she was hardly the picture of mental stability. It's worse for the clairvoyants, though. If this Faye is well, fey, how can she help?"

"She can, with effort, clear her thoughts temporarily," Lucas said. "I have an open invitation to use her powers, but given the strain it would place on her already fragile condition, I've never accepted her offer. I haven't visited her at all this trip, knowing that she's likely heard about the case and would want to help."

"She's here?" I said. "In Miami?"

Lucas nodded. "In a private nursing home, a Cortez-run mental-health facility."

"So your dad's looking after her?" I said.

"He should. He's the reason she's in there."

The dictionary defines a clairvoyant as someone who can see objects or actions beyond the natural boundaries of sight. That's a near-perfect description of a true clairvoyant. With the right cues, they can see through the eyes of a person miles away. A good clairvoyant can go beyond mere sight and pick up a sense of their target's intentions or emotions. It's not mind reading, but it's as close as any supernatural can get.

A clairvoyant is also the closest thing the supernatural world has to a soothsayer. None of us can truly foresee the future, yet a clairvoyant can make educated guesses about a person's future actions based on their current situation. For example, if they "see" a person nursing a sore tooth, they can "foresee" that person visiting a dentist in the near future. Some clairvoyants attune this deductive skill to the point where they appear to have the gift of prophecy.

I'd never actually met a clairvoyant. Even my mother met only one in her long life. Like spell-casting, it is an inherited gift, but so few people carry the gene that there are only a handful of clairvoyants born each generation, and they learn to hide their gift right from the cradle. Why? Because their powers are so valuable that anyone who finds a clairvoyant, and reports it to the Cabals, would reap a lottery-size reward.

To a Cabal, a clairvoyant is a prize beyond measure. They are the living equivalent of a crystal ball. Tell me what my enemies are plotting. Tell me what my allies are plotting. Tell me what my family is plotting. A Cabal CEO with a good clairvoyant on staff can double his profits and cut his internal problems in half. And the Cabals fully acknowledge the clairvoyants' value, treating and rewarding them better than any other nonsorcerer employee. So why do the clairvoyants go to extremes to avoid such a dream job? Because it will cost them their sanity.

Good necromancers are plagued by demanding spirits. They're taught how to erect the mental ramparts but, over time, the cracks begin to show, and the best necromancers almost invariably are driven mad by late middle age. To maintain their sanity for as long as possible they must regularly relieve the pressure by lowering the gate and communicating with the spirit world. It's like when Savannah wants something I don't think she should have—after enough pestering, I'll negotiate a compromise, knowing that will grant me a few months of peace before the pleading starts again. Clairvoyants also live with constant encroachments on their mental barricades, images and visions of other lives. When they lower the gate, though, it doesn't quite close properly, and gapes a little more each time.

In effect, the Cabals take the clairvoyants and use them up. The power, and the temptation to use it, is so great that they force the clairvoyant to keep "seeing" until the gates crash down and they are swept into a nightmare world of endless visions, seeing everyone else's lives and losing sight of their own.

That is what Benicio did with Faye Ashton. Lucas's grandfather had taken Faye as a child, then put her aside for safekeeping until she came into her full powers. By then Benicio was CEO. For twenty years, Faye had been the Cortez clairvoyant. A long life span for a clairvoyant, which may suggest that Benicio tried to conserve her powers, but the end result was the same. She went mad, and he put her in the home where she'd lived for the last decade.

Along with some of her powers, she'd retained enough of her sanity to never let Benicio near her again. Lucas, though, was another matter. Not only had she known him since he was a child, but she never turned down the opportunity to help anyone who fought the Cabals. So she'd given Lucas carte blanche to use her powers. Yet he never had. Although she assured him that the occasional "seeing" wasn't going to damage her already ruined mind, he'd always been unwilling to take the chance. Now, though, we had nowhere else to turn.

The nursing home was a century-old manor in a neighborhood where most homes had long since been converted to medical and legal offices, as the cost of maintaining the monstrosities overshadowed their historical value. From the street, the nursing home appeared to be one of the few still used as a private residence, with no signage and a front yard that hadn't been converted into a parking lot.

We parked in the driveway, behind a minivan. At the door, Lucas rang the bell. A few minutes later, an elderly black man opened the door and ushered us inside. When the door closed, it was like stepping into Cortez headquarters. All street noise vanished; I suspected the house had first-rate soundproofing, probably to keep the neighbors from realizing this wasn't a private home.

Inside, nothing disturbed this veneer of domestic normalcy, not a reception desk or nurse's station, not even the usual hospital stink of disinfectant and overcooked food. The front door opened into a tastefully decorated hallway with a parlor to one side and a library on the other. A woman's laugh fluttered down from the second level, followed by a low murmur of conversation. The only smells that greeted us were fresh-cut flowers and fresher-baked bread.

Lucas exchanged greetings with the caretaker, Oscar, and introduced me. As Lucas had explained earlier, both Oscar and his wife, Jeanne, were shamans, a race whose reputation for compassion and stability made them excellent nurses for the mentally ill. This was a long-term care facility, and none of the eight residents were ever expected to leave. All were former Cabal employees. All were here ostensibly because of excellent employee benefits packages, but in reality because the Cortez Cabal was responsible for their madness.

"It's good to see you," Oscar said, patting Lucas on the back as we headed down the hallway. "Been over a year, hasn't it?"

"I've been—"

"Busy." Oscar smiled. "It was an observation, not an accusation. We all know how busy you are."

"How is Faye?"

"No better. No worse. I told her you were coming, so she's ready. Woman's got the strength of a bull. She can be completely catatonic, but the moment I say someone's coming to see her, she pulls it together." He grinned over at me. "Well, unless she doesn't want to see them, in which case she plays possum. I suppose you two are here about those kids being killed."

Lucas nodded. "Does Faye know about it?"

"The damn woman's clairvoyant, boy. Course she knows. We tried to keep the news from her, but she sensed something was up and badgered one of her outside friends into spilling the beans. Been pestering us to get hold of you ever since, but we said, no, Faye, if he wants your help, he'll come get it."

"Has she . . . seen anything?"

"If she had, I'd have tracked you down. Everyone's been careful not to give her any details. That way she won't start fishing around that big psychic pond and strain herself."

"We can provide her with sufficient details to avoid that," Lucas said. "Yet, if you feel it would still be too great a strain—"

"Don't you answer that," called a strident voice. A small, white-haired woman wheeled herself into the doorway. "You send him away, Oscar Gale, and I'll make your life hell. You know I will."

Oscar smiled. "I wasn't going to do that, Faye. You'll be fine. You always are."

Faye reversed her wheelchair, vanishing into the room. We followed.

Black Hole of Hate

FAYE ASHTON WAS A TINY WOMAN WHO, HAD SHE STOOD, probably wouldn't have topped five feet. I doubted she weighed more than a hundred pounds. Though she was only in her late fifties, her hair was pure white and her face was lined with wrinkles. Her dark eyes danced with energy, giving her face the haunted look of a young spirit trapped within a body that had grown old before its time.

The wheelchair wasn't the result of age or mental infirmity. Faye had been in one since a childhood battle with polio. That was how the Cabal found her. When Faye's father, her clairvoyant parent, had been unable to cope with her growing medical bills, he'd contacted the Cortez Cabal and made them an offer. If they would give Faye the best possible care, they could take her. And they had.

As Oscar closed the door behind us, Faye wheeled her chair in a sharp 180.

"Took you long enough . . . and don't give me any of that crap about not wanting to hurt me. There's not enough left to hurt."

"We had other leads to pursue," Lucas said.

Faye grinned. "Good answer." She looked at me. "You must be Ruth Winterbourne's girl."

"Paige," I said, offering my hand.

She took my hand and, with a shockingly firm grip, pulled me down to kiss my cheek. Then she put her hands on either side of my face and held it in front of hers, eyes searching mine. A sheen of perspiration covered her forehead. After a minute, she released me and smiled.

"Wonderful," she said.

"I think so," Lucas said.

Faye laughed. "You should. You couldn't do better. Now, what do you have for me?"

Lucas told her the details, particularly those about Edward. He also gave her a photo of Edward and Natasha that he'd taken from their house, plus a shirt he'd removed from Edward's laundry hamper. I hadn't known he'd taken either. He must have already been considering contacting Faye.

As Faye listened, the sheen of perspiration spread to her cheeks and jaw, then beaded into rivulets of sweat. The room was cool, with a faint air-conditioned breeze that set goose bumps springing up on my bare arms, but obviously that wasn't enough for Faye. When Lucas finished, I offered to find Oscar and see if we could get Faye a fan or a cold drink.

"It's not the temperature, hon," she said. "It's me. Keeping the old brain clear takes some effort."

I remembered something my mother had done for a necromancer friend when she'd begun losing her battle with the spirit world.

"Can I try something?" I asked. "A spell?"

"You're welcome to try."

I cast a calming spell, then recast it for added strength. Faye closed her eyes. Her lips moved soundlessly, then she peeked one eye open.

"Not bad," she said, then opened the other eye. She smiled and rolled her shoulders. "Well, that gives a bit of relief. What was it?"

"Just a calming spell. Any witch can do one. I'm surprised they don't have a witch here. Shamans are great caretakers, but for a nurse, you really should have a witch."

Faye snorted. "Try telling that to those damned sorcerers."

"I will," I said. "I'll speak to Benicio next time I see him."

Faye's eyebrows shot up, and her lips curved just a fraction, as if waiting to burst into a laugh when I acknowledged the joke.

"She's quite serious," Lucas said. "She'll tell him and, even more shocking, he'll probably listen."

"I have leverage," I said, slanting a look toward Lucas.

Faye threw back her head, laughter filling the room. "You found the bastard's weakness, did you? Clever girl. If you can get me a witch, you'll move to the top of my approved visitors list. Now, let's see what I can do for *you*."

Faye laid Edward's photo on her lap and stared down at it. I took a chair slightly behind Faye, knowing it was always easier to concentrate when your audience was out of sight. Lucas pulled a chair over beside mine.

After a moment, Faye's shoulders dropped and she slouched forward. I glanced at Lucas. He nodded, telling me this was normal. At least ten minutes of silence passed. Then Faye's body tensed. Her mouth opened.

"I have—"

She gasped and her body jerked upright, eyes rolling to the whites. Lucas leapt up. She blinked, recovering, and shooed Lucas away.

"Sorry," she said. "Wrong tactic. I was too open. Got an emotional shock wave."

"You found him?" Lucas said.

"Big black hole of hate? That'd be him. Damn thing nearly sucked me right in." She shivered, then straightened. "Okay, round two coming up. This time, I'll turn off the emotional radar and stick to the visuals."

Faye dropped her head and, this time, took only a minute to hone in on Edward.

"He's sitting on the edge of a bed, staring at the wall. That doesn't help you much. Let me look around. Bed, dresser, television, two doors . . . wait, there's something on the back of the door. A fire escape plan. So we're talking motel or hotel. No surprise there. Details, details . . . I see a window. Looks out over the top of buildings, so let's narrow that down to hotel, something with at least three floors, he's probably on the third or fourth. The room's clean. Not so much as a sock on the floor. Okay, start directing."

"Back to the window," Lucas said. "Describe the buildings you see outside."

"Two. Both concrete, lots of windows. A tall one in the far distance, the shorter one in front of it, maybe fifty feet from the window. Doesn't leave much of a view."

"Any distinguishing marks on either?"

"No—wait, there's a sign on the farther one, on the roof, but it's too far to read."

"Do you see the sun?"

"No."

"Shadows?"

"There's one cast by the window."

"Which direction is the shadow falling?"

Faye smiled. "Clever boy. The shadow slants straight into the room, meaning the window points south."

"Back to the fire evacuation notice. Can you get close enough to read it?"

"Yes, but it doesn't list the hotel name or room number. Already thought of that."

"Does it have the room rate?"

"Ah, yes. One hundred dollars even."

"Good."

Lucas directed Faye around the room some more, but found nothing useful. Though I cast the occasional calming spell, she was starting to sweat again, so Lucas concluded the search.

"One last thing," Faye said. "Let me do a quick read. He's still sitting there, so he must be thinking. If he's planning something, I might be able to give you a heads up."

She went quiet, dropping her head to her chest again. A minute of silence passed, then she shuddered and her head jerked back, pupils flicking like someone in REM sleep. Lucas laid his hand on her shoulder. After a moment, she shuddered again.

"Sorry, it's that damned black hole again. It's... I've never felt anything like it. She meant so much to him." Faye swallowed. "Well, even Hitler loved his dog, right? Doesn't make someone a good person, and this one definitely isn't. Only thing he cared about was her. Okay, let me have another go—"

"Maybe you shouldn't."

"I've got it. Just hold on." She exhaled and let her head fall again. "He's frustrated. The killing—it doesn't help, doesn't fill the void. He needs more. There's one he was saving for last, but he can't wait. He's going to—" Her head snapped back, hitting the wheelchair headrest so hard it jumped.

"Oh." The single word came like a gasp.

Her arms gripped the sides of her wheelchair as her

body stiffened, torso rising out of the chair. Lucas and I both jumped up. Before we could reach her, her body went as straight as a board, and she slid from the chair. Lucas lunged and grabbed her before she hit the floor. She convulsed, eyes rolling, mouth open. I grabbed a pen from a nearby table, opened her mouth, and stuck it in to hold her tongue down. Then she stopped. Just stopped, as if frozen in place. Lucas gently lowered her to the floor.

"I'll get Oscar," he said.

"Is she—"

"She'll be okay. This is, I fear, her normal state. Catatonic."

As he left, I rearranged Faye's arms, trying to make her more comfortable, though I knew she was beyond caring. As I adjusted her head, I caught a glimpse of her eyes, wide and unseeing. No, not unseeing. Leaning over her, I saw movement there, her pupils contracting and flickering, ever so slightly, like someone watching television. Only it wasn't a television screen she was seeing, but the tiny screen in her own mind, playing a hundred movies of a hundred lives, all glimmering past so fast her brain could no longer make any sense of them.

I *would* talk to Benicio about getting Faye a witch nurse. It wouldn't cure her, but anything had to be better than . . . this. Yes, that would mean advocating that a witch take a job with a Cabal, something I'd never thought I'd do, but the sad truth was that there were dozens of witches eager for Cabal employment, and if it meant they could help someone like Faye, well, for now, that was the best I could do.

Hotel Shopping

BY EVENING WE'D CHECKED OUT NEARLY HALF THE HOTELS in Miami as we'd searched for one with a view that matched what Faye had seen outside Edward's window. We'd started by targeting those hotels with rack rates of a hundred dollars. Tougher than it might sound. It was a nice, even number, and many hotels had at least a few rooms at that rate.

When we first left Faye, we'd called Jaime, who'd offered to split the phone-book list with us. After we found a few possibilities, Jaime suggested she and Cassandra take over the phone calls while we did the footwork. A wise arrangement, except that Jaime and Cassandra found so many hotels with rooms at a hundred dollars that we couldn't begin to keep up.

At eight, Jaime called.

"We're still working on the last batch," I said when I answered.

"That's what I figured. I'm calling to say we're holding the rest of the list hostage. You guys have been at it for six hours, and I know you haven't eaten dinner. Probably skipped lunch, too."

"We just need to—"

"No. Seriously, Paige. Time to call it a day. Better to quit now, get food, get sleep, and get cracking again at daybreak."

As much as I hated to quit, this did make sense. With night falling, we could barely make out the buildings surrounding the hotels. I relayed the advice to Lucas, who agreed.

"Good," Jaime said when I told her. "There's a bar down the road here, advertises full-kitchen service until midnight. I'll meet you there in half an hour. If you keep working, you'll keep me waiting. I can cause a lot of trouble left alone in a bar. Remember that."

We did keep Jaime waiting fifteen minutes, but only because Lucas had another idea that he wanted to pursue immediately. The Cabal had satellite photos of Miami. Maybe with those we'd have more luck picking out the configuration of buildings Faye had described. Cortez headquarters was on the way, so we stopped by, and had copies of the photos in less than twenty minutes.

Despite her threat, Jaime hadn't caused any trouble at the bar. She wasn't alone, either. When I noticed a figure across the table from her, I immediately thought male, then noticed that it was Cassandra. The three of us ordered dinner, while Cassandra nursed her wine.

Jaime had managed to bully Lucas into not examining the photos while we ate, but the moment the plates left the table, he had them out. I tried helping, but we only had one magnifying glass, and the details were too small to see with the naked eye, so I let Jaime talk me into a post-dinner drink.

Halfway through the drinks, Cassandra got off a

"celebrity necro" jab at Jaime, who responded by bringing up her favorite issue.

"I'm not dead," Cassandra said, barely ungritting her teeth enough to let the words out.

"Care to test that theory? Let's say you find a guy lying on the ground, and you're not sure if he's dead or alive. How do you tell? Three ways. Heartbeat, pulse, breathing. Here, Cass, give me your wrist, let me check your pulse."

Cassandra glared and sipped her wine.

"Not seeing any condensation on that glass, Cass. Something tells me you're not breathing."

Cassandra's glass rapped against the tabletop. "I'm not dead."

"Geez, you sound like that Monty Python skit. You guys ever see that one? They're cleaning up the plague victims and one keeps saying: 'I'm not dead yet.' Sounds just like you, Cassandra. Well, except he had a British accent." Jaime sipped her drink. "Anyway, I don't see what the big deal is. You *look* like you're alive. Now zombies, there's a nasty afterlife."

"Speaking of zombies," I began, eager to segue off this subject. "I heard some necro in Hollywood raised a real one for that movie, oh, what was it called—"

"*Night of the Living Dead*?" Lucas said.

His leg brushed mine under the table. Last spring we'd tried to overcome a hellish day by watching that movie, before moving on to better methods of distraction. Our first night together. Our eyes met and we both grinned, then Lucas returned to his work.

"No, not that one," I said. "Something recent."

"I heard the rumor," Jaime said. "Makes a good story, but it's not true. The only living dead in Hollywood is Clint Eastwood."

I sputtered my drink. Jaime patted my back and laughed.

"Oh, I'm kidding. But he kinda looks it, don't you think? The man has not aged well."

"I wouldn't say that," Cassandra murmured.

"Well, I would," Jaime said. "And what I want to know is why, in every goddamned movie, he gets paired up with some hot little number a quarter his age."

"Jealous?" Cassandra said.

Jaime snorted. "Yeah, like I want to walk around with an eighteen-year-old guy on my arm. Nothing wrong with having fun, but you gotta keep your dignity. My rule: no guys more than a decade older or five years younger. The whole cougar thing is so . . ." She shuddered and pulled a face.

"Cougar?" Lucas said, glancing up from his photos.

"Women who date significantly younger men," I said.

"Why are you looking at me, Paige?" Cassandra said.

"I wasn't—"

"I can hardly date men my own age, can I?" Cassandra added.

Jaime laughed. "Got a point there, Cass. How old were you when you die—changed? About my age, I'll bet."

"Forty-five."

Jaime nodded. "If I could stop aging at some point, it'd be here. I know, most women—hell, most *people*—they'd go for their twenties, maybe thirties, but I like forty. Got the experience under your belt, but the body is still in perfect working order. A damn fine age for a woman." She lifted her glass. "Take that, Clint."

We ordered another round of drinks, talked a bit longer, then headed back to the hotel.

* * *

On the plane we'd agreed to meet Benicio for breakfast the next day, to share progress on the case. Now that we had a solid lead, we hated to waste time on something as trivial as eating. Yet when Lucas suggested that we needed to start our day early, Benicio offered to meet us at our hotel for breakfast at six, and keep his visit short. Not much we could say about that.

When we got to the restaurant, Troy slipped in ahead of us. He cornered the hostess, murmured something, and passed her a folded bill. A minute later, the hostess returned and escorted us to the patio. Our table was in the far corner. The three closest tables sported RESERVED tent cards. I supposed that was what the extra tip was for, guaranteeing our privacy. Since the restaurant was almost empty at this hour, it was a request easily accommodated. Troy and Morris took the next nearest table.

After we ordered our meal, I asked Benicio about hiring a witch nurse for Faye.

"A calming spell, hmm?" he said, unfolding his napkin. "Never could get that one to work myself. Do you think it would help the other residents as well?"

I hesitated, not because I wasn't ready with an answer, but because the thought of Benicio Cortez practicing witch magic . . . well, it was enough to render even me momentarily speechless.

"Er, yes," I said. "I think it would. That's just an educated guess, of course. You'd have to test it on the others."

He nodded. "I'll hire a witch part-time for Faye then, and if she can help the others, we'll make it a full-time position. Now, my contacts in the witch community are, as you might guess, quite poor. We'll discuss this later, but I may need your help finding someone qualified—"

"I'm sure you can do so without Paige's assistance,

Papá," Lucas said. "Witches apply for Cabal positions all the time. Human resources should be able to provide all the contact names you need."

"Perhaps, but if I have any questions, Paige, may I call you?"

I glanced at Lucas, who gave a soft sigh, then the barest nod.

"If it means getting a good witch nurse for Faye, you can call me," I said.

Benicio opened his mouth with what I was sure was another "request," but was diverted by the arrival of our coffee. We spent the next minute in silence, each fixing our drinks.

"So, Paige," Benicio said after his first sip of coffee. "How do you like Miami?"

A new topic. Thank God. I relaxed into my chair. "Can't say I've had much time for sightseeing, but I've certainly enjoyed the sunshine."

"Miami has its charms, though the pace isn't to everyone's taste. Nor the violence. Before you go, Lucas, you should take Paige for a drive, show her where you grew up." He turned to me. "It's a beautiful area. A fraction of Miami's crime rate, the safest streets in Florida, an excellent school system—"

"Any news regarding the case?" Lucas asked.

There wasn't. We told Benicio that we were pursuing a lead, but he didn't press for details, only offered us full use of the Cabal resources, should we need them. We spent the rest of breakfast discussing what the Cabals were doing to find Edward. The Nasts, as we'd expected, had been searching for him since Friday. Unfortunately, they hadn't found any clues . . . or any they cared to share.

As we neared the end of the meal, Benicio said, "As I was saying earlier, Lucas should take you on a tour of the area. Now, I know, I have a vested interest in wanting my son living closer than Oregon, but there is Savannah to consider. You've already had one bad experience keeping custody of her and, although you handled that very well, it was the *second* attempt, was it not?"

"Second attempt, but same person ... who is not going to be making any more."

"Maybe so, but now the news of Savannah's desirability has spread across the supernatural world. You must consider that—"

"Both Paige and Savannah are quite happy with Portland," Lucas said.

"I understand, but before you put down permanent roots, you must give the matter serious thought. You don't want to buy a house in Portland only to realize six months from now that it's unsafe for Savannah."

"I know that," I said. "Which is why I'm not house-shopping until we've been there a year."

"Oh?" Benicio frowned. "I thought you had a house picked out. Lucas said ..." His voice trailed off as he saw my look of confusion. "Oh, I see he hasn't mentioned it."

"No, I had not," Lucas said, his voice tight. "But thank you for doing so for me." He turned to me and lowered his voice. "I'll explain later."

We finished the meal in silence.

"What house?" I said before the hotel room door closed behind us.

"I believe I mentioned a potential arrangement with my last client, who, feeling indebted—"

"What house?" I said, throwing my purse onto the sofa. "The condensed version."

"You're understandably upset—"

"Hell, yes, I'm upset. You're making long-term plans for us and I have to hear it from your *father*?"

"It's not as it sounds. When he first called me in Chicago, he wanted to talk about our apartment. He didn't think it was right, me expecting you and Savannah to live there because I refuse to dip into my trust fund. I told him the apartment was short-term. He wouldn't listen, so I said that I had a lead on a house in Portland."

"Why didn't you tell me? We haven't discussed this, Lucas." I thumped down onto the couch and rubbed my temples. "If this was meant to be a surprise—"

"No, certainly not. I would never presume anything like that. Once this was over, I planned to show you the house and, if you liked it, then it would be yours to take at the offered price, whether you chose to share it with me or not."

"Whether I chose—? What the hell is that supposed to mean?"

He sat on the couch beside me, close but not touching. "I would have mentioned it, but I wanted to get through this first. It seemed unfair to discuss long-term plans now, when you were getting your first glimpse of what a life with me might entail—the . . . familial issues."

"So, you think I'm going to turn tail and run?"

He managed a wry smile. "I'm surprised you haven't already."

"No, I'm serious. Is that really what you think? That I care so little for you that I'd—" I shifted down the couch, away from him. "I knew all about your 'familial issues' when we got together, Lucas."

"Yes, but you may have been unprepared for the impact it could have on our lives. I would completely understand—"

"Would you?" I said, springing to my feet. "You'd understand if I walked out the door? Said 'Sorry, not for me'? Just like you'd understand if you showed me this house and I said, 'I'll take it . . . now where are you going to live?'"

"I don't want to pressure you, Paige. Of course, I don't want you to leave, and, yes, I want to get this house with you, but if that's not what you want—" He reached for my arm, but I yanked it back.

"You have no idea how I feel about you, do you?"

When he hesitated, I strode to the door. Then I paused, hand on the knob. I couldn't do this. Not now.

"Come on," I said. "We have work to do."

The Cabal photos of Miami had given Lucas a half-dozen possible hotels, which we now needed to check. As for our spat, neither of us mentioned it, though the heavy silence in the car said we were both thinking about it. As much as I wanted to resolve the problem and get past it, I told myself it was better to ignore it for now. Plenty of time to fix things later.

On the fourth possibility, we found a match. A five-story mid-price hotel, with a southern view that matched Faye's description.

We were walking up the side alley, heading for the front of the building, when Lucas's cell phone rang.

"That was Oscar," he said when he hung up. "Faye's awake and very upset. All he can make out is that she wants to see me—immediately."

"Damn," I said.

"If she has new information on the case, it almost certainly relates to Edward's whereabouts, which we've probably found, rendering her information welcome but potentially unnecessary. At this point—" He looked up at the hotel. "I'm loath to walk away, however briefly, from the best lead we've had."

"I could go talk to Faye," I said. "But if Edward's in this hotel, I'd rather back you up."

"And I'd rather have you backing me up."

"What about sending Jaime? She's good with people, and it sounds like she's had some experience with Faye's type of condition, with her grandmother."

"Good idea."

Lucas called. Jaime was still in bed, but once she had woken up enough to understand what he was asking, she agreed to speak to Faye. If it was important, she'd call me back. So Lucas turned off his phone, I switched mine to vibrate, and we headed into the hotel.

"Sure, yeah," the young desk clerk said, head bobbing as he looked at the photo Lucas held. "Room three-seventeen. That's him."

"He's still checked in?"

"Right."

"Has he gone out yet this morning?"

"Not this way." He checked his watch. "And not this early. He usually heads out around noon, comes back after my shift."

Lucas wrote down a phone number. "If he comes down, wait until he's gone, then call this number. But only after he's left. Don't do anything to make him suspicious."

"Sure." The young man's head bobbed. "Okay. Sure."

Lucas strode through the front doors, face grim.

"Time to call the SWAT team?" I said.

"I'm afraid we have more immediate concerns. Right now that clerk is on the phone to Edward, warning him we're here."

"What?"

Lucas rounded the building corner, walking so fast I had to jog to keep up. "I introduced us as NSA, told him we needed to find this man immediately. The first thing he should think, given the current climate, is 'terrorist.' But he doesn't ask any questions, even after I tell him not to raise the man's suspicions, implying he's dangerous. He tells us what we want to know and gets us out of there fast so he can call Edward, collect whatever reward Edward offered for warning him."

"And once Edward gets that call, he'll grab his things and bail."

"Precisely. Now—" He stopped halfway between the front of the hotel and the side door. "I want you to stand here. Cast a cover spell. If he comes out, don't do anything. Let him go, but watch where he heads, then get me. I'll be around back watching that door."

I nodded, but Lucas had already broken into a jog, heading toward the rear. I stood against the wall opposite the hotel, and hid behind a cover spell.

Less than two minutes later, the side door opened. A man stepped out. He wore a baggy windbreaker, sweatpants, sunglasses, and a ball cap pulled low, but none of that left any question that it was the man from the photograph: Edward.

Edward stepped out from behind the door and looked both ways. When his gaze passed over me, I resisted the urge to hold my breath, and concentrated instead on staying perfectly still. He eased the door shut. Then he lowered his backpack to the ground, bent, and opened it. As he crouched there, I couldn't help thinking how easy it would be to trap him in a binding spell. All I needed to do was break cover for a second and—

Edward pulled a gun from the knapsack and my idea died mid-thought.

He fiddled with the gun, then tucked it into the pocket of his windbreaker, hoisted his knapsack onto his back, and headed toward the rear of the building. Damn it! If only Lucas and I had practiced my long-range communication spell more, I could warn him. He'd be hiding, but not under a cover spell, since his cast wasn't reliable yet. I reassured myself that Lucas knew better than to pop out of hiding the moment he heard someone. Not that he'd even hear Edward. The man walked across the gravel like it was a foam cushion, not so much as rattling a stone underfoot. He stuck to the shadows, glancing over his shoulder with every few steps. Right before he reached the back of the building, he turned left and seemed to walk right through the wall I stood against.

I counted to three, then broke cover and leaned out to see an adjoining alley farther down. I took one slow step. The crunch of gravel under my feet resounded like thunder. I quickly recast my cover, but Edward didn't return. Again, I broke cover. Again, I took a single step. Again, the gravel crackled underfoot.

This wasn't working. After a moment's thought, I cast a light-ball and tossed it down the alley, praying Edward didn't pick that very moment to look behind him. When Lucas saw the ball, he peered around the corner. I gestured to the side alley. He nodded, darted across the alley, and pressed himself against the far wall. Then he inched to the opening and peeked down it. As he pulled back, he waved me forward.

When I got to the adjoining alley it was empty. Lucas

motioned that Edward had slipped into a corridor farther down.

"He has a gun," I mouthed, pantomiming a pistol with my hand.

Lucas nodded and we set off in pursuit.

The Target

WE HURRIED ALONG THE PASSAGE, THEN PEEKED INTO the cross-alley Edward had taken. It ended at a street. Edward stepped onto the sidewalk and turned right. We hustled to the end of the alley and looked out. Edward was poised on the curb of a busy road, as if debating whether to dodge through traffic. Lucas motioned for me to get into a better viewing position and cast a cover spell. I did.

After a moment on the curb, Edward wheeled and headed left along the sidewalk. At the first stoplight, he joined a small crowd and waited, rocking on the balls of his feet. When the light changed, he wove through the other pedestrians, then darted into the first door on the other side.

I broke cover.

"He went into a coffee shop," I said. "Lying low?"

"Perhaps. I'll take a look. Once I verify he's there, I'll call for backup. Best not to try taking him in on our own, not when he's armed."

"But he's in a public place. He wouldn't dare shoot—"

"Are you sure?"

"You're right. In that case, though, I'm not sure I even

want you peeking in the window. We need a spell. What about that glamor spell? The one you used with Savannah, to make me look like Eve."

"It only works if the viewer wants or expects to see someone else. I don't know how much information that desk clerk gave Edward, but I suspect he knows who he's watching out for. I believe we're down to the most obvious, and least satisfactory, choice. Arm myself with a good spell, slip in there, and hope for the best."

"Arm *ourselves*. I'll cover you."

Edward wasn't in the café. Lucas even popped into the men's washroom to be sure, but came out shaking his head. I did a visual sweep of the room. Next to the bathrooms was a short hall with three doors. Two were marked STAFF ONLY. The third had a push bar on it—a back exit.

We peeked out the rear door, then stepped into the alley. The empty corridor stretched a half-block in either direction.

"Damn," I muttered.

Lucas surveyed the ground. Water dripped from a leaky eaves-trough. During the cool night, a puddle had formed but now, in the heat of morning, it was drying fast. There were several footprints in the hardening mud, but only one still had water pooled between the tread marks. Lucas gestured in the direction the print pointed.

A dozen yards down, the alley branched off, heading farther away from the street. Lucas motioned for me to wait, then peered around the wall. A second later, he pulled back, brows knitting, and motioned for me to look.

I glanced around the corner. Edward was there, less than thirty feet away. I started to pull back fast, then noticed he'd stopped with his back to us. His knapsack lay at his feet and he was pulling out a map. Lucas tugged me back, then bent down to my ear.

"Go into the shop," he whispered. "Call my father."

I leaned over to his ear. "What if he leaves?"

"I'll follow and call you."

We'd let the café rear exit close behind us, so I had to walk all the way around the building. I was still in the alley when my phone vibrated. I glanced over my shoulder, but Lucas hadn't moved. I picked up the pace to get to the sidewalk, where I could answer without fear of my voice carrying to Edward. Before I was there, the phone stopped. I'd just set foot on the sidewalk when it vibrated again. I checked the number, but didn't recognize it.

"Hello?"

"Where are you?" Jaime's voice, words rushing out.

"We're—"

"Get over here now. Stop whatever you're doing, grab Lucas, and get over here."

"We can't. We're following Edward. We have him on the run—"

"Shit! No, leave him. Just back off and leave him alone. Where are you? I'll get the Cabal to send someone. Get back here—no, just get someplace—"

"Slow down, Jamie. What's—?"

The line buzzed, then Cassandra came on.

"Paige? Listen to me. We're with Faye. She knows who Edward's next target is. It's—"

I knew what she was going to say even before the name left her lips. I hit disconnect and fumbled to shove the phone back into my pocket, but it slipped and fell to the sidewalk. Ignoring it, I raced back into the alley.

Coup de Grâce

WHEN I REACHED THE ALLEY BEHIND THE CAFÉ, LUCAS
was gone. Edward was on the move. Of course he was.
He knew who was chasing him. He wasn't running from
Lucas; he was luring him in.

I raced down the adjoining alley, where we'd last seen
Edward. I didn't worry about how much noise I made. If
Lucas heard me, he'd come running, away from Edward,
which was exactly what I wanted.

When I rounded the first junction, I saw Lucas. He
was walking carefully, looking from side to side, his back
to me. I opened my mouth to shout to him, then stopped.
If Edward was lying in wait around the next corner, any
disruption could spook him. I wasn't about to spook a
vampire with a gun.

I jogged down the alley. A few yards from Lucas, as I
ran under a fire escape, a shadow moved overhead. I
whirled and looked up to see Edward, crouched on the
fire escape.

"Lucas!" I yelled.

As I raced toward Lucas, I realized that we were in a
blind alley, with only an alcove adjoining at the end. I

wheeled just as Edward leapt to the ground. He raised his gun. I side-lunged into his firing path, and started casting a binding spell. Edward trained the gun on my chest.

"I'll fire before you finish," he said. His sunglasses were gone, and his eyes were as flat and emotionless as his voice. He looked over my shoulder at Lucas, who'd also frozen mid-incantation. "You, too. Cast and I'll shoot her."

"Paige," Lucas said. "Step aside. Please."

"So he can shoot you? You're the one he's after. That was the message Faye was trying to give us. You're the target."

"Do you really think I won't shoot because you're in the way?" Edward said.

Yet he didn't. He lifted the gun, as if considering firing over my shoulder at Lucas, then lowered it back to my chest, clearly not comfortable enough with his marksmanship to try for anything but a torso shot. He might not care about adding me to his body count, but he wouldn't take the chance that, in the time it took to shoot me, Lucas could cast a spell and escape.

"Do you know what Benicio will do to you if you kill Lucas?" I said.

"Same thing everyone else wants to do. Hunt me down and kill me. Do you think I care? I stopped caring the day I came back to my hotel room and found those Cabal assassins had finished their job."

"We—"

"I walked into that room, and do you know what I saw?" His gaze skewered mine. "Her head on the bedpost. My wife's head on the bedpost!"

I tried to summon up some sympathy, but all I could think about were the dozens of bodies buried behind that cabin.

A soft breeze fluttered down the alley, coming from behind us. Though I didn't dare peek over my shoulder, I knew there was a three-story wall behind Lucas. No breeze could come through that. Was I casting without knowing it? I'd done that once before, under stress. Could I do it again? But no, I couldn't rely on magic. Not now. I plowed ahead.

"So you took what was dearest to them," I said. "But when Benicio finds out—"

"Are you listening? Have you heard a word I've said? I don't care!"

"But you wanted immortality—"

"I wanted eternal life with my *wife*. Without her, it doesn't matter."

A gust of wind whipped through the alley, making us all freeze. It came again, not so much a wind now as a quaking, as if the air itself was heaving, churning.

Edward stepped to the side fast and raised the gun at Lucas. I pitched sideways, throwing myself into his path, but the air around us vibrated so violently that I lost my balance and fell to one knee. As I twisted, the still-healing knife wounds blazed and I gasped.

"Don't move, Paige," Lucas said, his voice tight. "Please, don't move."

I shifted my eyes, straining to see Edward. He had the gun pointed at my chest.

"Don't do this," Lucas said. "She hasn't done anything to you. If you let her go, I can promise you—"

Edward swung the gun toward Lucas. "Shut up."

"Listen to him, Edward," I said. "If you stop now, you can be with Natasha."

"Natasha is gone!"

"No, she's not. She's a ghost."

His lips twisted. "You lying bitch. You'd say anything to save him, wouldn't you?"

He started to turn the gun on me. Then the air around us crackled and popped, and he swung the gun back toward Lucas.

"I told you, any magic and—"

Behind Lucas, the air darkened, then the backdrop shattered, like a mirror breaking. Light streamed through. A woman's figure appeared in the light. Edward looked up. He blinked.

"Nat—? Natasha?"

She reached for him. Edward took a slow, cautious step forward. Then suddenly, Natasha's body jerked ramrod straight. The hole shimmered around her. Her eyes went wide and her mouth opened in a silent scream, and she tumbled back into the yawning hole, arms still stretching toward Edward.

"No!" Edward shouted.

The gun jerked, then fell from his hand as he raced for the portal. I saw the gun fall. I swear that is the first thing I saw, and in that moment I knew Lucas was safe. Then Lucas toppled backward, a dark hole in his breast pocket. Then, only then, I heard the shot echoing through the alley.

I twisted around. Lucas was still falling into the hole. The light swallowed his head, then his chest, and finally his feet.

I dove in after him.

Through the Back Door

I WAS JUMPING ON A BED, LEAPING AS HIGH AS I COULD, shrieking each time my feet struck down. Someone was singing. My mother? No, a younger voice, struggling to sing without laughing.

"Five little monkeys jumping on the bed.
One fell off and bumped his head.
Momma called the doctor and the doctor said,
'No more monkeys jumping on the bed!'"

"Again!" I screamed. "Again!"

"Again?" the voice laughed. "If you break your mother's bed, she'll have both our hides."

I threw my chubby fists in the air as I jumped, then lost my footing and collapsed face first into the pillows. Hands reached down to pick me up, but I pushed them back, got up and whirled around, bouncing.

"Again! Again!"

A dramatic sigh. "One more time, Paige. I mean it. This is the last time."

I giggled, knowing this would be far from the last time. *Five little monkeys . . .*

I groaned and the dream faded, but I could still hear the song, that same person singing it. The voice tickled a memory, but it evaporated before I could seize it.

I opened my eyes, but could see nothing. A cold, damp darkness enveloped me and I shivered. I blinked and tried to clear my fogged brain. I was lying on my side. I reached out and touched something cold but smooth and solid. As I ran my hand across it, I felt bumps and sharp edges. Rock. I was lying on rock.

Four little monkeys jumping on the bed . . .

I squeezed my eyes shut, but the tune kept playing in my head. What was that song? Now that I heard it, I could say every word by heart, as they bubbled up from my subconscious. An image came to mind. Me, no more than two years old, jumping on my mother's bed as someone sang.

"No more monkeys jumping on the bed!"

Three little monkeys—

"Oh, God, stop!" I said, cradling my booming head.

The song stopped.

A voice sighed, that same dramatic sigh I'd heard in my dream. "Well, it was either that or scream until you woke up. Be glad I took the musical approach."

I scrambled up and looked around. My eyes had adjusted enough that I could make out dim shapes around me, but none looked remotely human. I blinked hard and focused. Scattered around me were huge boulders, rising up from the stone bed on which I lay.

"Rock," I said. "It's all rock."

"Weird, huh? We have some very strange places here. Looks like you landed in one of them. Let's just hope nothing nasty pops out."

My head whipped around, searching for the source of the voice, but I saw only rocks.

Two little monkeys . . .

"Stop that," I said.

"Hey, I'm trying to jar your memory. You used to love that song. Savannah did, too. Both of you, crazy for it, though I think you just liked the excuse to jump on the bed."

Savannah? How did she know—? I swallowed, making the only association I could.

"Eve?" I said.

"Who else? Don't tell me you've forgotten."

When I didn't answer, she said. "Oh, come on. You must remember your favorite babysitter. I looked after you every Wednesday night for nearly two years. If I couldn't make it, you wouldn't let your mom get anyone else. You'd cry so hard she had to cancel the Elders meeting and stay home."

Eve paused. When I still said nothing, she sighed. "You really don't remember, do you? Damn. I usually leave more of an impression."

"Where are you?" I said.

"Hold on. I'm working on that part. Just give me a—" A shimmer of movement to my left. The shape winked, then started coming into focus. "Almost there. This ain't easy, let me tell you."

An audible pop. And there stood a grown-up version of Savannah, a tall, exotically beautiful woman with a wide mouth, strong nose and chin, and long, straight black hair. Only the eyes were different, dark instead of the bright blue Savannah had inherited from Kristof Nast.

She hunkered down before me, then touched the ground and shivered.

"Damn cold. You sure picked a helluva place to pop through. If I'd known, I'd have dressed warmer." She caught my eye, her wide grin a mirror of Savannah's.

"Ghost humor." She looked down at her clothes: jeans, sneakers, and a dark green embroidered blouse. "You know, I used to really like this blouse, but after wearing it for a year straight . . . Time to figure out how to change clothes." She sized up my ensemble. "Not bad. Could have been worse."

"I'm not—I'm not a ghost. I didn't—"

"Die? Jury's still out on that one. All I know is you're here, and if you're here, you should be dead." Eve shook her head. "Never expected you to go all Romeo and Juliet on me, Paige. I know, once you commit yourself to someone, you go all the way, like you did with Savannah, but, really—" She waved at our surroundings. "This is too far."

"Lucas," I said, scrambling up.

"Easy, girl. He's right over—" Eve stood. "Now where . . . ? Oh, there."

I hurried past her. As I skirted an outcropping of rock, I saw Lucas's shoes. I raced around a large boulder to find him lying on his back, eyes closed. I dropped down beside him, fingers going to his throat, feeling for a pulse.

"Uh, you won't find that, Paige," Eve said behind me. "Not on yourself, either. Part of the passing-over package deal. You can jog all you want and never run out of breath. First time in a week your stomach hasn't hurt, I'll bet."

I touched Lucas's cheek. His skin was warm. I leaned down, bringing my face to his, and gently shook his shoulder as I called his name.

"You could try kissing him," Eve said. "But I don't think that works in real life . . . or real afterlife."

I glared at her. She held up her hands.

"Sorry, not the time for quips." She walked around Lucas and knelt on his other side. "He's okay, baby. This is normal. It's death shock. Takes a day or two to recover.

Normally, you'd come through into one of the waiting areas, where there are people to look after you, but you guys took the back door."

"D—death shock?"

I looked down at Lucas's chest. His shirt was whole. I slid my hand under it, but found no bullet hole.

"No, he's okay," I said. "He didn't get shot. He just fell through the rift, like I did."

Eve said nothing.

I turned to face her. "He didn't get shot. Look, no hole."

She nodded, eyes not meeting mine. I swallowed hard, then pulled up my blouse. On my stomach, where Weber had stabbed me, the skin was now smooth and unblemished.

Eve bent over Lucas and adjusted his glasses, which had slipped in the fall. "No need for these here, but they still pass through. Weird, huh?" She leaned back for a better look, then straightened the glasses again and brushed strands of hair off Lucas's forehead. "Poor kid. All these years, being Ben's son was the only thing that protected him, and now it's what killed him." She shook her head. "Did Lucas ever tell you we met?"

I struggled to focus, then nodded. The memory flashed and a tiny smile tweaked my lips. "He said 'encountered' was a more accurate word than 'met.'"

Eve laughed. "That's Lucas, isn't it? Got to be precise." She rocked back on her heels. "How long ago was that? Shit, it has to be four, five years. He couldn't have been more than twenty. Tried to confiscate some of my grimoires. But I caught him. Trounced him good, too."

"So he said."

Eve's left brow shot up. "He admitted it? Well, that's real strength, isn't it? Not being able to knock someone down, but being able to admit it when you're the one who hit the floor. He's a good kid. Good for Savannah, too. You both are." She looked from me to Lucas, then thumped down and pulled her knees up. "Ah, shit, what are we going to do?"

"We need to go back."

"Hey, I'm with you on that one, but it's easier said than done. Normally, it's a one-way ticket, but you guys didn't take that train in, so maybe we can find a way—" Her head snapped back and she glared at something over my head. "Goddamn it, you're worse than a bloodhound. Track me down no matter where I hide." She waved her hands. "Shoo. I'm busy. Go away."

I craned my neck to look behind me, but there was no one there.

"Of course I'm helping her get out of here," she snapped. "What, you want our daughter raised by wolves?"

I hesitated. "Kristof?"

"Yeah. You can't hear him?"

I shook my head.

Eve laughed. "Ha! Hear that, Mr. Almighty Cabal Sorcerer? You can't even project far enough into this dimension for her to hear you. I broke right though. In living color."

"Dimension?"

"Dimension, level, layer," she said, "It's complicated."

"So the real ghosts are all in your layer? The one Kristof's in now?"

"Nah, they're scattered everywhere. That's the bitch of it, really. You pass over, thinking you'll see everyone who left before you, and you don't, because they're not all in your dimension. Some of us, the magical races, can blur a layer or two, see through to the other side, like Kristof's doing. But to pass through—" She grinned in Kristof's direction. "That takes a real spell-caster."

"So my . . . my mother. Is she here?"

Eve shook her head. "Sorry, baby. Not in this layer or in mine. There are others, though. I just haven't figured out how to see through them."

Her gaze shot up again. "Yeah, yeah, funny guy. Go find someone else to pester. I need to talk to Paige."

A pause.

"Is he leaving?" I asked.

"Nah, just sitting there. Being quiet, though, which is the best I can hope for. Now, let's see what we've got here. That vamp bitch Natasha somehow ripped open a hole in her layer. I have no idea how she did that. Hell, I didn't even think vamps *had* a layer. It's all very strange. Almost makes me wonder if the Fates *let* her open it up, so she could suck her fiend-partner into hell with her."

"Uh-huh."

"Nice theory, but it doesn't help you out, right? Point is, you guys fell through by accident, and we need to get you back. Now, since you came through here, this spot must be important. A portal, if you want to get all Trekkie about it."

I looked around.

"Damned ugly place to stick one, isn't it?" she continued. "Which is probably the point. No one comes here sightseeing."

"So, can you break through?"

Eve shot a glare behind me. "Finish that sentence at your peril, Kris." She paused. "That's what I thought." She turned to me. "No can do. Not yet anyway. We need a necromancer."

"Good, I know just where to find one."

"Jaime Vegas?" Eve made a face. "Not my first choice,

but I guess any necro will do. Between her and me, we should be able to rip this thing open enough for you to go through."

"*Lucas* and me."

"Uh, right. Now, I can't say it'll work for sure, because I know there's no way for *me* to go back permanently. Believe me, I've tried."

Her eyes cut to Kristof and, for a split second I caught a glimpse of something in those eyes that sent a shiver down my spine, and reminded me of who and what Eve was. She locked glares with the air behind me.

I suspected whatever Kristof said, it had something to do with Eve trying to cross back into the world of the living. From the way she said it, I guessed she'd been trying damned hard to return to life and, for a moment, I wondered at that. She seemed happy and comfortable enough. It wasn't like she was in some kind of hell dimension. So why fight to return to life?

Even as the question flitted through my brain, I thought of my own situation. I was here, in the afterlife, and not for one second did I consider staying. Why? Because my life was on that other side, and no matter how pleasant it might be to live in a world free of pain and discomfort, I wanted to finish my "real" life before I embarked on my afterlife. That real life, though, included Lucas. It had to.

"So if you can't get back," I said, "then you think maybe we . . . ?"

"I don't know, but I'm sure as hell gonna try. You're a special case, so there's gotta be a way."

"Okay, so let's do it. You're a ghost, so you contact Jaime—"

"It's not that easy. First, we have to find her."

"Find her? She's in Miami."

"Obstacle number one, though it's not as bad as it seems. Miami exists here, too, only it's not quite . . . well, it's different. Distance isn't a problem. It's all very . . . relative."

"Uh-huh."

Eve shook her head. "I can't explain. Even I don't understand it all yet. Obstacle number two, though——" She looked down at Lucas. "We can't carry him."

"I'm not leaving him here."

"Well, then we have a real problem. He'll wake up in a day or two, but by then, the Searchers will have found us, and once they do, you're taking up permanent residence. Now, we can——" She stopped and looked up at Kristof, then nodded. "Kristof is offering to stay here with Lucas."

When I hesitated, she looked back toward Kristof. "You ripped the poor girl's life apart. That doesn't encourage trust, Kris." She looked at me. "It's okay, Paige. If Kristof says he'll watch Lucas, he will. He has nothing to gain if you and Lucas don't make it back to Savannah. He knows now this is what I want, what I wanted from the start, for Savannah to be with you. He won't interfere again."

Eve stood. I squeezed Lucas's hand, took one last look at him, then followed Eve across the rocky plain.

Primeval Swamp

WE HIKED ACROSS THE ROCKY PLAIN FOR WHAT MUST HAVE been two hours. One problem with the ghost world? Serious lack of public transportation. Yet, even with all that walking, I didn't suffer so much as sore feet. I suppose that renders motorized vehicles unnecessary. That and the fact that, here, you have all the time in the world to get wherever you're going.

Normally, I guess, travel in the ghost world is like a Sunday stroll, relax and enjoy the scenery. Where we were, though, there was no scenery to enjoy, unless you were a geologist. Rock, rock, and more rock. Not exactly the Elysian fields I'd hoped for. Of course, this was a temporary stay—the more temporary, the better—but I couldn't help being curious, if only to take my mind off the worries that were gnawing through my gut. This was the afterlife, the greatest mystery in the world unfolding before me. Yet my attempts to get more information from Eve were blocked with witticisms and non sequiturs. I can, however, be somewhat persistent, and finally she was forced to address the issue.

"I can't tell you anything, Paige. I know you're curious,

but if we're going to get you out of this world, then the less you know—"

"The better," I finished.

"The better for *me,* too," she said. "I'm already in the Fates' bad books, and once they find out—"

"So the Fates are real?"

"Oh, yeah, only they don't just sit around spinning yarn—" She shot me a mock glare. "Stop that. You're going to trick me into talking, and then they'll find out and I won't just be up to my neck in shit anymore, I'll be drowning in it. Believe me, they *will* find out—hopefully just not until you're gone."

"How will they find us? Those Searchers you mentioned?"

Eve kept walking.

I continued, "If I need to be on the lookout for these things, then I have to know what to look for."

"No, you don't. If you see them, they've already seen you, and we're both going down. Not a whole lotta laws in this place, but we're breaking most of them."

"What if—"

I stopped and stared. The rocky plains ended less than a dozen yards in front of us. Beyond that was . . . nothing. They didn't end in a cliff or a wall of darkness or anything so dramatic. They just ended, like hitting the last page in a book. I can't describe it any better than that.

"Well, come on," she said.

I couldn't move. There was something indescribably terrifying about the view in front of me, the yawning nothingness of it.

"Oh, hell," Eve said. "It's just a way station."

She grabbed my elbow and propelled me forward. When we reached the end of the plain, my brain went wild, digging in its mental heels. That response shot down to my legs and they stopped moving. Eve sighed and, without a word, stepped behind me, and pushed.

I'd been tricked. In that last second before Eve shoved me through, I realized the truth. Eve wasn't helping me. She didn't want me going back to Savannah. She hated me, hated what I was doing to her daughter, hated how I was raising her. This was her revenge. She was—

"There," Eve said, stepping beside me. "That's not so bad, is it?"

I looked around. Fog surrounded me, a strange, cold, bluish mist.

I rubbed my upper arms. "So what is this place? A way station between what?"

"Between planes, the nonearthly realms of the ghost world, like where you landed. From here I can transport us to another plane, or to any place on earth. Well, our version of earth."

"But how—"

"Think of it as a cosmic elevator. A modern one, though. No elevator attendant on duty. Can't just walk up and say 'Miami, please.' Don't I wish. No, it's strictly do-it-yourself, and you have to figure out the right incantation to get to each place, like breaking a code. Different place, different code."

"So I assume they don't like ghosts traveling."

Eve shrugged. "They aren't totally against it, but they'd rather you found a place and stuck to it, at least for a while. Frequent commuting is not encouraged. It confuses the older ghosts, seeing new faces popping in and out all the time."

"But you know the codes."

She grinned. "Not as many as I'd like, but I'm racking up far more frequent flier miles than the Fates would like. They've rapped my knuckles a few times. Not about using the codes, because, technically, that's allowed, but they don't always approve of the methods I use to get them."

"Uh-huh."

"And that's all you need to know about that. Now hold on."

Eve murmured an incantation in a language I'd never heard. Then she turned and walked back in the direction we'd come.

"It didn't work?" I said as I hurried after her. "So now what—"

"More walking, less talking, Paige."

I took one more step and my foot sank into what felt like a steaming pile of horse shit. I yelped and jumped back. I looked down. Warm, slimy mud oozed into my sandals.

"Gross, huh?" Eve said. "Come on."

I followed. The mist still swirled around us. I opened my mouth to ask Eve something, then caught a whiff of the air and gagged. In grade school, a sadistic teacher had forced our class on an educational tour of a sewer plant. It had smelled like this, only better. One more cautious step, and a wave of humid heat washed over me. Then the mist cleared.

I looked around. The first association that clicked was: the Everglades. But it wasn't. It had the same smell, the same feel, the same general look, but everything was multiplied a hundredfold. I touched the nearest overhanging fern. The leaf was bigger than I was. Massive twisted trees loomed overhead, pale moss dangling all around them, like a tattered wedding dress on a bridal corpse. An insect the size of a swallow buzzed past. As I turned to get a better look at it, something deep within the swamp shrieked. I jumped. Eve laughed and steadied me.

"Welcome to Miami," she said. "Population: a few hundred...none of whom you want to meet."

"This is Miami?" I said.

"Weird, huh? Watch this."

She murmured an incantation, then rubbed her hand in front of us, as if cleaning glass. There, in the spot she'd cleared, was a tunnel view of a city street, neon signs blazing. A pair of headlights rounded the corner and headed straight for us. I locked my knees so I wouldn't bolt. The car zoomed to the edge of the "window," then disappeared.

"That's your Miami," she said, then pointed at the swamp. "This is ours."

She swiped her hand over the image, and it dissolved. I took a few steps, shoes squelching in the mud.

"Stick close," she said. "I'm serious about there being things out there you don't want to meet."

I looked around and shook my head. "So all the cities are gone in the ghost world?"

"Nah. Miami's special."

"What are the other cities like? Do they look like ours?"

"Kind of. That's the cool thing. They look like the real ones, but they're stuck in the past, at some important point in their history, their heyday or whatever."

I looked around. "So Miami's heyday was back when it was a primeval swamp?"

Eve grinned. "All downhill from there, huh? Or maybe it's a metaphorical thing."

"You said ghosts live in the other cities. What if you lived in Miami while you were alive? Would you have to relocate?"

"Mostly, yes. But those things I was mentioning, the ones that live here? Rumor has it that they used to be—"

She grimaced and made a zipping motion over her mouth. "No more questions, Paige."

"But shouldn't I know—"

"No, you shouldn't. You don't need to. You just want to. God, I'd forgotten how curious you are. When you were little, I swore your first word wasn't 'Momma,' it was 'why.'"

"Just one last—"

"One last question? Ha! Do you have any idea how many times I fell for that one?" She started walking. "One last question. One last game. One last song."

"I just—"

"Stop talking and get moving or you'll learn more about this swamp than you ever cared to know."

Blindsided

EVE KNEW HER WAY AROUND THE GHOST-WORLD MIAMI from her frequent visits over the last two weeks. What had lured her to this hell swamp? Us. She'd been keeping tabs on Lucas and me since we'd arrived in Miami, as she'd been periodically checking in on Savannah while she was under Elena's care. Apparently, she'd been doing this since her death, reassuring herself that her daughter was safe, and now keeping track of her guardians as well. It was a strictly visual supervision, but only because she hadn't figured out a way to extend her protectorship to a more active form. Not surprisingly, the Fates frowned on the whole guardian-angel routine. Interfering with the living was forbidden. Even checking in on loved ones, as Eve was doing, was discouraged. To make the full transition to ghost life, you had to break all ties with the living world. Eve was having some difficulty with the concept.

We had to walk two miles to get to where our hotel would be in the living world. I hoped Jaime was there. Otherwise, we were in for a long hunt.

Two miles wasn't relatively far, given the size of Miami, but when you were walking through a swamp, up to your ankles in muck, blazing a trail through the vegetation with fire spells, every few yards seemed like miles. Fortunately, Eve had forged some paths earlier, including one to our hotel. Otherwise the vegetation would have been impassable. Already, in the half day she'd been gone, the vines had wound over her trail, the lush vegetation filling in so fast you could almost see it growing.

As we hacked through a particularly overgrown area, I thought I *did* see the vegetation growing, as ferns a few yards ahead swished in the still, fetid air. Then I saw a shape move behind the fronds.

"Shit!" Eve said.

The figure shambled forward, taking shape in the dim light. I made out a vaguely humanoid form, then everything went dark. I bit back a yelp, and started casting a light spell. Eve grasped my forearm and leaned down to my ear.

"It's me, Paige. I did it."

Did what? Before I could ask, I remembered that Eve was also a half-demon, having been sired by an Aspicio. An Aspicio's power is sight, and its progeny can inflict temporary blindness.

"What?" I hissed. "Don't—I can't see!"

"That's the idea."

Mud squelched as the thing moved through the swamp, coming closer with each step. I blinked hard, but saw only darkness.

"Eve!" I whispered. "Stop this. I'm not a little girl anymore. I've seen things, lots of things. Demons, corpses, *reanimated* corpses—multiple reanimated corpses. Whatever's out there, I can handle—"

I stopped mid-sentence, mouth open, frozen, not in fear, but in a binding spell. Eve's hair tickled my ear as she leaned down over me.

"Maybe you can handle it, Paige, but you don't need to."

I glared at her—or in the direction I assumed she was.

"Don't worry," she whispered. "I've dealt with these things before. Most times if you just stand still, they'll go away."

Stand still? Did I have a choice? I couldn't see. I couldn't move. I couldn't speak. I could hear, though. I was frozen there, blinded, listening to the squelching of some unknown horror as it shambled toward me. Then another sense kicked in. Smell. A sickly sweet smell, worse than the stink of the rotting vegetation. My gut clenched.

As the thing drew close, I caught a faint, papery sound, like dry leaves rustling in the breeze. The noise took on a rhythm, then a clear sound, a steady, raspy "ung-ung-ung." The hairs on my arms shot up and I struggled against the binding spell. The smell grew stronger, until it was so overwhelming, I felt the gag reflex in my throat. But, caught in the binding spell, I couldn't gag. My mouth filled with bile. I fought harder against the spell, but it didn't crack.

"Ung-ung-ung."

The sound was so close now I knew the creature was right in front of us, just off to my left, where Eve stood. The noise stopped, replaced by a dry snuffling.

"It's okay, Paige," she whispered. "Just let it sniff you, and it'll—" A chomping sound. Then a gasp. "You fucking—!"

She cast a spell, something I didn't recognize. A high-pitched shriek rent the air, then a bellow, and fast footfalls through the mud.

"You'd better run," Eve said. "Goddamned—"

"Ung-ung-ung!" The cry, loud now, came from somewhere to our left, immediately followed by another to our right.

"Holy shit," Eve whispered.

She snapped the binding spell and I stumbled forward, my sight returning just in time for me to see the ground rushing up. Eve grabbed my arm and yanked me upright. I made out three, maybe four humanoid shapes rushing at us before Eve whipped me around and we started to run.

We raced, slipping and sliding and scrambling, through the swamp. Apparently unaccustomed to moving fast, the creatures were having just as much trouble. We retraced our steps through the path we'd cut coming in, which made it easier.

As we rounded a corner, Eve skidded across a muddy patch. I caught her before she fell.

"I hate running away," she muttered as we plowed forward again. "Hate it, hate it, hate it."

"Should we stop and fight?"

"As soon as we get enough of a head start to cast. They're falling behind, aren't they?"

"Seems like it."

"Good. Fucking bastards. I can't believe they attacked me."

"Look on the bright side," I said as we tore around another curve. "At least they can't kill us."

Eve's laugh rang through the swamp. "This is true. Being dead has its—"

Eve's body jerked, as if someone yanked her legs out from under her. Her lips parted in an oath, but before any sound came out, she was sucked into the swamp.

"Eve!" I shouted.

Something grabbed my left foot. I pulled my right foot back to kick it, but a tremendous yank pulled me off balance, and the swamp sailed up to swallow me.

Busted

BEFORE I HAD TIME TO PANIC, THE SWAMP VANISHED, AND I was plunked down onto a cold, hard surface. Back to the rocky plain? I looked around, but a mist surrounded me. Unlike the cold fog in the way station, this was warm and almost tangibly soft. As I child, I'd often lain on the grass, stared up at the clouds, and wondered what they'd feel like. The mist around me was almost exactly what I'd imagined. A sudden image of clouds and harps and trumpeting angels sprang to mind. Had I died—again—and gone to heaven?

"Ah, shit," Eve muttered somewhere beside me. "Busted."

Okay, not heaven. Whew. Monotonous bliss was not what I had in mind for my eternity.

As the mist withdrew, it contracted, growing denser. For a split second, something like a face appeared in the mist. Then it stretched into a pale ribbon, twisting as it wended toward the roof and disappeared.

"Damn Searchers," Eve muttered. "There's gotta be a way to outsmart them. Gotta be." She glanced over at me. "Don't worry. Everything will be okay. Just keep quiet and let me do the talking."

The mist now completely gone, I looked around. What I saw was so overwhelming that, for a moment, I could only stare, uncomprehending. The room we were in—no, it wasn't a room, there couldn't be a room this large. The bluish-white marble walls seemed to extend into infinity, the dark marble floor stretching to meet it like the earth reaching to the horizon. The vaulted white ceiling and huge pillars gave it the look of a Grecian temple, but the mosaics and paintings decorating the walls seemed to come from every culture imaginable. Each frieze portrayed a scene from life. Every part of life, every celebration, every tragedy, every mundane moment seemed to be pictured on those walls. As my gaze passed a bloody battle scene, a rearing horse's front leg moved, infinitesimally. I blinked. The rider's mouth opened, so slowly that the casual glance would miss it.

I was about to say something to Eve when the floor began to turn.

"An audience has been granted," Eve muttered. "About time."

The floor rotated until we were faced with an open space at least as inconceivably huge as the one on the other side. Across the expanse, vines hung from the ceiling, thousands, tens of thousands of them, suspended from every inch of space. The sight was so incongruous that I blinked and rubbed my thumb and forefinger over my eyes. When I looked again, I saw that they weren't vines at all, but pieces of yarn, colored every shade in the rainbow, and all exactly the same length.

"What the—?" I began.

"Shhh," Eve hissed. "Let me talk, remember?"

It was then that I saw the woman. She stood on a dais, behind an old-fashioned spinning wheel. Neither young nor old, ugly nor beautiful, thin nor fat, short nor tall, she was a perfect average of everything female, a middle-aged matron with skin the color of honey and long graying dark hair.

Her head down, she pumped a length of yarn from the wheel until it looked the same length as those hanging all around her. Then in a transition so fast and seamless it seemed a trick of the eyes, the woman aged fifty years, becoming an elderly crone, back bent, long hair as coarse and gray as wire, the simple mauve dress now white with the palest hint of violet. Her sunken eyes gleamed, dark and quick, like a crow's. One wizened hand lifted the length of yarn. The other, wrapped around a pair of black scissors, reached up and snipped it off. A man—so pale he looked albino—appeared from the jungle of dangling yarn, took the newly cut piece, and disappeared back into the dark depths of wool.

I looked back at the crone, but in her place stood a child no more than five or six, so small she couldn't see over the spinning wheel. Like the others, she had long hair, but hers was gleaming golden brown, and her eyes were cornflower blue. Her dress was an equally vivid purple.

The girl threaded the wheel, standing on tiptoes to reach it. Once it was ready, she changed to the middle-aged woman, who began to spin the yarn.

Beside me, Eve sighed loudly. "See? Even the Fates aren't above petty sadism, making us sit here and stew."

The woman, now the old crone, pinned Eve with her sharp eyes. "Petty? Never. We're enjoying a rare moment of peace, when we don't need to worry what you're up to."

She clipped the yarn. As the albino man retrieved it, the girl appeared. Before she could load the wheel, she stopped, her head cocked, a frown flitting across her pretty face. The albino appeared, holding a length of yarn in his hands. The girl nodded gravely, then morphed into the middle-aged woman, who took the yarn. She slid it through her fingers, then closed her eyes. A single tear squeezed out as her fingers slipped up the yarn nearly to the top. The woman became the crone, who looked at the tiny length of yarn pinched between her fingers.

"So young," she murmured, and clipped it off.

She handed the tiny piece of yarn back to the albino, who took it and walked into a hallway to our left. The old woman turned into the girl.

"So this is the problem we heard about," the girl said, her voice high and musical. "And you're involved, Eve? Shocking."

"Hey, I didn't—"

The girl smiled. "Didn't do anything? Or didn't cause the original problem? We're well aware of your innocence in the latter, but we'd beg to differ on the former. Exactly how many rules have you broken today, Eve? I'm not sure I can count that high."

"Sarcastic deities," Eve muttered. "Just what every afterlife needs."

The girl changed into the woman. "We'll discuss your transgressions later, Eve. Right now—" Her voice softened as her gaze moved to me. "We have a more distressing situation to contend with. Not that you're to blame, child, but we must fix this immediately. We'll send you back, of course. You'll still remember your visit. We hate to tamper with memory, and we see no need for it in your case." A smile. "You're not the type to turn this experience into a best-selling memoir. Now, all we need—"

"Is Lucas," I said.

Eve elbowed me. I ignored her.

"We need Lucas. We left him—"

The woman shook her head. "He can't go, child. He died. He must stay here."

"No, he didn't—"

"We know you don't want to believe that, but—"

"Wait," I said, lifting my hands. "I'm arguing the fact, not the interpretation. The bullet hit Lucas and he fell into the portal."

"We know what happened."

"Then you know it takes longer than that split second to die after being shot in the chest. Therefore, when he fell through the portal, he wasn't dead."

The woman shook her head, smiling. "Always the logical one, aren't you? I'm afraid it's a matter of semantics, child. The shot would have killed him. We know that."

My heart seized in my chest, but I pushed on. "Okay, you know that because you know it was his time, but—"

"His time?" the old woman said as she appeared. She swept a hand at the yarn jungle behind her. "It's never anyone's time, girl. We don't make that decision. What happens happens, and what happened was that Lucas Cortez died—"

The middle sister cut in. "Which is a tragedy, of course. But here he'll be able to continue his work. There's good and evil in this world, too. We can use Lucas here and, when you die, you will join him. You'll be together. That's already been determined. That's why you came through to the same dimension. You just have to wait—"

"I won't wait. If he stays, I stay."

The woman's lips curved in a sympathetic smile. "That's not a choice you really want to make. It won't go the way you hoped."

"I'm not hoping for anything. I'm making a statement of fact. Lucas stays, I stay."

"Don't do this," Eve hissed in my ear. "You can't trick them."

"It isn't a bluff."

The crone appeared. "Whether you go or stay isn't your decision to make, girl."

"But if you send me back, I can make it my decision. You've said there's no predestination, so I can choose my own time of death."

"Doesn't matter. Even if you kill yourself, there's no guarantee you'll ever see him again."

"Of course there is. You said so yourself. It's been decided—we'll be together. I suppose you could change things, but that would be petty, and you said you're never petty."

The woman appeared with a sigh. "I do so prefer the ghosts who cower and quake in our presence."

"Oh, she's awful, isn't she?" Eve said. "Been like this since she was a child. Always questioning everything and everybody. No respect for authority. My advice? Send her and Lucas back and spare yourselves sixty, seventy unnecessary years of grief."

"Thank you, Eve, for considering our feelings in the matter. However, your bias in the matter is well known. You want Paige for your daughter's guardian."

"Have you considered that, Paige?" asked the old woman, popping back to fix me with that soul-piercing stare. "If you stayed here, you'd abandon Savannah, after all you've—"

The middle sister cut in. "No, that's not fair. We won't make you choose, child. The decision must be ours. That is the only truly equitable—" She stopped, head tilted. "Yes, sister, that's an idea."

The woman vanished, then the child appeared, then the crone, then the three began flipping so quickly I couldn't tell who I was seeing. Snatches of conversation flew past, meaningless, out of context. Then the middle-aged woman took over.

"Eve, you want Paige and Lucas as Savannah's guardians. Would you be willing to barter for it?"

Eve lifted her chin, meeting the other woman's gaze squarely. "I am. You want me to obey the rules, right? Send them back—both of them—and I'll do it."

The woman smiled and shook her head. "Obedience without acceptance is meaningless. When you under-stand the rules, you'll obey them. Until then—" She shrugged and waved at the yarn hanging behind them. "You make your own mistakes. You determine your own fate. We don't do that for you."

Eve frowned. "Then what's the price?"

"You will owe us a favor. A chit, which we may call in whenever we wish."

"I'll do it."

"Are you sure?"

"No, but I'm agreeing anyway. Do this for me, and I'll owe you one. Now, we left Lucas—"

The Fate cut Eve off with a wave. "We know." She closed her eyes and the three forms flipped past in a blur, then returned to the middle sister. "There. Lucas is back in the living world. Paige, we'll see you again someday, hopefully after a long and—"

"Wait!" Eve said. "Don't I get to say good-bye?"

"Yes, after I do. Now, Paige, turn around."

I did. Twenty feet away, the air shimmered, like heat rising off hot asphalt.

"That's the portal. When you're done with Eve, just walk through it. Be quick, though. I've sent Lucas back to where he left, and he'll likely be disoriented. There was no danger there a moment ago but—well, be quick."

I looked back at the Fates. "Thank you."

The woman nodded. "You're welcome. Just remember the cardinal rule of leaving the afterlife." She morphed into the child, who grinned. "Don't look back."

I smiled, turned, and headed for the portal. Eve walked beside me. Neither of us said anything until we reached it. Then I turned to her.

"Thank you," I said. "For everything."

"Hey, you're raising my kid. I owe you everything. Tell Savannah . . . No, I won't waste our last minute with that. You know what to tell her. And I won't tell you to take good care of her, because I know you will. So I'll settle for telling you to take care of yourself. You grew up good, Paige. Maybe more 'good' than I'd like, but I'm still proud of you." She leaned over, kissed my forehead, and whispered, "Have a good life, Paige. You deserve it."

"I—"

She took my shoulders, turned me around, and pushed me into the portal.

Bad Guy Dead?

I CAME TO IN THE ALLEY. WHEN I OPENED MY EYES, I SAW only darkness. I blinked and the world took focus as my eyes adjusted. It took a moment for my numbed brain to understand why it was dark out, to make that most obvious deductive leap. Night. It was nighttime. How long had we—? The thought slid from my brain. Too much effort. I tried lifting my head, but that also seemed like too much work. Everything was so . . . heavy. The very air had a weight that went beyond the dampness of a wet Miami night.

I yawned and closed my eyes. As I drifted toward sleep, my brain replayed snatches from the last eight hours and I shot upright, remembering everything.

"Lucas?" I scrambled to my feet. "Lucas!"

Pitching forward into the darkness, I stumbled over something and fell to my knees. My hands felt for the object that had tripped me, praying that it was Lucas. I touched the cold rough surface of broken concrete. Staying on all fours, I felt around wildly. When I over-reached, pain shot through my abdomen, the first twinge I'd felt since jumping through the portal. The sudden shock of the pain made me stop long enough to think. I closed my eyes, took a deep breath, and cast a light spell.

After casting, I kept my eyes closed, telling myself that when I did look I'd see Lucas, but still afraid . . . I opened my eyes. He wasn't there.

"Lucas!"

I flew to my feet, waving the light-ball about. He had to be here. They promised, they promised, they—

My light illuminated an outstretched hand near the end of the alley. Lucas lay on his back, arms out, face to the sky, eyes closed. He's sleeping, I told myself. Sleeping like I was. Then I saw the blood on his shirt front.

As I shot forward, an image raced through my mind, a scene from some half-remembered movie where a man had been granted a wish and, before he could use it, his wife died. So he made the obvious wish. He wanted her alive again. But he hadn't been specific, hadn't said he'd wanted her as she'd been before the accident, and the last scene had been of her mutilated body lurching toward the front door.

"You weren't specific!" I shouted to myself, my mental voice reverberating through my head. I said I wanted Lucas to be sent back to this world with me and the Fates had done exactly that. They'd brought him back as he'd been when he left it—shot through the heart.

People always say that after someone dies, the first thing they think of is everything they regret not having told them. My own regrets were enough to bury me alive, but they never crossed my mind, not in the ghost world, when I'd refused to believe he was dead, and not now, when I was certain he was. Instead, the only thought going through my head at that moment was that his death was my fault. I'd had the chance to save him, to deal with Fate, and I'd been my usual impetuous self, demanding something before thinking it through.

As I knelt beside Lucas, his eyelids flickered. My

breath caught. For a long moment, I didn't breathe, certain that somehow my dropping to the pavement had caused a vibration that made his eyelids move. Fingers trembling, I touched the side of his neck.

"Mmmm," he murmured.

My hands went to his shirt and I fumbled with the buttons, then gave up and ripped the sodden fabric. Beneath the bloodied hole, Lucas's chest was unmarked. Unable to believe it, I touched the spot where the bullet should have gone through, and felt his heart beating as strong as ever. I dropped my head onto his chest, and all the fear and anxiety I'd repressed in the ghost world bubbled forth in a chest-wrenching sob.

When I gasped for breath, a distant sound made me stop and listen. It came again, a soft rhythmic scraping against the concrete. A pale shape floated into the darkness a few yards away. I tensed and waved my light-ball higher, until it cast a dim glow down the length of the alley. A ghostly-white wolf stood at the other end, head tilted as if as surprised to see me as I was to see it. Our eyes met. The wolf dove back into the darkness.

"Did you just see . . . ?" Lucas croaked, lifting his head and squinting into the darkness.

"I think so."

"Then are we . . . back? Or still on the other side?"

"I have no idea. I'm just glad you're okay." I gave him a fierce hug, then pulled back fast. "Did that hurt? You *are* okay, aren't you?"

He smiled. "I'm fine. Just a little stiff . . . like someone hit me in the chest with a bullet."

"You remember?"

"I remember a lot of things," he said, then gave a confused frown. "Including things I really ought not to remember, considering I was unconscious at the time. It was very ... strange. I was—" His lips curved in a slow smile. "Oh."

"Oh what?"

"I just remembered how I got back here." His smile broadened to a lazy grin that lit up his eyes. "The Fates. You talked to the Fates. You told them—" He paused, and the grin dissipated, eyes sobering. "I must say, though, you were taking a serious risk, Paige. If they'd called your bluff—"

"Bluff?" I squawked. "You think I was bluffing? I couldn't tell a lie to save my own life, let alone someone else's. I can't believe you'd think—"

He tugged me down to him in a kiss. "I had to check." A smile. "Just in case."

"Well, you shouldn't have to, and if you think you do, then that's my fault. No more head games. You're stuck with me. I even followed you into the next world. Now that's commitment ... of the scariest stalker-chick kind."

His grin broadened. "Are you sure I'm alive? Because if this is my afterlife, I must have been a very good boy."

"The best," I said, bending over him.

As our lips met, Lucas reached up and pulled me down on top of him. I entwined my fingers behind his head and kissed him with ferocity that surprised me and sent a chuckle rippling through him. He returned the kiss full-strength, his lips parting mine, the tip of his tongue tickling mine. We kissed for a few minutes, then his hands slid to my rear, pulling me against him—

"Uh, sorry to interrupt," a voice wafted from down the alley. "But if any clothing is about to be shed, could you toss it this way?"

I jumped off Lucas so fast I nearly kneed him in a place I really didn't want him injured.

"Elena?" I said.

She peeked out from the end of the alley, her face a pale blob in the blackness.

"Uh, yeah. I am so sorry, guys, but I thought I'd better cut in before it was too late."

"So that was you. The wolf."

"Sorry if I startled you. I'd been by here about a half-dozen times tonight, so when I picked up your scent, I figured it was the old trail, from this morning. Then there you were."

I walked forward. She hadn't moved from her spot behind a garbage bin.

"Why are you—" I began, then grinned. "Oh, wait. You weren't kidding about the clothes, were you?"

Lucas had been coming up behind me, but now stopped in mid-stride.

"That's okay, Lucas," she said. "I'll stay back here. But if anyone has a spare piece of apparel . . ."

Lucas already had his shirt half-unbuttoned. He handed it to me and I took it to Elena.

"Always the gentleman," she said as he turned his back. "Thank you. I promise I'll get it back in one piece—Oh." She fingered the bloodied bullet hole, eyes widening. "What happened?"

"Got shot through the heart," I said. "But he's fine now."

"Uh-huh," she said, brows arching. "That must have been some healing spell."

"It's a long story. I'll explain later. So what the heck are you doing here, anyway?"

"Looking for you two," she said as she shrugged on Lucas's shirt. "When you missed your eleven o'clock check-in yesterday morning, I started to worry. I phoned your cell and left messages, then I kept phoning and finally someone answered—a guy who found your phone lying in an alley near here. Not a good sign. So we caught the next flight for Miami."

Elena tugged down the shirt, craning her neck to see how far it fell.

"Everything's covered." I leaned around the corner. "Lucas? She's decent."

"So long as I don't bend over," she said with a sigh. "I really have to start leaving my clothing in more convenient places."

"Or you could buy a big fanny pack," I said. "Strap it around your waist before you Change."

"Don't laugh. I've actually considered that."

"Where's Clayton?" Lucas asked. "I assume you didn't come alone."

"Oh!" I said. "Savannah. Did you—"

"She's with Jeremy at a hotel near here. Very worried and mad as hell about being left out of the search. You should call right away. I have my cell phone . . ." She grimaced. ". . . which is with my clothing. Sorry."

"Fanny pack," I said.

"No kidding. Now, Clay . . ." She looked around. "We split up to cover more ground. I should have howled for him before I Changed back, but I was so surprised seeing you two here that I completely forgot."

"You could howl now," I said.

She fixed me with a look. "No, thank you."

"Can you whistle?" Lucas asked.

"A much less embarrassing choice," she said. "Now let's just hope he recognizes it."

Elena put her fingers in her mouth, but only managed a squeal that sounded more like a stuck pig. A laugh sounded behind us.

"You sure howling wouldn't have been less embarrassing, darling?" Clay asked as he rounded the corner into the alley. He lifted a bundle of clothes. "Forgot something?"

"Thank you." Elena took the pile, rooted into her jeans pocket, and handed me her cell phone. "Just hit redial for the hotel."

I spoke to Jeremy, then to Savannah. I told them we were fine and we'd be there in a few minutes. By the time I hung up, Elena was walking out from an adjacent alley, twisting her hair back in a ponytail. Lucas and Clay were talking off to the side.

"We're too late, darling," Clay said as Elena approached. "They finished without us."

She glanced at me. "Bad guy dead?"

I nodded. "Bad guy dead."

"Damn," she muttered. "Well, that's good, of course . . ."

"But not much fun."

She grinned. "I'll survive. So what happened?"

"His dead lover tore open a portal into the ghost world and we all jumped through. Well, Lucas fell in, I jumped in after him, and Edward jumped in after her. We came back, which is good. He didn't come back, which is also good . . . except that it means that in punishment for his crimes he gets exactly what he wanted all along—eternal life with the woman he loves."

"Uh-huh. I think I'd better get the uncondensed version after we get back to the hotel. Oh, wait, you guys must be starving. First stop: food."

"What time is it?" Lucas asked, tapping his watch and frowning at it.

"Mine stopped, too," I said. "I don't think they survived that return trip."

"It's just past four A.M.," Elena said.

"You might have some difficulty locating a restaurant," Lucas said.

"Don't worry," Clay said. "We'll find food. We always do."

We stood at the take-out counter of a twenty-four-hour Cuban restaurant. Neither Elena nor Clay had ever eaten Cuban, so they were soliciting opinions and advice from Lucas. After placing the order, we took our coffees into the dining area to wait. After a few minutes, I realized we were getting a lot of attention. The restaurant had only eight other patrons, but every eye had slid our way a couple of times and, by the time my coffee was half-finished, I swear every busboy and cook had peeked out from the kitchen. Now, I'll admit, Elena and Clay made an eye-catching couple, but this seemed a tad excessive. The next time someone looked our way, I followed his gaze to Lucas's shirt.

"Uh, Lucas?" I said.

When I had his attention, I tapped my fingers against my left breast. He arched one eyebrow, lips curving in a slow grin. I rolled my eyes and discreetly pointed at his shirt. His gaze slid down to the bloody bullet hole.

"Ah," he said. "Perhaps I should wait outside . . . in the alley or someplace suitably dark."

"I'll come with you," I said. "Elena? Can I borrow your cell? I should call Cassandra, let her know we're okay, in case she's noticed we've been missing for eighteen hours."

"Not likely," Clay muttered. "Ten bucks says she hasn't noticed you've left the hotel room yet."

"That, I believe, is a wager I just might win," Lucas

said. "In fact, I'll raise it to twenty and postulate that she's not only noticed, but started looking for us."

Clay shook his head. "Hate to take advantage of youthful optimism, but, sure, you're on. Twenty bucks it is."

It turned out that we didn't need Elena's cell phone after all. Lucas's was still working—though I really hoped no one had called while we'd been in the ghost world, or they'd have racked up a hell of a long-distance charge.

Cassandra wasn't at the hotel. She was out, with Aaron, looking for us, and had been since early the previous afternoon.

"How'd you know that?" I whispered to Lucas when Jaime told me the news.

He only gave a small smile and waved for me to continue talking to Jaime, who'd just returned to the hotel an hour ago, too exhausted from her nights of haunting to continue the search. I told her I'd track down Cassandra via Aaron's cell.

"Better call Benicio first," she said. "He's going nuts. I swear, the city's crawling with supernaturals tonight looking for you two. I heard he called in every Cortez security force in the country. We notified him as soon as we realized you guys were missing." She paused. "Hope that was okay."

"It was. Thanks. Will we see you later? Or are you taking off already?"

"Taking off?"

"Back on tour. Now that everything is over—"

"Over? What about Edward?"

"Oh, right. Sorry. Let me back up."

I told her what she didn't know. Then she told me what I didn't know. When Elena and Clay came out of the restaurant, Lucas and I were huddled together, talking quietly as we tried to absorb the news.

"What's up?" Elena said.

"We have a problem," I said.

"What?"

"Bad guy *not* dead."

Standoff

LAST TIME I'D SEEN EDWARD, HE'D BEEN RUNNING FOR the portal, so we assumed he'd jumped through right after us. He hadn't made it. Less than an hour after we disappeared, Edward phoned John in New Orleans asking to be put in contact with Cassandra. John had the good sense to hand over Aaron's number, rather than try negotiating with Edward himself. When Edward finally got in touch with Cassandra, he demanded that she, as the vampire delegate to the council, negotiate on his behalf with the Cortez Cabal.

This made no sense to me. If Edward knew Natasha was waiting on the other side, why would he want to bargain his way out of a death sentence? Turned out he didn't. As Cassandra explained, Edward knew he'd be executed for his crimes, and he accepted that . . . so long as his punishment ended there. In a Cabal court, there is a sentence worse than execution: execution plus an afterlife curse, which sends your soul into limbo. For a vampire, the threat held little power, since most assumed they didn't have an afterlife. Can't curse a soul that doesn't exist. But now Edward knew better. Natasha still lived, in some form, in some place, and he wanted to be with her. Maybe this was why Natasha had been trying to contact Jaime, to somehow negotiate with us or pass along a message to Edward, telling him to stop and accept execution before he went too far. But now he had gone too far. In killing Lucas, he'd ensured that his death would come with every curse Benicio could dream up. His only hope was to negotiate an ironclad settlement before Benicio knew his beloved youngest son was gone.

The problem was that Cassandra knew nothing about portals and Cabal curses, and didn't even know for certain that we'd found Edward. She knew only that we were missing and he might be to blame. So she did the obvious: demanded to know where we were, whereupon Edward realized everyone knew we'd disappeared, which meant any hope of negotiating with the Cabals had also disappeared, which meant he didn't need Cassandra to mediate for him. So he'd hung up.

Not surprisingly, no one had heard from Edward since. My first thought was that it was still over. Edward would go into hiding, no more Cabal kids would die, and the problem would be resolved, however unsatisfying that resolution might be. Again, Jaime knew differently. When Edward had been trying to persuade Cassandra to negotiate for him, his terms were that he would stop the killings if the Cabal reopened a portal for him. Of course that made no sense to Cassandra, and Edward hung up before she could demand an explanation. Once I told Jaime what happened, though, she knew exactly what he'd meant.

Once a portal to the ghost world had been ripped open, it remained "hot" for about forty-eight hours. That meant, with the right materials, it could be reactivated. As for what material such a reopening required, Jaime knew only that it involved a sacrifice—a human sacrifice. Yet she also knew it wasn't as easy as selecting a random victim from the street. She had an idea where she could find details on the ritual, and promised to do so immediately. While I'd explained the situation to Elena and Clay, Lucas had called his father. We talked for another couple of minutes, then set out for our respective rental cars, which were parked in a lot near Edward's hotel. We got less than a block before a familiar black SUV squealed a U-turn in front of us.

"How the hell . . . ?" I said.

"Cell phone tracking, I would presume," Lucas murmured.

As the SUV pulled to the curbside, I turned to say something else to Lucas, then saw the bloodstained bullet hole on his shirt.

"Shit!" I said. "Your shirt. A jacket, does anyone have—"

No one did, but it didn't matter. Before the SUV even stopped rolling, the rear door opened and Benicio flew out. And, of course, the first thing he saw was that bullet hole.

Benicio stopped in mid-stride, gaze glued to that bloodied hole in Lucas's shirt. All color drained from his face. He took one unsteady step toward his son. Lucas hesitated only a split second, then met Benicio in an embrace.

As the two hugged, Elena slipped off to the side, then returned, grabbed Clay's arm, and tugged him away, motioning to me that they'd wait around the corner to give us privacy.

Lucas tried to explain away the hole, but it was too late. Benicio had already been to see Faye and she'd told him that Lucas was Edward's next target. She hadn't known Lucas had been shot, but the moment Benicio saw that shirt, he knew, and there was no sense fudging the facts. We did, however, gloss over our afterlife visit, saying only that we'd fallen through the portal and reawakened here.

Later, Benicio would undoubtedly press for details, but for now he didn't care. Lucas was safe. That was all that mattered.

"So now we still need to find Edward," Lucas said. "He'll probably lie low—"

Benicio shook his head. "He'll want to reopen the portal."

"We did . . . entertain that possibility," Lucas said. "We have Jaime looking into it now."

"And I'll get our researchers on it right away. For now, though, my first priority is you. I've made arrangements for you and Paige to be flown to the safe house, where you'll—"

"No, Papá," Lucas said quietly.

Benicio met his son's gaze. "Don't argue with me on this, Lucas. You are going—"

"I am going to continue what I started. As long as Edward is free, I still have a job to do."

"Your job is done. It ends here, Lucas. I have never interfered before—"

Lucas gave him a look.

Benicio's mouth set. "Not with this, I haven't. I have never tried to stop these crusades of yours or dissuade you from them." He stepped back. "Do you think I don't know how often your life is in danger, Lucas? Do you know how many nights I've spent worrying? Wondering what kind of trouble you'll get into next? But I have *never* said a word. You jaunt off to Boston to take on Kristof Nast over a witch, and I say nothing. You fly to California to confront a potential serial killer, and I say nothing. But now I am saying something. This time, my name isn't enough to protect you, so I'm damned well going to do it myself. You are going to that—"

"No, Papá."

They locked gazes and for a minute, just stood there, staring at one another. Then Lucas gave a slow shake of his head.

"No, Papá. This is my fight, just as much as anything else I've ever done. You're right. All the 'risks' I've ever taken haven't been risks at all, because of you and who I am. That has always kept me safe. So now, when I am—possibly for the first time—in real danger, do you honestly expect me to hide behind you? What kind of man would that make me?"

"A safe one."

Lucas met his father's glare with an unblinking stare. After a moment, Benicio turned away. From his profile, I could see his jaw working, struggling to rein in his anger. Finally, he turned back to Lucas.

"You're taking Troy," he said.

"I don't need a bodyguard, Papá," Lucas said.

"You—"

"He already has one," drawled a voice behind us.

We turned to see Clay heading our way. Although they'd been twenty feet away, and around the corner, they couldn't help eavesdropping—one drawback to a werewolf's enhanced hearing.

"I've got it covered," Clay said. "He needs a bodyguard; he's got me."

Benicio looked at Clay. Then his gaze slid to Elena, who was coming up behind Clay. He gave the barest nod, as if making the mental connection.

"Clayton Danvers, I presume," Benicio said. "Your reputation precedes you."

"Then you know your son is in good hands."

Benicio hesitated only a moment, then looked at Lucas. "You'll keep your cell phone on?"

Lucas nodded. "And keep you updated."

With that, Benicio let us go. A relatively easy victory. Too easy. When Benicio was gone, Lucas told us to expect to be tailed to the hotel by another car, one carrying a Cortez security team. And we were. So Benicio had assigned long-distance bodyguards. An inconvenience, but better than having Troy oversee our every move—and relay our every move back to Benicio.

We took the food back to Jeremy and Savannah, and filled them in.

After we'd finished, Jeremy walked to the nearest window and parted the curtains. "We have about an hour of darkness left. Elena . . ."

"Get back to the alley and get sniffing," she said. "Do you guys have anything belonging to Edward?"

"A shirt taken from his clothes hamper," Lucas said. When Elena gave him an odd look, he explained, "We needed a personal item for a clairvoyant."

"Clair—? You mean like—?" Elena stopped and shook her head. "My world was so much less confusing when it only had werewolves. A worn shirt is perfect." She shot a grin at Clay. "Even you could track from that."

"Yeah? Well, in that case, you won't mind me coming along . . . unless you're afraid I'll find him first, show you up."

Her grin broadened. "Never."

"Good. So—" Clay stopped and looked at Lucas. "Or maybe you'll need to handle this one on your own, darling. I promised Lucas's dad—"

"Go on," Lucas said. "Even my father would admit I'm safe here. Edward could hardly break in and overpower all of us."

Both Clay and Elena looked over at Jeremy, waiting for

permission. I still find that very strange, the idea that Pack werewolves don't act without their Alpha's approval. And stranger still that they don't seem to mind. I'm sure it helps that Jeremy never makes a big deal out of it— he'd never jump in when they're in the middle of making plans and yell, "Hey, I never said you could do that!" Instead, he does what he did now, intercepted their questioning looks with the barest of nods.

After visiting Faye, we'd left Edward's shirt in our rental car. Lucas gave Clayton the keys and told him where to find the shirt.

"Paige?" Elena said as they headed for the door. "You want to come along?"

Of course I did, but I also knew it wouldn't score me any points with Clayton.

"You two go on," I said. "I should wait here for Jaime's call."

"Can I go?" Savannah said, jumping up.

A chorus of nos answered her. She scowled and thumped back onto the sofa.

"Have you tried the *arepas*?" Lucas asked her. "These are stuffed with chicken, and those over there are beef."

She sighed, but allowed Lucas to put some *arepas* on her plate and explain how they were made.

Next, Jeremy suggested that we invite Cassandra and Aaron to join us, so we could all discuss a plan of action. I'd intended to propose this myself, but had been waiting for Elena and Clay to leave. I suspect Jeremy had been waiting for the same thing, knowing neither of them would be pleased at the prospect of working with Cassandra.

Jeremy also suggested that Jaime join us. This was a

more difficult decision to make. Aaron and Cassandra already knew the werewolves; Jaime did not. The Pack had only rejoined the interracial council last year, after more than a century of cutting themselves off from the rest of the supernatural world. Elena might joke about her world being easier when it contained only werewolves, but there was a lot of truth in that. For the Pack, coming back to the council meant a trade-off between gaining allies and giving up the layer of protection that came with isolation.

Outside of the interracial council, few supernaturals could name the members of the Pack, and even fewer could put names to faces. Jeremy was happy to keep it that way, and I didn't blame him. In this case, though, he weighed the danger of identifying themselves to Jaime against the help she could provide with the portal, and decided she had to join us.

At six, Jaime phoned to say she had something, and was coming right over to explain it. Aaron hadn't returned our messages yet, likely having turned off his cell phone while they hunted for us, so we left another, giving him the hotel address, and told them to meet us here. Moments later Elena called. They'd hit a dead end and were heading back.

While we'd been waiting for Jaime's call, I'd talked to Jeremy about the case, hoping he might see some clue we'd overlooked. After about twenty minutes, I noticed Lucas had gone quiet, looked over, and found he was asleep. I suppose dying does take a lot out of a person. I'll admit, though, that on pretense of removing his glasses, I did surreptitiously check to make sure he was breathing. I'd probably be doing that for a while.

The Leader of the Pack

WHEN ELENA CALLED, JEREMY TOLD THEM TO SKIP THE food run on the way back. Savannah was getting restless, so he was taking her out to hunt down breakfast. They'd been gone about ten minutes when Jaime arrived.

"God, it's quiet in here," she said as I ushered her into the room. "I thought werewolves were supposed to be rowdy—" She saw Lucas asleep on the sofa. "Shit, I'm sorry."

I waved her out onto the balcony, then slid the patio door closed so we could talk. Of course, the first thing she wanted to know was what had happened to us. On the way to the hotel, Lucas and I had decided we'd tell the others the basics of our adventure, but keep the specifics secret. Ghosts are forbidden to reveal details of their world, so we assumed we were expected to do the same. Better to claim we didn't remember what had happened, as we had with Benicio.

"And then, here we were, back on this side. Spit out by the ghost world."

"Nan used to tell stories about things like that, portals opening and the living going through ... or the ghosts coming out. I'll keep my mouth shut about this one, though. If people knew you guys had passed over and come back—" She leaned over the second-story railing. "Hey, is that your ward? Savannah?"

I glanced down and nodded.

"Then those must be the werewolves," Jaime said.

She leaned out farther for a better look. Elena and Clay had either met Jeremy and Savannah in the parking lot or picked them up on the street, because all four were now crossing the parking lot together. Jaime stared down at them, lips curved in the tiny smile of a woman who sees something she really likes . . . almost always something of the opposite sex.

"That'd be Clayton," I said.

"Ah," she said, tearing her gaze away after one last regret-filled look. "The one Cassandra tried to jump. Damn, can't even be original, can I?" She peered down at the quartet. "Huh. Now I'd have guessed the blonde would have been her choice. He looks a bit like Aaron, and I get the impression that's one ex Cass isn't completely over."

I looked at Clay. "I didn't notice it before, but I guess there is a slight resemblance. In the coloring at least, maybe the build. But that *is* Clayton. So who were you—" I followed her gaze. "You meant *Jeremy*?"

I should point out that there was nothing wrong with Jeremy Danvers. He wasn't what you'd call conventionally good-looking, but he was attractive enough, more striking than handsome, just over six feet tall, and lean, with black hair, high cheekbones, and a slight slant to his black eyes, which suggested Asian blood somewhere in his family tree. If I was surprised, it was because Jaime's choice *was* original. Put Jeremy next to blond-haired, blue-eyed Clayton, and it would be a rare woman who'd notice Clayton wasn't alone. To be honest, I wouldn't have guessed Jaime would be that woman.

"Jeremy Danvers?" Jaime said. "Isn't he the, uh, leader—oh, God, what's the word?"

"Alpha. The lead wolf in a pack is the Alpha. Werewolves use the same terminology."

"So that guy—the dark-haired one—We *are* talking about the dark-haired one, right?"

"The dark-haired one is Jeremy. He's the Alpha. The blonde is Clayton. He was Jeremy's adopted son; now he's the Pack muscle and Jeremy's self-appointed bodyguard. Elena is the woman, of course. She's Clay's partner and acts as Jeremy's representative outside the Pack. Clay and Elena are the beta wolves, though I don't think they use that terminology."

"Uh, right," Jaime said, gaze once again glued to Jeremy. I suspected she'd be asking me ten minutes from now to explain the relationships again, having not heard a word I'd said about Clayton or Elena. "So he's the leader? I thought the Alpha would be some old guy. He can't be much older than me." She squinted for a better look. "Shit, no, he could be younger than me. He isn't, is he?"

She turned from the view and rubbed her hands over her face. "Ack! Is it just me or was I suddenly channeling the ghost of a love-struck fifteen-year-old girl? Don't ask me where that came from." She inhaled and exhaled. "There, all better. So, uh, how old is he, anyway?"

I grinned. "Too old for someone who doesn't date men more than a decade her senior."

"Bullshit. I mean, that he's that old, not that I won't—it's not a hard-and-fast rule, so if he was that old . . . But he's not. Can't be."

"Werewolves get prolonged youth. He's fifty-three, I think. Maybe fifty-four."

"No way." She sighed. "Damn, everyone else gets cool powers, and I get hauntings. Doesn't seem fair. What the hell does a werewolf need a fountain of youth for, anyway?"

"Same reason vamps have regeneration," I said, holding open the patio door and waving her back inside. "With the hunters, it's all about survival. Prolonged youth means prolonged strength, which means you'll be able to defend yourself longer."

"And look really good doing it."

The door slammed open and we both jumped. Savannah rushed in ahead of Jeremy, with Elena and Clay bringing up the rear.

Seeing Jaime, Savannah skidded to a stop. "Oh, my god! It's—it's you." She shot a glare my way. "You didn't say it was *her*!"

"Jaime, meet Savannah," I said. "A fan."

"Oh, my—I don't believe it. See, Paige? I told you she could really contact the dead and you said"—Savannah switched to the unflattering impersonation every teen uses for adults—"'Only a necromancer can contact the dead, Savannah.' Well, ha! She is a necromancer. This is so cool! You're the best, Jaime. I watch you on *The Keni Bales Show* every month—well, I can't always watch it, because I'm usually in school, but I tape it."

Jaime fairly glowed, sneaking quick glances at Jeremy to see what kind of impression this display of adoration was making on him.

Savannah continued, "I saw your show last month—Whoa, what happened to your face?" As Jaime's hands flew to the scratches down her cheek, Savannah studied her closer. "You don't look so good. Well, not like you do on TV. Are you sick?"

I grabbed Savannah's arm and tugged her aside. "We're

still teaching her manners. Normally, we keep her confined to a locked room in the attic, but today she escaped."

"Very funny, Paige. I just meant—"

"Jaime's been going through a very nasty haunting, her reward for helping us out. Now for the proper introductions. Jaime, this is Jeremy Danvers. Jeremy, Jaime Vegas."

As Jeremy shook Jaime's hand, his face revealed nothing more than a glimmering of polite interest—not surprising, given that Jeremy can make Lucas look overemotional. Disappointment darted across Jaime's face. Savannah, obviously thinking Jeremy wasn't nearly impressed enough, scurried back to stand beside her.

"Jaime's on TV," Savannah said.

"TV?" Jeremy repeated.

Elena swung up beside him, grinning. "Yes, TV. Small box, pretty pictures that move . . ." She stage-whispered to Jaime. "He's very old. Not quite used to the industrial age yet." She extended a hand. "I'm Elena." She looked around. "And the rude one who walked past you without saying hello is Clayton."

She paused, waiting for Clayton to offer a belated greeting, but he just kept heading toward the sofa, where Lucas was slowly waking up. He handed Lucas his coffee, sat down beside him and passed him his glasses from the side table.

"Sorry," Elena muttered. "Just ignore him. Please. You know, I read an article about you a few months ago. At the time, I thought it was pretty interesting. Then when Paige told me who she was working with, the name sounded familiar, so I plugged it into a search engine and realized you were the one I'd read about."

"*You* knew who she was, too, and you didn't tell me?" Savannah sputtered.

"Edward got into a car," Clay announced from across the room.

For a moment, everyone was silent, struggling to fit this statement into the present conversation, then realizing it didn't fit and wasn't supposed to.

"Yeah, yeah," Elena said. "We'll get to that in a second. Don't be so impatient."

We all headed into the room. Lucas was still fighting back yawns, but managed a tired smile for me and shifted over to let me sit down beside him. Clay stayed on his other side and Elena perched on the sofa arm beside him, leaving the armchair for Jeremy. Jaime and Savannah grabbed chairs from the dinette table.

"So Edward got into a car?" I said. "Can't track him that way, I guess. Damn."

"Was it in a parking lot?" Lucas asked.

Clay shook his head. "Street in front of his hotel."

"Did you happen to notice a bus stop nearby?" Lucas asked.

"Oh, very good," Elena said. "Nope. No bus stop, and no street parking. So he must have hailed a cab. Does that help?"

"It might," he said. "I have a contact at one of the taxi companies, who can usually obtain information from the others for a small fee. I'll go call him."

When Lucas slipped into the next room, I turned to Jaime. "How have things been with you since we left? Natasha making any noise?"

Jaime shook her head. "She's gone. Disappeared, probably at the same time she ripped open that portal. Mission accomplished, I guess."

"Maybe, but something happened to her when she

opened the portal, and from the look on her face, it wasn't something good. She might not be haunting you now because she *can't*. Someone shut her down, or—"

Lucas reappeared.

I studied his expression. "Not good, I take it."

"Edward did call a cab, one from Peter's company, which made it easy. Unfortunately, he asked to be dropped off in Little Haiti, at the Caribbean market-place, which doesn't help us at all." He settled onto the couch. "What about this portal ritual, Jaime? Did you have any luck researching it?"

"Yep," Jaime said. "Found exactly what I was looking for. First, though, the warning. I have no idea whether this would even work. Like I told Paige, people don't. punch holes into the ghost world every day. Portals and how to reopen them are the stuff of necro myth. I knew I'd read something about it years ago, going through my Nan's books. I had some trouble finding another necro who knew the details, though."

"Do you have the books at your place?" I said. "If it'd help, we could send someone from the Cabal to get them. Save relying on secondhand info."

"I, uh, don't have the books," Jaime said, gaze skitter-ing across the floor. "Back when I left home, I didn't take them. My mother pitched them out."

"That's okay," I said. "We don't need them. You got the information from someone else, so we're good. What did they say?"

"Well, the first three necros I called had no clue what I was talking about. Then I found two who did, and they tried to tell me any necromancer could reopen the portal, no special tools required. But I knew that was wrong. Nan's books were the best there were, the real thing, not like the crap that's out there today." Another wave of regret flooded her eyes. She shook it off. "Anyway, I knew that reopening a portal called for human sacrifice of a specific kind, so I kept calling around and finally found someone who'd read the same book my Nan had. We need—"

A knock came at the door. Everyone looked up. Elena's nostrils flared and she leaned over to whisper something to Clay.

"Fuck," he muttered. "Keep talking, Jaime. It's only Cassandra. She can wait. Forever, if we're lucky."

"I heard that, Clayton," Cassandra said as she walked in.

"Who the hell forgot to lock the door?" Clay said.

"You were the last one in," Elena murmured.

"Damn."

Black-Magic Standby

AARON ARRIVED A FEW MINUTES LATER, HAVING LIKELY been parking the car. He got a warmer reception than Cassandra, but the meet-and-greet phase was cut even shorter this time, now that we were all eager to hear what Jaime had found. First, though, we had to bring Cassandra and Aaron up to speed.

"So now Jaime was about to tell us what Edward needs to reopen the portal," I finished.

"Well, like I said, the key ingredient is the black-magic standby, a good ol' human sacrifice. If Edward performs the sacrifice on the exact spot that the portal opened, it'll reopen for a couple of minutes."

"So what's to say he hasn't done this already?" Cassandra said. "He's a vampire. He could have taken a victim by now and gone through the portal."

"I'm getting to that," Jaime said. "As I told Paige, I knew he needed a specific victim. According to the necromantic ritual book, he needs to shed the blood of someone who passed through the portal."

"What?" Cassandra said. "That's ridiculous. You've made a mistake, Jaime. Obviously, if they passed through the portal, they aren't here to—"

Aaron clamped a hand over Cassandra's mouth. "Continue, please, Jaime."

"Cassandra's right," Jaime said. "Most people who pass through a portal never return, so the ritual doesn't actually mean you need to kill—or rekill—the person who went through. That *would* work, but the ritual means figurative blood—the blood of the closest same-sex relative. That leaves four possibilities, since two of you went through. Someone could use Paige's mother or daughter, or Lucas's father or son. Now, I know Paige's mom has passed over, so unless one of you guys has a kid stashed away—which I seriously doubt—that leaves one possibility."

"My father," Lucas murmured.

"And Edward has how long left?" I said. "About twenty-four hours before the portal closes for good? That leaves him one day to kidnap and kill the Cortez Cabal CEO. Right now, I bet Edward's seriously researching the 'hidden child' theory. It would be near-impossible to get Benicio."

"Perhaps," Jeremy said. "But if he's as determined as he seems, he'll certainly try."

"I should warn him," Lucas said.

As he rose, he brushed his hand against my arm. I looked up and he nodded, almost imperceptibly, toward the bedroom, asking me to join him. I followed. Less than thirty seconds into the call, I understood why he felt the need for a little moral support.

"No, Papá," he said firmly. "I am in absolutely no danger. This is about you—" Pause. "No, my blood—" Pause. "My blood won't—" Pause. "Papá, listen to me. Please. Edward can't use my blood for the ritual."

The lie flowed so smoothly even I almost wondered whether I'd misunderstood Jaime.

"Consider it logically, Papá," Lucas continued. "Why would the ritual require the blood of the person who passed through? That person is gone and, in almost every case, not coming back. In most sacrificial rituals, if the original subject is no longer available, you must use the nearest same-sex blood relative, correct?"

A brief pause. Lucas's lips parted in a silent sigh of relief.

"Yes, that's right," he said. "Therefore *you* are the one in danger. I know you're extremely security-conscious already, but this will require additional protection. For the next twenty-four hours, you should excuse yourself from public life and—"

Lucas stopped and listened, frown lines deepening with each passing second.

"Yes, yes, I do remember your mentioning it, but—" Pause. "In this one case, I believe you have a reasonable excuse for not attending—" Pause. "Yes, perhaps it would be a way to trap him, but—" Another sigh, this one audible. His eyes cut to me. "Let me speak to Paige, and I'll phone you back."

"What's this about trapping Edward?" I said as Lucas hung up.

"My father is scheduled to make an appearance tonight—a semipublic appearance—and he refuses to bow out. He hopes Edward will show up."

"The charity masquerade," I said. "For the New York firefighters."

"Precisely."

"Would Edward know he's there?"

"It's a large event, well covered in the media. The Cortez Corporation is a cosponsor, and my father is expected to attend. Edward would only need to pick up today's paper to see that. That may also explain why the cab dropped him off at the Caribbean marketplace. It would be an excellent place to get costume fixings." He swore under his breath and pinched the bridge of his nose. "Perhaps I can still talk him out of it—"

"You won't," I said. "He's not going to that safe house any more than you are. We have to deal with it. Let's go talk to the others."

As we walked back into the main room, Elena was talking.

"Okay," she said. "This is dead obvious so, since no one else is bringing it up, I know I'm missing something. We're assuming that Edward wants to go back through the portal to get to Natasha. My question is: Why doesn't he just kill himself?"

"I know that sounds easy, Elena, but for a vampire, it's more complicated than that." Cassandra's voice held none of the impatient snap she used with the rest of us. "The only way we can die is by being beheaded."

"Not the easiest method of suicide. Okay, I get it. But why . . ." She hesitated, as if reluctant to question something if no one else was.

"Why not get someone else to do it?" Clay said.

Elena nodded. "Right."

"Because he can't guarantee he'll end up with Natasha," I said as I took my place on the sofa. "We have no idea where she is, whether it was some kind of vampire afterlife, or a side effect of their immortality experiments. The best way for Edward to ensure he'd be with Natasha is to use the portal she opened. In the meantime, we have a new problem."

I told them about Benicio's plan.

"Maybe this is for the best," Cassandra said. "You've

done your share—more than your share. Let the Cabals finish this. I would prefer to see Edward taken quietly and allowed a fair trial, but if he's killed while attempting to kidnap a Cabal CEO, there's little I can do about that."

She glanced at Aaron as if for confirmation.

He nodded. "Not much chance they'll behead the guy in the middle of a charity gala. They'll probably settle for taking him into custody; then we could intervene later. If not, well, Cassandra and I can deal with any fallout in the vampire community. Edward has committed enough crimes that I'm not going to put someone else in danger just to make sure he gets a fair trial."

I looked at Lucas. Stone-faced, he was struggling not to argue, but I could see concern simmering in his eyes.

"Your father invited us to the masquerade," I said softly. "Maybe we should go."

"As backup, I hope," Clay said. "Because if you mean what I think you mean—"

I lifted a hand. "Hear me out, okay? Yes, I mean Lucas and I go as guests, that we set ourselves up as bait."

Clay's mouth opened, but Elena shushed him.

"It makes sense, doesn't it?" I said. "Edward thinks we're dead. If he sees us there, it'll throw him off and divert his attention from Benicio. We'd be the easier targets—" I stopped and looked at Lucas. "Unless your dad finds out Edward *can* use our blood. Didn't he have his researchers looking into the ritual?"

"They didn't find anything."

"Good. So he might have a couple of guards tailing us, but he knows Edward's focus will be on opening that portal, not getting revenge by killing you. So he'd assume *he's* the main target. When Edward sees us, though, he'll realize we'd be easier to capture."

"But you're only trading one decoy for another," Clay said.

"True, but it's not an equal trade," Lucas said. "Paige and I know more about vampires than my father does. And we're certainly better equipped to deal with a direct threat than he is. It's been many years since he's needed to defend himself."

"I can pull bodyguard duty," Aaron said. "Watch over you from the sidelines."

Elena glanced over at Jeremy, who nodded.

"Count me in," Elena said.

"Us," Clay said.

"Not sure what I can do, but I'm in, too," Jaime said.

"I'll go as well," Cassandra said.

"Cool," Savannah said. "Do I get to dress up in a costume, too? Or should I help Elena and Clay?"

Everyone turned and looked at her. As her gaze went from my face to Lucas's to Jeremy's, her eyes narrowed.

"No way," she said. "Uh-uh. I'm not staying behind. I can help out. I'm at least as good a spell-caster as Paige—"

"Better," I said. "But you're also thirteen years old. No matter how good you are, I'm responsible for you. Not only might you get hurt by Edward, but you're still a prize for the Cabals."

"You're special, remember?" Elena said, offering a smile. "Just like Jeremy. You two can keep each other company, man the control center, eat lots of pizza, and stay up really late."

Savannah rolled her eyes at Jeremy. "Sucks being special sometimes, doesn't it?"

"It certainly does," Jeremy said.

*   *   *

Benicio was thrilled with our offer to attend the gala as backup for him, though I'm sure he had no intention of letting us watch his back. That was a job for a half-demon employee, not a sorcerer heir, but if it meant Lucas willingly appeared by his side at a public function, Benicio would humor us . . . especially if it also meant he could keep a closer eye on his son.

We devoted the day to preparing for the night. Our first concern was costumes. Though it was by no means our *primary* concern, it did need to be attended to first. Since it wasn't safe for us to be combing costume shops, where Edward might see us, we accepted Benicio's offer to bring materials to us. We left the guys to work on something for Lucas, while Cassandra, Jaime, Elena, and Savannah helped me. Once we came up with an outfit that could be put together quickly, I called Benicio and gave him my material list.

Next Lucas obtained blueprints for the hall and maps of the grounds. We used these to scope out routes Edward could take, plus the best places from which the others could hide and watch us. Then we spent the rest of the afternoon making plans.

At five we started getting dressed. The basis of my costume was a green silk dress. I used the minimal dressmaking skills I'd learned from my mother to sew on scraps and strips of green and brown taffeta. Next, I added real leaves and feathers. Then onto grooming. Cassandra did my makeup in golds and browns. Savannah painted my nails a mossy green. Jaime styled my hair in a messy, upswept do, and added leaves and feathers. Elena held the mirror.

Clayton flung open the bedroom door as Cassandra was zipping up my dress.

"Closed door means *knock*," Elena said, shooing him out.

"You've been in here for two hours," he said. "She can't need that much work." He frowned as he examined my outfit. "What the hell is she? A tree?"

"A dryad," Elena said, cuffing him in the arm.

"Oh, my god," Jaime said, surveying my outfit. "We forgot the bag!"

"Bag?" Clay said. "What does a dryad need with—"

"An evening bag," Cassandra said. "A purse."

"She's got a purse. It's right there on the bed."

"That's a day purse," Cassandra snapped.

"What, do they expire when the sun goes down?"

Elena pushed him out of the room. "Okay, do we still have time for someone to run out and buy something?"

"No!" Clay called back through the closed door. "Car comes in fifteen minutes."

"I'll have to skip the purse," I said. "I can slip my lipstick into Lucas's pocket. He's got his cell phone. That'll have to do."

Jaime opened the door and announced me with due fanfare. I accepted the obligatory gracious compliments from Jeremy and Aaron. Lucas smiled, walked over, and offered his compliments privately into my ear.

"Lucas!" Savannah cried. "Where's your costume?"

"I'm wearing it."

"That's not a costume, that's a suit! The same thing you wear almost every day."

"It's a tux," I said. "And a very nice one."

"But what are you supposed to be?" Cassandra said. "A cocktail waiter?"

"I was going to say James Bond," Jaime said.

"Don't look at me," Aaron said. "I was pushing for a

knight costume, but these two"—he gestured at Lucas and Clay—"shut me down."

"And I wisely decided to keep my mouth shut," Jeremy said.

"If he doesn't want to wear a costume, he doesn't have to wear a costume," Clay said. "Hell, he's got a mask. Good enough."

Lucas held up a plain black eye-mask.

"They don't come in colors?" Savannah sighed. "At least you put in your contacts." She looked out the balcony window. "So do you get a limo?"

Lucas shook his head. "A chauffeured car, but not a limousine. My father finds them too ostentatious, even for formal occasions."

"Limos are for high school graduations," Cassandra said.

"And weddings," Jaime said.

"Not good ones," Cassandra said.

"I like limos," Savannah said.

"So do I," I said, sneaking a grin at Lucas. "Lots of room to . . . stretch out."

He paused, then the corners of his mouth twitched and he reached for his cell phone. "I believe we still have time to request a change of vehicle."

"Uh-uh," Jaime said. "I just spent an hour doing Paige's hair. No limos. Tell you what, though. You guys finish this and I'll rent you a limo for the whole trip back to Portland."

"Cool," Savannah said.

"Uh, right," Jaime said. "Okay, scrap that idea. How about a shorter limo ride and free baby-sitting?"

"Car's here," Clay said from his spot at the window.

"You guys scoot, then," Jaime said. "We'll meet you there."

Masquerade

THE CHARITY BALL ORGANIZERS HAD CHOSEN A MASQUER-
ade because of the event's timing—the night before
Halloween. The party planners, though, had avoided the
usual Halloween fare in favor of something more whim-
sical, accentuating the fantastical rather than the frightening. The ballroom was ringed with mannequins in
incredibly elaborate costumes from children's fiction,
from the Queen of Hearts to Puss-in-Boots to the Swan
Princess. Paper dragons guarded the door, heads dipping
and swaying in an invisible breeze. The buffet tables
were floating magic carpets, the food forming the patterns of the rugs. Punch flowed from the mouth of an
ice-sculpture phoenix, backlit by a small fire that melted
the bird, only to have a fresh one arise from the bowl below. It was a glorious paean to everything magical, and I
would have loved it . . . had I not spent every minute worrying about a certain murderous vampire. Mythical creatures make lovely ice sculptures, but far less enchanting
enemies.

Most people wore costumes even less definable than
mine—rainbow-hued designer dresses and tuxes, intri-
cate body makeup and gorgeous masks—that didn't trans-

form them into any recognizable character or creature. But hey, they looked great, and that, I think, was the point.

Like Lucas, Benicio had opted for the basic black tux. His mask, though, was anything but basic—it was an elaborate red hand-painted devil's face that extended to his upper lip, leaving only his mouth and chin bare. It was gorgeous, and the devil/CEO metaphor was wryly clever, but hardly matched Benicio's normal understated style. After a momentary burst of surprise, Lucas and I had to agree the disguise was good thinking on Benicio's part. Between the simple black tux and the brilliant red mask, there was little chance he'd get lost in the crowd tonight. Keeping an eye on him would be a snap.

Of the Cortez family, the only other members in attendance were William and William's wife. I have no idea what William's wife's name was, because I never met her. From the time we arrived, William found it convenient to be elsewhere, and kept his wife with him, so I know only that she was short, plump, and Hispanic.

As for Benicio's wife, Delores, our invitation apparently revoked hers. Delores was forbidden to attend any function where Lucas might be present. I bet that went over well, informing her this morning that she couldn't come to the event of the season. According to Lucas, Benicio and Delores's marriage had long since become a union of formality. Both lived in their own homes and appeared together only at public events. And if I felt sorry for Delores missing the charity gala, I only had to remind myself that Benicio had instituted the no-shared-events rule eight years ago when Delores tried to poison Lucas at his high school graduation dinner.

Speaking of wishing Lucas dead, the eldest Cortez son, Hector, had been detained in New York, and was expected to miss tonight's event. A damned shame, really. I knew someday I'd have to face Hector but, in this case, sooner was definitely not better. I had enough to worry about without that.

One thing we *didn't* need to worry about was letting Benicio out of our sight. As I expected, he wasn't letting Lucas out of his. We spent the first half hour being escorted around the room, introduced to what seemed like every politician and business leader in the state. I know I should have been impressed, but I couldn't help thinking that I was in the same room with quite possibly every person responsible for the Florida election snafu, and the subsequent election of George W. Bush, and somehow I couldn't muster a proper feeling of awe.

As Benicio led us about the room, I kept sneaking glances at Lucas, knowing how much he must have hated this. Given the choice between facing down a gun-toting vampire again and attending a charity ball with his father, I suspect he'd pick the near-death experience. After roughly fifty rounds of being introduced as the next CEO of the Cortez Corporation, he was probably cursing me for bringing him back from the ghost world. Yet he never showed it. Instead he only deflected questions about his future with a smile and a deft change of subject. Finally, when the constant introductions threatened to start us both yawning, Lucas begged leave to take me onto the dance floor.

"Thought you couldn't dance," I murmured as he led me out among the other couples.

"I can't." A small smile. "But I can fake it for a few minutes."

He positioned us where we could both see Benicio and could be easily seen by anyone watching the dance floor.

"Seems you're learning the steps of another dance, too," I said.

"Hmmm?"

"With your father. I saw what you were doing. He introduces you as his heir, you say nothing. You don't deny it, but nor do you say anything that would confirm it."

"I think I've realized that the harder I protest, the harder he pushes."

"And while that might not wear down your resolve, it does wear *you* down."

Lucas pulled me closer and brushed his lips across the top of my head. "Yes, I've noticed that. With you here, I've been seeing it though your eyes, imagining how it must look to you, and I haven't been too pleased with the image I saw reflected."

"Well, the image I see is fine. Always has been."

A soft laugh. "That's good to hear. But I can't continue that way, running away, avoiding him, hoping he'll leave me alone. He won't. I'm his son. He wants some kind of relationship with me, and I think I want the same thing. I need to learn to deal with him on his terms, because he isn't going to change. Yes, if I associate with my father, some people will take that as a sign of backsliding, but I can't worry about that. *I* know I'm not taking over the Cabal. And if you know it, too, then that's all that matters. Which leads me to another area of resolve. Regarding you. Or, I should say, us."

"I hope it's along the same lines," I said. "Standing firm instead of running."

"I've been resolved on that point for four months. Since the first flicker of interest on your part, I knew I wasn't going anywhere without a fight." He paused and frowned, eyes scanning the crowd.

"Talking to two women near the bar," I said. "Can't miss that mask."

"Ah, yes, I see him. Now, what was I . . . ? Resolve. It relates to your participation in my investigations."

"You don't want me there. I understand—"

He pressed his forefinger to my lips. "No, my resolve is to see this conversation through to the end, saying what I want to say without backing down for fear of frightening you off with a proposal that may impose upon your need for independence."

"Uh-huh. Once more, please . . . in translation."

He leaned down to my ear. "I'd like . . . no, I would *love* for you to be my partner, Paige. In my work, in my life, everything. I know you have your own aspirations, and if you don't wish to share my life quite so completely, I understand. But if you do, you are more than welcome to play as large a role in my investigations as you want."

I smiled up at him. "You may regret saying that."

"No, I don't think I will. Is that a yes?"

"It's a 'we need to discuss this more, but I'm definitely interested.'"

He grinned then, a grin so broad Benicio did a double take from across the room.

Lucas noticed his father's reaction and laughed softly. "He probably thinks I just proposed."

I tried to glance over at Benicio, but another couple blocked my view.

"We'd better hurry over and set him straight," I said. "Before he has a coronary."

"No, he looks quite pleased," Lucas said. "I believe he'll be disappointed when he learns I *didn't* propose. He'll have to wait for that. I know better than to push my luck. I'll give it some time before I take that plunge." His grin broadened. "At least a week."

I laughed, but before I could respond, he checked his watch.

"Speaking of time, we're late for our rendezvous with the others. We should go—"

"I'll go. Your dad's not letting you out of his sight tonight. Don't worry, I'll be careful."

"Then I'll track down a couple glasses of champagne for your return."

We disengaged and I slipped from the dance floor.

I found Jaime alone in our agreed meeting place, a nook between the kitchen and the bathroom hall.

"Sorry I'm late," I said. "The others get tired of waiting?"

"More worried than impatient," she said. "Elena didn't like us all hanging out here where we can't see what's going on, so I nominated myself for the job. Not like I can do much else. If I try following them around, I just get in the way. I've *had* stalkers, but never quite developed a talent for it myself, and all four of them are pros."

"Hunters."

She shivered. "Yeah, well, I try not to think about that. Werewolves, uh, they only hunt animals, right? The four-legged variety?"

"Pack wolves, yes. Other werewolves . . . you take your chances."

"Uh-huh. Well, there's nothing to report. No sign of Edward. No Natasha, either. I think I've seen the last of her. Which leads me to something else. I'm really not doing any good here, Paige. If you think I'm helping, I'll stay, but if not—"

"If you want to leave, that's fine."

"No, no. Well, yes, I want to leave, but for a reason. I'm thinking I might be more help if I keep looking into this ritual, call some more people, see whether I missed something. I could go back to the hotel room with Jeremy and Savannah, make my calls, and help them man the control center."

"Manning the control center, hmm?" I said with a grin. "Sure, that sounds like a plan. Go for it."

"I didn't mean that," she said, reddening. "Seriously, I think I'd be more use checking out this lead, don't you? Okay, the control center probably doesn't need extra manning. Maybe I should make the calls from our hotel instead—"

"No, go stay with Jeremy. That's safer all around, and you can bounce ideas off him. He might not know much about necromantic ritual, but he's a smart guy and he's very easy to talk to."

"He is, isn't he? I mean, for a werewolf, and an Alpha werewolf at that, you'd expect the guy to be all high-and-mighty, brawn-over-brains, but he's not, and he just seems like such a—" She buried her hands in her face with a moan. "Oh, God, I'm too old for this shit." She peeked up at me. "Lack of sleep. It's lack of sleep . . . and emotional trauma. I've been traumatized by this vamp-spook, and I'm not thinking straight."

"Exactly."

"Right. So, I'll just go over there and start making my calls. If Jeremy can help, that's great, but otherwise, I'll just do my thing, and he can keep Savannah company. He's great with Savannah, isn't he? I mean, other guys would tell her to go off and play a video game or watch TV, but he pays attention to her and—" She inhaled and exhaled. "Okay. Fine now. Leaving now. If you need me, I'm heading straight to the hotel." She paused. "Well, after I swing by my hotel room for a quick shower—I think I spritzed myself with your hairspray earlier and I'm all sticky. So I'll shower, change my clothes, and then head to their hotel."

"Got it," I said, biting my cheek to keep from smiling.

"First, I'll find Elena and tell her I'm taking off. She seems nice. We haven't really talked, but she seems nice. Down-to-earth."

"She is."

With that, Jaime left, and I headed back to the party. I found Lucas near the buffet tables, holding the promised champagne flutes.

"Your dad hasn't shanghaied you yet?" I said.

"He's heading in this direction, but keeps being way-laid by other guests. In light of my new strategy for paternal relations, I am not using the situation as an opportunity to initiate a game of hide-and-seek, but standing firm and allowing him to make his way here, however long that may take."

I told Lucas about Jaime, and he agreed there was lit-tle for her to do here. Between the vampires and the werewolves, security detail was covered.

"I'll admit, I am concerned that Edward has yet to make an appearance," Lucas said. "Given the time con-straints he's under, this would be the opportune moment to grab my father, and quite possibly the only chance he'll get before morning."

"Maybe he's having trouble getting past security," I said. "It is tight."

"It *appears* to be tight," he said. "Yet the others had no problem getting past it and they've been skulking about the perimeter for nearly two hours now without inci-dent."

"It doesn't help that this is a masquerade." I looked out over the crowd. "But Elena or Clay would still have scented Edward, or Aaron and Cassandra would have sensed him, so—"

"Champagne, I see." Benicio appeared at Lucas's side and clapped a hand on his shoulder, beaming a smile. "May I assume that congratulations are in order?"

"They are. Paige has agreed to join my investigations on a permanent basis."

Benicio's smile faltered, but only for a second. "Well, that's a start, then. You've made an excellent team so far, and working together will certainly give you more time together, which I know was one of your concerns."

Lucas snuck a look at me. "It was," he murmured.

"And the house?" Benicio said.

"We're buying *a* house," I said. "Maybe the one in Portland, maybe not, but we're definitely buying a house."

"Good, good."

We braced ourselves, waiting for Benicio to start offering advice, but instead he turned to me.

"May I have a dance?"

"Uh, sure."

We walked on to the dance floor.

"Have you considered Seattle?" Benicio asked as we launched into our dance. "If you like Portland, I'm sure you'd like Seattle."

"Portland seems fine, but we'll probably look elsewhere, too, just to be sure."

"As you should. Buying a house is a major commitment. You also have Savannah's security to consider. Has Lucas mentioned that we have a satellite office in Seattle?"

"Really. How . . . surprising."

I caught Lucas's gaze across the floor. He put his fingers into his ears and mouthed "Ignore him." I grinned back.

Benicio plowed ahead, explaining all the benefits of living in a city with a Cortez corporate office. How much safer it would be. How we could share resources. How we could keep an eye on local corporate operations to ensure no serious crimes against supernaturals were "accidentally" being committed. As I listened, I realized Lucas had the right idea. There was only one way to deal with Benicio. Let him talk. Let him "suggest." Don't argue. Don't even answer. Just listen . . . and let it all flow out the other ear.

While we danced, and Benicio talked, I tried to keep an eye on Lucas, but it proved increasingly difficult. Benicio seemed determined to steer me away from Lucas, probably so his son wouldn't notice he was using the opportunity to "advise" me. Soon we were so deep in the mass of other dancers that I lost sight of him.

When we finished our dance, Benicio accompanied me back to where Lucas had been standing. He wasn't there. Benicio lifted one hand, just slightly, and Troy appeared.

"Where's Lucas?" Benicio asked.

"Morris was watching him; I was watching you."

Troy glanced around, then waved Morris over. As Morris approached, Troy slipped away.

Morris admitted he'd seen Lucas head away from the buffet table, but when he tried to follow, couldn't find him.

"I figured he just went to the bathroom. You said not to crowd him, and he was heading in that direction."

Troy returned. "Tim saw Lucas leave, sir. He tried to follow, but Lucas said he needed to use the washroom, so Tim backed off. He's waiting at the end of the hallway. Lucas hasn't come out yet."

"That's right," I said, turning to scan the room so Benicio wouldn't see the lie in my face. "Just before our dance he asked whether I'd seen where the bathrooms were. He probably decided to slip away while we were busy. Now that you mention it, I could use a quick trip myself. If Lucas comes back before I do . . ."

"I'll tell him where you are," Benicio said.

"Thanks."

I hurried off.

I did hope Lucas had gone to the bathroom, but I doubted it. Knowing I was already worried about his safety, he wouldn't take off for something so trivial without telling me. The only thing that would make him leave his post would be spotting Edward or, rather, catching so fleeting a glimpse of the vampire that he knew if he didn't follow immediately, he'd lose him. When he'd seen the Cortez security guard following, he would have used the bathroom excuse to get rid of him.

Edward had already lured Lucas to his death once. Could the same ruse work twice? I told myself it couldn't, that Lucas was too savvy for that. Yet, if the situation were reversed, and I'd seen Edward while Lucas was otherwise engaged, would I say, "Humph, not falling for that one again," and stand my ground? No. I'd realize it could be another trick but, given the choice between protecting myself and catching Edward before he killed again, I'd prep a good spell and proceed with caution. But I *would* proceed. And so would Lucas.

As I surveyed the partygoers, I tried to evaluate the situation logically. The last thing we needed was for me to panic and rush headlong into a back corridor, and straight into Edward's grasp, while Lucas returned from an emergency bathroom visit. First, I should try his cell phone. I reached for my purse...and remembered I didn't have one. Nor did I have a cell phone.

I hurried to the bathroom. Standing outside the men's room, I cast a sensing spell within. It picked up one person. Good. Then the door opened and an elderly man walked out. Once he was gone, I cast the spell again, but the bathroom was empty.

"Damn, damn, damn," I muttered.

I had to find Lucas—no, I had to find the others, who would help me find Lucas. As much as I bristled at losing a few precious minutes tracking down the others, I knew the extra effort would be worth it. They could track Lucas in a fraction of the time it would take me.

I shot one last look around the ballroom, then headed into the warren of back halls, where the others were supposed to be prowling. As the noise of the gala settled to a distant murmur, I realized I was entering uncharted—and unoccupied—territory. Time to ready a self-defense spell. I started my suffocation spell, then stopped. Would that work on a vampire? Of course not. They didn't breathe. Fireball spell? Nonlethal, but it could startle him enough for me to make a getaway. Or would it? Fire didn't hurt a vampire. Goddamn it! Why didn't I think of this—

"Hello, Paige."

I jumped and spun around. There behind me was, not a green-eyed, sandy-haired vampire, but a dark-eyed, dark-haired sorcerer. Hector Cortez.

A Coward's Plan

"WE NEED TO TALK," HECTOR SAID, BEARING DOWN ON ME.

Of all the moments Hector Cortez could choose to reenter my life, this was quite possibly the worst. A voice in my head told me to run, forget how bad it would look, forget how embarrassing it would be, get away from him and continue looking for Lucas. But my feet wouldn't obey me. After a lifetime of refusing to run from confrontations, they were damned if they were going to start now.

"I don't believe we've been properly introduced," I said. "Well, we have, but at the time I was bound and gagged, and I don't think you ever expected to see me alive again, so you skipped the formalities. I'm Paige Winterbourne. You're Hector Cortez. I'd say I'm pleased to meet you, but we both know I'd be lying. So your meeting didn't run as late as Benicio expected? Sorry to hear it. Now, if you'll excuse me . . ."

I turned to go. Hector swung in front of me.

"A late meeting? Is that the excuse he used? I didn't have a meeting. I've been exiled in New York for the past two weeks, on my father's orders. Any idea why he'd do that?"

"Besides to keep you from killing Lucas? No, I can't imagine why." I stopped, seeing the hard glint in his eye, the glare of a hawk confronting the sparrow who'd chased him off his turf. "You think *I* got you banished? That I told Benicio that you tried to have me killed in Boston? Well, gee, I'd hope if I did tattle, you'd get something a little worse than an extended New York vacation. No, I didn't tell your father. Now, if you'll excuse me—"

Hector stepped into my path. "I never said you told my *father*."

"What? Oh, so you think I told Lucas and he asked your father to keep you away?" I met Hector's glare with one of my own. "No, I didn't. And I won't. What happened at that house is between you and me, and it stays there. Now get out of my way."

"Is that your plan, then, witch? Hold it over my head?" He stepped closer, looming over me. "I may make a mistake once, but never twice. I'm not getting out of your way, you're getting out of mine. Stay with Lucas, and the only question is when I'll decide to move you aside... permanently."

"How about now?" said a slow drawl behind him. "First, though, you gotta move me aside."

Hector turned to see Clayton behind him. His gaze skimmed over the other man with a dismissive twist of his lips. He lifted his fingers to flick Clay aside with a knock-back spell, but Clay grabbed his hand before the first words left his mouth.

"You think you're going to kill Paige to hurt Lucas?" he said, leaning in, putting his face to Hector's. "That sound like a clever plan to you? Sounds like a coward's plan to me."

Hector tried to wrench his hand free, but couldn't so much as twist it in Clay's grasp.

"Who are you?" Hector demanded.

"The question isn't really who, but what," Clay said. "You want to find out? Lay a hand on Paige or Lucas and you will."

Clay clapped his free hand over Hector's mouth, then squeezed his other hand around Hector's fingers. There was a sickening crunch of bone and Hector's eyes bulged, his scream muffled by Clay's hand.

"You think that hurt?" Clay said. "Imagine what I'd do if I was really pissed off."

He shoved Hector away and turned to me. "Come on."

I followed Clay around two corners before he slowed enough to let me catch up.

"He tried to kill you in Boston?" Clay asked.

"You overheard?"

"I was waiting around the corner. Didn't figure you'd appreciate me interfering too soon. So Lucas doesn't know?"

"No, he doesn't, and please don't tell him. Maybe it seems he has a right to know, but—"

"He shouldn't. He worries enough about putting you in danger. If you want to accept the risk, then that's your decision to make, not his. Just take precautions, and if what's-his-name—"

"Hector. He's Lucas's oldest brother."

"Fucked-up family," Clay said, shaking his head. "If this Hector comes after you again, you let me know. Yeah, I know, that's not how you like to handle things, but with something like this, you're not going to get anywhere jabbing each other back and forth. Give one big shove and be done with it."

He looked each way down an intersecting corridor,

tilted his head in a quick sniff, then jerked his chin to the left and set out.

"I take it we're following Lucas?" I said.

"Yeah. Well, no. Elena's following Lucas. I'm following Elena. We figure Lucas is following Edward."

"Uh-huh."

"We saw Lucas take off, so Elena sent me to get you while she tracks him."

He rounded another corner, walked a dozen feet, then wheeled and backtracked to an exit door. He opened the door and stuck his head out, then waved for me to follow.

"Wait," I said. "Benicio. Is anyone watching—"

"Aaron."

I was about to step outside when Cassandra hailed us from down the hall.

"Come out and shut the door," Clay said. "Maybe she'll take the hint."

"Hold on. It might be important."

"What's going on, Paige?" Cassandra said when she caught up. "Why aren't you in the ballroom?" She peered out the door. "Clayton? Who are you looking for out here?"

"Elena."

Cassandra rolled her eyes. "What a surprise. The poor woman gets ten feet from you and you're off like a shot—"

"She's following Lucas, who's following Edward," I said.

"Oh."

Clay was already heading into the shadows.

I glanced at Cassandra. "Aaron's watching Benicio. Would you mind helping him? In case Edward circles back?"

I expected her to argue, but she nodded. "Have Elena phone Aaron if you need us."

I jogged to catch up with Clayton. Well, I tried anyway—one does not "jog" in two-inch heels. Instead I stumbled along until I drew close enough to see him standing by the wall, arms crossed, shaking his head. Once he was in sight, I stopped, yanked off my shoes, and broke into as near a jog as I could approximate in my dress.

"Good idea," he said, waving at the shoes in my hand. "But watch your step. Ground's rough."

"Think it's safe enough for a light spell?"

He nodded. After I'd cast the spell, we started off again. We'd gone about twenty yards when Lucas and Elena appeared, walking along a path leading to the parking lot.

"Lost him?" I called.

"Wasn't him," Elena called back. She drew nearer before continuing. "When I caught up with Lucas, he already had his doubts, so I conducted a sniff test. Guy failed, but we decided to trail him a bit farther, just to be sure. Followed him into the parking lot, where he climbed into the back of an SUV and met a woman I really doubt was his wife. We left before the show started."

As she spoke, Lucas kept sneaking concerned looks in the direction of the main building.

"Aaron and Cassandra are watching your dad," I said. "But we should get back inside."

We found Benicio showing an associate's wife around the dance floor. After an uneventful forty-five minutes, we joined the others in a side room, from which we could still see Benicio.

With less than an hour of the event left, the chances of Edward showing up were growing slim. He might try to nab Benicio in the confusion at the end, when everyone poured out to their cars. Yet he had no way of knowing whether Benicio intended to stay until the final moments, so he should still be here somewhere, watching in case Benicio left early. He could try to kidnap Benicio between here and his home, but that would mean taking on an armored car filled with bodyguards. And obviously Benicio's home would be at least as well guarded as his car. Grabbing him here made the most sense. So where was Edward?

Before we returned to the party, I decided to check in with Jaime. The most probable explanation for Edward's failure to appear was that he'd found an easier way to open the portal. If Jaime had uncovered a second ritual, I'm sure she would have called, but it never hurt to check.

Jaime's cell phone rang four times, then her answering service clicked on. That probably meant she was on the line, calling her necromancer contacts. So I phoned Jeremy's hotel room. He answered on the second ring.

"It's Paige," I said. "Nothing to report, I'm afraid. We were hoping Jaime might have something. May I speak to her?"

"Jaime?"

"Uh, right. Redhead? Necromancer? Hanging out in your hotel room right now? And hopefully not being pestered by Savannah ..."

"Yes, I know who you meant, Paige. But Jaime isn't here."

"Did she leave? Damn it, was she trying to call us? We've been running around—"

"Slow down, Paige. Jaime hasn't been here. Not since she left with the rest of you. Was she heading here?"

"Two hours ago. I know she was stopping by her hotel room first, but . . . two hours?"

"Have you called her hotel room?"

"No, I'll do that now."

"If she's not there, check with the hotel front desk, see whether anyone saw her come in."

I did as he'd suggested. No answer at the hotel room. No answer again on her cell. The desk clerk said he hadn't seen her come in. When I suggested maybe she'd slipped past, he swore he would have noticed, and from his stammer, I guessed he'd been keeping an eye out for this semifamous, fully attractive guest. He offered to run up to her room, and left me hanging on the line before I could respond. Five minutes later he returned saying there was no sign of Jaime. He'd even checked inside her room, which was doubtless against company policy, but I wasn't going to call him on it. I thanked him for his help, then relayed the news to the others.

"Oh, for God's sake," Cassandra said. "The woman has the attention span of a gnat. She probably drove halfway to the hotel, saw a shoe sale, and forgot all about us."

Lucas shook his head. "While Jaime may cultivate the appearance of flightiness, she has far more gravitas than that, and far more dedication. She's stayed with us so far, despite some serious battering."

"Lucas is right," I said. "Jaime really wanted to help, and it would take something far more serious than a shoe sale to distract her from that."

"Ladies' night at the strip club, perhaps?" Cassandra said.

"Mrrow," Aaron said. "Retract your claws, Cass, before you cut yourself. I'm with Lucas and Paige on this one."

"It's settled, then," Clay said. "Jaime is missing, so someone needs to look for her, and Elena and I are the best trackers. Aaron and Cassandra can stay here and keep an eye out for their fellow vampire. Lucas and Paige? Take your pick."

I looked toward Benicio on the dance floor. "We'd better stay."

"No," Lucas said. "We'll go. My father is well protected by his guards, and Aaron and Cassandra can handle Edward if he shows up, which I'm strongly beginning to doubt. We have a portal that must be reopened using a necromantic ritual, and now we have a missing necromancer. I suspect the two are not unconnected."

"Oh, shit."

"My thoughts exactly."

Missing: One Celeb Necromancer

IN THE HOTEL PARKING LOT, ELENA PICKED UP A SCENT. But it wasn't Jaime's. It was Edward's. She trailed it to an empty parking space, where I found Jaime's designer cell phone lying on the asphalt. Elena and Clay could detect traces of Jaime's scent at the site, but no trail, as if she'd stepped from the car, but gone no farther. And, unless Edward had perfectly retraced his own path, he hadn't gone any farther, either. The logical conclusion: Edward had surprised Jaime getting out of her car; she'd had time to fumble for her cell phone, but dropped it as he overwhelmed her. Then he'd driven off, in her rental car, with her in it.

I cursed myself for not seeing this coming. Yet as Lucas insisted, kidnapping Jaime wasn't the obvious scenario. Reopening a portal was considered a necromantic ritual only because it involved access to the dead. Edward didn't need a necromancer to carry it out. If he had the right victim, he only needed to slit that person's throat over the portal site. Without that blood, he couldn't open the portal at all, not even with a dozen necromancers helping him.

What we had overlooked, though, was the very real

possibility that Edward had no idea how to reopen the portal. As Jaime had said, it was an obscure ritual. Edward might not have even known any necromancers to ask about it. Yet he did know where to find one. Given Jaime's celebrity, her involvement in our case had to be all over the supernatural grapevine. Even John in New Orleans had probably known about it. And to find a photo of Jaime, all Edward had to do was run an Internet search, as Elena had done.

Did I think Jaime would tell Edward what he needed to complete the ceremony? Yes, and that's no reflection on her character. What reason did she have not to tell him? She knew Benicio was safely under guard, and if she steered Edward in his direction, she'd be steering him into ours, which was exactly what we wanted. Our main concern was that, after Edward got what he wanted from Jaime, he'd kill her. We could only hope he wouldn't trust Jaime's word enough to kill her before he had the portal reopened.

We planned our attack from both ends, the first end being the gala, where Edward would find Benicio, and the other end being the portal site, where he had to return if his mission was successful. Elena and Clay would join Aaron and Cassandra at the gala; with that kind of supernatural firepower on the alert, Edward would find it nearly impossible to capture Benicio. But, just in case, Lucas and I would stand guard at the portal site.

Lucas drove us back to the neighborhood where the portal had been opened. On the way, I drew a map of the surrounding area, noting all the possible points of entry and all the best locations for perimeter spells. Then we considered places to lie in wait. We were still debating our choices when Lucas's cell phone rang. He checked the call display, then passed it to me.

I didn't even get a chance to say hello before Aaron cut in. "Lucas? Where are you?"

"Uh, it's Paige, and we're still heading to the portal site. Do you want to talk to—"

"No, not if I can help it." His voice sounded strained, and a bit breathless. "Shit! I am so sorry, guys. We fucked up. Fucked up big-time."

"What's wrong?"

I tried to keep my voice steady, but Lucas's gaze shot over the moment the words left my mouth. I mouthed, "It's okay," and pointed at the road.

"We were watching Benicio," Aaron said. "Cass and I. He was on the dance floor. Couldn't miss him with that mask. Then Cass saw his bodyguard leaving. The one with the freaky blue eyes."

"Troy."

"Right, and she wanted me to follow him. She said he sticks pretty close to Benicio, and if he was taking off, something was up. So I went after him while she watched Benicio. I caught the guy sneaking out the back. Tried to get him to talk to me, but he wasn't in a talking mood. We scuffled and just as I took him down, Cass came running out. Said the guy on the dance floor wasn't Benicio."

My gut went cold. "Wasn't—?"

"It was a stand-in. With the mask—Fuck! We saw that mask and we were sure it was him."

"So Benicio's go—"

I stopped myself, but it was too late. Lucas veered the car to the curbside and hit the brakes so hard the seat belt snapped me back against the seat. I passed him the phone.

"Aaron?" he said. "Let me talk to Troy."

Within minutes later, Lucas had the whole story, which he relayed to me as he drove hell-for-leather for the portal site. The Cabal researchers *had* found the ritual, so Benicio had always known that Edward could use Lucas's blood to reopen the portal. He'd played along with us because it had seemed the best way to ensure Lucas would be at the masquerade, safely under Cabal guard. As a precaution, he'd brought in a look-alike, who could take his place with that distinctive mask.

When Lucas and I took off after Jaime, Benicio feared the worst. And he'd feared that calling in a full Cabal SWAT team could result in a California-like fiasco, which would only endanger Lucas yet again. This had to be handled delicately. Earlier that day Benicio had sworn to us that if his name was no longer enough to protect his son, he'd do so himself; that was what he'd decided to do.

Benicio had grabbed Morris, told Troy to stay behind in case we reappeared. Then he'd left for the portal site, knowing that was where Edward had to end up. Troy, though, hadn't been about to let his boss take on a murderous vampire aided only by a temporary bodyguard. So he waited until Benicio was gone, then went after him. And that's when Aaron had intercepted him.

Now Benicio was indeed headed to the portal site, with only Morris for backup. But not for long. We were only a few minutes from the site. Aaron, Cassandra, and Troy were also on their way, and Aaron was phoning Elena to tell her to turn around and head over to the portal. In half an hour, we'd have seven supernaturals ready to take on Edward. We only prayed we'd get to him before Benicio did.

We parked as close to the site as we dared. As anxious as we both were to get there, we had to be careful. And there was very likely no need to rush. Benicio might have arrived ahead of us, but if Jaime had told Edward who he needed for the sacrifice, he was probably across the city by now, heading for the masquerade gala. The greatest danger we likely faced was Benicio himself. As Lucas said, it had been years—if not decades—since Benicio had needed to defend himself. If we came flying down the alley, we might find ourselves on the receiving end of a lethal energy bolt.

Once out of the car, we hurried to the café. I cast perimeter spells at the alley on either side, and across the rear door. That covered the east side. Now on to the west, on the other side of the dead-end alley where we'd met Edward.

We'd gone only a few steps when Lucas lifted a hand to stop me. I followed his gaze down to the ground. A fingerlike puddle snaked around the corner, moving almost imperceptibly, expanding. The puddle shone black in the darkness. Without even casting a light spell, I knew it wasn't water.

As Lucas peered around the corner, I kept my gaze glued to his face, braced for a reaction I prayed I wouldn't see. His eyes closed in a soft wince, and my breath whooshed out. I slipped over to him, and looked.

Morris sat braced against the wall. He was dead. His shirt was ripped apart, and his hands still clutched the bloodied missing half to his throat, a frantic final attempt to save himself. Over the cloth I could see long jagged holes where Edward had ripped at his throat. Then he'd left Morris to bleed out while he turned his attention to the secondary threat: Benicio.

Lucas darted around the corner, moving as quietly as he could. As I set out after him, the whisper of voices fluttered across the still night. We both froze and listened.

"...won't help..." a woman said.

I looked up at Lucas and mouthed, "Jaime?" He nodded.

"You said...sacrifice." Edward, his words clipped with anger.

Had Jaime betrayed us? Had she been betraying us all along? I told myself there was no motivation, nothing to be gained by this, but nor did I have time to think it through. If I did, maybe I would find a motive. For now, we had a far more pressing concern.

As we crept forward, the voices came clear.

"I'm telling you it *won't* work," Jaime said. "You can't use him. It needs to be a very specific sacrifice. I was trying to tell you that—"

"You weren't trying to tell me anything," Edward snarled. "You said I needed a sacrifice. *Any* sacrifice."

"Well, I lied, okay?"

"Oh, and now you're telling the truth?"

Lucas motioned for me to pass him. I ducked down before peeking out, then cast a fast cover spell. Jaime knelt before a makeshift altar...bound hand and foot. Beside her, Benicio lay on his side, also bound. His eyes were closed. My gut went cold.

"Yes, *now* I'm telling the truth," Jaime said. "Why? Because I'm scared shitless, okay? Maybe I did lie earlier, but that was before you killed a Cabal bodyguard and captured the damned CEO."

A humorless laugh. "So now you take me seriously?"

"Look, you can't kill Benicio, okay?"

Beside me, Lucas exhaled and slumped against the wall. I stifled my own sigh of relief, for fear of breaking my cover spell.

Jaime continued, "It won't reopen the portal."

"Oh, but I could try...and I think I will. Just to be sure."

Edward stepped toward Benicio. I broke my cover, a spell flying to my lips. Lucas started to swing around the corner.

"Wait!" Jaime said. "If you kill him, you can't get Lucas."

Edward stopped. Lucas yanked me back behind the wall.

"You need Lucas," Jaime said. "You need someone who went through the portal."

"And what does that have to do with keeping this bastard alive?"

"Think about it. What would happen if you called Lucas and said you have his dad? If you can prove you have his dad? The kid puts his life on the line for total strangers. You think he's not going to come running to save his father?"

"Good," Lucas whispered. "Thank you, Jaime."

I nodded. This was, of course, the perfect plan. Edward wouldn't kill Benicio until he had Lucas, and Jaime knew that when Lucas received that call, he would indeed come running—backed by a small army of supernaturals.

"My phone's gone, but you can use his," Jaime said. "I'm sure he has Lucas on speed-dial. Probably right at the top."

Lucas tensed, ready to dash back toward the café so he could answer his phone without being heard.

"In a minute," Edward said. "First, I need to wake this one up . . . at least long enough to make that call for me. After that, though, I think I'll test your word. Better hope you don't fail."

"W—what?"

"All I need him for is to phone Lucas. Once that's done, he'll have outlived his usefulness. And, if his blood does reopen the portal, you'll have outlived yours. Believe me, if you are lying about that, I'll take you with me to the other side. And if you aren't? Well, then, the boy is in for a double surprise when he comes around that corner, though he won't have long to grieve before he's reunited with his old man."

Lucas and I looked at one another. I cast a privacy spell, so I could speak without whispering.

"D—don't answer the phone," I said. "Just don't answer it."

He cast his own spell. "I wasn't going to. If he can't get through, it'll buy us some time. But not long enough to wait for the others. We'll have to handle this ourselves." He laid his fingers on my arm. They trembled against my skin. He squeezed his eyes shut, pushing past the fear. "We can handle it. We have spells, and we have the element of surprise."

"But we don't know what spells work on vampires. We—" I took a deep breath and fought my own panic down. "A binding spell will work. But I need a way to get close enough to cast it without his seeing me. Maybe a distraction. But I don't know what—"

"I might," whispered a voice to our left.

Jeremy appeared beside us. He motioned for us to follow him to the other end of the alley, where Savannah waited.

"Aaron called the hotel for Elena's number," Jeremy

whispered. "I thought you could use help, and we were closer than the others. Now what's happened?"

We told him, as quickly as possible.

"Paige was right," he said. "Distraction followed by attack is our best bet. I can provide the first, and assist you with the second."

"Me, too," Savannah said. "I can help."

"Uh-uh," I said. "You're staying—"

"No, Savannah's right," Jeremy said. "She can help me with the distraction."

He told us his idea, then turned to Savannah. "Now, you'll wait with Paige and Lucas. As soon as you see me, you can start, but not until you see me."

She nodded, and Jeremy headed down the side alley to loop around the north building. We returned to our hiding place at the head of the portal alley.

Nice Doggie

WE ARRIVED BACK AT THE CORNER JUST AS EDWARD finished telling a now-conscious Benicio that he needed to make a phone call. As we waited for Jeremy, I slid off my heels, in case we needed to dash down that alley.

"And if I refuse?" Benicio said.

A slap resounded through the silence. Benicio didn't so much as gasp.

"This isn't some business deal you can negotiate your way out of," Edward hissed. "What do you *think* happens to you if you refuse?"

"You'll kill me," Benicio said calmly. "And if I do call Lucas, and he comes, you'll kill him. Do you honestly think I would exchange my life for my son's?"

Edward gave a short laugh. "So you're offering to sacrifice yourself to save him. Very noble, but it won't work. I'll still find him and kill him."

"But you wouldn't need to. Kill me, use my blood on that portal, and it *will* reopen."

Lucas's eyes went round and his lips formed a silent no. I gripped his arm and looked anxiously down the alley for Jeremy, knowing it was still too soon, that he'd never be ready yet.

"N—no," Jaime said. "It won't work. Don't listen to him. You need Lucas's blood—"

"Try mine," Benicio said, voice still as calm as if he were dickering over the cost of his lunch. "If I am lying, you've lost nothing. As you say, you could probably still capture Lucas without my help, which you'll never get. Kill me, though, and I guarantee your portal will reopen."

Lucas lunged forward, breaking from my grip. At that moment, Jeremy stepped around the other corner. Lucas stopped. Our eyes met, and I knew what he was thinking. Did we still dare try Jeremy's plan? Both of us would have been much happier blazing in there, spells flying. But was that the smart move? The safe move? Savannah looked over at us. Lucas swallowed, then motioned for her to go. As she turned away, he took my hand and squeezed it so hard I heard the bones crackle. I squeezed his back.

As I watched Savannah go, a thousand new doubts skittered through my brain. She was so young. What if she couldn't pull this off? What if she froze up? What if that happened, and we couldn't cast before Edward pounced on her? What if Jeremy couldn't stop him in time? I took a deep breath and closed my eyes. Jeremy thought this would work, and I trusted that he'd never put Savannah in danger.

She stepped into the alley. Edward had his back turned to her, still talking to Benicio. Jaime and Benicio saw her, though. Jaime's eyes widened. I leaned as far from my hiding place as I dared, and, seeing me, Jaime shuttered her look of surprise. Benicio hesitated, then gave a tiny nod, and said something to Edward, keeping him engaged.

I cast a cover spell, then readied a fireball. For the few seconds it took me to prep the spell, I was visible, but the cloak of invisibility fell again the moment I stopped. Behind me, Lucas had a knock-back spell ready—far from lethal, but one of the few spells we knew would work on a vampire.

Savannah crept down the alley. Edward was too intent on Benicio to notice her. When she'd reached the mark we'd agreed upon, she stopped.

"Hey," she said. "Cool altar."

Edward whirled around and stared, momentarily dumbfounded by the sight of a thirteen-year-old alone in an alley at midnight.

Savannah took another step forward. "Is that, like, a satanic altar? Are you guys gonna call up a demon or something?" She walked over near Jaime and pretended to notice Jaime and Benicio's bindings for the first time. "A sacrifice? Cool. I've never seen anyone get sacrificed before. Can I watch?"

Edward's mouth opened, then shut, as if his brain was still muddling through this. I glanced over at Jeremy, but he was already on his way, creeping along the far wall, out of Edward's sight. He moved as soundlessly as a vampire. Within seconds he was less than a yard from Edward.

Savannah's eyes rounded to saucers, mouth opening in an O of delighted surprise.

"Wow," she said. "Is that your dog, mister?"

Edward followed her gaze, then backpedaled fast. Behind him stood a jet-black wolf the size of a Great Dane. When Jeremy looked up at Edward, his black eyes blended perfectly with his fur, so the effect was one of eerily unrelieved darkness, more like the shadow of a wolf than an animal itself. With Elena, I could easily mistake her for a large dog. With Jeremy, no one getting close enough could make that error. I could tell by Edward's face that he knew this was no stray mutt.

Savannah strolled over and ran her fingers through the ruff around Jeremy's neck. Edward gave a sharp intake of breath, as if expecting her to lose that hand, but Jeremy didn't move.

"He's beautiful," Savannah said. "What's his name?"

She kept her hand on the back of Jeremy's neck. Jeremy looked up, eyes meeting Edward's. He drew his lips back and growled so softly that the sound seemed more felt than heard as it vibrated down the alley.

"Oooh," Savannah said. "I don't think your dog likes you, mister."

She scrunched her face in a thoughtful frown as she studied Jeremy's face. "You know, I think he's hungry." She looked at Edward and smiled. "Maybe you should feed him."

Jeremy pounced.

He caught Edward in the stomach and knocked him across the alley, away from Jaime and Savannah. Lucas and I bolted from our hiding spot and raced down the alley. By the time we got there, Jeremy was on top of Edward and had his teeth buried in his shoulder. Edward kicked and punched, but to no effect. Unfortunately, Jeremy's bite had no effect either. Not a single drop of blood flowed from the wound and the moment Jeremy released his grip, the tears in Edward's flesh knitted together.

Edward's head jerked up, teeth bared, aiming for Jeremy's foreleg.

"Jeremy!" I shouted.

Jeremy yanked his leg out of the way. We didn't know whether the sedative in Edward's bite would knock out a werewolf, but this wasn't the time to find out. Jeremy planted his forepaws on Edward's shoulders to pin him, then slashed at his throat, ripping the flesh in a slice that would have been lethal to anything mortal. Edward snarled in pain, but the moment Jeremy lifted his head from the bite, Edward's neck was whole again.

I turned to say something to Lucas, but he was already hurrying toward the altar. He grabbed the length of rope left over from tying Jaime, and jogged to Edward and Jeremy. As strong as Jeremy might be, unless he could behead Edward, this fight required a pair of human hands.

As Lucas approached, Jeremy lifted his head and met his gaze. Then he sank his teeth into Edward's side and lifted him, to flip him onto his back so Lucas could tie him. Edward slammed his fist into the back of Jeremy's left foreleg joint. Jeremy's leg buckled and his grip on Edward slid.

Beside me, Savannah began to cast. I prepped a knock-back spell, then heard Savannah's incantation and whirled.

"No!" I yelled. "Don't—"

The last words to the spell left her lips as Jeremy regained his hold and tossed Edward up. As Jeremy swung Edward, he moved into the path of Savannah's binding spell and stopped dead. Edward landed on top of Jeremy. Savannah broke the spell, but Edward already had hold of Jeremy's rear leg. He bit it. Jeremy recovered and twisted, but Edward kept his teeth firmly planted in Jeremy's leg, drawing blood and injecting his sedative. Lucas lunged at the pair. He caught Edward in the side and knocked him away from Jeremy. As the two skidded across the alley, Jeremy stayed where he was, looking around as if confused. Then he snorted, and slid to the pavement.

Lucas and Edward hit the ground fighting, each grappling for a hold on the other. I prepped a binding spell. I knew I couldn't use it while they were tumbling together, but nor could I risk using anything dangerous. I felt useless enough standing there watching. At least the binding spell made me feel I could stop Edward if things went wrong.

The two men were an equal match in size and strength. Lucas had one forearm jammed under Edward's throat, so he couldn't bite, but every time Lucas lifted his free hand to cast, Edward knocked it down.

Edward wrenched away from Lucas and managed to get halfway to his feet before Lucas yanked him down again. They rolled together. When they reached the wall, Edward reared up and twisted. Lucas's head slammed into the brick.

The blow dazed Lucas only for a moment, but in that moment Edward saw his chance. His head arched back, mouth opening. I cast my binding spell—cast it too fast and knew before I even finished that it hadn't worked. Savannah and I both raced toward them, but we were ten feet away, too far to cover the distance in time. As Edward's head swung down for the bite, Lucas recovered and ducked. Edward's fangs still caught the skin of his neck. As Lucas tore himself away, a fine mist of blood sprayed across the alley. The air surrounding Lucas started to shimmer. He dove out of the way. I grabbed Savannah and yanked her backward.

Edward stopped. He saw that first glimmer of the portal and his lips curved in a slow smile.

"Natasha," he whispered.

Lucas pitched himself at Edward, trying to shove him away from the portal. And Edward let him. He knew the portal wasn't about to open. Not yet. He hadn't spilled nearly enough of Lucas's blood. Edward grabbed Lucas by the hair and snapped his head back, teeth arcing down to tear through his throat. Lucas's eyes went wide as he realized his mistake.

"Binding spell!" I shouted at Savannah.

As she cast, I dove for Edward. I caught the back of his shirt and threw myself sideways. I managed to rip him away from Lucas, but not before his fangs made contact. More blood sprayed. The ground began to vibrate.

Edward wrenched away from me. As my grasp on his shirt slipped, Savannah cast her binding spell. Edward froze. Lucas wheeled to grab him.

"No!" I yelled. "Go!"

He hesitated.

"Get away from the portal!"

Lucas's gaze darted from me to his father to the portal, shimmering behind me. Then he turned and jogged toward the other end of the alley.

"Keep holding him," I said to Savannah. "I'll grab the rope."

Something moved behind Savannah. It was just Jeremy waking and lurching to his feet, but the sudden motion startled her and the binding spell snapped. Edward tore free of my grasp. Lucas spun around, saw Edward, and lifted his hands to cast.

"No!" I shouted. "Keep going!"

Lucas hesitated only a second before racing down the alley. Edward shot after him. And I followed, passing Jeremy as he tried to shake off the sedative, growling softly.

Ahead, the two men disappeared around the corner. A moment of silence. Then trash cans crashed like cymbals, the sound not quite drowning out a yelp of pain. I hiked up my skirt and tore down the alley.

I rounded the corner as Edward sprang to his feet, recovering from whatever spell Lucas had cast at him. With a roar, Edward threw himself at Lucas. Lucas backpedaled and lifted his hands to cast again. Then Jeremy skidded around the corner. He whipped past me and launched himself at Edward. As Edward fell, Jeremy clamped his jaws around the back of his neck. Then he pinned him to the pavement, forepaws on his shoulders, mouth still on his neck. I raced in with the rope. Lucas grabbed Edward's hands, yanked them behind his back, and I tied them with the best knots I knew, then let Lucas add his own, just to be sure.

When we'd finished, I turned to Savannah, and nodded. She cast a binding spell on Edward. And it was over.

As Jeremy Changed back, I cared for Lucas, casting a spell to staunch the dribbling blood flow, then wrapping his neck with strips of fabric from my dress. Then, leaving Savannah in charge of the binding spell, we hurried into the alley to free Jaime and Benicio. Lucas headed straight for his father.

Jaime had her head down, but on hearing me, she looked up and flashed a wide grin.

"Hey," she said. "Everything under control?"

"Yes," I said, kneeling behind her. "Thank you so much. You were amazing."

At a noise of assent behind me, Jaime looked up and, from the sudden light in her face, I knew who was standing there. I glanced up at Jeremy and motioned to the ropes.

"Do you mind?" I said. "My fingers are too slippery. Sweating pretty hard, I guess."

He nodded and circled Jaime. "I'll start with your hands. If I pull too tight, just say so."

"Ummm, not yet, okay? Hold on for a minute. I'm still trying to figure out how to escape."

"You don't need to escape, Jaime," he said gently. "It's all over. I can untie you now."

"Oh, I know, and you can, just as soon as I figure out how I *could* have done it. It's humiliating enough to be kidnapped, tied up, and need rescuing. At least I have to be able to say, 'Thanks for setting me free, but I was actually just minutes away from doing it myself.'"

A low chuckle. "I see."

"What do you think of lip gloss?"

"In general? Or as an instrument of escape?"

"Escape. I have some in my pocket and I can almost reach it. What if I'd smeared lip gloss on the ropes? Could I have slid out?"

As Jeremy answered, I felt a hand on my shoulder. I looked up to see Benicio. As I stood, he embraced me.

"Well done," he whispered in my ear.

"I've just called the Cabal, Papá," Lucas said. "They're sending an extraction team."

"Oh, I don't believe that will be necessary."

Benicio pulled back from me. As Lucas and I exchanged a look, Benicio headed for the end of the alley.

"He's quite secure, Papá," Lucas called after him. "Perhaps—"

Benicio lifted a finger, and kept walking. His voice floated back to us, barely above a whisper. Lucas frowned and jogged after him. I followed, trying to hear what Benicio was saying. Then I caught a few words of Latin and knew he was casting. Lucas realized it at the same moment and broke into a run. When we reached the corner, though, Benicio had stopped the incantation. He was leaning over Edward, who lay on his back, staring up, cold-eyed and defiant. Benicio's lips curved in a small smile.

"Vampires are indeed the race of arrogance, aren't they?" he said, his tone pleasant, even congenial. "And perhaps not without reason. You did manage to kill my son once. Almost managed to do it twice. Did you really think you'd get away with it? If you had, I'd have pursued you through every level of Hell to wreak my revenge. As it is, though, things are a bit"—his smile broadened, showing his teeth—"easier."

Benicio lifted his hands and said the last three words of the incantation. As his hands flew down, a lightning bolt severed Edward's head from his neck.

No one moved. We all stood in shock, watching Edward's head roll across the alley.

Benicio lifted his hands again. This time, his voice boomed down the alley, as he cursed Edward's soul for eternity.

Full Circle

FOR ME, THE CASE TRULY ENDED ONLY WHEN IT RETURNED to where it had begun: with a teenage witch named Dana MacArthur.

While we'd been tracking Edward, Randy MacArthur had finally arrived in Miami to see his daughter. When the initial flurry of activity over Edward's execution died down, we admitted to Benicio that Dana was gone. Of course, the Cortez Cabal wasn't taking Jaime's say-so, but their necromancers tried to contact Dana and confirmed that she had indeed passed over. So, two days later, Lucas, Savannah, and I stood in a Cabal cemetery and said good-bye to a girl we'd never known.

Since I'd now seen what lay on the other side, Dana's passing pained me less than it might have. Yet I still felt the full weight of the tragedy her death brought for her father and her younger sister, and maybe even her mother. Even for Dana herself, there was tragedy here. She'd gone to a good place, and I was sure she'd be happy, but that didn't mean her life hadn't been cut short, that she hadn't missed out on so much. And for what? To avenge the death of a vampire who had herself killed so many, gone so far beyond the needs of her nature? As I stood in that cemetery, listening to the minister try to eulogize a girl he'd never met, I looked out across the graves and thought of all the other fresh graves in other Cabal cemeteries. I glanced over at Savannah, and thought about Joey Nast, the cousin she never knew. On the other side of the group of mourners, I could see Holden Wyngaard, a plump red-haired boy, now the lone survivor. I thought of the others. Jacob Sorenson. Stephen St. Cloud. Colby Washington. Sarah Dermack. Michael Shane. Matthew Tucker. All gone. And how many tombstones would it take to commemorate the lives of everyone else Edward and Natasha had killed, the scores of humans they'd murdered trying to become immortal? I thought of that, of all those lives, and I couldn't for one second disagree with what Benicio had done. No matter what kind of hell Edward now faced, it was no less than he deserved.

I looked out at the small crowd gathered around Dana's open grave. Her mother wasn't there. I still wondered what had gone wrong in that woman's life to make her abandon her daughter, and I couldn't help but wonder whether having a Coven would have helped. I'm sure it would have, at least for Dana. If she'd had other witches to turn to, she would never have ended up on the streets of Atlanta, and now here.

Yet, as bad as I felt for Dana, I had to accept that the responsibility for starting a second Coven did not lie squarely on my shoulders. I was willing to start one. I would always be willing, and I'd make that willingness known, but I would no longer actively try to convince witches that they needed a Coven. They had to come to see that for themselves. In the meantime, I certainly didn't lack for work. I had an interracial council to reform and a new partnership with Lucas to pursue. Yes, I would have been more comfortable pouring my energy into a dream that started with me, but I think part of growing up is realizing that everything doesn't have to be *mine*. It could be *ours,* and that wasn't a show of weakness or dependence. I liked what Lucas did. I believed in it. I wanted to share it. And, if he wanted to share it back, well, that was damned near perfect.

When the service ended, Benicio leaned over and whispered an invitation to lunch, before we left for Portland. We agreed, and he slipped away to offer final condolences to Randy MacArthur.

The others had all gone their separate ways. The werewolves left Miami the morning after the showdown with Edward. Cassandra and Aaron had followed later that day, after they'd met with Benicio and the other CEOs to discuss possible fallout between the Cabals and the vampire community. Jaime had done her Halloween show in Memphis the night before, then zipped back to attend Dana's morning memorial service before returning to Tennessee for her next show.

As the mourners drifted away from the grave site, I glanced back one last time. Lucas took my hand and squeezed it.

"She'll be okay," he said.

I managed a smile. "I know she will."

"Mr. Cortez? Ms. Winterbourne?"

We turned to see Randy MacArthur behind us, looking uncomfortable in a too-tight black suit. His hand rested on the shoulder of an equally uncomfortable-looking young girl with Dana's long blond hair.

"I—we wanted to thank you," he said. "For stopping him. This—it should never—I don't know how it happened. I had no idea how bad things were—"

"It's okay, Dad," the girl murmured, her red-rimmed eyes fixed on the ground. "It was Mom's fault. Her and that guy. He didn't want kids, and she let him chase Dana off."

"This is Gillian," Randy said. "Dana's sister. I'm going to be looking after her now. Mr. Cortez is giving me a job in town here, so I can stay with her."

"That's great," I said. I tried to catch Gillian's eye and smiled. "You must be what, thirteen? Fourteen? Just starting your second-level spells, I bet."

Gillian looked up at me and for a moment, her eyes were blank, then she realized what I meant. "Spells, no, we don't do that. My mom, I mean. She never . . . well, not much."

"That was, uh, one reason I wanted to speak to you before you left," Randy said. "I know Miss Nast here is about Gillian's age . . ."

It took a moment for me to realize he meant Savannah.

Randy continued. "I know that you're teaching her, and that you used to be with the Coven and you did some teaching there, so I thought maybe you could help Gillian. Long-distance, of course. By phone or e-mail or whatever, maybe visit when you're in town, or we could visit up there. I'll pay you, of course. I hate to impose, but I don't know any other witches. My ex-wife didn't keep in contact with her sister, and I wouldn't even know where to find her, but I really want Gillian to know more, to be able to cast spells, so she can protect herself"—a quick glance at his daughter's grave—"against everything."

"And so she should," I said. "I would love to help her, in any way I can."

"Are you sure?" Randy asked.

I met Gillian's shy gaze with a wide smile. "I'm positive."

About the Author

KELLEY ARMSTRONG lives in Ontario with her family.
Visit her website at www.kelleyarmstrong.com.

Be sure not to miss Eve's book:

HAUNTED

The next exciting novel in
The Women of the Otherworld series

by

Kelley Armstrong

Available now

Here's a special preview:

HAUNTED

on sale now

"Come on," Savannah whispered, tugging the young man's hand. "This way."

She climbed a wooden fence into the backyard of an old three-story row house.

"Watch out for the roses," she said. "We gotta come this way, though, or the old bat across the road will bitch about me having friends over when no one's home."

"Yeah," the boy said. "I get shit from my folks about that, too."

"Oh, Paige and Lucas don't care, as long as I clean up and don't have any parties. Well, they might care if they found out I was bringing a guy over. They're pretty cool about stuff, though. But that old bat sees me having friends over and she starts telling people Paige and Lucas are crappy guardians, shit like that. Makes me want to—" She swallowed her next words and shrugged. "Throw quicklime on her roses or something."

I followed less than a half-dozen paces behind the two, but they never turned around, never even peered over their shoulder. Sometimes that really pisses me off. Sure, all teenagers ignore their mothers. And, sure, Savannah had a good excuse, since I'd been dead for three years. Still, you'd think maybe we'd have a deeper connection, that she'd somehow hear me, if only as a voice in her head that said "Don't listen to that girl" or "That boy's not worth the trouble." Never happened, though. In life I'd been one of the most powerful women in the supernatural world. Now I was a third-rate ghost who couldn't even contact her own daughter. My afterlife sucked.

Savannah took the boy through the lean-to, dragged him away from Lucas's latest motorcycle restoration project, opened the back door and led him inside. The door swung shut in my face. I walked through it.

They shed their shoes, then climbed the small set of stairs from the landing to the kitchen. Savannah headed straight for the fridge and started grabbing sandwich fixings. I wandered past them into the living room, headed for my favorite seat, a butter-yellow leather armchair.

I'd done the right thing, sending Savannah to Paige. Quite possibly the smartest thing I've ever done. Of course, if I'd been really smart, Savannah wouldn't have needed caring for at all. I wouldn't have been in such a hellfire rush to escape that compound, wouldn't have gotten myself killed, wouldn't have endangered my little girl—

Enough with the whipping. Yes, I'd screwed up, but I was going to fix that. I'd promised to look after my daughter, and I would . . . just as soon as I figured out how.

Savannah and her friend took their sandwiches into the dining room. I leaned forward to peer around the corner, just a quick check in case . . . In case what, Eve? In case she chokes on a pickle? I silenced the too-familiar voice and started to settle back into my chair when I noticed a third person in the dining room. A gray-haired woman sitting in a chair pulled up to the window, head bent, shoulder racked with silent sobs. Savannah circled the table, brushing past the woman, and took her seat on the opposite side.

"Did you hear Ms. Lenke might not be back before the

city finals?" Savannah said. "She'd better be. Callohan doesn't know the difference between a dead ball and a free ball."

The boy snorted. "I'd be surprised if that moron could tell a basketball from a football. At last week's practice . . ."

I tuned them out and crossed the room. As I drew near, I could hear the woman's quiet sobs. I sighed and leaned against the doorway.

"Look," I said. "Whatever happened to you, I'm sure it was bad, but you have to move on. Go into the light or click your heels three times or whatever. Get thee to the other side, ghost."

The woman didn't even look up. Only thing worse than a stubborn spirit was a rude one. I'd seen her here at least a dozen times in the eighteen months since the kids had moved in, and not once had she so much as acknowledged my presence. Never spoke. Never left that chair. Never stopped crying. And I thought I had a lousy afterlife.

I softened my tone. "You have to get over it. You're wasting your time—"

She faded, and was gone. Really. Some people.

"Where's that new stereo you got for Easter?" the boy asked Savannah through a mouthful of multigrain bread.

"In my room." She hesitated. "You wanna go up and see it?"

The boy jumped to his feet so fast the chair tumbled over backward. Savannah laughed and helped him right it. Then she grabbed his hand and led him to the stairs.

I stayed at the bottom.

A moment later, music rocked the rafters. It didn't sound like anything I recognized. Dead three years, and I was already a pop culture has-been. No, wait. I did recognize the song. "Don't Fear the Reaper" . . . but with a techno beat. Who the hell was this? Not Blue Oyster Cult, that's for sure. What kind of crap—? Oh God, I was turning into my mother. I'd avoided it all my life and now—

A man walked through the wall. Two inches taller than me, and a decade older. Broad shoulders. Thickening middle.

Thinning blond hair. Gorgeous blue eyes, which followed my gaze to the stairs.

"And what does our daughter desperately need your help with today?"

Savannah's father, Kristof Nast. His contribution to "our daughter" had been purely biological, having not entered her life until just days before the end of his. My choice, not his. After I'd become pregnant, I'd skedaddled. Took him thirteen years and a life-ending blow to the head, but he'd finally caught up with me.

He cocked his head, listened to the music and pulled a face. "Well, at least she's out of the boy-band stage. And it could be worse. Bryce went through heavy metal, then rap, then hip-hop, and at each phase I swore the next one couldn't be any worse, but he always found something guaranteed to make me—" Kristof noticed my inattention and waved a hand in front of my eyes.

"Come on, Eve," he said. "Savannah's taste may be questionable, but she doesn't require musical supervision. I need to talk to you. Remember—"

"Shhh. Can you hear anything?"

He arched his brows. "Besides a badly tuned bass guitar and vocals worthy of a castrated stray cat?"

"She has a boy up there."

Another frown, deeper this time. "What kind of boy?"

"Human."

"I meant what 'sort' of boy? This isn't the same one—" He closed his mouth with an audible click of his teeth, then launched into a voice I knew only too well, one I heard in my own head when he wasn't around. "All right. Savannah has a boy in her room. And exactly what are you going to do about it? She's fifteen. We both know they aren't up there on a study date. As for exactly what they're doing . . . is that really any of your business?"

"I'm not worried about sex, Kris. She's a smart girl. If she's ready—and I don't think she is—she'll take precautions. But what if *he's* ready? I barely know this guy. He could—"

"Force her to do something she doesn't want?" His laugh

boomed through the foyer. "When's the last time anyone ever forced you to do something against your will? She's your daughter, Eve. In every way. First guy that puts a hand where she doesn't want it will be lucky if he doesn't lose it."

"I know, but—"

"But what? What if they *do* turn that music down? Do you really want to hear what's going on up there?"

"Of course not. That's why I'm staying down here. I'm just making sure—"

"Making sure of what? You can't make sure of anything, Eve. You're dead. That boy could pull a gun on her and there's not a damn thing you could do about it."

"I'm working on that."

He sighed. "You've been working on it for three years. And you're no further than when you started. It's time to—"

"I'm not giving up."

He stepped closer, and hooked his pinkie finger with mine as he leaned down to me. "I was going to say take a break. A vacation. You need to step back from it for a little while."

"And do what?"

"Well, funny you should ask. That's what I wanted to talk to you about. I may happen to have the perfect getaway for you. Full of adventure, mystery, maybe even a little danger . . ."

"Just a little?"

He grinned. "Depends on how you play it."

"So what is it?"

"Just some . . . odd jobs down at the courthouse. I'm headed there now. Why don't you come with me and check them out yourself, see if anything catches your interest?"

"You go on. We'll talk about it later."

Kristof looked from me to the steps, then threw up his hands and disappeared into the wall. I plunked down onto the step. He didn't understand. Savannah and I had a special bond, and he couldn't possibly understand. I only wish that was true. Kris had single-parented both his sons after his wife had left while his youngest was still in diapers. As for what kind of parent he'd been . . . soon after we'd first met, his secretary had paged him because Sean had been hit in the head during a baseball game. Barely more than a bump on the head, but he'd blown off an important business dinner meeting to catch the next plane home. And that's when my opinion of him began the slow but steady shift that led to Savannah.

It had ended there, though. I'd realized I was a black witch carrying the bastard child of a Cabal heir, and hadn't been dumb enough to stick around and see what his family thought of that. But now, after two years of telling him that just because we'd ended up in the same afterlife didn't mean we were getting back together, he'd proven me wrong. And, really, the only thing I regretted was that I hadn't given in sooner.

Upstairs, the music ended. Savannah popped in another CD . . . or switched MP3s . . . or whatever music came on these days. Yep, a pop culture has-been. The next song began, something slow, and definitely soft enough for me to hear the giggles and murmurs from the bedroom above.

Damn it, Kris was right. Following my fifteen-year-old daughter to the mall was one thing. Listening to her make out with a boy was wrong. And creepy. But now I was stuck here. If Kristof found out I'd left right after him, he'd know I'd seen his point, and I wasn't ready to admit that. Maybe—

A sharp oath erupted from the living room. I stood and took a cautious step toward the corner. A human intruder? Or ghostly? I hated being so cautious. In life, I would have strode over there, defensive spell at the ready. But here? Well, here things were different. There were a lot of things here that I could no longer handle with a good roundhouse kick and an energy bolt spell.

Kristof stepped from behind the sofa, picking what looked like cobwebs from his rumpled shirt. The back of his hair stuck straight up, as if someone had run a static-charged hand through it. Dirt smeared a ragged line from his cheek to his chin. His tie was shredded.

"Let me guess," I said. "Wrong turn . . . again?"

He gave a fierce wet-dog shake. When he stopped, he was as immaculate as he'd been when he'd first arrived . . . except for his tie. It was whole again, but the end was tucked into his shirt. I plucked it out and straightened it.

"Thank you," he said. "It's ang-taliwala-balay, isn't it? To get to the central hub?"

"From our dimension. If you go straight from here, it's ang-taliwala-balay." I put the emphasis on the second syllable in the last two words.

He repeated it, but his pronunciation was still off.

He gave a helpless shrug. "You know how I am with spells."

"Uh-huh."

I glanced back at the stairs. A sigh floated down.

I turned back to Kris. "Want a lift?"

"Please."

I took his hand, said the incantation, and teleported us to the courthouse.

Transportation is my afterlife specialty. In other areas of ghost activity, well, I wasn't so good, though I didn't think the Fates really needed to send me through that damned orientation course three times. Hell, I wasn't stupid. I just had other priorities. One other priority to be exact. Savannah. To help her, I needed to be able to influence the living world, which isn't as easy as all those haunted house stories make it sound. So far, I'd gotten nowhere, but I'd spent a lot of time tracking down sources, which meant I'd learned a lot about transportation.

I dropped Kris off right on the courthouse steps. Yes, we have courts here. The Fates take care of all major disciplinary issues in our world, but when it comes to disputes between ghosts, they let us handle those ourselves, and we do so in the only way we understand: a judicial system, which was staffed by volunteers. Which begs the question, what kind of person spends his afterlife voluntarily working as a lawyer? Kristof hadn't even practiced law in real life. The day he'd passed the bar exam, he'd gone into business with his family. But here he was, playing lawyer on the ghost world judiciary circuit. Crazy man. Even Kris admitted this wasn't his first choice for an afterlife career. Yet until they started a ghost world NHL franchise, he was stuck with it.

As for those "odd jobs," I told Kris we'd discuss those later. Right now, I had some thinking to do. So I teleported over to Savannah. No, not to check in on my daughter again—to the city, Savannah, in Georgia. This was where I lived now. Before Savannah was born, I'd scoured the supernatural world for greater sources of power, and a few of those stops had been in Savannah. I'd loved the place. I don't know why. Savannah was the epitome of genteel Southern charm, and there wasn't an ounce of gentility or charm in my body, nor did I want there to be. Yet something about the city struck a chord in me, so much so that I'd named my daughter after it. After I died, and had my pick of places to live, I'd chosen Savannah.

My afterlife world was a version of Earth, with some weird sub-dimensions that we really tried to avoid. Everyone here was a supernatural, but not every supernatural was here. When I'd died, my first thought on waking had been "great, now I finally find out what comes next." Well, actually that had been my *second* thought, right after "hmmm, I thought it would be hotter." Yes, I'd escaped the fiery hell my mother and many others had prophesied for me, but in dying, I hadn't found out what comes next, only what came next for me. Was there fire and brimstone somewhere else? Were there angels and heavenly harps? I have no idea. I only know that where I am is better than where I expected to be, so I'm not complaining.

I knew the code for teleporting just down the street from my house, but instead I went for a walk along the river bluffs. I think better on my feet. Kristof was right. I needed a break. I'd known that for a while now, but couldn't bring myself to admit it. Maybe I should find out more about those jobs Kris had mentioned. I knew they wouldn't be the kind of employment the Fates would approve of, but that wasn't a problem.

That thought had no more left my mind than a bluish fog blew in off the Savannah River.

"Hey, I didn't say I was going to do anything," I said as the warm fog swirled around my legs. "I was just—"

The fog sucked me into the ground.

The Searchers deposited me in the Fates' throne room. I have no idea what a real throne room looks like, but this is pretty much what I picture, a huge cavern of a room, guaranteed to make the subjects feel as tiny as possible while the king sits high up on his dais and passes judgment on them.

When the Searchers first drop you off, they leave you facing the back of the room, so it seems like you're alone in this big empty place, left to dwell on your sins and worry about the punishment to come. Then, when you've had proper time to reflect and repent, the floor turns and you find that you're not alone at all, but that the Fates have been standing there, behind you, the whole time. Now, it's a great effect . . . the first time. But once you've figured out the trick, I'm not sure why they keep doing it. Maybe because most ghosts aren't dragged before the Fates quite as often as I am.

The Fates are the guardians of the supernatural layers of the ghost world. They presumably answer to someone, but most of us are a little unclear on "who." Doesn't matter. Allah, Jehovah, God, Jupiter, Mother Nature, whoever is up there, he or she doesn't play any noticeable role in our afterlife. Our top dogs are the Fates, and they are ours alone, which means we don't have to compete for their attention with ten billion ghosts. Nope, we screw up, we feel the full force of their wrath up close and personal.

So when the floor began to turn, I braced myself for the

gale. When it didn't turn fast enough, I twisted around to face the Fates myself. A pretty dark-haired girl threaded yarn onto a spinning wheel. She looked no more than five or six years old, with bright violet eyes that matched her dress.

"Okay," I said. "What did I do?"

The girl grinned. "Isn't the question: what did I do *now*?"

I sighed, the deep sigh of a ghost most misunderstood. In less time than it takes to blink, the girl morphed into a middle-aged version of herself.

"We have a problem, Eve."

"What did I do?" I said, mentally adding the "now."

"You haven't done anything, although that's about to change. You made us a promise."

"Look, I said I wouldn't use the codes for *excessive* unauthorized travel. I never said—"

"This isn't about unauthorized travel."

I thought for a moment. "Visiting Adena Milan for spell-swapping? Hey, that was an honest mistake. No one told me she was on the black list."

The middle-aged Fate shook her head, eyes twinkling. "Although, admittedly, there might be some amusement to be had in making you recite the whole list of your infractions, I'm afraid we don't have that much time. Eighteen months ago, you made a deal with us. If we returned Paige and Lucas to the living world, you'd owe us a favor."

"Oh . . . that."

Damn. In the last eighteen months, they hadn't mentioned it again, so I'd hoped they'd forgotten. Like that's going to happen. The Fates can remember what Noah ate for breakfast on the morning of the flood. They sure as hell aren't going to forget that I owe them a favor. My first instinct, as always, was to weasel out of it. Hell, what's the worst thing that could happen? Well, for starters, they could undo their end of the bargain and bring Paige and Lucas back to the ghost world. Okay, no weaseling out of this one.

Besides, I *had* been looking for a distraction. Which made this all seem very coincidental.

"Have you been talking to Kristof?" I asked. "Did he put you up to this? Finding me something to do?"

The Fate morphed into her oldest sister, a hunchbacked crone with a wizened face permanently set in a scowl . . . well, at least whenever I was around.

"Put us up to it?" she snapped. "Kristof Nast does not 'put us up' to anything."

"I didn't mean—"

"Nor are we going to be doing favors for the likes of him. Several hundred thousand ghosts in our domains and I can count on my fingers the number of them who give us more trouble than you two. We thought that lawyer job would keep him busy." She snorted. "And it does. Keeps him busy getting into more trouble."

"If you mean the Agito case, that wasn't Kris's fault. The plaintiff started lying, so he had to do something about it. It wasn't *really* witness tampering. Just—"

"Just a means to an end," she said, fixing me with that bright glare. "That's how you two think, isn't it? Doesn't matter *how* you get there, as long as you do."

The middle sister took over. "An interesting philosophy. Not one we share but, in some cases . . . useful. This particular job we need done may require some of those unique skills."

I perked up. "Oh?"

"We have a spirit who's escaped from the lower realms. We need you to bring her in."

The lower realms are where they keep the ghosts who can't be allowed to mingle with the rest of us—the seriously nasty criminals, mass murderers, serial killers and the like. Hmmm, interesting.

"Sounds easy enough," I said. "How much of a head start does she have? A day or two?"

"A bit longer than that. She's been gone a little over a hundred years."

"What? And you haven't sent anyone after her yet?"

"Of course we have. Several people. But they ran into

some . . . complications." She smiled down at me. "But we're sure you'll do much better."

The child Fate popped in, grinning. "Or so we hope."

Something told me I was really going to regret making that promise.